ANCIENT CANADA

A MYTHOLOGICAL TALE

ANCIENT CANADA

A MYTHOLOGICAL TALE

CLINTON FESTA

CamCat
Books

CamCat Publishing, LLC
Brentwood, Tennessee 37027
camcatpublishing.com

Hardcover ISBN 9780744304350
Paperback ISBN 9780744304367
Large-Print Paperback ISBN 9780744304381
eBook ISBN 9780744304411
Audiobook ISBN 9780744304459

Library of Congress Control Number: 2021945663

Cover and book design by Maryann Appel
Map illustration by Jerome Eyquem

5   3   1   2   4

Table of Contents

Mainland
Siberia

Canada

Ellesmere
Island

York   Fort Alert

Lichen's
Clearing

Fort Alert

Svalbard   Nyebyen

Kildebyen

Arbor
Beach

Windfall

The Pa...

Windfall

Arbor
Beach

Bog

Jan Mayen Island

The Royal Asylum on Emberlnd
(The King's Closet)

Marigold's Prologue

If I were to describe my sister in one word, it would be oversimplified. To define her solely by her gift would be equally unfair, although a common and convenient indulgence taken by some.

To say this is her story exclusively would also be untrue. It is many stories, each told from the perspective of a different narrator, and I merely fill these pages with their words. In doing so, I hope the word to be, as I am to Lavender, sibling to the deed and not its cousin.

Polaris proclaimed himself the religious, military, and otherwise autonomous leader of our people, our country, and its capital of York. With her words and actions, my younger sister challenged his authority. In recounting her story, I stand beside her.

Our journey bridges the lands of the known world, through both the wild and domestic, lasting an entire season of light and into a season of darkness. The encounters you read about are recalled by those we passed throughout our wandering. You will therefore not rely solely on my partiality but hear many perspectives on my sister. The narrators have directly formed their opinions, and through them you will likely form your own. In doing so, and objectively, you will have fulfilled my hope for this document.

1 / The Summoner

"Treason, then," said Polaris.

"How do you read that, sir?" I asked.

And just like that I crossed the line. He turned his six-generations-old head toward me and glared with his famous red, glowing eyes. I turned away quickly and straightened my back.

"You don't think so?"

"I don't recall writing it in my report, sir."

"You didn't. It's right here," he concluded, reading the colorful brochure from the Mystic Garden. "Services. Predictions of life and death. Verification of pregnancy, and how many. For just three tiles, our seer will tell you if you will live or die based on your current condition. Should those conditions change, your future may change with it. All receive a flower regardless of their fortune."

"Treason, then, sir?"

He flared up as if possessed by internal combustion. "Is she not accepting a fee for a spiritual service? Is that not infringing on my authority?" He hated to be doubted, but as any summoner knows, a hypersensitive reaction reveals a level of preexisting guilt. Polaris had an agenda. "Treason and blasphemy. Go back and arrest her, Summoner."

"But . . . the penalty for either of those is execution. Won't she know I'm coming? If she can predict life and death, that is."

"You're not intimidated by a teenage fortune-teller, are you?"

"No, sir."

He took a few steps around the private briefing chamber and dug his overgrown nails into the back of an empty wooden chair. "Let me tell you something I learned when I was a young man: All human behavior follows one simple rule. We weigh penalties and rewards, and in the moment of decision, we choose the path of least apparent resistance. Every one of us, every time. That's not to say we take the easy way out. We choose based on what we can see. But simple minds will be clouded and nearsighted, so it's up to the master to make sure the servant sees far enough into their future to make the wisest possible decision. Treason and blasphemy cannot be tolerated."

"You make your point perfectly clear, sir."

"Stop procrastinating. Put on your uniform and make your arrest. You may use any of the cathedral's exit points. I'll see you in the marketplace. Crimes like these require an immediate public trial."

I am a summoner. I have sworn an oath to protect the Polarian mandates. When I arrest you, you won't know who I am, and you won't see it coming.

The Cathedral at York has a series of discreet entries and exits, each of which connects to a web of underground passageways and briefing rooms. This allows a summoner to enter plainly clothed, descend deep into the lowest levels above only the catacombs, and receive an assignment. We then return aboveground fully hooded, robed, cloaked, gloved, and strapped to the boot in dense gray garments.

To some, blood tastes sweet and savory; to others, it's bitter and sour. When fully uniformed, a summoner cannot be recognized and does not speak, so as not to be identified by any other means. We're ordered to arrest the mark, and in the event of resistance, use fatal measures. Should this be necessary in a public setting, or even with just one bystander, the summoner can return to life without judgment or resentment as the public reaction is unpredictable. Merely researching a summoner's true identity is punishable by death. Call me Denton if you like. It's not my real name.

I thought I understood the profile of a typical mark, and it was not a girl of fifteen seasons under suspicion of treason or blasphemy. However, most assignments are not ordered directly by Polaris himself, as in this case, concerning a young lady named Lavender. I needed to know more. I needed the man from the heavens to answer questions no one could ask. But when light shines on an agenda, it casts a permanent shadow, and he knew this. So, it was no accident that I never learned the real reasons why Polaris wanted her dead.

———

My assignment had started one day prior. In plain clothes I bought a small, fidgety bird in the marketplace, planning to then seek out the new business where this girl predicted the future. It was by no means difficult, as the report had not exaggerated about her older sister Marigold. Even in the commotion of desperate vendors and haggling customers, you could see and hear her without effort. She wore eye-catching pastels and stood on a salesman's stool. Her hair was blonde, healthy, and well-managed, but so long that I wondered if it had ever been cut. In a sharp, high-pitched note above the droning of the marketplace, she hollered to the crowd, "Trade a small fortune for a great one?"

Marigold even pointed to her and her sister's studio to suggest that potential patrons enter their street-level dwelling—which rested alongside the busiest section of the marketplace—unwittingly guiding my investigation.

A long line spilled out the open door, the patrons pressing against the structure's wall so those waiting nervously would not collide with the other vendors in the open-air bazaar. The door between the private-turned-professional dwelling and the market stayed propped open, the entrance-way draped with plush violet curtains, above which hung a large wooden panel artistically decorated as if a tympanum. The entrance's resemblance to a place of worship certainly didn't prove blasphemy, but it didn't help. The large wooden panel was semicircular, with a single large painted eye: white around a purple iris, and a small, beady, black circle for the pupil. Above the eye on the wooden panel read the title banner of their business: THE MYSTIC GARDEN.

My briefing had included the category of the girl's commerce permit: "parlor amusement." There was nothing subtle about what I had seen up to that point, including the flamboyant Marigold, with whom I avoided eye contact and conversation in passing. I scanned the crowd for her younger sister but saw no girl with glowing purple eyes in the market.

I got in line, expecting, like the other patrons, to find Lavender inside. Looking at those in front of me and at those who stood behind me as we progressed, I felt certain that as an undercover summoner holding a small bird I was the least curious of the lot. Every third woman of childbearing age was pregnant, most only starting to show. There were older couples, often one spouse the other's crutch. Men with diseased skin waited elbow to elbow with other guests. A curious boy stood in front of me, carrying a small serpent in a mold-formed glass cage. Some seemed to be holding a brochure, the one from which Polaris would later conclude Lavender's guilt.

Another and another exited the dwelling, each holding a flower. Most returned to the outer marketplace with a mundane indifference, perhaps also with some relief.

The crowd grew hushed, staring at an older gentleman as he exited, weeping. He held a small, white-petaled stem in his left hand and was joined in arms with an older woman who appeared quite afflicted, presumably dying. Following them were an elated young man and woman, loudly discussing what to name the child in her womb. They held a small, tasteful, red-petaled flower, but otherwise it was an indulgent, inconsiderate display following the elder pair.

After some waiting and slow, forward shuffling, I passed to the inside of the dwelling, step for step with the child and his limbless creature, a small, thankfully caged, white-feathered serpent. When it was the child and his creature's turn, the entire line laughed at the predictable shriek as he brought his pet behind Lavender's cloth barrier. Next for services behind the boy and therefore closest to this utility curtain, I could hear every word.

"Don't remove it from its cage, please!" said the teenage girl hidden behind the drapes.

"I caught him in the forest, and I'd like to know if he's venomous," said the boy.

"Him? How do you know it's a boy?" she asked. "Are *all* serpents boys?"

"Yes," he confirmed.

Hearing everything, the crowd laughed. The girl, aware of it, paused and told the boy, "Not this one. She's pregnant."

This time the crowd did not laugh. A general reaction of repulsion was the response.

"I see fourteen . . . fifteen . . . sixteen are alive, but I'm sorry to say two of the unborn appear to have died inside of her," said Lavender, counting.

"But you didn't believe her to be female, and this is not why you said you came to me."

"No. I would like to know if she's venomous."

"Well then, I suppose we're going to have to take her out of her cage," said the teen, sighing. "Not yet though. Don't open it now."

As Lavender emerged from behind the curtain I had the first glimpse of my mark. She was as described: neither tall nor large. Her hair was black, likely from dye, and cropped with short bangs. Her eyes were the color promised, although the beadiness of the painted version above their entryway was of course exaggerated. And possibly because it was late afternoon and the sun still shone, I saw no noticeable glow. "This will only take a moment," she announced, addressing the patrons as they stared. She stepped into the kitchen, grabbed a pair of wooden tongs, and returned to the boy.

From behind the curtain, she said, "Stand back. I'm going to hold her head securely and slowly bring it to my arm . . . "

Those in the line inside the studio froze.

"Venomous! Venomous!" yelled the girl, slamming the glass cage shut.

"I'll have to take her back to the forest, I suppose," said the dejected boy.

"Yes, please do," insisted the girl. "Here. You are the newest owner of wooden tongs. And give this flower to your mother. You may need to if she's already seen the serpent."

The boy left with his creature secured inside the cage, and I entered with my bird.

"Your bird's not venomous, is she?" asked Lavender, the mystic of the Mystic Garden. I saw the purple eyes, steadily now, and noticed a faint glow, aided from reduced light behind the curtain.

"Why all the rocks, crystals, and strange orbs?" I asked. The room behind the curtain was ridiculous—cramped as it was but even more densely decorated than the remainder of the studio.

"Oh, my sister . . . the flowers were her idea. 'Mystic Garden,' her idea. And the garish purple eye above our entrance . . . I am not to be blamed for that, either. But the flowers . . . we don't always predict good fortunes, and we believe a sendoff with a small flower helps." She lifted her chin and added, "So you are to live but I'm sorry to say your bird is going to die. Was that why you came?"

"Yes, but I'm curious now about what happened with the boy."

She demonstrated with her hands as she explained, "With the tongs, I held the creature's neck and slowly brought it to my forearm. Had that continued, I would have died, because the animal was indeed venomous. So, I drew it back and pulled away my arm. Sorry for the commotion, but this is a new service my sister and I are providing. We're still developing policy. I can tell you I won't do that in the future. And if I may, also in the future, ask that when you bring even a small animal that it be caged or harnessed. For the comfort of the other patrons."

"Of course." I had failed to follow the letter of their rules, whatever they were. "So, you essentially tricked your own gift with the serpent?"

"It works." She shrugged. "I can't explain why, although it seems to predict based on the extension of the circumstances and conditions of your life, which can change."

"Thank you. So, what of my bird? What will cause her death?"

"Distemper," she said. She paused. She scanned my face and said, "No, that's not true. I presume you will eat her." There was a second delay before she spoke, "Yes, I believe you or perhaps your family will eat her."

"How can you tell these things?"

"The cause of death? Just a guess. When I lied and told you she was contaminated, she was then no longer ill-fated. From that point, the conclusion was that you originally planned to eat her. She is now, as I see her, again doomed, likely because I have told you she is not tainted. I'm sorry for the lie, but may I ask why you would bring a bird to me, one you planned on eating, and ask me to predict its cause of death?"

"I . . . I wanted to be sure it wasn't sick. If it were sick, could you treat it?"

"I could not. It doesn't work like that. Forgive my rudeness . . . I wish I could spend more time explaining, but we've printed some literature that should help."

"I'd like two copies."

"My sister . . ." Lavender looked beneath her seat for their brochures without success. "Marigold was distributing them."

I knew precisely where Marigold was, advertising in the market street, but remained silent to observe my mark. Lavender called for her sister in a volume appropriate to the inside of the studio, then a bit louder, and with no reply to either attempt, broke from behind the curtain. She peered out and scanned the crowd. She quickly focused on an older man, fifth or sixth from his turn at the front of the line.

"Somebody fetch a medic!" Lavender yelled. "Immediately!"

The man's skin looked like a fish and had the texture as well. If he were not leaning on his much smaller wife, he probably would have been unable to stand.

"Hey, we were in line long before he arrived!" said the couple in front of the dying man.

"You'll live," said Lavender as she glanced at them. "Medic!"

The man who was next in line complained, "Excuse me, miss, I've already paid. I don't believe that man has paid quite yet."

The lineup ignored Lavender's attempts to call for help, and likewise, she ignored their complaints. I believe most of the dregs of society I've summoned throughout my career would have acted more appropriately than these patrons, and certainly faster.

Hearing her sister's scream, Marigold ran inside from the street only to notice Lavender rushing into their bedroom, pulling out her own mattress, tossing off her sheets, and coming back again to where the patrons stood in the studio.

"Marigold, grab a corner! These people are sessile, useless, and this man is dying."

Finally, as if waking from some strange trance, three men from the line stepped forward to grab a corner of the mattress as the old man mounted it as if it were a gurney. I volunteered as the fourth, but Lavender wouldn't release her grip on her corner.

"We're carting this couple to the hospital. It's more sensible for me to be there anyway," she announced.

"I'll handle the customers," Marigold said. "You go ahead, and hurry." She waited for her sister's exit, then announced loudly, "Clearly there has been an emergency, but if you require services today, you are welcome to follow me to the hospital where we shall continue, free of charge."

"Will Lavender be able to save that man?" asked a patron near the doorway.

"It doesn't work like that," barked two other patrons in unison.

"They're correct. Why does nobody read these?" asked Marigold, holding up her stack of brochures. I laughed quietly at her comment.

———

With my dinner squirming under the pit of my arm, I followed about a quarter of the crowd—perhaps thirty in our flock—out of the market district and on toward the old stone hospital. The sun was in our eyes, and the building was not near.

We found only Lavender at the hospital. We never saw the elderly man again. By our arrival he was dead. Our herd entered and stood back from the gifted girl, who was alone in the common waiting area, tears streaming from her eyes. She hunched into herself on an unpadded wood chair, not comforted by her own soft mattress propped beside her.

I assumed she was not permitted in the treatment areas, which allowed only hospital staff. From what I saw, I doubt the staff even thanked her. The older woman, now widowed, wasn't there, nor were the three men who carried the mattress. It was clear the emergency had ended, and her old patron had died.

We stared across the empty space in silence. Lavender had been alone with her burden in the common area, and now was joined by thirty solemn sets of eyes. Marigold made the journey across the square, hollow room. The crowd held back and watched as Lavender barely stood. The two embraced, then Marigold held Lavender by her shoulders. The older sister's lips moved, then Lavender nodded. I don't know what Marigold said to her younger sister, but Lavender looked up, dried her eyes, and said, quivering, "I can see whoever was next."

The crowd consoled her one by one as she told their fortunes. Marigold, as promised and with good business sense, did not charge any of these customers who walked to the hospital. I lingered long enough to finally receive two copies of the brochure Marigold had been providing, then returned home to prepare my report.

Leaving the cathedral following my briefing with Polaris, on my way to arrest Lavender, I decided to perform a disobedient act. I hoped for the girl to feel little pain, and so I planned to smother her with a rag soaked in a concentrated ether solution hidden under my attire. I knew I would eventually have this opportunity during the arrest, and the crowd would then see a disoriented, sedated girl unfit for execution.

The dense crowd of the marketplace parted at the sight of me, or rather the sight of me in my gray robes, and the drone of their voices turned to silence.

Transactions stalled, heads turned, and eyes stared, perhaps while an opportunistic thief stole a necklace to no one's notice. The smell of blood came to the crowd, but not yet the taste.

I wondered how long it might have lasted for some of the hundreds of bystanders who stared, as I marched directly toward the street-side studio business called the Mystic Garden. Since they would not hear my voice, they would wait to learn the identity of my mark. With so many present in this area, I doubted less than half of their heartbeats quickened.

Marigold was again advertising in the street as their business thrived. The stretch of patrons was again cramped with the sick, aged, and pregnant. The line parted with much more urgent accommodation than it had the day prior when the elderly man waited for death.

I moved quickly into the studio. The whispers of the crowd breezed, "Oh, he's here for the girl."

I tore the inner drapery from its post, the curtain that shielded Lavender and her patron from those waiting in line. A seated sickly woman startled and turned to look at me. Lavender's iridescent purple eyes latched on to me as well. All were watching. Someone in the crowd murmured, repeating, "Yes, he's here for the girl."

I swept the curtains around Lavender and tightly swaddled her arms and face, ensuring the process would leave her blindfolded but able to breathe. I carried her under my arm, squirming. I palmed the ether-dampened rag I had prepared and snuck it through the curtain onto her nose and mouth.

She had no choice but to breathe it in.

She wasn't heavy, and the best she could do to resist was kick her legs. She fought off the ether, as I'd preferred, never allowing it to make her unconscious. I carried her past the frozen, shocked line of people and proceeded through the studio doorway into the crowded marketplace.

Easily, a thousand eyes eagerly attended the writhing, protesting creature wrapped in the curtain under my arm, and her concealed identity only compounded their curiosity. Seconds prior, all these eyes had observed a summoner in gray march into a crowded dwelling to make an arrest. Without releasing the girl, I searched left and right again for her execution squadron. Until their arrival, I could do nothing but absorb the stares of the crowd.

A yellow patch caught my eye.

It was Marigold, stunned and no doubt hoping that I held a patron and not her sister squirming under my arm.

The next thing I noticed was to me a shock, as Polaris himself walked purposefully from the rear of the crowd toward me accompanied by several guardsmen in heavy, dark green armor and carrying nets and spears as if they expected the girl to transform into a hissing, winged jackal.

From four corners of the market next came the execution squadron: men of significant stature, easily three times the girl's weight, with shoulders so broad they could torque her neck and spine simply with their own hands. And yet they carried their instruments of execution: one, a small wooden platform; another, a broad axe for her neck; a third, a bucket and mop; and the fourth, a towering pike on which to mount her head once separated.

I stood barely three steps from the Mystic Garden's entrance and pressed my back against its outer wall, Lavender struggling lethargically because of the ether. The commoners of the marketplace parted for Polaris to pass, many kneeling in reverence, reminding me that I too once viewed him with the same mystique. Marching with his guardsmen to within several paces of us, the crowd and I awaiting his command, Polaris instructed, "Reveal her!"

"Lavender!" yelled Marigold from within the crowd. Lavender's eyelids drooped. She recognized the familiar voice and turned her head but did not respond.

"Quiet!" commanded Polaris as his guards turned to face Marigold and gripped their spears. Addressing the crowd, he continued, "This girl has committed treason and blasphemy. She is a threat to both our faith and our state. She has failed to follow mandate as the rest of you work so hard to do, and as such, you are promised a public execution."

The squadron collected near me, moving quite quickly. But before the wooden platform could even be mounted, a voice came anonymously from the crowd. "Does mandate not promise the offering of a split sentence?"

"Who speaks?" shouted Polaris.

The bold man continued, "Is she not entitled a divide if she is able to persuade someone to host the other half of her penalty?" Squinting through my hood, I spotted him: a peddler, a poor man . . . unshaved and in dirty brown garments but with luminous green eyes.

The law was old but valid, written in a time of famine. A desperate man caught habitually stealing could be spared if his wife or child—be it for love or simply reliance—could not survive without him but was willing to endure exile. I was as discouraged as I was surprised that a commoner, and a poor man, was in this case more deeply and usefully educated than I in my own field.

It didn't matter who made the suggestion, simply that someone had. Had Polaris not ordered this public execution, he would not have triggered this trap.

Polaris stood in a small clearing that had formed around me and the girl, his guards posted along its perimeter. He responded, "Who would share a split sentence with a traitor against our country? Who would want this unholy girl to escape execution only to join her in exile?"

"Me. I will," declared Marigold, emerging from her shock.

I studied Polaris's face and watched his wrinkles ease. I certainly didn't believe he'd expected the public spectacle he'd orchestrated to turn into a split sentence, but the idea of exiling the girl and her sister had to appeal to him.

"Arrest her!" yelled Polaris. His men seized Marigold as the execution squadron disassembled their small platform and stood back. The haste in which Polaris verified Marigold's name and intentions left still-hazy Lavender no time to protest her sister's decision. It also left me now more convinced Polaris wanted to be rid of both girls. Speaking to them loudly enough for the crowd to hear, he said, "You are hereby convicted of blasphemy and treason. You are sentenced to exile from the Canadian capital city of York and her surrounding rural districts. If you are found within these limits, you will be executed on site."

As Polaris was speaking, the guards blindfolded and shackled the girls.

"You will be escorted by your summoner to a remote location and released into the wilderness. You may wander the remainder of Canadian soil but are hereby no longer considered Canadians, both civically and in the eyes of the faith."

———

My final instructions were to load the sisters into a carriage and discard them to the northwest. I nodded in silence as they embarked for exile.

Traveling beyond the limits of the city, I recall the conversation along the way. Still affected by the ether and now likely numb, Lavender began to speak coherently but slowly to her sister. "I appreciate this, Marigold . . . but I hope you know . . . because I don't . . . where we're going."

"I do not," responded Marigold quickly. "Remember when we were children, and we would run into fences or trip on rocks? And Grandmother would say, 'Never move in a direction you're not looking?'"

"Well, we're blindfolded now." Lavender struggled to speak. "What are our . . . that we do . . . when this carriage stops?"

"Well, my intention is to interrupt frequently and reminisce about our home for the rest of our lives."

"Marigold . . . please, not now. Please, no manipulative . . . no attempts . . . humor greatly trivializes . . ."

"Do you know what I miss?" said Marigold in the middle of her sister's sentence. "The bakery back home. Oh, the aroma!"

By my estimation, Lavender was still somewhat under the ether's influence. I had almost forgotten that I used no ether on Marigold, and yet strangely her mood did not seem indicative of a girl who had just . . . well, I need not defend her. I shall simply state that she is responsible for herself with no behavioral explanation that I am aware of.

Lavender sighed at her sister's comments, numb now also with defeat, although that wasn't her sister's intention. "I played well . . . into that one. I should be . . . your inappropriate timing . . . I know. If it consoles you . . . a smile . . . half of my lips."

"Of course. That was the original purpose."

"This feels . . . surreal. Not five hours ago . . . was sleeping."

"In a bed. No reminders, I beg you," said Marigold in continued flippancy. "I don't enjoy camping."

Lavender responded, "Do you . . . take anything seriously?"

"Why would that be necessary when I have you?" Marigold shifted to speak to me, and I may have detected humor mixed with ironic flirtation as she asked, "Summoner? Might this carriage stop by my grandparents' farm? We're not interested in bidding permanent farewell to our family. Rather, if I am to be exiled, I'll require a fresh pair of stockings."

I laughed.

"You're the man with the bird! I never forget a man's laugh. You might say I have a gift."

"Wonderful, Marigold. You have . . . discovered him. Now he is . . . he'll kill us."

"Well, are we glowing white?"

"I'm . . . blindfolded, Marigold."

I looked around and saw nothing but trees and dirt country roads. I stopped the carriage, went to its rear platform where the girls were bound and removed their blindfolds.

There was no longer a need for silence. "I'll bring you to your grandparents' farm."

The day prior, an old man was dying while people stared. Today the people Lavender served nearly let her be executed . . . but this was not unfamiliar to me. A crowd expects the individual to emerge, someone else to step forward and assume the duty, risk, or responsibility. If this were not so common, leaders such as Polaris would not come to power. He never did consider the immeasurable benefit she could have had to our military. Or maybe he feared she would be stolen by the Siberians. One thing had made sense: the man with the green eyes knew to be in the marketplace, ready to save Lavender. If the execution were ever a threat to her, she would have glowed white; she would have seen it coming. But it was never that way. The green-eyed man had anticipated it.

After two hours, the girls emerged tearfully from their family's farmhouse. They reboarded the carriage peacefully and we went northwest until we reached the district limits.

2 / Heather

I never thought I'd give birth to a goddess, though I suppose I should be careful calling her that.

I was heavily pregnant, traveling in darkness to the far north to see my husband, when one of my five weary livestock nearly trampled a woman crossing a shallow river. Her silhouette knelt gently on the far side of the cool, flowing water. She was cradling something in her arms.

The silhouette approached, speaking unintelligible, guttural phrases, all while retching and grunting. *This is no woman,* I thought. *She attempts the voice of one but is some female miscreation.*

She stepped through the water toward me, carefully avoiding my livestock. I retreated quickly behind them. "What are you?"

The guttural cries continued from the creature. I was too pregnant to run. With little room left for my lungs, I would lose my breath quickly if I tried. I used the livestock as a living shield. She came right to my feet.

The clear sky and its stars revealed a human face trapped within a distorted woman's body. Thorns protruded from her skin, her body a weapon, and yet she looked at me with desperation. What I saw was not simply a play of the moonlight; her skin was gray. She repeated her pattern of noises. She began pointing to her treasure but held it hidden beneath her robe.

"You're a Siberian?" I asked.

"Siberia? Siberia?" she repeated excitedly, standing beneath me in ankle-deep water.

I had never seen a Siberian before. No Canadian had, except the few soldiers who had encountered them in battle and survived. From his training my husband had learned that they are lean, gray-skinned, and thorned. A sort of genetic abnormality, sharp protrusions of bone extend from their skeleton outward, piercing naturally through the skin. They are fashioned for violence, and their military invades Canadian soil relentlessly. "Go. I will not help a Siberian."

"Canada! Canada!" she cried.

"Go! Flee! Do you understand?" I shouted, pointing to the shore of the stream.

She stared hopelessly, finally pulling her treasure from her robe. It was a naked infant, held out not for me to take but for me to see.

"Oh my . . ." The child was not thorned; I wondered if this was even his mother. "Give me that child! Give him to me!" I shouted and gestured. She drew back defensively, took several steps toward the shore, but did not run. "You Siberia! He Canada! Give the child to me!"

I hoped to avoid violence, and believing that she held a small Canadian boy as her hostage, I pleaded, "Bread? Fruit? I will help! I . . . will . . . help . . . you! Do . . . not . . . eat . . . the . . . child!"

She returned to the shore and waited. She didn't run, and she didn't wish to end our encounter. But she had the child. I moved slowly, went toward her, and crossed the cool stream. I brought bread and fruit; slowly I placed them on a large rock while she watched. I cringed, thinking that beneath her robe, the thorns of her forearms might be burrowing into the child's soft skin.

Words were useless. I slowly pointed to the food, stood several paces aside, and prepared myself for pain as the desperate cannibal stared at me, confused. I reached into her arms, finding the child. She permitted a gentle touch, but once I tugged on the boy, the Siberian woman flailed a thorned backhand and struck me across the cheek.

I stumbled backward from the blow. She carefully set the child aside on the soil and charged as I retreated to the river. She reached me quickly, as if she wished to attack my womb, searching for another treasure, another infant to rip out and steal from its mother. She stopped and did not attack. Staring at me with her thorned forearms exposed, she might have slashed me anywhere she liked, but she hesitated. A jolt from a tollimore, loose and charging, knocked the barbarian upstream.

The unbridled animal came to my side. We were both a bit shredded, the tollimore bleeding from her scalp simply from burying it in the thorned Siberian's flank. The woman rose to her feet, and a man shouted from the shoreline, "Stop!"

A lantern illuminated the source of the voice, from where the woman had left the infant boy. A man stood holding the child in one arm and a light in the other. The Siberian approached him desperately, but he would not return the child. "Take the bread and fruit and be gone," he commanded. "Find your way off Canadian soil." He tossed a handful of tiles onto the ground.

The woman cried, whimpered, and yowled, but stayed on the shore of the shallow river as the man handed me the boy and I got on his cart.

"Thank you," I said.

"The woman has food and Canadian currency. The child is safe and will not be eaten," he said quietly amid the Siberian's howls.

He was nearly forty, a half-generation my elder. He looked to be a poor man, for a merchant. He was overweight, unshaven, and smelled unwashed. He wore layers of brown garments, which I don't doubt he slept in. But he had one remarkable feature: glowing, shimmering eyes, which were green like a celestial flare. I had seen green eyes before but nothing quite like this.

"Had you not been here, I might have been killed. The child too."

"You may thank me, but you have a fine tollimore if she is willing to defend you. Be faithful to her, and she will help you again. Eventually."

"Thank you," I said, looking over at my weary livestock keeping pace with the cart.

"I'm sorry you were injured. The cart has bandages and balm if you can find them. Among the herbs I have lavender, for any wounds. Please, I insist you use it."

"I will."

"Is your daughter all right?"

"Excuse me?" I looked him in the eyes as we rode. Without blinking I asked, "You say I am to have a girl?"

"A girl, yes. And please, have the lavender."

"She's fine. I feel her moving."

"What are you doing so far from the capital?" he asked.

"I'm a farmer's daughter from the rural districts north of York. I have a daughter, Marigold, with a man named Simon, whom I am traveling to see. Marigold is with my parents, on the farm. She's not quite one and a half seasons, close in age to her younger brother or sister."

"Sister."

"So you say. Simon is my husband, a soldier in the Canadian military. He's stationed at Fort Alert here on Ellesmere Island, and I would like him to see his second child. The Siberians invade Ellesmere as predictably as the long sunset. I worry what will become of my Simon. Blow the horn, signal the next horn blower to the south? This chain of horns may reach us back home . . . but of Simon and the others furthest north? I want him to see his second child at least once, in case . . . he doesn't get another chance. My father provided five livestock from our farm for milk, protection, and a shepherd's camouflage. In return I insisted on going alone. He wouldn't have it, so I snuck out."

"And here you are." He smiled.

"But I'm not there yet."

"I'll make sure you get to where you need to be," he said. "And your daughter."

The journey to Fort Alert continued without any trouble, though the peddler believed we had a Canadian scout following us. He oddly asked that I not attempt to nurse the boy we had saved until we reached Simon, concerned that it could trigger labor. Along the horizon veils of green and violet rolled over the sky like thin curtains shifted by a breeze. It was the dawn of the Celestial Lights, illuminating our path and painting a peaceful smile on the peddler's face. He said he didn't want my child to be born until we reached the lights.

We approached a clearing in sight of Fort Alert. "I should go no further," he said, stopping his cart behind a clump of thick trees. "Only military are allowed this far north, not visitors. I know as well as you that this is against Canadian mandate."

He got out of the cart to release and return my protective tollimore. He kept the rest of the livestock, saying he would return them one day. I wouldn't have been able to bring them home alive anyway.

"I suppose I'll be arrested. But I worry much more about my husband's destiny, as well as that of this boy, and my own children."

"We have a future, not a destiny," he replied.

"You don't believe in destiny?"

"No. Destiny, or fate, is the absurd idea that moments in your life, other than death, will make certain they occur for you, and that the entire universe will orchestrate itself in preparation for those moments in your life. Young lady, these are the best words I can leave you with: do not fear the future and what it will do to us. Worry only about what you will do. Though if you were willing to make this journey, I'd bet you already knew that."

"Thank you for your help, sir. I would be lost in the forests if not for you."

"It's good that you came here."

From the clearing I walked, child in womb and carrying a child not my own in my arms, alongside my one faithful tollimore. The Celestial Lights were blooming and hanging, casting shimmering shadows behind us. Their beauty was pastoral to the heavens, so viewed with admiration by the sea that her waters reflected her sister's display in echo and applause. I casually approached the battalion encampment in hopes to find Simon, so welcomed by the sky's meadow that I didn't consider how to approach the shoreline fort without causing an alarm.

None could have been more vulnerable than I was, and yet the lights were so convincing in their harmony that I considered danger impossible. How could this be the site of persistent Siberian invasion? How could human discord exist here? Or anywhere when your eyes look up? *There must be no better place to have a child*, I thought.

"Halt!"

Facing the fort, I replied, "I am Heather, wife of Simon."

"Quiet!" came the voice again. I placed it behind me, from the forest, not the fort.

I turned to find a Canadian scout, bow readied and arrow drawn. He came toward me, body frozen above the waist, keeping the bow drawn.

"I come to see my . . ." I began, interrupted by a horn now coming from behind, from the fort.

The horn blew once more, and footsteps shuffled on creaking wood planks. Doors slammed, latches squealed, and a voice from the fort boomed, "You, with the weapon! Who are you?"

With tension still on his bow, I hoped the archer's shoulder held strong. He answered, "A Canadian scout. I serve Polaris."

"Very well," boomed the fort. "Who are you then, with the tollimore?"

"My name is Heather, wife of Simon. I come to . . . "

Another voice. "Heather? Heather, you've gotten so much bigger!"

"Simon! Simon, where are you?"

"Simon, hold your position!" came the first voice. "Woman, go with the scout. Leave here. It's not safe for you, or for us to have you. It compromises our fort, all of our country."

"I cannot! I cannot leave!" After a pause and no reply from the fort, I yelled, "I'm in labor!"

When I was carrying Marigold, the midwife explained that there is labor and there is false labor. This was *very* false labor—my own variety. I moved the infant boy, already beneath my coat for warmth, to my breast. "Ho, you're a strong one," I mumbled. The child found me and latched on with incredible pull. He was a survivor. I stood frozen, biting my cheek to adjust to the suckling, waiting for either the scout or the fort to do something, anything.

The scout relaxed his bow finally, and a single medic emerged from the fort to inspect me. I stood as Fort Alert remained silent, perhaps while a hundred young men stared from behind binoculars.

"Heather is your name?" asked the medic as he reached me, exposed in the field before the fort's gate.

"Ye-yes." I grimaced.

"And you are in labor . . . with Simon's child?"

I nodded.

"You shouldn't be here, Heather. But if you are indeed in labor, we'll care for you."

He walked around me the way a carriage driver would inspect his cart before a long ride. "What are you holding under your coat?"

"A child. A boy. Not my own."

He waved for the scout. "Archer! Come here; we'll need you to return to York quickly. Bring this baby to safety."

"He has no parents," I explained. "Please, I will nurse him. Let me keep him. I can raise the child."

The voice from the fort commanded: "Heather, do as the medic says and give the boy to the scout. If you wish to adopt him, do so formally through the orphanage in York."

"No!" My body had not yet responded, and I still needed the child to induce labor.

"Please, I must inspect you," explained the medic.

"Clean your hands first! Give me a moment to nurse the—" and my water broke.

He shuffled me away from the fort because I was not permitted inside, even considering my condition. Simon was excused from duty to be with me. We were together, finally, in a small grove under the sky, under the lights.

I embraced and kissed my husband and between contractions tried to explain my journey and its purpose.

The scout left with the infant. Explaining the red lines of blood across my face, I told Simon about the Siberian creature from whom we rescued the child. He said, "Canadians often say that Siberians eat babies, but until now I assumed those to be words of ignorance and intolerance, or at least exaggeration."

"She was a monster."

The medic rejoined us with his kit full of sharp tools and bandages, reminding me of the pain and blood that lay before me. The joy in Simon's face faded as he said: "Heather, thank you for coming here, but you'll be arrested, and possibly our child as well."

"At this point, I'm relying on it. I have no other means of returning home. I have little supplies, no tiles, no protection, and soon a child."

"Well then, I won't wait to tell you," announced the impatient medic. "You and I, your tollimore and your son or daughter, will be returning to York once you've given birth."

"My daughter," I explained. "I am to have a girl."

Simon and the medic glanced at each other but chose not to argue with a woman in labor.

The colors in the sky continued to dance while the two men stayed by my side, politely bored as I battled nature. "Have some milk from the tollimore," I offered. "She would appreciate it if you took some out of her."

I needed something to focus on to get through the pain, so I studied the tollimore. A tollimore's head is waist-high to a human. The animal is four-legged and hoofed, with long, usually black, shiny fur clinging to its body. Tassels hang beneath its chin and behind each hoof. Its lower jaw protrudes a bit more than the upper, with thick, flat, grazing teeth that grind left to right, a sight that is always worth a smile. Each eye's pupil resembles an hourglass on its side. Its abdomen bulges behind its ribs, as if the creature carries a treasure inside, but the greatest value of the breed is the female's well-developed udder, the result of generations of selection.

I studied the tollimore again. *A tollimore's head is waist-high to a human, four-legged and hoofed, with long, usually black, shiny fur clinging to its body . . .*

I paced around the grove, leaned against nearby trees with the palms of my hands, and howled through the contractions. My parents more accurately remember the details from Marigold's delivery than I do, as I inexplicably forgot much of my own experience of the process. However, with Lavender, none present in her grove or inside the fort could forget the display in the sky, which provided such a beautiful distraction. It was clear and cloudless with the Celestial Lights glowing like a broad, delicate ribbon. Iridescent jades, identical in color to the peddler's eyes, and fresh lavenders shimmered in spectral bloom and pleasantly occupied me in labor. Only these visions, along with Simon, the animal, and the fort's medic accompanied the birth of my second daughter. The illumination poured down on our clearing as she was born and remained there for some time.

It had happened.

Simon had seen his second child.

Quietly and peacefully, she opened her eyes, quite soon after birth. Perhaps the brilliance of the sky overhead opened them itself, and if so, it was our first indication that she had the ability of sight.

"I've never seen that color before," said the medic.

"Nor I," said Simon. "They're clear, not even murky like Marigold's when she was first born. Are those truly purple eyes, or is that just an effect of the Lights?"

"No, they really are purple. Or maybe a sort of violet," said the medic.

"Or maybe lavender," said Simon. Once I told him what the peddler had said earlier, about the lavender I traded from him, we agreed on her name. I didn't expect the color to be her permanent shade, but to this day they are identical to when she first opened them, when they were soaked in the Lights.

Immediately after Lavender's arrival, once the medic had finished performing his duties, he returned to the fort to inform the battalion leader of the birth. The medic then circled hastily back to our clearing. We had little time to recover as a family before he instructed Simon and me to bid our farewells. For my entire journey to this moment, I had been certain this farewell would not feel so ominous. I reminded my husband of his two daughters who needed him, my father's farm, and anything my mind could produce in the moment to encourage him not to be a hero in battle. But in the end it would be our final good-bye.

The medic escorted me south, directly to York, where I was imprisoned with my newborn daughter. They did not separate us. The justice we would receive for disobeying a widely known war mandate—that a civilian must not enter a military zone—would quite possibly require the attention of the great Polaris himself.

After two nights my father and mother were permitted to visit. Marigold, one and a half at the time, stayed with neighbors. She would have to wait patiently to meet her younger sister.

My parents and I shared explanations. The animals were gone, aside from the one tollimore, which the medic returned to their farm. When I saw that they weren't bothered by my news, I knew something much worse had happened. My father explained that all the men of Fort Alert had been killed when the Siberians attacked, with the exception of the medic who escorted me to prison. The invasion was held off at the fort nearest to the south, but Fort Alert and its men had been destroyed.

I would in time grieve for my husband, and still do, but throughout it all I held a newborn child in my arms.

Then I was confronted. On the third night in prison, I received a visit by the great Polaris, the celestial ruler of Canada's military and leader of our faith. He wore a white-and-black robe, black on the left and right, the middle, a white stripe from his neck to his feet.

"Why are the men of Fort Alert dead?" he questioned. "Why am I wearing a robe of mourning?"

"The Siberians, I understand, sir." Lavender's cries competed with Polaris's voice.

"And where was the medic?" He lunged toward my cell, as if to insist I was only safe from him because of the bars that protected me.

I didn't retreat from the bars, not with my child in my arms, simply because he advanced too quickly. Standing near him but with bars between, I noticed what rumors had told me. He was older than anyone you know, beyond a number, already a grown man when he came to our ancestors from the sky. When he approached, the color from his red eyes almost vanished, his skin became ashy, and I saw just how old he was. There were wrinkles of course, many of them, and nearly as many scars like the one I would soon have across my cheek from the Siberian's backhand. And yet if he retreated only slightly none of this was discernable.

"The medic was with me, sir," I answered after gathering my courage.

"Yes, he certainly was. And do you know what happens when it's very cold, and a Siberian sword, or even just one of their thorns grazes a soldier's shoulder, or a Siberian arrow lands on a Canadian's toe?" he asked rhetorically, yet obviously demanded a response.

"No, sir, I don't."

"The wounds become fatal!" he shouted, flaring up like a furnace, ignoring Lavender's continual screams. Noticing the bandages on my arms, he continued: "You see when a soldier is inflicted with a minor injury and does not have the luxury of comfortable temperature, they will experience one of two hands: the hand of a medic to heal their wound, or the hand of death. It's just one of many reasons Canadian mandate clearly insists only soldiers occupy certain regions. Why, young lady, did the poor soldiers of Fort Alert experience the hand of death and not that of a Canadian medic?"

"Well, sir, I had just given birth and the medic was . . . "

"I know what happened!" He continued to smolder, asking, "Are you Siberian yourself?"

"No, sir," I said, confused as to how he could think that. "I don't have thorns."

"That doesn't matter," he scoffed. "You and your child, whom I might add also broke mandate, would be fortunate to be exiled and not beheaded."

"My husband is dead because of this! How could that be the work of a Siberian? How could I have wanted this to happen? I'm left to raise two young girls alone."

"That's true. Perhaps knowing your actions have killed your husband will be punishment enough," he said calmly, extinguishing his rage abruptly, like a snuffed flame. With this, his rant seemed to have been so deliberate and almost calculated. I was relieved, but his words were scorched into my mind. Every day since then has convinced me that I truly received a crueler punishment than death.

He released me from prison but warned me that he was doing so after an act of treason. From that day on, he kept a file on Lavender. I know he did. I could see it in the way he looked at her bright, beautiful eyes.

I returned to the same farm, yet a different home. Simon had died, Lavender had arrived, and I wished to adopt the infant boy. After several days I walked to the orphanage in York and asked for him. He was not there and never had been. I never saw the child again, not since he left the fort in the hands of the scout. I don't know what his future held but decided to take the peddler's advice. I stopped worrying about the future.

3 / The Lichen

I used to be a monster, but now I'm not.

Sister Lavender and Sister Marigold were the first two humans to come to my clearing, speak to me, and survive. When I first heard them talking, they were discussing their next meal. The horizon was dim but not entirely dark, as it was the time of season when Brother Sun dips only a little below the horizon at night. I went into my usual performance when I heard the humans: a territorial scream, stomping my stone fists against the ground and against each other, and went into a slow crawl to follow their voices.

"What are those noises?" one of the girls asked the other.

"I see nothing. I'll tell you if we're in danger," she responded.

A thick, dead tree made my threats more convincing. With one stone fist I swept it up by the roots and smashed it into the ground while its brittle branches snapped.

"Stop, please!" yelled one of the girls.

I searched for them in the dim light, but for voices that sounded so near, I still couldn't see them. I pounded the tree again and swung it left and right to vibrate both the earth and the air.

"Peace! Peace!" cried the voice again.

"Yes, peace!" yelled the other. "And happiness! Rainbows, sunshine, fresh bread, and all good things. Please, rock man; just stop!"

I finally saw them, hiding behind a poison-berry bush.

"Are we okay?" asked the yellow-haired one of her sister, still fixing her gaze on me.

"Yes, Marigold. We're fine. I told you I'd say something if we were in danger."

"You didn't even look at me," said Marigold. "It would make me feel better if you looked at me."

"Why didn't you run?" I asked.

"We were never in any danger," said the one with the short, dark hair and purple eyes.

"How did you know that?" I asked.

"My name's Lavender, and this is my sister Marigold. I have the ability to tell if someone is about to die. Are you the Lichen?"

"Yes. And this is my lake. You have wandered into my clearing."

"You're huge. You scared us, you know. You sounded like a geyser," said Marigold.

"When have you ever heard a geyser?" asked Lavender.

"This would be my first. If it were one."

"You're really the Lichen?" asked Lavender. "We've heard legends about you."

"Oh? And what do the humans say about me?"

"That you're a large creature with arms but no legs, made of a series of stones held together by some kind of dry lichen plant. All of which appears to be true."

"And that you kill anyone who comes to your clearing," added Marigold. "But you don't seem like you're going to."

"I'm not going to kill you. I've never killed anyone. You'll find more danger in the berry from that bush than you will from me."

"Yes, we know," said Lavender. "These berries are poisonous."

I set the dead tree down and told them, "That's the only danger you face here: the mushrooms and berries."

Lavender paused, stared, and asked, "So you're a friend?"

"I can be. I'd like to be."

"Then why the attack?" asked Sister Marigold.

"To scare you away. It's true; if any human comes to my clearing, they die. But I'm not the one who kills them. It's the food that grows around my lake. All of it is poisonous."

"Not all the berries are," explained Sister Lavender. "We're figuring out which are edible, and which aren't."

"How?"

"Trial and error," smiled Marigold. "I slowly bring a berry or mushroom to my mouth, and if my sister yells 'Poison!' then I don't eat it."

"That's very trusting."

Marigold continued, "It's that or we starve. We've been exiled."

They waited for me to speak. "You've been exiled? Then come with me. I have a pile of curiosities that I've stripped from every traveler who has died in my clearing. You may take what you like."

"How long have people been dying in your clearing?" asked Sister Lavender.

"Centuries."

I used to be stones in a crater, but now I'm alive. In my earliest memories I was alone. Facing toward Brother Sky, I watched as a pale green lattice—some type of a fungus or flora, with a dry texture—spread throughout the rocks within my view.

The rocks to which it spread were dark brown, red, and black. Eventually I was able to command motion of these rocks, but only after the lattice had reached them from their origin, the region which provides me with thought and sight. Each discovery of new motion was as the others before: awkward, heavy, and gracelessly uncoordinated. In time, and only with the flourishing of the lattice across the rocks, I developed command of two limbs and a torso.

I am a series of many dark, dense stones, which would never hold together or even stack against gravity without the assembling lattice. The stones are my flesh; some are small, some large. I'm only able to move slowly, but every patch of lattice can be traced across my body to any other patch, as all are thoroughly connected—and I believe in unity—while concentrating densely around my two eyes.

I came to be in a crater, broad in diameter but not deeply set into the terrain. Its rim served as a barrier to escape, but by using my arms I was able to drag myself out of it.

In times of drought I became weak, clumsy, and after a severely and perpetually rainless sky, immobile. This would last only until the next rain, which would refresh the lattice and revive my strength and mobility. For this reason, I began observing Brother Cloud. Then came the deluge.

The deluge originated from the horizon to the slight right of where the sun rises and came during the transitioning days from persistent light to the season of darkness. The deluge moved slowly, as do I, by the grasp of its arms. It refused to dissipate. When it grew near, it revealed a peculiar rotation I've never seen even from the strongest storm. Facing it as it approached, I could see it turned from left to right. So spun its arms, which hurled the air with such force that I began to believe even I would be lifted from the soil. As it passed overhead, for which it required a full day, there was a brief sense of peace as the sky dissolved from darkness to clear blue and Brother Wind rested. Soon and in succession followed the remainder of the storm, as powerful as its first attack. With both stages, rain fell onto the soil and drenched the ground until rain fell only upon more rain.

In the trail of the deluge lay crippled trees, flooded soil, and adjusted terrain. Most noticeably altered was my crater, now full of rainwater. The crater became my lake, which provided the solution to my only natural need. Should I become weak or begin to lose mobility, I need only bathe in this new lake. I dare not stray far from my lake.

Sister Lake persisted long after the deluge had ended, and in time became murky green as vegetation began to grow in her water. Soon, fungus appeared along the damp shore, with shrubs, berries, and eventually larger trees. If the deluge brought the gift of the lake, and the lake brought the gift of flora, then all brought the gift of the crowned elk.

The crowned elk were magnificent and noble, and by no accident to their name, quite regal. They arrived from the same direction every season preceding the session of darkness. They reversed their path once the darkness began to concede to the sun and retraced their migration. With each pass, my lake became a landmark of their journey, although this I tell of is still thousands of seasons in the past.

With the gift of the elk came Brother and Sister Human, and a fascinating new model of behavior. In proportion to the crowned elk, these humans were much smaller. In proportion to me, they were less than one tenth my size. Because of my stone body, I was over one hundred times their weight.

The first tribe of humans to come to my clearing wore hide sandals with hide straps, furs, and in some cases feather arrangements around their waists. The furs appeared to be that of the elk, and often I saw a buck human wearing the trophy antlers of a crowned elk, for both status and decoration. When I realized the humans wished to hurt the elk, I wished ill on the humans. I assumed they wanted to make me lonely. I didn't understand them.

As the elk migrated and drank from my lake, the humans followed. Though the elk and other creatures could tolerate the wild fruits and mushrooms around my clearing, Brother and Sister Human could not. I found the first dead human after a hunt passed through. He had black-stained fingers and tongue. Then I found another, and a third.

I wasn't happy to see the humans suffer, and I feared my ill will had caused the deaths of the three. I dragged their corpses to a mound for collection. I stripped their personal effects, which were no more than their fur garments, and started a curiosity pile. Upset now that the clearing had taken the lives of three humans, and afraid they would not venture near my lake again as a result, I set to eradicate the toxins of my home.

I patrolled my territory, seeking ill will only to the mushrooms and berries that grew there. I smashed them, ripped them up from the soil, buried them, or immersed them in water, but every attempt was a failure . . . ten more appeared in the same location mere days later, particularly the mushrooms. I even attempted uprooting, dragging my stone arms and disrupting the soil, but nothing proved permanently effective. I struggled to accept Brother Mushroom and Sister Berry, and they refused to be rejected.

My lake continued to be a landmark to both Sister Elk and the nomadic human for centuries. With every season, I would see the mothers nursing their new spotted fawns and find at least several poisoned humans in my clearing. Over time, the migration pattern shifted, and humans began settling in cities. But still on occasion a merchant or traveler succumbed to the berries by my lake.

As one human lay dying, I dragged myself over to hear his final words. He spoke first. "You beast! I've seen your vulgar trophies. You won't have the satisfaction of killing me as you have the others. I am the victim of a berry! A tiny, poisoned berry, and not you, you hideous monster!"

"Monster?" I asked. "I've never killed anything."

"I've seen your mound of corpses. How many have you killed? Do you eat their bodies? Eat mine and be poisoned."

"You wish ill on me. You see me as a monster."

"I see you as you are! Have any escaped this place?" he mocked, still searching for victory in death.

"Only those too afraid to come into my clearing," I answered, realizing the truth.

After his death, I set up crude, intentionally harmless and escapable traps as deterrents. If any human died from the berries or mushrooms, I mounted their bodies along the clearing's perimeter, usually suspended on an old wooden spear. At first sight of a wandering human or even merely smoke in the distance, I would growl and moan, since sound travels much faster than I do. Pounding my fists into the dirt, I would drag myself as quickly as was possible for a creature of stone.

As the seasons passed, I saw fewer and fewer of the fascinating creatures, but they never disappeared or stopped dying by my lake. Even if it was hurtful to me, I always sought to learn something from their final words, to gain something from their death that could help the next human. I gathered much in their final moments, caught between life and death, with a brief understanding of both.

On occasion I would strip something new from one of their corpses, be it a coin, garment, or tool, each representing a failure, a lapse in my duty to keep humans and death from my territory. Some would flee on sight of my amassed pile of artifacts, and in those I found success. On several occasions I attempted peaceful greetings, a quickly abandoned campaign; always my efforts were met with terror, after which the human would flee, yelling, "The Lichen!"

And so, I gathered, "the Lichen" was a monster to be feared. Their fear would save them. But I still wished no ill on the poison berries or mushrooms.

There was no reason to.

———————

I told Sister Lavender and Sister Marigold my story as I led them around the lake to my collection of artifacts. I silently studied them as they listened. Forgive my detail; I enjoy studying humans.

Sister Marigold had long, yellow hair. She wore elevated, strapped yellow sandals. I had never seen a traveler wear such inconvenient footwear before. She wore a dress dyed the color of the sky. Her dress had flamboyant patterns of embroidered flowers and delicate vines. For form, I believe, and not for comfort, she cinched her dress just above her waist with a thin beaded belt. Her dress was decorated with more beads and ruffles. I don't believe any of it would be practical for hunting or throwing a spear. On top of this dress I didn't understand, she carried small merchant's pouches around her waist and a strong satchel of treated leather, worn as a sling from left shoulder to right hip. On her right wrist were several thin metal bracelets, whose functions were their decoration, I believe, and not spiritual protection. Her eyes were hazel. Her face and its features were proportionate and balanced, but, as I learned, she was quick to smile asymmetrically, tilt her head, or raise one eyebrow and not the other.

Sister Lavender stood behind Marigold in wooden shoes lined with fleece that formed cuffs around the ankles. On her legs were stockings, thin and black. She wore a sand-colored tunic ending above the knee and a brown braided rope cinched around her waist. Over this was a thick hooded robe, double layered to be outwardly black and the green of the forest within. It ended at her ankles and gathered with the tunic around her neck. Strapped to her back was her satchel, stained black. Her face resembled her sister's, though it was more reserved and less likely to exaggerate its features. The two dressed quite differently, yet there was a certain similarity of structure. Their complexions were different. Lavender's skin was paler, and her hair was dark brown if not black. She wore it short, with most strands ending below her chin but above her shoulder. The hair above her forehead was cut short and not allowed below her brow, preventing obstruction of her unusual purple eyes and their dim glow. Her eyes were the single feature she possessed that was not hidden or understated.

I am so fascinated by living humans, with such fleeting opportunity to study them, that I attempt to quickly absorb every detail. I also noticed that the robe and tunic were held together with a patterned clasp at the neckline.

As we came within sight of my items, I asked, "What's the symbol on your clasp?"

"Oh, it's"—she stalled—"it was a friend. Her name was Ellie."

"Does your friend have four legs?"

"She did, yes," answered Lavender as we walked. "She's gone now."

"She was a tollimore," explained Marigold. "A farm animal that saved our mother from an attacker when she was about to give birth to Lavender."

"Ellie's buried back home." Lavender looked down at the soil. "On the family plot. She lived as long as can be expected of a tollimore, but I still miss her. She was a good friend growing up."

"I used to have many friends with four legs, but they're gone now. Brother and Sister Elk don't come to my clearing anymore. So, there's nothing spiritual about your clasp?"

"No. Just a memory of an old friend."

"I wonder. If you're exiled, are you still of the Canadian faith?"

They both paused.

"It's molded us, and that doesn't change, however . . ." responded Marigold only to interrupt herself. "Sister Lavender, I don't specifically remember Polaris's words. Does this exile include excommunication?"

"Marigold, where is the cathedral?" asked Lavender, knowing the answer.

"York."

"And where were we exiled from?"

"So, you're nomads now?" I asked. "It's been many, many seasons since I've seen nomads."

"Yes," answered Lavender. "We came to your clearing to sleep, and in searching for food we found berries and mushrooms."

"You said you had a method to sort the edible from the poison ones. But if you aren't careful, your personal effects and all of your clothing will be strewn in a pile with my collection."

"Do you promise?" said the yellow-haired girl as she confusingly closed one of her eyes and smiled at me.

"Marigold! Don't tease!" corrected Lavender.

"Why? He must be terribly lonely."

"That . . . may . . . be . . . but . . . he's . . . made . . . of . . . stone."

"Yes, and so are you, apparently," said Marigold to her sister.

"I'm sorry. I don't understand what you're saying."

"My sister," said Lavender, sighing. "She flirts with the populace."

Marigold smiled. "And occasionally with death itself. But I'm not to be blamed for that relationship. Lavender introduced us."

"Marigold, please," said Lavender.

Nothing seemed to bother the yellow-haired girl. I enjoyed their company, both of them.

Lavender asked, "So you've devoted your existence to protecting humans from poison, though they fear you and see you as a beast?"

"Yes. For thousands of seasons."

"Well, don't reveal your intent to help them, unless you want to be punished for it," she said. "You're better off if they fear you and think of you as a monster."

"Lavender, stop," said Marigold.

"They do think of me as a monster," I stated. "Any human who has seen my collection of artifacts surely would conclude I've murdered hundreds. I hope it won't be this way forever."

"Yes, perhaps the filth you're trying to serve will not continue to paint you as an outcast," said Lavender.

"You've made your point," replied her sister.

"You've been misunderstood. How would the Canadian faith have you respond in this situation?" I asked.

Lavender answered, "Polaris is the sole author of all scripture read at the cathedral. He writes in quatrains. Marigold, help me . . . If violence serves . . ."

Marigold quoted with ease:

If violence serves reaction to profound
Then wasted words, on deafness you have preached
Defend yourself, an enemy you've found
Protect your ears from minds that can't be reached

"So, all who disagree with his preaching are his enemy? I could not disagree more. Yet, if I protect my ears as he suggests, how will I understand him?"

"Why would you need to understand him?" asked the gifted girl.

"Far better to understand those you disagree with than those of common mind. Lavender, if I may, I sense the Canadian faith hasn't prepared you for a moment like this."

"The Canadian faith has declared me an abomination."

"That's how the world sees me too," I said as we continued to walk together. "If I'm being punished for helping the ones who say this, so be it. They don't accept me, but neither the martyr nor the violent sociopath has the approval of society. The one difference is, with the violent sociopath, it's mutual."

There was a silence. I had done one of three things with the girl: struck an epiphany, offended her terribly, or simply confused her.

"How is it you speak of society, having never been its member?"

"Those thoughts were derived from a poisoned man's final words. I've learned a great deal from listening to the thoughts of the dying. This man believed himself to be the first to die of the toxins, but he was far from it."

"He believed he was unique," concluded Marigold. "He sounds a little self-absorbed."

"Self-absorbed?" asked Lavender, taken aback.

"Maybe. But he only had a few words left, and he chose them well," I said.

Marigold meanwhile was dancing around behind me. I had never been in a human conversation like this one before.

"Marigold, careful!" yelled Lavender.

"Well, am I glowing?"

I felt a foot on my back, then another.

"No."

"Then join me! He's as tall as a tree! Even in the twilight, the view is magnificent!"

I laughed, still dragging one pillar-arm in front of the other and undulating toward my pile of human artifacts. I smiled and thought, *Not since the curious elk has anything like this happened.*

———————

I used to take artifacts off dead bodies. Now I give them away.

Reaching the pile, I pulled back a canvas tarp as Lavender and Marigold dismounted my rocky backside and began to search for anything they could use in their travels. They grabbed coins—from many different countries, they said—and collected them in a pouch.

They took stones the humans had worn around their necks, and different colored metals from pockets.

"I'm glad you've already discarded the bodies," said Marigold, rummaging through my pile.

"What's this?" asked Lavender, finding a small tool of wood, clear glass, and metal. It bore several alphabetic symbols.

"Where did you find it?"

"With some very large, bizarre, porous armor. It was near a huge, serrated sword of a similar design," answered Lavender.

"Ah, the great bird creature," I remembered. "He was as big as I am, but his body much lighter. He had feathers and even scales. He died here, fell from the sky. In a storm, actually. I don't believe he consumed the berries or mushrooms, but I don't know."

"What was his tool for?"

"With the swiveling needle? I don't believe it still functions as it should. It spins erratically."

Confused, Lavender explained, "For me it only points in a single direction."

Marigold hopped over to her sister to form her own speculation. "Then it's a man finder. There are four letters. N for 'No!', E for 'Eh,' S for 'You may have my Sister . . .'"

"Hey!" chirped Lavender.

". . . and W for 'When can we schedule the Wedding?'"

I smiled and asked, "What am I reading?"

"You're reading 'S,'" joked Marigold.

"Give me," blurted Lavender, repossessing the device from her sister. "The needle points in only one direction as I pivot the base. The letters seem meaningless."

"I've never seen that," I commented, now curious myself.

I planted my fists in the ground to drag myself over to where she stood, and within an arm's reach—one of mine, that is—Lavender commanded, "Stop!"

"What?"

"Now it does spin," she said. She walked slowly toward me, focused on the device's needle, and repeated, "It spins faster as I get closer to you."

"Correct. A man finder," confirmed Marigold to herself.

"If it just spins when near me, I'll never observe it otherwise. It's useless to me and you may have it. I hope you discover its function and make use of it someday."

"This is doubtful, but thank you," said Lavender. "I believe its only function is in my sister's novelties."

"Hmm . . . " said Marigold.

"What?" asked Lavender.

"Someone was an artist. I found some brushes."

"So?"

"I have an idea," explained Sister Marigold. She dug further into my pile, sorting through garments and grabbing any pale-colored blouses or trousers. "Lavender, fetch one mushroom and berry of every kind."

We sorted them out into the two standard mushroom categories: edible and poisonous. Lavender used the technique she mentioned earlier with Marigold but brought the mushroom toward her own mouth instead. If it was poisonous, her arm would stop and she would say, "Poison." If not, the mushroom would fall in a different pile. I cringed at how rapidly she worked, advancing so quickly on death only to stop suddenly and always just beyond its reach.

By then Marigold had rummaged a second time through my artifacts, and in this sweep searched for ink. She began to draw on the garments, creating pictures of each mushroom and berry. Limited in color with only black ink, she described them in writing on the cloth's space beside the picture. She seemed to enter a state of flow as she worked, one of strong focus yet freedom from worry. It reminded me of the deluge.

"You use the tool with your left hand," I noted. "When the nomads assembled in formation with spears, a left-holding spear thrower always drew attention."

She laughed as she painted. "So you've met my ancestors. They probably believed themselves modern and contemporary. Few realize themselves to be living in both Ancient Canada and its distant future, or any country for that matter. Had I lived then, however, they would not have given me a spear. I would have been given a paintbrush and told to decorate the caves . . . and I would have painted some windows."

"And if you lived in the distant future?" I asked.

"I do! By their reference, at least."

Their work took several hours. Nearing completion, Sister Marigold told Sister Lavender and me to fetch all the spears and wood we could find from my pile. We stretched out the garments so they were taut and attached each between two spears.

Marigold explained, "You can mount these throughout your clearing. They warn which mushrooms are poisonous and which are not. On each is a note to not eat the berries. There's only one kind and it's not safe to consume."

"I notice a familiar design on the bottom of each sign. Is that me, Marigold?"

"Why, yes, it is."

"And what are those words beside my image?"

"It reads: 'Brother Lichen—friendly, not poisonous.' Accepted?"

"Embraced," I responded, feeling light as a human. "I used to be without a friend, but now I have two."

The two sisters came over, spread their arms as far out as they could, and wrapped their flesh around my stone torso. I opened my palms and hugged back.

"So, what's next for you, Brother Lichen?" asked Marigold. "Travel the world?"

"I think I'll stay near my clearing and meet her people first. Thanks to you. What about you? Where will you go next?"

Lavender's face sank. "We can't go home. We have no home."

"Not now, maybe. But I have one more idea," said Marigold. "A book, inspired by Brother Lichen. And it does require travel. We can catalog every mushroom, berry, herb, leaf, flower petal, and even small game in the known world, in the same way we were able to determine the edibility of the food in this clearing. I already have a title: The Field Guide to Life and Death."

"So travelers will know what they can eat in the wild?" asked Lavender.

"Exactly!"

"That's a good idea," said Lavender.

"You'd be using your gift for great good," I noted.

Marigold added, "Who knows? It may even be enough good for Polaris to forget our conviction and allow us to return home."

"Return to York?" scoffed Lavender. "You're kissing the moon, Marigold. Polaris hates me."

"I doubt it," said Marigold. "He hardly even knew you."

"He wanted me dead. I shouldn't have to defend that."

"Sister Lavender, are we friends?" I asked.

"Yes, of course, Brother Lichen."

"And among human friends, is it best to be honest?"

"Yes," she said with hesitation.

"I may not know Polaris, but I would suggest he doesn't hate you. What he did likely had nothing to do with you."

"How would you know?" asked Lavender. "I think it had an awful lot to do with me."

"But it wasn't to hurt you. I've never seen humans act with sole motivation to hurt anyone."

"Oh really? An innocent girl whose assistance of the people of York, in matters of life and death, earns her the mark of exile and nearly execution? You don't think he hates me? You don't think he's trying to hurt me?"

Marigold interrupted, "I haven't digested this exile yet either, but I agree with Brother Lichen. All I know is that Polaris has a country to run, and until yesterday, I might have said a prosperous, free, safe one."

Lavender sighed. "Thank you, Marigold. Thank you both so very much for the sermon."

"Lavender, I think what your sister means is that your persecution was incidental to some separate method of benefit. Exactly what, I don't know. But nobody persecutes anyone for its own sake. By thinking it was about you, you'll never learn what his motives were. Knowing his motives . . . that's how you might find your way back home. But the path lies through you, and what you will do. Your actions are what matter, not his. In that sense, you have no enemy but yourself."

She glared at Marigold, then at me like a cornered elk. "My good deeds were lost on him. How can I understand him if he refuses to understand me?"

"Your good deeds may have been lost back in York, but not on me," I said. "Thank you for hearing my thoughts."

"Thank you, Brother Lichen," said Lavender with a strained smile. "But you don't understand him. He blamed my mother for our father's death, and recently he tried to kill me for wanting to do good. He's just evil."

"It's never that simple," said Marigold.

Lavender snapped back, "Either he's evil or I am, then."

"The evil ones always believe themselves to be the good. The good are not as certain," I said. She stared, waiting for me to admit: "Those were the final words of another traveler who died in my clearing."

"He still wants me dead," mumbled Lavender to herself, looking at her forearms.

"We should rest," said Marigold, her back turned.

Lavender shook her head. "No, we can't. He's still persecuting us. Even now."

"I'm exhausted," answered Marigold, taking off her shoes.

"Marigold?"

She recognized something in the tone of her sister's voice. "We're glowing, aren't we?"

"Both of us. It just started," said Lavender.

"You didn't eat the berries, did you?" I asked.

"No," said Lavender, scrambling to gather what she could. "It happened just now while we were standing here talking. Something somewhere changed, or someone decided something. Whatever it is, if we don't do something about it, we'll be dead soon."

Likewise gathering up her belongings, Marigold guessed: "It could just be a wild animal that picked up our scent; we don't know."

"Polaris," said Lavender. "It's always Polaris. It's always going to be Polaris. He didn't get the execution he wanted, so now he wants to kill us in the bush."

"You may be right," said Marigold, strapping her shoes back on. "But we don't know."

"Of course I'm right."

"I wonder. Are we to live the rest of our lives like this?"

"You chose exile, Marigold. I didn't tell you to save me," said Lavender, latching her satchel and swinging it over her shoulder.

"I hope to see you again someday," I said.

"Good-bye, Brother Lichen," said Marigold, smiling. "Peace and all good."

I watched them dash away on foot, keeping stride close together as they disappeared beyond the clearing into the trees. I wished they could have stayed longer, but I was glad not to watch another human die in my clearing.

They used to live in Canada, but now they were running for their lives.

4 / The Commander

Polaris wanted to meet with me alone. I had heard of the public exile of the two young women, Lavender and Marigold. It seemed of little importance at the time, though the source of a lot of superstitious talk.

Polaris is the man from the heavens. He is the highest-ranking member of the Canadian military, and always my professional superior. We met alone in the lower levels of the cathedral, in the military briefing chambers one level above the dead. He wore his green and white livery. His skin was textured with age, wisdom, and scars.

His red eyes were burning.

We exchanged professional and military formalities. With some anxiety he detailed the specifics of our audience.

"First, I must state that I admire your service, Commander Markham. I know you are a professional soldier, and a skilled officer, and I'm familiar with your impeccable record. Everything you've done as a member of our military has shown patriotism and obedience, which I feel qualifies you as the one officer in my ranks to accept the mission I present to you today."

"Thank you, sir."

"There are two evils that were exiled but should have been executed recently. Through unfortunate exceptions of our mandate, they have escaped justice. The threat they pose, rather one of them in particular, requires they be handled immediately and silently, hence the secrecy of this assignment."

"Who or what are the two evils, sir? And which is the particular threat?"

"Their names are Lavender and Marigold."

"Yes, I recall my wife mentioned them. They are two young women, sir?"

"To think of them as such is to fail in your mission," he insisted. "Lavender is not a young woman. She is an evil threat to the freedom and equality we cherish here in this country and everywhere."

He briefed me of their supposed intent to defect to Siberia and employ Lavender's gift for the benefit of the Siberian military. Once within the Siberians' power, the gift would serve them never to fight an unwinnable battle.

Our enemy would be impossible to ambush and could use her to predict if entire battalions would live or die.

Considering the great numbers of the Siberian forces, they would therefore engage in battle too frugally to be defeated. They would only fight when the outcome was prophesized a victory. To fail in my assignment would be to commission a bleak, nearly impossible mission of the future, a death march for not only me but also every other soldier alive who served Polaris's military.

"So then I assume she and her sister are to be killed?"

"Certainly. In the field and returned dead, to me. Marigold is to be killed but left in the ground if necessary."

"They have defected, sir, but they have been exiled. Therefore, when I find them, under what authority are they to be killed?"

"By what authority?" he responded, quickly upset like gas spilled near a flame. "By your sword, Commander."

"Yes, sir," I responded to his sudden flare. "And I return with proof of her full corpse?"

"At the very least, carve out and retrieve her eyes."

"Yes, sir." I stood to attention. "Sir, what men shall I take?"

"There are two soldiers awaiting your command outside the cathedral doors. Low-ranking and obedient. Do the names Lyell or Ellard sound familiar?"

"I've trained many front liners. But yes, I believe I recall a Lyell."

"You did train Lyell," he said, smiling. "In a way, briefly."

"Yes. The Wooden Sword. So, he's grown now and is one of our soldiers. Excellent."

"He should be eager to follow your command." He continued with disgust, "I don't believe you know Ellard, though you may have seen him."

"Sir?"

"He's not within the physical standards of a Canadian soldier."

"I don't understand, sir."

"He's been told he needs to lose weight."

"Sir," I hesitated, nervous to question him again. "For a long trek in the wilderness?"

"You three have all been selected for your obedience," he said. "Lyell knows life only as an orphan and a soldier. In your one visit nearly nine seasons past you may be, we may be, his one form of a father. He will follow you. Where Ellard joins this mission is in his jeopardized career. I have spoken directly with his commanding officer, and by now Ellard understands his profession is at risk unless he can meet our physical standards. He should be the most obedient of all."

"Yes, sir. I will return to his commanding officer a much-improved soldier."

———————

I looked forward to working with Lyell. Nine seasons and several ranks in the past, as a lieutenant, I volunteered for the Wooden Sword program. We delivered beautifully crafted sugar-maple swords to poor boys, including the ones living in the York Orphans' Home. The Wooden Sword is a campaign originating with and managed by the Canadian military. They do not solely target orphans, but any son of a poor family which may not have the means to provide much beyond a meager gift for their boy's tenth birthday. Its purpose is, through a carefully crafted wooden sword, to deliver a message of joy and belonging to the boy along with a sense of purpose and patriotism. The child then learns to embrace our nation's priorities with pride and enthusiasm.

The swords were carved and crafted with care, made to be manageable in the hands of a boy of ten. With a rich stain, finish, and shine, but no excessive ornamentation, they resembled the double-edged metal swords used in battle.

I arrived at the home in full ceremonial uniform that day, nine seasons prior, young Lyell's estimated tenth birthday. A blue-eyed boy filled with expectation and excitement waited for me at the gate. Having witnessed several of his older friends' tenth birthdays, he would have been devastated had I been sent a day later.

"Lyell?" I asked, just outside the iron gate.

"Yes," he responded with restraint, as several others had quickly collected near him.

"I've been told it's your tenth birthday. Is that true?"

"Yes, sir," he said, shy about finding himself on display for his friends.

"Do you know how I know it's your birthday?"

"No, sir," he answered. All of the children watching struggled to pry their eyes from the wooden sword in my hands. I tucked the distraction behind my back and pointed to my eyes.

"All the soldiers are speaking of it today, Lyell. We know it's your birthday. We all do."

The entranced, youthful audience gasped, and as expected, the celebrated child blushed. "Do I . . . do I receive a sword?" he said, insecure in what was, to an adult, an obvious inevitability.

"Yes, you do, Lyell." I handed him the wooden sword, which was met with another collective gasp.

I took some time to instruct young Lyell in sword technique. I drew another gasp from his audience when I pulled my own metal sword from its scabbard.

"Shall we spar?" I asked.

Immediately he swung his gift, flailing it with an elated smile. Ready to enjoy his new toy with or without an understanding of it, he entirely dismissed everything I had just taught him.

"Remember your technique, Lyell," I reminded him as I danced and parried his erratic swings.

After a moment, resting and breathing heavily, he asked, "Was I victorious?"

"I am too weary to continue," I lied. "I yield. You are too expert the swordsman for me."

The seven or eight in his group cheered and saw this break in ceremony as their opportunity to crowd around their friend's new gift.

"Children, I must speak with Lyell for a moment, please. He will be free to play with you soon."

Alone with the boy, I told him, "Lyell, you handled the wooden sword very well. I think you should hold my metal sword once before I leave."

He gasped as I passed it to him carefully, making sure he received the handle gracefully.

"So, what will you do when you're grown?" I asked.

He gawked at the thin, sparkling ceremonial sword in his hands. "I want to be a merchant, and travel."

"Wonderful," I said while he looked at the reflection of his blue eyes in the blade's broadest part. "I travel a great deal as a soldier. If you were to become a foot soldier, you would learn about survival in the bush; you would learn cartography—that's mapmaking; and you would master many weapons, not only the sword. You would receive a uniform. And clothing. Proper clothing."

"When I'm older and finished with my courses I'll be permitted to leave the home," he responded, with a distinct desire to please.

"I look forward to fighting alongside you one day."

Lyell remembered me immediately when we met outside the cathedral in the morning. Now a grown, young man, he still had the same look of enthusiasm in his blue eyes.

We talked for a moment and reminisced over our meeting nine seasons prior. Sensing he was on the outside of the conversation, Ellard tried to worm a way in. "Do you like a joke, sir?"

"As you desire, soldier," I responded without endorsement.

"All right, so there's a foot soldier and his commanding officer, right? And they're in the bush around the campfire. They finish their rations, but the foot soldier hasn't bitten into his dessert."

"Dessert in a field ration?" I asked.

"Yes, uh, they're Svalbards, not Canadian." He improvised. "So, you see, the foot soldier offers the pastry to his commanding officer and the officer responds, 'What, are you offering your dessert to me? Cold? You haven't even bothered to warm it up in the fire! And what is it filled with, fruit? I much prefer cream! Ah, it must be at least a day old! Is this all you think of me? Have you not bothered to consider what I might want? I cannot believe I am sharing a camp with a man so inconsiderate!' Then the officer pauses, and if the foot soldier wasn't surprised enough, the officer finishes, 'However, I shall accept your gift so as not to appear rude.'"

Ellard laughed with deliberate volume, Lyell laughed genuinely, and I forced a brief, polite, dishonest chuckle. Having been warned by Polaris of Ellard's predicament, I wanted to be utterly clear and early in our mission to disabuse him of any notion that he would preserve his career simply by befriending a commander. "Fine joke, front liner. But promotions aren't earned through regaling officers with comedy."

"Oh no, sir! You've got me wrong! I never intended the joke to polish your armor, simply to improve morale! Initiate camaraderie at the start of our mission!"

My point had been made, so for the sake of peace within our unit, I teased: "What, a commander can't open with a joke as well?"

"Oh, you got me, sir!" said Ellard.

What irritated me immediately about Ellard was his moral high ground. When challenged as to his intentions, he claimed that he never intended to lick my boots but only wanted to "improve morale" and "initiate camaraderie." I'm no stranger to this. The moral high road is the shortcut to winning any argument, and so often abused as such. I didn't have that problem with Lyell.

Meeting Lyell again was an endearing reunion from our one day in the past. Seeing a grown man, still young and able, showed me particularly what formed the spine of our military. He contrasted with Ellard in this sense.

I led them into the wilderness without a word about our mission.

Somewhere in the forest, around midday, Ellard whined, "Sir, when will we be briefed on the details of our assignment? We've been marching for hours and still don't know where."

I responded, "To whom, Ellard. Not where." As I did, he removed his helmet, realizing by my tone that he would not be told how to pace himself. I continued: "For now, follow my track. And Ellard?"

"Yes, sir?"

"Keep your helmet on. Keep your full armor on."

"Yes, sir." He sighed. "Must be quite a powerful enemy."

We continued through the forest for hours, tracking signs of the sisters' paths to a broad clearing around a lake.

"Fresh footprints," said Ellard. "Looks like two people."

"A lot of footprints scattered around this spot," observed Lyell. "I suppose they were just wandering around?"

"No," I responded. "Look at the three or four paces they took to the south, toward the direction from which we approached. See how they're spread apart? Those are running strides, but only a few before they tried another direction. Notice how the final footstep tossed up a clump of dirt. Then follow them east, west, and the same. Then north . . . to the north the footprints are spaced farther apart and appear to continue in that direction."

"They ran from this spot?" asked Ellard.

"From us?" asked Lyell. "How would they know?"

"Whoever they are, they know they're being hunted," said Ellard.

"Our targets must not be far," I said. "And they ran north, headed for the sea."

"Not the biggest footprints I've ever seen," murmured Ellard, comparing his footprint to theirs.

We continued. The path of the footprints curved, then changed direction more than once. Before long, the landscape flattened and broadened further, and the footing dampened. We were in the pure marsh, nearly to the sea. Searching for Lavender and Marigold on the horizon, I saw instead a tremendous object in the far distance. At first I took it for a mountain, but it would be out of place here, on smooth, wet silt.

"Over there, sir!" yelled Ellard from behind, noticing with keen eyesight two objects in motion. Had they not been moving, they would have remained hidden by the dark object on the horizon. They were between the spectacle and us.

Lavender and Marigold ran several hundred paces ahead and appeared to be staggering, with occasional slight changes in direction. This explained the footprints. The adjustments I did not understand, but they had set course for the mountainlike object, which was for them another several hundred paces. My two men and I proceeded to lumber through the marsh, and with us all breathing too heavily to speak, I relied on a soldier's sense to instruct them onward.

We may have gained some ground on the girls, but it was clear they would reach the object before any of us, even Lyell, the fastest. Coming into focus, the object appeared not to be made of rock or wood. It was not a fortress or a design of human architecture.

"It's moving!" yelled Lyell, using as few words as possible, and on the exhale.

And it was. It was rising, and beneath it, what appeared to be six pillars or thick trees straightened into legs. And a mouth, an opening, an enormous mouth . . . one that comprised the entire height and width of its right side. It didn't open evenly from the middle such as some creatures, but rather its large jaw, even disproportionately large for its size, creased from the top and opened toward the soil. With jaw fully extended, the mouth was dark and cavernous, at least from what I was able to see in my one opportunity still a hundred paces away. I didn't see its mouth open but once. Lavender and Marigold were there, on the jaw's threshold. They were no longer running. Still out of our reach, they were within swallowing distance of the creature. The beast did not lunge for them but rather awaited their decision. They stared at it while we gained strides on them. They looked back at us, fifty paces to Lyell, our closest man. They attempted to run left. They stopped quickly, kicking up some silt. They tried another direction, stopped, and ran toward the creature's open jaw. They hesitated in front of the jaw, but only briefly. They looked at Lyell, twenty paces behind. I watched as they then stepped inside the beast carefully.

It collapsed its jaw shut, consuming the sisters, but showed no further sign of chewing, grinding, or swallowing. They had disappeared inside the creature, and in the moment, I didn't have the time to decide if that determined our assignment a success or failure. It relieved its six legs of its massive weight as it rested again on its belly. When it did, we all instantly broke stride, breathing heavily, leaning over in the marsh with our hands on our knees.

The creature didn't move or take notice of us. Only twenty paces from it, we regrouped. Its astonishing size reminded us that we were tempting fate simply by being so close to something that had just consumed two others of our species.

"Two teenage girls, sir?" asked Ellard.

"Lavender and Marigold. They were exiled from York recently." I finally explained.

"I heard about them," said Lyell. "Her eyes can see life and death."

"We were to retrieve those eyes," I informed.

"They're dead," said Ellard. "We all saw them walk into the creature and be swallowed."

"Yes, but the creature isn't moving. Sir, perhaps we can still retrieve her head," suggested Lyell.

"Wait a moment," I instructed, looking up at the inhaling and exhaling creature. Our existence was still unknown to it in spite of our voices. "Don't move quite yet."

We regained our breath in preparation for our next move. Studying the creature, I did not observe much more than a few legs and a closed jaw on an incredible reddish-black core—at least it appeared that color in the dawn light. The original architect of the largest wooden boat operated by the Canadian military may have been the only other human to see this creature and survive. No other segment to its abdomen could I see. This led me to believe the creature swam submerged in the water and not buoyant on the surface. Its skin was smooth, not scaled, and appeared damp. I watched it labor as it breathed but it was so featureless that I failed to locate a nostril or spiracle. It was not amorphous; it had an elliptical shape, but my eye was brought to the region of detail: its legs. There were six and not four. If its jaw was its front, of which I am still uncertain, then its front was to our right and we observed it broadside, facing its right flank. We therefore saw its three right appendages as it rested on its hull. I studied the detail of its closest leg to my position, its front right, although it was partially tucked under its body, claws facing forward. Perhaps they were not terribly large in proportion to its size, but each claw was easily longer than one of our swords. The peculiarity was that the same appendage on its trailing edge appeared finlike. It was long and broad and if the creature were moving in the opposite direction, through the water with the jaw trailing, these fins could provide its motion as the clawed appendages either steered or simply dangled.

I considered the mission and realized Lavender and Marigold were almost certainly dead. Perhaps through a technicality they were not killed by the authority of my sword, but their demise was a great relief, regardless. There would be no fear of unholy advantage for the Siberians, and York would remain as safe as it ever was. Yet as the creature ignored us, and as I saw no ocular adaptation—on what I began to believe was a blind, seaborne creature that beached itself ashore to die—I felt encouraged to finish our mission. "Lyell, Ellard, advance carefully. Take its legs first. I'll attempt to occupy its attention if I can find a set of eyes."

Lyell began walking as Ellard began protesting. "Are they not dead, sir? Why instead do we not watch for several moments to be confident they have suffocated, then return to York?"

"Because we are not to return to York without the objective's eyes. And those eyes are inside the creature. Now advance slowly."

To my surprise he did not protest further. I suppose he saw that the end of our mission was in sight. Lyell advanced on the front right appendage, Ellard on the middle right, and I positioned to face its huge jaw. Still, I saw no eyes on the creature. Looking at one another nervously, we advanced to within steps of it. Able to speak casually without alarming the beast, I instructed, "Strike your swords into its claw on my command, understood?"

"Yes sir," they responded.

I waited for them to draw their weapons and raise them above their heads. "Now!" I yelled.

They drove their blades downward, piercing the flesh of the creature's claws, an attack met by a low-registered screech. The beast, now alarmed and aware of our presence, let out a terrible bellow that not only deafened us but also rattled our armor and even our bones. Ellard fell backward as Lyell, more committed to his assault, continued to drive and twist his sword into his assigned claw.

A seventh appendage emerged from directly opposite its jaw, coming from the distant end of its huge body, far from where I stood. What I could not officially determine as its rear was where this whip-like, tentacle-like, tail-like adaptation appeared.

It had been entirely tucked beneath the hull, buried in the silt, but now rose above its back and was long enough to reach the Canadian soldier of its choice.

At first appearing to be a tail, it lashed at its afflicted side. It defended itself where it was attacked, and with incredible force struck Lyell to the ground. Ellard, already apart from the creature by enough separation to survive, stepped back further with his mortality intact.

"Ellard, pull Lyell away!" I yelled. He approached Lyell to comply, but the creature continued to strike its own front right claw where Lyell's sword was buried in its flesh. It lashed several times as Ellard disobediently but wisely backed away, and each time the tentacle struck on or near Lyell's body within his armor.

The appendage opened a lid, a lens, and revealed the long-awaited eye. It was one eye only, which looked out from above and over its body. It stared briefly at Ellard and at me, then turned toward the sea, pivoting its entire body. Its jaws now faced Ellard, but the creature was retreating into the water. It escaped without favoring its foot. The swords had done nothing. By some grace or mercy, or simple rule of nature, the creature spared Ellard and me and slipped amphibiously into the depths of the sea, fins forward and presumably already in use.

"Lyell," said Ellard.

We approached where he lay motionless. We felt for a heartbeat and found none.

The force of the appendage had killed him.

I stared at his body, then at the sea, at the subsiding wake of the creature under the light of the sun. "Take a moment, then strip his armor," I said. With the danger beneath the water, we could grieve briefly before we began our next chore. "When that's done, toss him over your back. We must carry him home."

Ellard waited a moment, likely hoping I would change my command, and mournfully pleaded, "Sir, perhaps this is Lyell's grave. By the sea."

"We must return his body to York, for a proper fallen soldier's ceremony."

"Why?"

"Because that is what he has earned, Ellard."

"Yes, but for whom? He was an orphan, was he not? And not a husband or father, I don't believe. We can mourn him here, as his family . . . our brother in arms."

"Ellard, I'm aware of your agenda. Do you not expect me to realize that you are simply too fatigued or slothful to carry a man half your size back to York?"

"My weight," mumbled Ellard. Raising his voice, he said, "You believe my weight is the reason I can't understand why his full corpse should needlessly be dragged the long trek back to York? Polaris wanted the girl's eyes. We can simply dig out Lyell's and carry those back to York."

"The mission was to bring the evil objective's eyes back to York, not a fraudulent pair."

"So? You follow all instructions blindly and with needless obedience? The girls are dead, and we have two eyes, which will please Polaris."

"I also promised I would return an improved soldier to your commanding officer. Ellard, you will, in full plate armor, toss Lyell over your back and carry his corpse the entire return trek to York."

"Why is my weight of such concern to you?"

"Why is it of so little concern to you?"

"To each his own," he replied, smug.

"Simple messages complicate large groups, Ellard."

"Sir? That sounded like a simple message. Care to elaborate?"

"You can't run a military let alone a country when the group doesn't share a set of values. What your values are, I haven't figured out yet. But first in my nation is safety against our enemies, then our nation's prosperity. We all must do our part."

Ellard stared calmly at me. "Carve out your own eyes, sir. You're a blind man as it is. If you could think for yourself, you'd realize you just chased yourself into the ocean."

"You fool. You'll not serve another day in this military, you ignorant aberration. That creature crushed the wrong soldier."

He unbuckled his breastplate and left it in the sand. "Teenage girls," he scoffed. "Next time you think of your values, try not to forget the youth. Your value is greed and nothing else. Greed killed Lyell. That young woman's gift warned her we were coming to kill her. You are a greedy fool and so is Polaris. I may understand her gift no better than you, but we could have simply tried to capture her, and she may have never known our intentions. The girls would be in our custody today, and Lyell standing with a beating heart. Good-bye, Markham."

"Ellard, I declared that you will not serve another day in this military, not that this day is complete. You have not finished your duty."

"Good-bye, Markham."

"Leave now while the mission is incomplete and I will report you as having defected, not having been discharged."

But he defected. I will no longer criticize him, because at that moment he no longer was my soldier to command. He turned his back and walked away. For no sake other than to avoid crossing my path, I assume he took a less direct route home.

Returning to York was a dreary, lonely event. My final task upon return was to debrief Polaris on, aside from Lyell and Ellard, what I considered at the time the success of the mission.

We met in the same chamber below the cathedral as before, and again alone. I entered the room empty-handed aside from a small cloth pouch. Polaris welcomed me with a well-appointed feast. It was as if he were rewarding a mercenary, but it was still appreciated after several days in the bush. He stated: "We can't have parades for heroes of secure missions. I hope this will do."

"I'm honored, sir," I responded. I didn't want a parade. I wished for this mission to finally end, and to end quietly. The solitary feast was ideal. "Sir, thank you."

"Yes, please sit. So where is the head? We'll need something of her flesh to send to the catacomb's haunted hall of criminals."

"All I have gathered are her eyes, sir," I responded after my first bite of the meal.

"Where?" Polaris asked anxiously.

"This pouch, sir."

I watched for his reaction as I handed it to him. I continued to eat. He opened the bag and pulled out the two eyes.

"Blue eyes? Stand up, Commander!"

"Yes, sir!"

I was caught.

The old man was hotter than a flame, so intoxicated by his own temperature that he pulled the cloth from the table, spilling the meal, grabbing first the plates, then the meat, then the drink.

He grabbed them individually, sequentially hurling each one onto the floor or the wall to my right, even shattering one ceramic dish intentionally on his own feeble thigh.

Then the eyes, the no-longer-warm, somewhat bloody, sticky, blue eyes . . . he threw them into the wall as well.

"Whose eyes are those?" he shouted.

"Sir, the girls are dead. I'm sorry."

"Then where are her eyes?" he demanded, loudly, somehow knowing the ones I had given him were not Lavender's or even Marigold's.

"Likely hundreds of lengths beneath the sea," I responded, knowing I should have looked straight ahead at attention but finding it very difficult to pick my gaze up off the floor.

"Where?"

"The girls were swallowed by a tremendous beast, sir."

"So why did you not bring me the beast? With the head inside?" he shouted, slamming his frail fist on the table, spilling my drink. "You were instructed to bring the eyes!"

"Yes sir, and we tried. But sir, I lost a good man trying to retrieve the eyes from inside the creature."

"So?" he asked, still so focused on the eyes that he entirely neglected to inquire anything about the creature. "So, you lost an obedient man. I sent you two, did I not?"

"Sir, the girls are dead. I watched them walk into the jaw of a monster, then be swallowed by it, and carried into the depths. I really don't think there is the slightest . . ." I said, stopping there as my voice began to shake.

He then sat down. I remained standing, now perspiring. The fire inside him seemed to have flared up and burned out quickly, and did so by his design like an unnatural flame, never meant to burn. He appeared to be resting briefly, and in his old age was likely quite fatigued from the outburst. "How large was the creature?" he asked calmly.

"It might fit inside the cathedral, sir, but would have to pass through the doors in portions."

"The girls you say . . . both consumed by it?"

"Yes, sir."

He breathed deeply, closed his red eyes underneath their ripened lids, and ordered in a soft tone with a trace of apology: "Dismissed."

5 / Anders and Ylwa

"Love: the emotion that can do no wrong." These are the words of my love, a gentle creature named Ylwa.

The only one of my kind, I was discovered near a mountain pond on Svalbard's big island, shivering and still near my eggshell. I'm fortunate I wasn't eaten by wild creatures or by the men who found me. If I were a *roach* and the only of my kind, I'm sure I would have met the underside of a boot. But I was small and covered with gray down, and I'm told I made an adorable little chirping noise.

They called me Greta, meaning "pearl" in Old Svalbardian, until I began to speak after about three seasons. When I did speak, my adoptive parents realized I couldn't be their exotic little pet; I was now their foster child.

When they realized I wasn't female, they began dressing me in laboriously custom-made clothing and gave me a proper boy's name: Anders.

They saved everything, and not merely the clothes. My eggshell, the down from my early stages, and even the juvenile tooth from the tapered end of my short beak that they believe helped me hatch. It all went to the nearby Svalbardian Museum in our capital of Kildebyen. Kildebyen is in the northeast section of the big island, along the coastline and downslope from the mountain pond where I hatched. It's the largest Svalbardian city, home to the royal family, and has the densest concentration of their subjects. It's also the home of my adoptive parents, who raised me there, not far from the Svalbardian Museum and its exhibit of natural curiosities. This is where my eggshell, down, and tooth were displayed alongside speculated evidence of a Siberian's thorned skeleton in fragments, and artistically rendered sketches of a giant fabled amphibious creature known as the Host.

Unlike the others in my display, I lived and grew up among the Svalbards. A very homogeneous and unified people, Svalbards are not known for valuing diversity. Their culture is ancient, their streets clean and safe, and they find comfort in their rigid mentality. I didn't blend in. Even at my fullest inhale with plumage puffed, a slouching Svalbard, or almost any human, was twice my size.

My foster parents—my parents if I may—placed me in the civic academy to be educated among the children my own age, where I was very well accepted. They were drawn to me, or possibly my soft black and yellow feathers, and I was regularly embraced . . . literally, and usually with the full enthusiasm of a small child's arms. This would occur so much in fact that our instructor would threaten disallowing it as a means of controlling the classroom. I was likened with playtime; the children would argue over me as they would the tetherball or the puppets.

Being a living novelty makes you the recipient of affection, pity, and expectations. For this I did not object to the children's embraces, nor did I develop any resentment. I fulfilled my role, thankful that when done serving my novel purpose, I was not tossed aside like the tetherball or the puppets.

Although my birthday celebrations were quite crowded, my afternoons and other holidays were lonely. My parents were older, their two sons and daughter young adults who had left the home, and I was a child's age. It seemed that none of my classmates' parents were comfortable allowing their child to spend playtime with me alone.

Relief came from this on one miraculous day, one which at the time I was too young to appreciate.

I believe I was five seasons or so when the fisherman came to see my family. He sailed from the small northeast islands in the channel between Kildebyen and Nyebyen, a port town on the principal northeast island. When my parents heard his knock on our door, they first suspected him to be what they called a gawker: someone so overwhelmed with curiosity about me that they would arrive unannounced and disturb our household. My parents' approach toward these folks was to indulge them, believing their curiosity had to be embraced and informed. Refusing them, they felt, would lead to secrets, rumors, ignorance, and the resentment we fought so hard to avoid.

"Oh, that's her, most certainly," said the fisherman after his greeting and first glance at me. "Looks just like her."

"I'm a boy," I said, "at least I'm told."

"The yellow and black plumage, the short legs and webbed toes, the small face and dark eyes, the little frame and stature . . ."

"Yes, sir, this is Anders. Of course, everyone has taken to calling him 'Little Andy,'" said my father.

"And now you have seen him, sir," said my mother, not registering the stranger's mentioning of another like me. As was her habit with gawkers, she was now hoping for a handout or an exit on the part of the fisherman. Strangers often brought gifts in exchange for meeting me.

This man would do far better than that.

"I've found one just like him, madam. Three seasons past, a bit smaller than yours, and recently beginning to speak," announced the fisherman. "A female."

My parents' eyes grew large. As far as anyone knew, I was the only one of my kind. Feathered but flightless, awkward on land but adept in the water. I would have swum to her if necessary. In fact, I may have even attempted to fly. I briefly understood the curiosity others had about me when I realized I had to see her.

"So, there are two?" asked my mother. The man explained how he found her near an empty eggshell along the shoreline of his island, and how he had raised her on fish and vegetables. When she recently began speaking, he sought advice from other northeast islanders about how to properly raise such a creature. The other islanders shared rumors of me, and so he came to our doorstep.

"We must arrange for the two to meet!" said my mother. "Sir, where do you live?"

"Never mind that, madam. I'm a fisherman. Tomorrow I'll bring her with me across the water and come to see you along my route."

———————

Before their arrival, my mother was already weeping. It was confusing for a child to understand her happiness through tears, but I paid it little concern once the knock on the door came. The fisherman stood in the doorway, and with his arm around her was what from far away would have appeared to be a small child. Fully clothed, perhaps overdressed, and unmistakably in a young girl's garments.

A large-brimmed hat hid her face.

"Come on, darling; say hello," urged the fisherman.

The girl took two formal steps forward . . . the first to stand evenly with the man and the second to stand in front. She approached with reservation, looked up, and said, "Hello, I am Ylwa." I could see her face now. It was just like mine.

We played as the three guardians spoke, with only one interruption that I remember. My mother approached us with some cooking ware from the kitchen and Father's shoes. She encouraged us to play house. The rest of the time—and this I wouldn't know without my parents—the three debated notions of how we should be raised. Neither my parents nor the fisherman, nor anyone for that matter, had past experience in raising a creature like me, yet they disagreed. I was encouraged to socialize, as was unavoidable living in the more densely populated area of our country. He greatly limited Ylwa's exposure even within her remote island community, to protect her, as he said, "with dignity and humility," though my parents would say "with shame."

The playtime continued, usually once every several days or so, because both sides agreed we should have each other. In fact, all of Svalbard agreed we should have each other, and as we grew older, they became more interested.

When I was about twelve seasons to her ten, the fisherman finally agreed to a trip into town with Ylwa, my parents, and me. It would be Ylwa's first trip into Kildebyen, and she of course wore a long-sleeved dress that dragged on the ground and another wide-brimmed hat.

I don't believe the fisherman understood the extent to which the townspeople talked of Ylwa and me, or the attention we would receive along our short walk to the market. "Hey, Little Andy!" shouted a neighbor as we left. Ylwa tucked her small body behind the fisherman's, and the rest of us waved back politely.

Closer to town we received another, "Hey, Little Andy!" This time it was from a young man, about twenty.

The fisherman asked, "Who was that?"

"Oh, I don't know," I answered.

"But he knows you?"

"He knows of Andy," answered my father. "The whole town does."

"Do they know of Ylwa here as well?"

"Well, I would imagine so," said my mother softly. "People talk." She was also likely thinking of the museum exhibit, trying to recall if Ylwa is mentioned in the display. I suppose the fisherman didn't know about it, and if that's truly what my parents were thinking of at the time, they sensed it a terrible moment to inform him . . . particularly because they'd then have to explain how they were the ones to donate the items in the collection.

Loud greetings from strangers continued on the way to the market. One older couple approached us to say hello. They were strangers. Without asking permission, the man touched my head and began scratching the back of my neck. The woman knelt directly in front of Ylwa, lifted the brim of her hat and said kindly, "Well this must be little Ylwa!"

The fisherman smacked the older woman's arm away. Ylwa hid behind her father, and the older woman's husband stepped toward the fisherman aggressively. "Is there a reason you strike my wife?"

"Yes sir, there is. What business do you have putting your hands on our children? How should another parent react if I were to, without so much as an introduction, touch another man's son or daughter?"

The older couple left without an apology, or another word of any kind. Just a stare as they walked off, leaving the five of us again to ourselves. "Are all city dwellers as rude?" asked the fisherman.

"You can't have a child like ours and react as you do, sir," said my father. As offended as he was, fortunately the fisherman kept his mouth shut and didn't respond to this. But he insisted we return home, and we did. He walked several paces ahead, my parents walked in the middle, and Ylwa and I with our shorter legs shuffled behind. Ylwa whispered to me: "Love: the emotion that can do no wrong." I took comfort in her words after the unpleasant day. We returned home, and he left with Ylwa on his boat to go back to their northeast island.

An argument ensued between my mother and father.

"You simply cannot correct a man like that," said my mother.

"Me? How I corrected the fisherman, or how he corrected the stranger?" asked my father.

"You! You, you, you! We were quite fortunate the fisherman did not defend himself when you told him he overreacted."

"Perhaps what I said made sense to him."

"Are you joking? There's not so much of a slim chance that it did. The fisherman was correcting the older couple, and why would he do so if he didn't feel the situation warranted it? In his mind, he was doing what was right."

"But he wasn't," said my father. "I was."

"But by now you know how protective he is. I agree with what you said, but the fact that you said it was terribly out of place. Perhaps ten times you correct someone and once, at most, your audience will say to themselves, 'Yes, I was behaving incorrectly.' And what happens the other nine in ten? They defend themselves. So, you accomplish nothing, which is a tragic failure with truth on your side, and the man becomes more stubborn in the end."

"So, what am I to do?" asked Father. "Watch as he holds the child from society, blocking her from all human interaction?"

"You have just proven my point. I attempted to correct you as you attempted to correct the fisherman, as he attempted to correct the older couple. No one has changed. You have not changed. You will not, either. I must accept that. You believe what you have done was right and just, and are now more adamant about it than ever because I have challenged you. I have wasted both of our times," said Mother as she went to the bedroom, upset.

I was more worried I would never see Ylwa again than I was with the arguing of my parents. However, before long, the fisherman returned with Ylwa to spend time with me as before: in our house. My father, to seem apologetic, offered to the fisherman, "If you would ever like to return to market with Ylwa and Andy, it's fine with us if you three alone prefer to go." The fisherman thanked my father, but without committing to an agreement. Maybe in his reluctance he sensed not an apology but another attempt by my father to teach a lesson through example, this time one of allowing his own child more freedom and exposure.

It did happen, though, later and in a much-unexpected day. A storm thundered overhead. The rain was heavy and Ylwa and the fisherman stepped off their boat from his fishing route appropriately dressed for the weather. My parents asked them to come in and dry off. "No thank you," said the fisherman. "We were wondering if Andy would like to come out." The fisherman had called my father's bluff and was willing to see what the appropriate limit to a child's freedom and exposure really was, at least under my parents' method.

"You mean, into town? Now?" Mother asked.

Staring the fisherman in the eye, Father said, "I'll fetch his rain gear."

Ylwa, the fisherman, and I set off. As soon as the door to my house closed behind us, he said, "It will be better in the rain. There will be very few people to bother us."

The three of us walked the short distance to the market. He was right; in this weather no one was on the street, and for the first time I saw Ylwa extend her neck and move her head about, curious as she took in the surroundings of the tall houses and city streets I had traveled a hundred times or more.

"The only people we'll see today are other fishermen. Come now, there's a small port near here. I'm sure I can find a friend who will provide you both lunch," said her father.

We walked toward the harbor but when we got close, he asked that Ylwa and I wait behind some carts so as not to be seen while he went on to find our fish. For a moment we were alone, in silence, in the rain. I realized this was the first time in our lives we had even for a moment been left alone together. "Are you cold?" I asked.

"Yes."

I placed my wing around her and drew her into the warm spot on my body beneath it. She huddled closely and innocently. I peered around the side of the cart to see her father still looking at his friends' catches by the boats along the dockside. I looked in front at an empty street and at the rain falling, then down the short distance to her head tucked under my wing.

"Ylwa?" I said, only so that she would look up.

"Yes?"

I kissed her.

I kissed her as best I could, or could figure with a beak. Sensing the awkwardness, she affectionately rubbed the top of her head along the side of my face and neck. She turned to face me more directly, and we rubbed our cheeks together.

Footsteps approached and we separated. Her father came around a corner of the cart with two fish just brought in from the sea.

"Here you go," he said as he handed her one, which I believe still had some movement to it. I watched her gobble it down with the same beak I had just kissed . . . and yet this didn't bother me. In fact, I wanted to kiss her again, right then if I could. At the time I wondered what that meant, but of course now I know.

"Andy, I remember you like yours cooked," said her father, "but I didn't want to come back empty-handed."

"That's all right," I answered. "I know a place that sells cooked food. It's out of the rain too."

I've forgotten what we did with the second fish, but I remember clearly how kissing Ylwa made me feel invincible. I felt as tall as a human. Keeping this a secret was nearly impossible.

From there I showed them the way to the museum they had yet to visit.

When we arrived, the gatekeeper said to us: "Oh, what a special honor. We have two very valued guests here on this rainy day." Ylwa's father didn't understand what the man meant but took it as a condescending assessment of his unusual company. Accordingly, he delivered the man a silent, angry expression.

I rushed Ylwa and her father past the plant and seed rooms to my exhibit next to the thorned skeleton.

"What is this?" asked her father. "This looks like . . . is this yours?"

"It was. My parents donated it all."

"Down? Your eggshell? Feathers?"

Still feeling empowered and not correctly interpreting the situation, I continued: "There's more . . ." I brought him to the corner of the room, smiled, and placed my wing around a false-feathered facsimile of myself to scale. A plaque by the feet read: LITTLE ANDY HIMSELF.

"Almost as handsome as the real thing, isn't he?" I said.

Ylwa was crying. The swings of the day must have overborne her, and the museum alone was too much for the fisherman. He took his daughter and me out of the building, marching directly toward my home.

The skies were still gray but the rain had stopped, and a few more people walked the streets than had earlier. "Hey, Little Andy!" yelled one of them.

I stopped, put on a smile, and responded, "Hello, friend!"

The fisherman kept marching. "Hurry, Anders." I caught up with him and he continued his thought: "And what if you don't respond? What if you were just once to attempt a level of privacy, to not indulge their whims for the sake of your own dignity?"

"I'll show you what would happen," I said and stopped.

"Come now, Anders, don't stop here," said the fisherman.

"Andy . . ." started Ylwa.

"No," I said, now with all joy and invincibility imparted by the kiss completely washed away. "Stand in the alley and watch. It won't take long."

"Anders!" insisted the father.

"Would you like to know what it is to be the way I am? Then I'll show you. Please though, wait in the alley so no one sees you."

"Father?" pleaded Ylwa, finally to the aid of her own cause.

"Quickly." He compromised.

They snuck into an alleyway so I would appear to be standing alone in the street. Soon a family walked by, a husband, wife, and their small daughter. "Hey, Little Andy!" greeted the father.

I ignored them, not even turning my head.

"Hey, Little Andy!" he yelled again, slightly louder. It was impossible for me not to hear him, though. We were on opposing sides of an empty, fairly narrow street.

"Andy, can my daughter say hello?" asked the mother, as I continued to ignore them.

"Come on, forget it," said the father. "Something's wrong."

The family passed and I spoke to Ylwa and her father, who had of course seen everything. "Wait," I said as I saw a group of three older boys approaching. "Not yet."

"Hey, it's Little Andy!" they said, laughing, as they grew closer. "Hey Andy, give us a squawk!"

"Yeah, a loud one!" said another boy.

"Hey Andy, we're talking to you!"

A silent pause.

"Hey!" they yelled.

I continued to stare downward at the street, not reacting to the boys.

"Oh, I'll fix you!" said one as the other two started laughing. Not breaking my downward stare, I waited for it . . . and it hit. Just a cobblestone, fortunately, from the street, striking my shoulder. The boys walked on, laughing.

Ylwa and her father emerged from the alley and we all quietly continued to my home.

"Andy, are you all right?" asked Ylwa nervously, caught between her father and me.

"Fine," I answered. As I did, her father strode two steps in front of us, walking the rest of the way home like that. But I added loudly enough for the fisherman to hear, "So now you see. To be vulnerable is to be approachable. But to embrace it is to be invincible. The other choice is to be assaulted by cobblestones."

We finally returned, and before we even reached the door, my mother was opening it, asking, "So, how was everything?"

"A word?" asked the fisherman. He went inside while Ylwa and I waited outdoors under the gray clouds. It was now the second time I was alone with Ylwa, although it was certainly no time for our second kiss. After several minutes, the fisherman came out and spoke directly to his girl. "Say good-bye, Ylwa."

The two left and were heading back toward their boat when my mother, sobbing, called me in. The fisherman had decided that Ylwa was no longer to visit me, and I was not welcome to travel to see her.

———————

For four seasons I wrote and sent hundreds of letters, which were never answered. At one time I even feared Ylwa had met another, although a more logical mind would remember there was no other. I believe when I was sixteen or so, and she was fourteen, I finally questioned myself. Why would continuing the same actions result in a new outcome?

Of course, the fisherman had taken, and likely hid or destroyed, all of my letters. It was even possible that he was now keeping her from the world entirely.

I couldn't take the ferry to their island. I'd be spotted immediately. News would reach the man of my attempt to see Ylwa, and his grip on her would tighten. I did have another option, though. Something no Svalbard would attempt.

I would swim the distance to her island.

If I survived the swim, I fully expected to be taken home on an angry fisherman's boat. So be it. I told no one of my attempt and launched myself in darkness. Along the way, I unlocked some of the gifts of my species, whatever I am. Swimming became more natural with every moment; I found I could dive to great depths. However, I could not see in black water, even by moonlight.

For most of the swim, my only concern was becoming disoriented, that is until something touched my leg. Quite possibly only seaweed, but my reaction was to swim faster than I ever had before. I didn't stop until I reached the shoreline by their house.

There it was, just as I remembered from only a few seasons since I was last welcome. Wet and fatigued, I now had to alert Ylwa and not disturb the fisherman. Thankfully, their home was on one level. I quietly tapped outside her window.

"Andy? Is that you?" she said as she came to open the window.

She looked different. She looked like a woman now, and in her nightgown, the most beautiful one in our world. We embraced across the windowsill, and I explained everything from the letters to my long swim across the sea. She confirmed that she'd never received my letters.

For fear of waking her father, my visit was short. I spent far more time swimming that night than I spent with Ylwa. We arranged future meetings, and she promised we could write each other through a trusted friend's address.

Eventually the season changed, and the nights became too short for the journey without risk of being sighted. We spent the time writing letters. As difficult as it was to be apart, it became even more so when her responses suddenly stopped. I vowed to swim to her once again when the nights were long enough.

However, I did not have to wait that long to see her.

The fisherman arrived unannounced one day, about fifty days or so after the letters stopped. Ylwa was with him, in tears. My parents called me to the door, quite scared. "Ylwa!" I yelled. She looked up, but then her father glared at her, and so Ylwa gave me no reply.

He carried a heavy chest and delicately laid it on the floor. "Andy?" he shouted, opening the lid, "What is this?"

"It appears to be an egg, sir," I responded foolishly.

"Oh my," shrieked my mother. I turned to look at her and saw her face shift from stunned to joyously proud, thrilled even.

"Oh my," I murmured. I looked at Ylwa, but she focused her eyes on the floor, still sobbing.

"Andy, I know you've been sneaking off with my daughter."

"Yes sir, but I promise you we haven't . . . in fact, I don't think I'd even know how to—"

"You haven't what? You're telling me you haven't made any advances on my daughter? That you would swim at night across the water to visit her, and risk being caught or killed by the sea, and you did this simply for . . ."

"Love, yes," I answered.

"Oh Andy! It's all so romantic!" squealed my mother, with not the best timing.

"Well then, I suppose I'm to assume this egg is unfertilized, that there is no child of yours inside," added the fisherman facetiously. "I might as well smash it open."

"Don't you dare!" screamed my mother. "That's my grandchild!"

"No, it's not, Mother," I said, nauseous with humiliation.

"As I have told you, Father," confirmed Ylwa through her sobs.

The fisherman wound his fingers into a fist as though he was going to destroy the large egg.

"Why hesitate?" I asked. "I've told the truth. In fact, I would destroy it myself if it meant you would respect my intentions with your daughter."

He made a fist so tight, I could see his tendons push away the blood inside his knuckles. He raised up a bent elbow and did it. We all grimaced as the egg was smashed. Albumin fluid covered his wooden case and forearm. My mother shrieked and rushed to the egg, proving she didn't believe my honest words, as I assured her there was indeed nothing inside.

No child, no evidence of a spinal cord, no red speck, nothing. Defensively humiliated, the fisherman left the egg and his chest behind saying, "Put that in your museum."

I rushed to Ylwa, still by the doorway, where we embraced. "You're laying eggs now?" I whispered. She nodded, no doubt with the same nausea of her own. She hurried outside after her father. I'm not sure what she said to the man, but after a moment he came back inside.

"I'm terribly sorry," he said to all of us. And with that, Svalbard was again a unified people. He may have been the last to assimilate, but now anyone who knew of our existence desperately wanted us together. The broken eggshell did indeed find its way into the museum, something the fisherman was eventually able to laugh about, and so the community knew Ylwa to be of fertile age.

We dated openly; I'd estimate I was seventeen to her fifteen at the time, and we'd often appear publicly, in the market. No one dared accuse our young love of being simply an infatuation, as our uniqueness relieved us of that common parental reduction. Instead, our romance was supported wherever it was known, which was well beyond where we would travel. Ylwa was still quite shy and would cling to me, something truly endearing, but I would be tasked with politely deflecting the gawkers and any who would approach us with all too much curious ambition. They would ask her about the first egg, and I would answer while Ylwa stared at the ground. They would ask if she'd laid any more, and I would answer while Ylwa stared at the ground. They would ask eagerly if we planned to have a fertile egg in the future or if we were to be married . . . and I would freeze in silence while Ylwa stared at me.

We would occasionally receive gifts, often from strangers. Usually a hand-knitted garment in our proportions, but scaled for an infant.

"This is very thoughtful," I said on one occasion. "You know how hard it was for our parents to find clothing for us. It always had to be custom-made like this."

"We cannot accept this," Ylwa would oddly say of packages abandoned at my family's doorstep. "We don't have a child, and we shouldn't be in debt or favor to any strangers."

"What can we do?" I'd ask. "It's handmade and not designed to be of any use for a Svalbardian boy or girl."

In a moment of fleeting privacy on a nice evening together, we sat at a restaurant, where she told me nothing from the menu interested her.

"Yes, I know. Your father raised you on raw fish and rotten vegetables. Very convenient for a fisherman," I teased.

"He never fed me rotten vegetables."

"Of course not, just his leftover chum." Then a thought returned to me that I had conceived earlier. "Ylwa, we must find a name for our species."

"I'm more concerned with what species I'll be eating tonight, and if this restaurant is willing to serve it raw."

"What would you call us? If we don't give ourselves a name, the Svalbards may. And we might not like it."

"Well, you're definitely a jingleberry. I'm not sure what I am."

"Oh, and what is a jingleberry?"

"Something cute and silly," she teased. "Something that follows you home, that you just can't get rid of."

"And what do jingleberries eat?"

"Strange things. Very strange things."

"Like uncooked fish?" Pointing to the menu I told her, "Try this. It's fish, and it's hardly cooked. In fact, it's smoked."

"How do I know it won't kill me?" she asked, which was, in fairness, a lingering concern for the two of us when adventuring with new food.

"Truthfully, Ylwa, you don't unless you try. But I've eaten it before."

"Oh dear," she said, flirting, "then it will surely turn me mad."

"Hey, Little Andy!" interrupted a voice from across the room. Ylwa sighed.

"Hello, friend!" I shouted back in a perfunctory effort.

"Andy," she whispered, "please, this is a table for two."

"Ylwa, they're twice our size," I said softly, speaking of all Svalbards. "It's gracious of them to accept us, and we should work to keep it so. We're fortunate we haven't been placed in a zoo somewhere."

"We haven't? Oh, if only we could have our own island . . . just a small one. There must be so many . . ." She spoke of her dreams as I had heard many times before, when I would swim the great distance across the sea to visit her.

She did try the smoked fish that night, and she rather enjoyed it. I watched her eat her meal for a moment and thought how several seasons ago I had first kissed her. I had an idea, although this one would require more careful planning than spontaneity.

In his recent miraculous shift in trust, the fisherman now allowed Ylwa to spend nights with our family in our spare bedroom. I woke up early one morning while she still slept, and I escaped to a meadow to pick wildflowers. I returned home and placed the flowers in the last of our water so they would remain fresh. I went to the market alone. Though it was early, the fish vendors were at their stands. I planned to also stop by the rainwater collection sites to bring back more fresh water, but in my haste to finish my project before Ylwa awoke, I simply forgot.

I returned home with the fish to quietly prepare it the simplest way I knew, the only way I knew. I would poach the filet in boiling water. Realizing then that I had forgotten to bring back the fresh water, and that I doubtfully had time to return for more before Ylwa awoke, I turned to the vase holding the wildflowers. I pulled the flowers and bound their stalks with string and set them aside on the table. I drained the water from the vase to poach the fish. It was hardly enough, but it was successful.

I walked carefully to her room carrying five items. The fish and the flowers I carried on a platter. Hidden in my pockets were a poem and a separate letter that I had written that morning, and finally a jewelry box. Inside the box was all that I could afford: a delicate, finely chained necklace with two pearls mounted cleverly around a small medallion, which was to hang as the focus of the piece. It was custom-made by an eager, cooperative jeweler who I believe would have asked for much more in return for his work had I not been "Little Andy."

I entered the room and Ylwa awoke pleasantly. I brought her meal and explained the fish was not raw or smoked; it was boiled. She received the flowers with a drowsy but peaceful smile and took several bites of the fish. I knew her father had long since forfeited the letters I had written, so when I handed her the poem first, I said, "There are two more letters that you still haven't received."

She opened it and read the verse I had written that morning, which I hope you judge kindly:

The Good Jingleberry

A day alone beneath a tree
when something fell quite harmlessly.
It dropped and struck atop my head,
"What now? A Jingleberry?" I think I said.
No pit, no worm, and it was clean—
sanitary, but still quite green.
I asked her where she thought she'd be
in several days. Here with me?
Because by then, if all goes right,
this Jingleberry will be ripe.
She said good-bye and then I warned
of vermin, weeds, and sprouting thorns.
It's nice to be one of a kind,
but a good Jingleberry is hard to find.

I was prepared for her to laugh or smile lovingly, and she did both. Before she was able to comment, I added, "And here is the final letter, which has, until now, gone undelivered."

She opened the much shorter message, which asked quite plainly, "Will you marry me?"

I was prepared as she reacted to the unembellished card, ready to reveal the two-pearled necklace, although slightly unprepared for her response.

"Anders, do you promise to find our very own island where we can be together, and I can live the rest of my life with you?" She had said this so many times before. I was beginning to believe this fantasy, although unrealistic, was something she truly wanted. "One in which no one will be there to stare at me?"

"I'll find us an island somewhere. I will stare at times, but no one else."

"Anders, of course I will marry you!"

The island was a fantasy to her, but her desire for isolation was a reality: to be separated from the relentless social attention we had to deal with our entire lives. We had spoken of it before, and I never understood how she planned to function without the very community that permitted us such little privacy.

It was a topic that concerned me as we planned our next step, but to bring it into discussion would have been to ruin the proposal.

"Anders, I don't feel well. Suddenly, in fact, I'm quite nauseous."

"It must be the fish," I said, laughing, at first, at my own cooking. "I'll throw away the rest."

"Anders, could you bring me some water?" she said, then groaned and added, "And possibly an empty bucket?"

I ran quickly and returned with the bucket. "I'm sorry; I used the last of the water to cook the fish. I can fetch some more from the sites if you're well enough to be alone for a while."

"Yes. I'll be all right. Thank you."

I returned after an hour or so with fresh water, and found my parents, now awake, caring for Ylwa in her room. "Andy, thank you for the water," said my mother in a tone deliberately void of panic, "but I think we'll need to send you back out again for a medic. Ylwa is shaking."

With no time to focus on anything but fetching a physician, I ran to Harskamp, an older gentleman whose practice was nearest our house. I pressed him to gather his tools and run with me to Ylwa's bedside. Thankfully, he came that far, but at the sight of Ylwa lying weak in her bed, he was reluctant to help any further. "Andy, I was trained in the physiology and anatomy of the Svalbards. I . . . I wouldn't even know where her digestive tract is."

"Sir, we're not looking for surgery just yet," said my mother. "We believe the girl has eaten something."

"Well at the very least I would suggest water. Have her drink a considerable amount of water," he answered.

"Oh dear . . ." I said. "The water."

"What is it, Andy?" asked my father, tending to Ylwa.

I grabbed the flowers and asked the medic, "Please, look at these. There are several different kinds. Are any of them not to be consumed?"

"Well, here's one," he said, pulling a long-stemmed flimsy flower with bluish, purplish petals. "'Iris.' It's not well known which wild vegetation is toxic, but I do recall an incident when a small boy, for whatever reason, consumed the roots of this flower . . . did she consume the flower?"

"It doesn't look like she did," said my mother, smiling with a false sense of hope.

"That's not true," I explained. "In a way, she did. The flowers soaked in the water I used to cook the fish."

Harskamp reasoned. "That would only put trace amounts in her system. I believe a Svalbard would have to consume quite a great many of . . ." He paused, interrupting himself. "Of course, a Svalbard is not sick."

I asked, "Sir, is there anything you can do to help?"

"Insist she drink plenty of water and eat simple sweets and salted foods when she can. Even if she can't hold them long. I would believe that advice to be universal."

The medic left and we continued to tend to Ylwa.

As she slept, I grew restless. Knowing my parents would stay by her bedside, I returned to town to find a second medic. I spoke with several, but with no further success. Each one repeated, "Have her drink substantial amounts of water," an extremely painful reminder of my mistake. After the medics, I even visited a livestock caretaker, which was rather humiliating, and asked for advice to help my fiancée. I made no progress there either.

I was, however, near the museum. I remembered the exhibit, the one next to my own, about a creature called the Host. I quickly revisited it and read every word, then returned to Ylwa and my parents.

Ylwa's father had returned as planned, intending to take Ylwa back to their island. My parents had, prior to my return, informed him of what had happened, and all agreed she was too weak to travel. Her father and his boat would stay on the big island for the present time.

I discussed what I had read about the Host. Ylwa was sleeping, though not improving, so I was only able to discuss this with her father and my parents. "It's a legend, but they say a way to sustain life. The Host is said to be a tremendous creature of both land and seagoing means. It's migratory and often crawls up along a certain island to the northwest of here in its seasonal path. They say if you are with the beast, as long as it lives, so shall you."

"I believe I would have seen if not heard of such a creature from another fisherman if it were real," said Ylwa's father.

"It's on exhibit at the museum alongside my down and eggshell. Do I not exist? And if it were not real, why are all accounts of the creature so consistent, always speaking of sighting it on a specific island to the northwest?"

"Andy, Ylwa is too weak to take to the sea, to chase after something like this," said my father.

"She's not improving, and no one is able to help us. Am I to idle as the woman I love, and possibly the future of our species, simply expires here in a bedroom?"

My family took me as irrational, but they harbored what I considered a foolish sense of optimism for Ylwa's recovery. They considered the illness in their own terms, how a Svalbard's body, accustomed to a varied diet, would react. The fisherman spent that night in our house to be near his daughter, but I vowed in silence he would wake up without his boat.

After all had gone to sleep, I quietly snuck into the room where Ylwa rested.

To my great relief she was alive and in fact somewhat alert.

"Andy?" she said.

"Hold on, Ylwa. We have to be quiet." I carried her with great difficulty through the window of the room. I brought the flowers as well, though starting to wilt, not knowing if they might hold a clue to finding a treatment.

"Where are we going?"

"To the boat."

"Oh, all right," she responded in delirium. I carried her along the brief walk from my house to the shoreline. When we reached her father's boat, I laid her down in the vessel, untied it, and launched it. Fortunately, it was not terribly large, or I might not have been able to maneuver it properly. The fisherman had shown me some things about handling the boat on past trips to or from their home. This time, however, I set off through the channel between the big island and the principle northeast island, heading to the northwest.

We wandered for several hours, but eventually I spotted another vessel. I hailed the ship, another small boat, planning to ask for help returning to shore. I decided I had made a great mistake taking Ylwa away from the fresh water and rest she'd need for her recovery. I got the attention of the captain of the other boat, and he quickly steered toward us in the open water. I had expected the first words from the man's mouth to be "Little Andy," but before he said that, or before I said anything, he shouted, "Turn around! Hurry!"

"What is it?" I asked.

"We spotted a terrible creature," spoke his mate, pointing. "It crested in and out of the water as though it wanted to consume our boat. It was big enough, and could have!"

"Where again?" I asked as the man pointed and told me how far away and how recently it was spotted. They explained that they were ending their trip early and returning to the big island because of what they had seen. They didn't want to stay long, and I didn't delay them. They steered toward Kildebyen, and I set off in the direction of the creature.

After another hour, something crested on the horizon.

It wasn't moving, and I saw it before I saw the island beneath it. Eventually running the boat aground on the island, I pulled Ylwa and the flowers up along the sand. It was the Host; it had to be. All accounts in the museum described what I also saw with my own eyes. Red and brown in color, a tremendous jaw, six oddly shaped legs, but no visible eyes or face. I stood alone on the small island, a hundred steps or so from the creature, with Ylwa lying unconscious next to the dried bouquet of flowers near her father's boat.

The creature breathed.

Its tremendous jaw opened and sucked in more air than I had breathed in my lifetime. I carefully walked around the island so that I could see inside the creature's mouth on its next breath. It took several minutes, and I was ready in my position, but when the creature's jaw opened again, the dawn shone into what looked like a living cave, and not an empty one. I had seen something in its darkness, several things in fact, but I wasn't sure what. I had to wait for the next breath. When the jaw opened once more, shouting came from within . . .

"Hurry!" "Come, quickly" "Now, hurry!" were several of the intelligible shouts, along with many in other languages. Something inside had seen me, and I was being called there. I returned to collect Ylwa, still unconscious, and the wilting flowers. Abandoning the boat, I positioned us close to the creature's jaw, nervously awaiting its next breath. I was ready to enter, but when it came, I was so close that we were sucked in by its intake of breath. Stumbling, I found myself inside the cavity of whatever this tremendous creature was.

Applause ensued from the darkness. Eventually came a greeting, from a man I was unable to see. "Do you speak Svalbardian?"

"Andy?" asked an alert Ylwa. "Are you there?"

"Ah, you do speak Svalbardian," came the disembodied voice.

"I'm here, Ylwa. Are you all right?" I asked.

"I feel wonderful."

"Well, let me tell you why," said the man. His name was Rangar and he had been living in the Host for over a hundred seasons. He had been a fisherman and had been in a terrible storm. His boat was destroyed. He washed up on the small island and began to bleed to death from a wound sustained in the breakup. When he saw the huge creature crawl up along the shoreline shortly after he had, he believed he was hallucinating and near death. He approached the creature and heard voices coming from within. He believed it a spiritual experience, thinking this creature would carry him to the afterlife. Instead, when he entered, he felt strong again and realized his vitality had returned. The belief of those inside the Host was that somehow the creature's life and immunity was able to support those within it, much like a barnacle on shellfish or a parasitic worm inside the intestinal tract of livestock.

They knew nearly nothing of the science behind it, but all agreed that we occupied the land lungs of the creature, because it spent most of its time deep underwater and would breathe differently then, not opening the giant jaw. Aside from any science, many had their own spiritual beliefs of the creature. Rangar did say with confidence that the creature could not cure you, simply sustain you. It would not be necessary to eat or drink, and we would not age. All physical needs would be met simply by sharing the air of the Host.

"So, this creature is over one hundred seasons old?" I asked.

"At least five hundred by my count," came another voice. It was difficult, not being able to see the sources of the voices in the darkness of the creature's lungs.

"So, if I leave?" asked Ylwa.

"It depends," answered Rangar. "If you were going to die on the outside, then you will die. Otherwise, I would have left a long time ago. I still have my wounds, same as the day I stepped inside this creature. Here they don't drain my life or cause me pain."

I searched around the ground to collect the flowers in the darkness. They were as firm again as several days ago, when I picked them.

"Tell us your story!" yelled someone from the depths. "With detail. Time is something that won't concern you ever again . . ."

They were right. As torturous as these last hectic hours had been, the arrested pace of living in the Host would be its own unique pain. Waiting and dying have too much in common.

We told our stories, and about our personal desperation over being perhaps the last of our species. Because the Host was migratory, not all residents shared the same language. There were sixty or so inside. Those who spoke Svalbardian told us their stories, one by one. Some were learning the language from others inside the creature and contributed their stories in broken Svalbardian. There were several elder couples, that is, older when they entered the creature. There was a murderer afraid of the fate he would face in death, a holy man facing the same fear, and even an older woman with a small, pampered pet whom she said she simply could not live without. All shared a desperation and, like me, felt themselves tremendously blessed to have found the beast. After sharing our stories, they asked Ylwa and me about the outside world, of any world news we had heard, and the date by the Svalbardian calendar or any others we knew.

Ylwa trembled when the creature first moved with us inside, crawling into the water and diving deep beneath the sea. She asked about her father, if I ever thought we'd see him again. I didn't know. I just felt it our responsibility to wait inside the creature as long as necessary for a cure. Maybe someone would join us one day, a medic from another land, with an herb or a drink that would rid her of the poison. It was unlikely, but if she were to die, what of our species?

"Andy, I appreciate what you have done for me," she said privately, during an extended lull while the creature traveled through the water. "I do not blame you for the flowers, and I do love you."

"I love you," I responded, adding foolishly, "and as you've taught me, love is the emotion that can do no wrong. We will make all of our decisions henceforth only with love."

"Love is the . . ." She paused, confused. "When did I say this?"

"Do you recall the older couple who approached us when we were younger? As poorly as your father reacted, I knew it was because he loved you."

"Oh dear," she said. "Oh my, no . . . Andy, no . . ."

"What?"

"Andy, love can cause so many problems if you aren't cautious and if you let it blind all rational thought. People become so misguided by love."

Embarrassed, I said, "Like when your father that day . . ."

"He wanted nothing more than to avoid attention. He couldn't even act clearly enough to accomplish that. In fact he accomplished quite the opposite, causing a scene."

"So, when you said, about love, the emotion that can . . ."

"Satire, irony," she said, devastating me. "I'm sorry, I'm so sorry for misleading you. I didn't realize you had misunderstood me."

"Be careful how you satire. You may be giving your victim an anthem," I murmured to myself. I was unable to accept the death of a part of me, part of a foundation I had built that I felt defined me well. I protested. "So what then? A sterile existence? There's no place for love in one's personal life? There's no room for emotions in your love life?"

"No, of course there is. Love is a wonderful thing and should be present in all of your decisions."

"Now you're contradicting yourself!"

"Andy, you're upset. Because you love me."

"I do love you." I began to weep. "And look at where it has brought us."

But Ylwa was honest, with no satire or irony when she said that she did not blame me.

Though sharing a dark cavern with sixty others, I felt a duty to at least discuss having a child together. This of course appalled Ylwa, because of not only the concern about privacy but also the uncertainty of our own futures. We fell into arguing over the topic, something we had never done in Svalbard. Often in the silence and boredom I was guilty of brooding over the topic, feeling it absolutely necessary to reopen the discussion. The "discussion" wouldn't last long and would end in drama.

Over time, it became cyclical, our relationship. Only drama could end the boredom, and only boredom could end the drama. In the end, there was no attempt made by us to have a child together, ever.

Whoever desires less from a relationship will always get what they want.

We had spent one full migration inside the creature, traveling in the darkness and usually, we presumed, deep below the surface. Occasionally it would crawl onto shore and rest for several days. Its occupants would rush to the jaw for a glimpse of where we were, then argue over the speculations. We as a group would also use this chance to look at each other, and over time I was able to match voices with appearances . . . but really we were looking outward for another like us, hoping to speak a familiar dialect to someone who, understandably, is reluctant to crawl into the jaw of a huge but benevolent creature.

Ylwa grew weary. She was physically repaired the instant I brought her inside but had emotionally deteriorated since that time. She stayed by my side at all times, partially out of shyness but also out of a silent obligation I believe she felt toward me. When the creature would crawl onto dry land, she'd never rush to the open jaw for a view of the outside like the rest of us.

I encouraged her, but she stayed seated the twenty or so steps away from the excitement.

One day, when the jaw opened, there were two figures standing near the creature's gateway. Quite special ones in fact. On the creature's first breath it's always hard to see clearly, as our eyes struggled to adjust to the light. Still, at the first sight of silhouettes we began cheering and encouraging them to join us.

What harm could a stranger do inside the Host, even with ill intent? On the third breath, the two silhouettes joined us.

They were two young women, Canadians. Their names were Lavender and Marigold. The group attempted their introductions, but the creature too soon made a horrible noise, began shuffling like we had never felt before, then slipped into the water. Once it had, we were able to try again. The girls had escaped from York, in Canada, though their Svalbardian was quite good. To this they credited their grandmother. They spent a great deal of time speaking with a young man in our darkness, a soldier I'm told, who had been attacked some fifteen seasons ago. I didn't understand the conversation; it was held in Canadian.

Ylwa and I did, however, have an opportunity to speak with the girls in our native language. "We're Lavender and Marigold, of York," came one of the voices. "Of Canada."

"Oh, you're from York?" asked Ylwa.

"Just outside of it," said one of the girls. "It's less confusing to tell people we're from York."

"So where exactly are you from?" asked Ylwa.

"The rural districts north of York."

"Oh, I'm not familiar," said Ylwa.

"Right, exactly," said one of the girls, Marigold. It was the most outgoing Ylwa had been since we'd come to the Host. I believe somehow she sensed that the girls could help her.

"So, they're saying you have a unique gift?" I asked.

"Yes," said Lavender, the other girl. She had a strange glow to her eyes, a purple I believe, although it was difficult to discern colors in the darkness. She continued, "I'm able to see if a person is to die, or if a female is carrying a child. But please remember, I cannot heal."

"Are you able to tell in this darkness?" asked Ylwa.

"I would be. But I believe the nature of this creature is interfering. Since we can't die inside of it, I won't be able to make such a prediction until we return to land and are able to step outside its jaw."

Ylwa was ecstatic. "So, you'll be able to tell me if I'm to die, or if I will be able to recover?"

"Essentially, yes. Marigold and I had discussed offering this service to anyone here, the next time we are on land."

"Oh, but I must go first!" insisted Ylwa.

It was several more days, but the creature did crawl back up to dry land. For the first time, Ylwa was waiting eagerly for what was outside the beast's jaw. Marigold and Lavender were ready as well. It drew its first breath, and leaving the flowers behind, the four of us rushed outside to feel the sun, the sand, and to breathe our own air. It must have been precisely one season, one full migration, because the creature had returned to exactly the small island, the same location where I had run the fisherman's ship ashore. There was no doubt; his boat was still there.

Marigold and Lavender first looked at each other and said something in Canadian. I believe Lavender was confirming that they were in fact safe from death. Lavender then looked at me, and although I had no reason to fear her next words, I was still relieved when she told me I was not to die.

Ylwa was next. Lavender looked at her, looked at her closely, then at me, and down to the sand. She picked her neck up and turned to Ylwa. "I'm sorry," she said.

"I don't feel well," confirmed Ylwa. The Canadian girls continued with the rest of the predictions, one by one as the others inside received the same service we had. I paid the scene no attention and stayed with Ylwa.

She knelt on the sand, crouching over her abdomen. "Come on; let's get back inside," I whispered.

"No. Let me try to stand." She was able to get back on her feet to take several steps but only managed five or six before she stumbled and was kneeling again.

"Ylwa, hurry," I said, squinting from the most intense light I had seen in a season, trying to lift her up and return to the Host.

"Anders, stop."

"No, Ylwa. Our wait isn't over."

"Mine is." She looked at me and smiled. "Anders, thank you for all you have done."

"Ylwa? Don't! We don't have a cure."

"I do," she answered. "It's here, in the light. You've done everything expected of you. By the Svalbards, by your community, and by your species. You've always done to them as you would have done to you. But not this time. I don't want to be dragged back into the darkness, my body preserved and my spirit as caged as it's been my entire life."

I wanted to understand what she was feeling but knew I could lose her at any moment.

"Then good-bye, Ylwa. I love you."

"Thank you, Anders. For everything. I love you as well."

She rose to her feet for a final embrace, then turned away from me to face the water. She took several strides upright before stumbling once more. I watched her from behind, not moving since our final farewell. She rose to her feet yet again, took several more paces, and finally collapsed. I rushed to her before a small crowd could form.

Ylwa had died.

I brought her body onto the boat and planned to return home. My parents, the fisherman, and everyone who had ever shouted "Little Andy" across the marketplace would receive our return. After a season's absence, they might have believed us both dead.

Hopefully, in spite of losing Ylwa, I would somewhat relieve them with my reappearance.

For their help, I offered Lavender and Marigold a trip to wherever the boat could go. They said they wanted only to come with me to Svalbard, to Kildebyen. We drained the rainwater out of the vessel and boarded. Not only were the girls with me but also several others from the Host who had recently received news that they were not to die. The survivors were exuberant, which made the trip all the more difficult for me. I not only had to mourn while the others celebrated, but I had to function, piloting the ship. All this while Ylwa's body was unavoidably within my view. She lay at my feet by my station, while those who celebrated clumped to the opposite side of the small boat, ignoring any sadness that would interfere with their joy.

I stopped the boat briefly on the open water and spoke to the others to explain myself. "Excuse me, there's something I must do." They stared as I, now sobbing, stood Ylwa upright. I embraced her but could not feel her presence within the body. I brought her to the side of the stern, as the stares turned into gawks. I released her into the water and watched her sink, rigid, deep below the surface. I turned to address the living and explained, "She would not have wanted to be confined to a museum."

———————————

Today I still live on the big island, studying languages and working to save. Both efforts are to someday travel in search of another like me . . . or rather, another like Ylwa. I'll never forget her but do hope to find the love we had again, and with another, if such a one exists.

6 / Marigold

Had it not been for the shouts of encouragement coming from within the giant beast, Lavender and I might not have dreamt it safe to—even as gingerly as we did—crawl into its mouth. And though three soldiers pursued us with intent to kill, even with Lavender's gift we might have taken our odds treading into the sea.

Yet the survival we found inside the lungs of the great water mammoth was more proof of my sister's vision.

We entered the creature and were soaked in darkness once its jaw shut behind us. The group that waited inside greeted us in their native tongues. Some had been there so long they spoke dead languages, like Old Svalbardian.

"Lavender, are you all right?" I asked as the creature seemed to settle.

"I'm fine. Marigold, is it dark in here to you?"

"Yes, of course," I answered, standing close. "I see nothing, but I hear many voices. All for us. I believe none are the soldiers that were chasing us."

"I can see everyone in this group."

"How? We're in total darkness."

"To me, we're all glowing," answered Lavender.

"Glowing? Oh no. We are going to die. We were swallowed by this creature and now we'll be consumed."

The group continued to shout their greetings in various languages.

"No, it's a new color: a pale yellow. I've never seen anything glow yellow like this before. Only red or white. I'm certain it's not white for death, but I don't know what it means."

———

Just a moment after we entered, the creature began to move. It seemed to absorb a strike to our left, from its exterior. Then we heard some sort of lashing sound, and we were off into the water. I felt little more than the pressure of texture and friction as we tumbled and collided while the creature seemed to shuffle into the sea and dive.

Once the voices quieted, we resumed our introductions. A Canadian man from the other side of the cavity asked, "Are your names Lavender and Marigold?"

"Yes, sir," I said. "It's nice to hear a familiar language. And what is your name?"

"Can you come closer?" he asked from across the creature.

"Yes!" I blurted out.

Able to see pale yellow silhouettes, Lavender guided me across the dark cavity.

"Sir, where do we know you?" she asked. "Were you one of our patrons at the Mystic Garden?"

"I don't believe so. I've been here a while. What garden?"

"It was our business," Lavender responded.

"You had a business? Oh, I've missed so much."

"But you're Canadian, aren't you? Where are you from?" I asked, still holding Lavender's hand, twisting behind her through the murmuring crowd.

"Where am I from?" He laughed politely. "First I want to be sure it's really you, before my hopes get too high."

I whispered, "Lavender, this may sound impossible, but I swear I recognize that laugh."

My sister halted a few paces short of his voice. "Sir, will you please tell us your name and how you know us?"

"Oh, it is you. It's definitely you," he said excitedly. "I've seen those eyes before. Only once, but they're just as I remember them."

"Sir?" she insisted. "Your name?"

"Simon. My name is Simon. I believe I'm your father."

The crowd stopped its murmuring and remained cooperatively silent. Time was frozen.

"Father?" I asked.

"Yes, here," he responded, still difficult to find. "Oh, you sound so much like your mother."

I gained a step or two and leaped in his direction to embrace him.

"No, Marigold, don't!" yelled Lavender, too late.

I screamed as something rough struck me along the neck.

"Oh dear, are you all right?" asked Father.

"I am," I realized. "I just reacted . . . to the feel of something along your back. I felt no pain, but I should have. What was that?" In a darkness only Lavender could navigate, something protruded slightly from Father's upper back.

"It's a thorned bone. From a Siberian soldier's leg. I'm sorry, I didn't mean to give you a Siberian hug," he joked. "We can try a gentler one if we can face each other."

Lavender stepped forward, and we both embraced the man. The crowd, now an audience, reacted to our reunion with a gasp and a sigh and then applause. So much happened, and so quickly. Hearing Father's voice initially forced me to question whether or not I was alive. Or had Lavender and I possibly been killed by the soldiers that had chased us through the marsh? And were we now, for better or worse, in the afterlife?

Father answered these questions as he explained the creature's technique, though likely unintentional, of sustaining life. To this Lavender and I attributed the pale yellow glow that she saw and concluded we had not been killed. We explained Lavender's gift to the man, who confirmed he was our father when he said, "Heather and I always knew there was something special about those luminous purple eyes."

There was still the matter of the Siberian's bone, lodged in his flesh, and the question of how it was possible that we were speaking with him.

"So, it's true that Siberians' bones are thorned?" asked Lavender.

"The only Siberians I have ever seen have been soldiers, but yes. Gray skinned, as a result of the altered blood flow around the thorns, our military believes. Their base skeleton is just as ours, but numerous spurs sprout along their bones. Arms, legs, ribs, even their spines . . . the spurs are just extensions of their bones, hereditary growths that taper into thorns. They protrude from the skin if the thorn is long enough, or if the flesh is shallow enough. And their country produces particularly lean men, at least those whom I have seen in battle. They may be slender, but their thorns extend formidably from throughout their body. As Canadian soldiers, we're trained in spears, pikes, broad and long swords, taught to fight at least at arm's length. Should they engage you directly in combat at short range, your chances of survival are poor. They can thrust or thrash almost any limb in any direction to pierce your skin."

"So then, a Siberian hug, as you said?" I asked.

"Is a fighting maneuver they employ. But used figuratively to mean when someone close to you hurts you."

"And is that how the thorned bone became lodged in your back?" asked Lavender.

"That would bring us to my story . . ."

Simon

I was serving on Ellesmere, at Fort Alert. It was well into the season of darkness, when Siberian invasions are most common. Their nation consists of mainland Siberia, a peninsula, and Severnaya Siberia, a series of islands to the north of the mainland. The islands serve as a barrier to the mainland, and so they keep a naval base there. From Severnaya they can navigate by the pole star, the very same that Polaris is from. They can easily reach the northern tip of Canadian soil. This is Fort Alert. They most often launch their invasions in the season of darkness, when there is little break in celestial navigation because sunlight is so minimal. They're able to see the stars at all times, if the weather is clear. It's also more difficult for us to spot a Siberian ship as it approaches in the darkness. To their further advantage, they can easily dock near the northwestern shore of Thule, then invade across the strait into Canadian territory. Even if we are expecting them, they're capable of an ambush, which is how they attacked Fort Alert during my time.

Following Heather's visit for Lavender's birth, and after a spectacular display of the Celestial Lights, we quickly returned our focus to guarding the edge of our country closest to Siberia. I believe Heather and Lavender had been gone at least a day but not much longer. I don't know for certain; time passes oddly without the sun and while on rotating guard shifts. I was off duty and wandering just south of the fort . . . we were permitted to wander if armed and protected, which I was. I was as ready as I could have hoped, and almost as though they waited for the Celestial Lights to disappear, the ambush began.

Walking outside the fort's perimeter and before I became aware of the ambush, I casually looked toward the guard post, curious as to who was on duty. I saw only a slumped-over Canadian soldier's corpse hanging, then drooping, then falling from the high post silently into the fort somewhere out of view. I drew my sword but had still not seen a Siberian. The fort began to burn from within; a fiery glow emanated through the gaps around the gate. There's a peculiar detail of our defense that I must mention. A Canadian fort is laced with vines, prunings and sap from a particular tree that, when burned, can cause a terrible skin reaction if you are exposed to its fumes. I don't know the name of the tree, but it produces egg-shaped fruit with red, green, or orange skin and orange flesh inside. A Canadian commander may issue the torching of his own fort to expose our invader to these fumes. Should the base be lost to our enemy, their lungs will itch and burn so horribly that they'll wait to be slaughtered by our next fort to the south, crippling their own invasion. In short, if Fort Alert is to fall, it should burn.

Fighting fire with fire makes the whole world burn, but Polaris knows no other way. And so, our fort was ablaze, yet I had not heard a single startling noise, nor had I heard a horn blow from the tower. The battle seemed lost before a Canadian knew it had begun.

I turned away from the fort to face south, considering an escape to warn the next post.

Standing in my way was a lone enemy soldier, expecting me. I engaged him one-on-one and immediately saw the thorns coming from the exposed parts of his arms and legs. Blood dripped from the top of his head and covered his body, though I don't believe his own. Siberians are known to drench themselves in the blood of animals they slaughter, and they feast upon the fresh carcasses shortly before a battle. The Canadian military's belief is that they do this so as to ignore their own injuries, and their own blood, allowing them to continue fighting without awareness of pain should they become wounded in battle.

Engaging the soldier, I fought carefully to keep a distance, and with a successful strike of a heavy sword I severed his right leg below his knee. He hadn't drawn any of my blood, and I had attacked the thorned, unarmored portion of his body. Though I hobbled him, I chose not to ensure the kill in favor of fleeing more quickly to the south to spread word of the invasion.

I hardly advanced ten strides before I was blocked by a second Siberian soldier, appearing out of the darkness and closing in to obstruct my path. He was a bit more skilled than the first, and just as thorned. I knew it necessary again to fight from a distance so he would be unable to pummel me with his limbs at short range. I believed for a moment at first that I fought properly and with patience, keeping the appropriate sword's length as we struggled, but I realize now he was merely toying with me, stalling my fleeting chance of escape.

From behind, the first soldier plunged his severed leg bone through the flesh and tissue of my upper back. The hobbled Siberian had pulled the flesh off his own limb and used the stripped bone as a weapon. His fresh and wet blood spilled from his mouth and he had bits of his leg flesh between his teeth.

Before I could react, I was secured and gripped from behind as the second soldier now found the break he needed to advance on me, giving me the Siberian hug.

Easily finding gaps in my armor from the rear, the second soldier's thorns dug into me and added to the pain of the first soldier's leg. He made new holes in my skin, while the hobbled soldier grappled my legs, dragging his thorns along my shins to spill more Canadian blood on Canadian soil. I was still upright, though they quickly brought me to the ground, hoping for a kill. Still with my sword in hand, the two slender men were not massive enough to secure me, and in desperation I recklessly flailed my sword in several wide arcs to fend them off. They released me, but I failed to harm them further, and I was dying. In my final moments of natural life, I realized heading south was not an option, as I was being approached by more able-bodied Siberians attempting to kill me.

Before they could get close enough, I fled northeast to the sea, where I soon heard voices calling. I believed them to be the sounds of relatives and elders who had died before me, other generations of long-ago-fallen Canadian soldiers perhaps, and that it was my time. They led me to what was a vessel, and with their urgency and how little we know about the afterlife, I believed the ship to be redemption and the Siberians following behind to be damnation. Escaping for my own eternity, I successfully reached the vessel, which now I know was this creature, and I have been within ever since. I believe the Siberians must have seen me consumed and kept their distance from this beast. No Canadian soldiers followed me here either; perhaps none were able.

Soon after arriving in the Host, or the Living Cave if you prefer, the pain of my injuries vanished, and I stood comfortably upright. Even in the darkness I knew that the bleeding had ceased. Without the thought of pain, I attempted to remove the lower right leg of the Siberian embedded in my upper back. I managed to smash apart the greater protruding portion of the bone but not the entire implant. So much is buried in my flesh that I'm unable to remove it, nor do I desire to shred my flesh, even without fear of pain.

And so, my life in the darkness began. How do I portray a life inside this creature to someone who has experienced it only for a matter of moments, not even a day? You may have noticed that not only do you not feel pain but you also feel almost nothing physically. Roughness, yes, but for example, if you have slept on your arms, you can only feel pressure, tingling, and other things that imply feeling but do not constitute it. You are not hot, and you are not cold. In addition to seeing nothing you smell nothing, if you have not noticed, even as you sit in the stagnant body cavity of a tremendous amphibious sea beast. Are you able to recall a dull day with little work and no recreation in which you spent every hour anticipating dinner? We have only dull days, and we have no dinners. There is no nourishment; we do not require sustenance. And if there were food to eat, we would taste nothing.

My mind rots. Yes, we have ways of entertaining ourselves, which do help. Of our sixty or so inhabitants, we have a small group who sing. We have some games we can play, but there is little you can do in darkness.

For a while I kept occupied by seeking ways of contacting Heather. Hardly anyone who wanders into the Living Cave will leave this creature, and I have not yet found it possible to send a message to the exterior. So, a note in a bottle, but where would I find either?

In time I felt it best for her to believe me dead, and in this she could have closure. I eventually decided it selfish to attempt to contact her in any way, not that I believe it possible.

I entered this creature believing it was salvation and the Siberians who trailed me were damnation . . . but all I have had is an existence with neither. And without the horrible threat of damnation, I have not had the hope of salvation.

Until now. My two daughters, young women, have made my wait worthwhile.

Marigold

He had been there for fifteen seasons, and we had been without him all the while. Lavender focused entirely on the Siberian ambush. She was oddly guarded against sharing any emotions with our father.

Still thinking of the attack, she said, "We've never heard that angle of the story before."

"What were you told?" he asked. "I'm curious. Were we hailed as heroes or failures?"

"Heroes, of course," I said. "At least we are told. By Mother."

He sighed. "How is she? Is Heather all right?" Hearing him call her that, and not "your mother" as our grandparents would, was when I realized he was effectively closer to our own age than to hers, having been in suspension inside the creature for so long.

"She's well," answered Lavender. "She hasn't remarried."

"Oh. I've spent so many days wondering if she had, and I always wondered if 'no' would be the answer I would want to hear. I now know it isn't."

"She speaks of you," I said, "and tries terribly to connect her stories of you with us. But it's nearly impossible. We were so young when this happened."

"It's difficult for her to speak of," said Lavender, "of course because she believes you dead, but also because Polaris blamed her for your death and the loss of the entire battle."

I hadn't been eager to mention this, to spare my father. Although I am quite glad in hindsight that Lavender did. Our father immediately protested, "What? That's not so."

"Mother says the fort's only medic returned to York with her, leaving its soldiers vulnerable," she told him.

"Oh no . . . that's simply a lie. We had three medics."

"What?" yelled Lavender.

"Yes, we had three medics."

"Three? You had three medics?" she yelled again, too angrily, her shouts echoing in the large cavity.

Father continued: "One initially, that's true, but when Heather arrived, we blew the horn for two more from the south. We knew we'd need them, and she may not realize we did this, or why the horn sounded when it did, but it was the best decision. After all, she was about to bear a child. We called for the others to tend to the soldiers inside the fort if necessary. When she returned home with you, only the original medic that had been by her side traveled with her. The other two reached Alert and stayed with us, but I presume were slaughtered or burned in the battle . . . How can medics aid a cause anyway, when trapped with their fellow soldiers inside an ambushed, burning fort?"

"Perhaps Polaris was not properly informed of these details," I said.

"Oh no, no, no, no, no!" said Lavender. "This makes no logical sense."

Father agreed. "It doesn't surprise me if he's lying, manipulating, and controlling people or their minds . . . all in the name of . . . well, himself. There's a side to that ancient man that no commoner in the cathedral sees in his celestial services. True, I'd rather be born Canadian than Siberian. And I do owe him for the many things I enjoyed about my country. We all do. But only those who carry Canadian swords know the real Polaris."

"No, I understand as well," added Lavender. "How were the other numbers, besides the medics?"

"I saw only a few Siberians, but it had the mark of a silent ambush, possibly even a suicide mission. They sought to destroy the stronghold only and to retreat. If they intended to push south to take the next fort, if it had been an invasion, I would have seen greater numbers. I'm certain we had them outnumbered. Our fort was stocked with men."

"But you lost?" asked Lavender.

"I believe all were in the fort as I watched it burn. The enemy's method was silent and brilliant, and their fighting technique highly skilled. Their metals, their weapons are more advanced . . . the soldiers themselves are weapons."

"Yes, and you lost," added Lavender, thinking.

"True, but please understand—"

"There it lies," interrupted my sister. "Polaris is the military leader of all of Canada and would not want belief to spread that his military was beaten because of inferiority."

"I'm not sure that I would use that word . . ."

"So," added Lavender, "he scapegoats Mother and me, an infant. Let the public believe the battle was a full-scale Siberian land invasion and was lost only as a result of the military's compassion toward the ones they serve to protect, not because of military incompetence."

"A little heavy, Lavender," I muttered.

"We tried," said Father. "I suppose."

"So, he scapegoats us, but what happens when the infant with the purple eyes resurfaces fifteen seasons later?" asked my sister.

"Well, now you ask an interesting question," I responded. "What happens when a scapegoat will not be gone?"

"You are constantly and involuntarily remembering the pain of past mistakes and failures," said Father. "Just like the bone stuck inside my back."

"Precisely," I said, joining in. "If a scapegoat refuses to serve its purpose, you'll kick it and kick it until it leaves."

"Almost," corrected Lavender with a sad sigh amid our epiphany. "Until it dies. You don't exile a scapegoat; you execute it. If you do not, you aren't exonerated. That's why Canadian soldiers chased us here. When his public vilification campaign failed, Polaris issued a private edict to have the execution done quietly and by as few soldiers as possible, far from civilization in the bush somewhere."

"They're trying to kill my daughters," murmured Father, knowing he was unable to help. "I served that army."

"They observed us being consumed by this beast," I added optimistically. "Perhaps they will abandon their attempts."

"Marigold?" said Lavender.

"Yes?"

"Usually you're equipped with novelties in times of despair. Your genuine optimism concerns me. Remember, I can see a pale yellow shadowy reflection of your face. You appear quite sad."

"I had almost forgotten," said Father. "When this creature rests on land, we'll see each other. Though it will be our good-bye. Your first safe opportunity to escape this creature should be taken, before your mind suffers. We will have some time until then. It doesn't resurface often, but when it does you should not look back. I'll miss you, but I will insist."

"You are our father," said Lavender. "We will oblige." She seemed too eager to be cooperative, and I was fully ready to dismiss all the man's thoughts about a mind rotting in darkness to spend as much time with him as possible, and so be it if this occurred inside the creature.

Lavender continued with her inquiry: "Father, you may not have much familiarity with our personalities yet. Typically, Marigold uses difficult moments like these to share her poorly timed humor."

"The optimism you mentioned," I answered, genuinely depressed at the moment, as was Lavender. "I'm fighting not to let hope die. Our book, a catalog of edible and poisonous wild food . . . I had hoped it would pave our reentry into Canada. If Polaris wishes us dead, I can bury that possibility."

"Yes, you can," insisted Lavender. "Polaris hates me. He *hates* me."

"It can't be that simple," I said.

"My existence threatens his own. I don't understand it, but he wants me dead. And it gets worse. It won't even be safe to write Mother and inform her that not only is Father alive but also that the lost battle was not her fault, as Polaris falsely claims."

"You're right. He may learn that we survived and send another party to kill us. I'm sorry, Father . . . you do wish us to tell Heather that you are alive, do you not?"

"Yes, you must, now, if you can do it safely. You cannot keep this secret from her."

"We'll find a way. But yes, Lavender, I am quite sad. The hope I had retained has died. But it's difficult to suppress the final shred of hope that Father may be able to walk out of this creature with us, alive and well."

"I . . . I would not survive outside this creature. Not with my injuries. They may not bleed or cause me pain here, but they haven't healed. I still have open wounds, just as they were the night I stumbled into this cavity."

———

Father remembered that my birthday was near, and that I would soon be seventeen. We shared with him every moment of every event he'd missed while the creature wandered the sea for several days. We did ask if any Siberian had ever stumbled into the Host, and he didn't believe the creature wandered far enough east for this to happen. But there was an old story he retold, one he had heard from another resident of the Living Cave: fifty or so seasons ago an uninjured, silent man they believed to be a rogue Siberian slave wandered inside.

The story goes that over time the man listened to and learned the Canadian language from the creature's other inhabitants, and suddenly one day began speaking Canadian. He claimed to be Canadian, yet he spoke with the residue of a Siberian accent. According to the story, he didn't have thorns. And once the creature beached itself on Canadian soil, the man quietly walked away to begin life anew.

Eventually it happened; with no harm to itself, the creature beached on the shore of a tiny island. With that, the Mystic Garden was open for business, all services free of charge, naturally. The two feathered creatures Anders and Ylwa were first, and sadly, only one of the two was to survive. Then the rush: those who were interested were very interested. And those who weren't felt just as strongly about staying inside the creature and not being told their fate, almost afraid we would force the information on them. It was completely different from our brief service back in York, where nearly everyone was to survive.

Lavender sorted them out, one by one, having to answer the question "Are you certain?" repeatedly. It was strange, though, and I still struggle to understand this: some who were told they were to survive went back inside the creature.

I suppose they would say that we will all die, eventually, and that is what the creature can allow them to avoid. Or maybe they simply did not care for the small island. Yet they seemed the least happy of the group. In any account, we felt it not appropriate to tell them how to live their lives or die their deaths. We were eager to get to Lavender's prediction about Father. He decided to be the final one to exit.

We were standing just outside. The creature, having relaxed its jaws to breathe openly on land, gave Father an opportunity to cross the threshold of the cavity into the direct sunlight of the island, where Lavender and I waited. It was the first time I can remember seeing him. I still remember it today. He was younger in appearance than Mother and disheveled but handsome. He had hardly crossed to the outside before instantly crouching, grabbing his upper back with both hands. He suffered further from the pain of lacerations on his legs, caused by a Siberian's thorns. We were able to see his injuries now, in the light, and they began oozing red. I do remember them as quite severe, but we had so little time to look at him.

Reacting more to a man in pain than to the sight of her father, Lavender spoke quickly, "Father, you best return to the creature if you are to survive. I'm terribly sorry."

We had expected that. Still, as hard as I worked to suppress my optimism, I had failed. I was devastated.

"Don't cry, Marigold," Father said, cringing and retreating to the creature with our assistance. "We knew."

We hugged him delicately.

"I just want to look at you," I said following our hug, sobbing and grabbing his face with both my palms, staring for the final moment in the sunlight before he was lost again inside the Host and its darkness. Lavender remained strangely and awkwardly distant. It was a rushed good-bye, as our father was in agony and quite clearly dying from standing not even three steps outside the Host's mouth. He returned inside, quickly regaining his strength. He said a father's supportive, encouraging farewell:

"Thank you. For all the good you have done for the people who live in this creature, and all the good I know you will do for those outside of it.

You know where I will be if you can find me. Good-bye, Lavender! Good-bye, Marigold! I will always remember you here, in the light."

We said our final good-byes, unfulfilling and rushed.

Anders, the small, feathered creature who had just lost his companion, Ylwa, had a boat and offered to transport anyone interested to the archipelago country of Svalbard's big island and capital city of Kildebyen. We boarded the small ship bound for a new country and embarked on the open sea.

Lavender finally expressed what had troubled her earlier.

"Marigold, do you believe that man was my father?"

"Yes, of course. Why else would Mother have gone through all the trouble she did when you were born for you to meet him if he were not your father?"

"Guilt, perhaps. Why then do you have blonde hair and mine is so dark brown?"

"Oh, well I always just assumed I was meant to be the bright one . . ."

"Simply thinking that makes you the funny one. Hysterical, Marigold. Truly. But you, that man, and Mother are passable as family. I always figured I looked different from you because our father looked so different from our mother, but he doesn't. At least not enough to explain me."

"Yes, confusing. Especially because we get our milk from Grandfather's tollimore."

"And not the milkman. I'm not the milkman's baby. Funny. Simply brilliant. A round of applause for Marigold," replied Lavender with a strained smile. "Now if you'll stop cracking jokes for a minute . . . where do you think my purple eyes are from?"

"Hmmm . . . the postal carrier? I don't remember; does he have purple eyes?"

"Marigold, please!"

"Lavender, I don't know where you got your eyes, but look at me and picture me in wooden shoes, a dark robe . . ." I said, shifting to a better argument. "No, never mind. You need only look at my face." I pulled back my hair and, using my hands to cover as much of my scalp as possible, I closed my eyes and said, "Do I not look just like you, like Mother, even like our father?"

"Yes, actually you do," replied Lavender after a pause. "Thank you," she said after another. "Do you think it's possible to have a third natural parent?"

"Only in our family."

"Perhaps I'm not the seed of evil."

"Of course not. You simply have Father's sense of guilt. But you can do a great deal of good for the world, if they will let you."

"Do you think when we reach Svalbard, they will let us?"

7 / Prince Oslo

"Let me go! I don't want to be here!" Lavender squirmed, hopelessly resisting my palace guard. I could hear the commotion as they came down the hall to the throne room.

"Wow. I've never been in a castle before," said Marigold looking at the high ceilings. "I wouldn't have gone with the blue tapestries. And it needs a little more natural light. But that wouldn't stop me from living here."

"Marigold, we need to go!"

"Quit your complaining, Canadian," barked the guard. "The prince wants to see you."

"And I would love to meet him!" Marigold smiled.

"No! Let us go!"

"Lavender, are we glowing?"

"No, but—"

"Then what are you upset about?"

"Marigold, I would know if we're going to be executed, but not imprisoned."

"You'll be neither," I said.

"Your Majesty," said the guard to me.

"Is that him? Is that the prince?" asked Marigold.

"Introducing Prince Oslo," grumbled the guard.

I gave the signal for him to release Lavender and excuse himself. Marigold was never restrained.

"So," said Marigold. "A prince." She did something strange as she said that. With a sweep of her neck, she tossed her waist-length blonde hair aside, stroked it, faced me sideways and made a small, repeated circular motion with her shoulder. Perhaps it was a Canadian greeting.

"Marigold, please."

"Lavender? Let me handle this. Your Majesty, my sister and I have come to your country from Canada. We were just setting up this morning to sell our book in the marketplace. It's titled *The Field Guide to Life and Death*."

"Yes," I said. "That's why you're here."

Lavender straightened the hood of her dark robe and looked around the throne room, I believe seeking an exit. "Just like Polaris. We try to help people, and we only end up being punished for it." She had a soft glow to her purple eyes.

"Lavender?"

"What, Marigold?"

"Don't ruin this. Prince Oslo, are we to be punished for our book, or is there something we can do to help? Your guard was not entirely clear on that when he snatched us from the marketplace."

"Punished?" I asked. "No. I believe our country needs you. That's why I sent for you. I'm sorry if he was rough."

"He wasn't," said Marigold.

"Oh yes, he was!" snapped Lavender.

"Only because you refused to go to the castle," said Marigold. "We're single. I'm single."

"Are you? Then they must have run out of princes in Canada. It does happen," I said.

Marigold laughed. "Clever and quick. I think we'll get along quite nicely."

"We're familiar with your book," said Sanna, entering the room. "The illustrations are beautiful. And you speak Svalbardian quite well."

"Thank you," said Marigold. "That's your girlfriend, isn't it?"

"Introducing my fiancée, Sanna," I answered.

Sanna looked at me with a pause and raised two eyebrows.

"But . . . we haven't announced it to the public yet," I explained. "I . . . shouldn't have told you that."

"Your secret's safe with me," promised Marigold. "It's a pleasure to meet you, Lady Sanna." She curtsied, while Lavender crossed her arms. "So how does one become a princess?"

"Never mind that. What does Svalbard ask of us?" inquired Lavender, uncrossing her arms.

Sanna answered, "I bought your book in the market yesterday. We believe someone is trying to poison the king. And I'm a suspect."

"So am I. My own father thinks I would kill him."

Lavender prompted: "Because . . ."

"The throne. Power."

"Comfort," added Sanna. "Impatience. But we have no such intentions."

"How do you know someone is trying to kill him?" asked Marigold.

"Quinby. The royal taste tester disappeared recently. Never a good sign," I told them.

Sanna said: "We want to try to help King Ulffr, but he's not making it easy. Your book details what wild food is edible and what's poison. Do you have knowledge of poisons and toxins?"

Lavender answered: "I will know if a food is toxic. Yes. I can make sure the king won't be poisoned. We will help."

"Great." I sighed, relieved. "Then we can focus on finding Quinby."

"Thank you," said Sanna. "It's not good when your future father-in-law thinks you're an assassin."

"Uh-huh. So how does one become a princess?" asked Marigold again.

––––––––––

My father, mother, and I were greatly concerned the day Quinby, the royal taste tester, began acting strangely. I had known him since I was a child. Being four seasons older than I was, he was twenty-five the day his behavior abruptly changed. If you were to approach him from behind, he would jump, that is, if you were successful. He was unstill, and his usually half-open eyes were widened to their fullest. He was not to be found at lunch one day, to my father's frustration, as his sole duty was to test the king's food and drink.

If Quinby consumed a small portion of that which was intended for the king and did not die or become blind—and this of course never occurred in his past—the king would know it safe to consume his meal. For this reason, when Quinby became scared and began neglecting his duties, my father suspected the tester had knowledge of an impending plot.

Quinby was orphaned as an infant, under the reign of my father's father. Strangely, my grandfather accepted care of Quinby, and although he intended it to be interpreted as an act of compassion, it was transparent to most that an orphan would serve a better poison filter than anyone with a family.

Immediately upon noticing Quinby's behavioral changes, my father, my mother, and I summoned him for a private audience in a small, quiet chamber in the castle. He tensely denied any change in behavior, as he also denied any knowledge or existence of an impending plot. Father dismissed him after little questioning, leaving only the three living members of the royal family in the room.

"That was amiss," said my father after Quinby left.

"The only mistake was that you did not continue to question him further," I said, still lightly tingling with unpleasant tension from our examination of Quinby.

"Do we all agree that there is a plot developing?" the king asked his wife and son.

"Yes," we answered.

"And the tester's life is therefore threatened, as any poison would pass through him before it would pass to me."

"Agreed," I said. "Unless it's at the end of a sword and not in your drink. You should have questioned him further."

"Oslo," began my mother, Queen Erika, "Quinby does not know how the assassination attempt will come. Rather, he knows it either will come, or may come, by poisoned food or by drink. He knows he may die, which is why he's tense and was scarce at mealtime."

"Your mother's correct, Oslo. And listen to us because you must understand these issues of security. You will face them as king."

I spoke with an unsteady voice. "The better security would be to treat people so that they don't want to kill you. Wouldn't you rather prevent a problem than correct one?" My father and I do agree on many things; it's how to act on them that often separates us.

My father looked at me, tensed his brow and said, "You're a naïve and foolish brat. If you become king with that weakness, your reign will not last a full season."

"And I suppose it would last longer if I'm threatened with assassination attempts?"

My mother interrupted: "If there is anything Quinby knows, he won't tell us. He either knows very little, and aggressive questioning would only gather the attention of the plotters, whoever they are. Or, if he does have knowledge of the plot, he'll never tell us. He knows he may be killed; this we see from his behavior. So, if he knows he may die, and won't help his own cause by revealing anything to us, then he is willing to die. His allegiance may be elsewhere, not with his king."

"Correct, Erika," said my father, looking at me. "Who could pry more allegiance from a man than his own king?"

I conceded: "That's what we need to figure out, then. To whom would Quinby be more devoted than his king? I don't have any guesses. He's an orphan." I paused and continued: "Let's consider motives, then. Who would want to kill you, Father?"

Laughing deliberately, he answered: "Motives? I am king! There are always motives to kill a king. Listen to us, learn, and let this be another lesson for you, Oslo."

Instantly tense again, I said: "So you don't believe it worthwhile to consider how your actions may have seeded a plot against you?"

"My actions as king are justified, as I am king."

"Quiet, Ulffr," whispered my mother.

"The first suspect," said my father, "is of course Quinby."

"I don't believe it's him," said Mother. "He's had ample opportunity. All he must do is test your drink, drop a poison into it, and pass it along to you."

"Agreed," said my father. "It's someone he knows."

"Who does he know?" I asked. "He's quiet, aloof, a loner . . . he has no family."

"You will learn this by following him," said my mother. "If this is a plot from within the castle, we can't reveal our awareness of it even to the guards."

"I can't follow him. I'm sorry, but remember my ship sails today for Arbor Beach."

"Yes, I had forgotten," she said. "You're going to visit Sanna at our mansion there."

"And propose to her," I reminded my mother.

"Such a joyous occasion ruined by this conspiracy. A shameful coincidence."

"It may be no coincidence," said Father.

"What? Excuse me, Father. That's ridiculous. You are ridiculous. She's not part of this. You believe a girl who has yet to become a princess-to-be has her thoughts on killing you to quickly seat herself as queen?"

"And render me a queen matron. Respected, but less powerful than a queen. I would believe it."

"I would not, Mother," I said, my hands somewhat shaky. Nothing abnormal, just another visceral effect of the daily royal aggravation.

"Oslo, you just don't understand," she said. "When there is so much attainable power . . . you haven't realized yet how it affects certain people."

"No. I do know how it affects certain people. And it's comfort, not power, that people hoard. Some people let their soul slip away to stay in comfort. But not Sanna."

"She would have much to gain," said my father.

"Such a wonderful way to welcome a new member of our royal family," I said.

"Don't blame me, Oslo! We must consider any potential suspect."

"I cannot blame you, Father. You will not allow it because you refuse to accept or discuss that perhaps your actions have seeded this plot. In fact, I'm surprised I have not yet become a suspect."

"You? You wouldn't kill me if it meant you could save all of Svalbard."

"Is that not a virtue? Never mind. Why frustrate ourselves in each other's presence? Perhaps it's time for me to embark for Arbor Beach."

"Yes, you have become quite irritating," said my father. "Please find your princess."

"I pity the man who has to be your taste tester," I hollered back on my way out.

Sanna had been waiting on Arbor Beach for days, our family's private resort estate. It's a secluded, quiet island where we could continue dating seriously without revealing our relationship to the public. My entire life, as any prince's would be, I suppose, was infused with the question of whom I would one day marry. Meeting Sanna was in that sense a relief, but the greater relief was finding her to be a virtuous woman and a capable, compassionate future princess and queen. My father had yet to see that side of her.

My yacht sailed from the dock at Kilde-av-Kimen, the royal castle at Kildebyen. The crew and I arrived at Arbor Beach, then rode in a carriage up the hill to my family's small mansion. It was dark by then. I entered the mansion through the main doors, where I was quietly greeted by the estate's head servant, an older man named Borg. Aside from his occasional acerbic tongue, Borg was notably distinguished and refined.

"Hello, Prince Oslo," he whispered as one would to not wake others who were asleep nearby. "Welcome back to Arbor Beach. You are here to find your princess?"

"Yes, Borg. I'm sorry I've come at such an hour."

"Don't apologize. The sooner this is decided, the sooner we will all be at peace," he said, almost taking my own rehearsed words from my mouth before I spoke them. Anticipation separates a trained servant from a talented one, and Borg was the best. "You do have the ring, don't you?"

"I do, Borg, thank you."

"Excellent," he said handing me a small document.

I took the note and proceeded alone to the room where Sanna had been waiting patiently for days. I glanced at the note, which read, *Prince Oslo, she is the one. She is trustworthy and kind. I have seen how luxury affects her. It doesn't.*

"Sanna?" I said, taking a deep breath and quietly knocking on her door.

She said yes, though I hardly remember it. The whole moment was ruined from what was developing in the castle. She smiled, we hugged, and we kissed. But all I could think about, all I'll ever think about when I look back, is how I didn't tell her that the moment she stepped in line to be princess, and one day queen, she became a suspect. But I had a plan for that.

We boarded the yacht together and returned to the castle. My mother met us at the gate with a hug. Sanna took it as a warm greeting, but the moment we were inside Kilde-av-Kimen, my mother ordered the doors sealed off until further notice.

"Where's Quinby?" I asked.

My mother looked at me, widened her eyelids, and then smiled at Sanna.

"He's fled the castle."

I looked over at Sanna and said: "It's never good when the taste tester disappears. It makes everybody suspicious of one another."

"Is something wrong?" asked Sanna.

"Mother, could you please tell her about it? If I recall, your last command to me was to follow Quinby. So, if you'll excuse me, I'd better do as you say."

"Of course." She smiled insincerely.

I walked off smiling with my back to Mother and Sanna. A master of psychology and reading people's behavior, my mother would soon see Sanna's honest, genuine response to learning of the plot involving the tester. She would know Sanna was innocent. She wouldn't be able to convince herself otherwise.

I marched directly for Quinby's quarters. The poor servant owned little other than several candles, all unlit, and some effects for writing, mostly personal letters, it seemed. I tossed the bedding and searched throughout the small bedroom but found nothing. Clothing and grooming supplies . . . stationery, ink, and envelopes. I found no written letters.

Quinby's room among the servants' quarters was near the stables, and from there I opened the door to the base of a rampart hoping to climb its stairway to reach the parapet walkway, seeking a view from above the castle grounds. I concluded that Quinby had indeed vanished from Kilde-av-Kimen. Likely nothing else was different inside the castle. I returned to my bedroom to wait for the inevitable visit from my mother. She didn't disappoint.

"Hello, Oslo. I was able to have a nice talk with Sanna."

"Did you show her to her new room?"

"Yes. She's resting now. I have also spoken with your father, and he has agreed to greet her, but under certain conditions."

"So, you were able to convince him she's innocent?"

She paused. I don't think she appreciated that I brought attention to the fact that I had outmaneuvered her.

"He will greet her for dinner, then be brief and retire to his chamber quickly."

"So, he's hungry? Knowing his relationship with food, he must be struggling without Quinby."

"You do know your father. He has vowed not to eat untested food, which thus far merely means that I am permitted the first nibble of my meals, and he consumes the rest. I suspect his agreeing to meet Sanna is merely to justify his return to the dining chambers for a proper meal, even if he considers it a risk."

"Of course, it is. Mother?"

"Yes, Oslo?"

"Sanna is innocent."

"She doesn't look like an assassin."

"She isn't an assassin."

"Of course," she said.

"And Mother?"

"Yes?"

"I will not be like my father."

"No. You're much more like me."

My mother left the room peacefully, stating that she would return to be by my father's side, and advised me to stay inside my chambers. I painfully waited and waited for the day to pass and night to come. My thoughts had been completely taken up with making progress on the investigation of the unknown assassin, yet no information seemed as though it would present itself within the castle walls. I focused my thoughts on my father and how his mind operated. He considered a king's actions infallible and had become defensive two days prior when I suggested the possibility that he had motivated the plot against him.

But I needed more information from him, faults he possessed or mistakes he had made but was unwilling to disclose. I needed him to reveal some clue as to what he could have done that would make someone want to kill him.

Finally, evening approached, and it was time for dinner. When we arrived in the dining hall, Father was eating his customary fried fowl and fried potatoes. All his food was arranged near his seat, within less than an arm's reach and in view. He'd started without us.

Mother walked in with Sanna and announced, "Ulffr, this is your future daughter-in-law and princess, Lady Sanna."

"Come, sit, eat!" Father waved without standing or picking up his head. He sat at the far end of the table in such a way to force Mother to sit by his side and placing Sanna at well more than an arm's length away. I don't believe Sanna noticed, and had no reason to question it.

"So how was the conservatory?" asked the king.

"My education, Your Majesty?" asked Sanna.

"Tell me about it."

I nodded for her to go ahead.

"First I should thank you, for the free education."

My mother interjected, "Yes, as soon as Oslo was born, Ulffr sponsored a free education for every girl born that season. A prerequisite to becoming princess."

"I wanted my boy to have options," he said without picking his head up. My mother rolled her eyes.

Sanna laughed, "All any of us talked about growing up was which one of us would one day become princess."

My father looked up at me with an "I told you so" face that needed to be slapped, but I couldn't.

Sanna continued: "But my father builds and repairs roofs. We could never have afforded the conservatory on his salary, and all I ever hoped for was a good education."

I looked back at my father and grinned like the brat he thought I was.

"Then one day the headmistress arranged a meeting between me and Oslo. I'm glad she did." Sanna smiled.

"Even a prince needs a little help from a matchmaker," teased my mother.

I laughed. "Especially a prince."

My mother confessed: "I may have had one of my fingers stirring that pot. I'm an old friend of the headmistress's. She told me she saw how it affected the others. Constant speculation of how the new princess would be selected. So much competition, so much animosity."

"Yes, the pursuit of power can corrupt one," said Ulffr.

"It's comfort, Father. Once people get used to comfort, they'll let it eat away their soul to maintain it. Power is only the tool."

Father stared dismissively at me and let Sanna tell us more about the other girls, those not recommended by the headmistress.

Eventually Mother commented on the fact that Father had begun his meal without us and continued to harass him for his dining habits. This was standard between Queen Erika and King Ulffr, but this time was different, and no doubt my mother's design. Ulffr was the butt of her jokes because Sanna was her audience; Queen Erika sympathized with her, which means she believed in her innocence. My strategy had taken hold. And certainly my father would not make any accusations . . . not in an effort to build a relationship with his new daughter-in-law-to-be, but as a strategic measure to investigate his suspicions.

After finishing, Father vanished without any formalities. I watched my mother excuse herself more appropriately, thanking Sanna for the time spent with her earlier and bidding her good night. I spoke with Sanna in the small dining area until both my mother and father had left and we were alone. I had observed my parents bicker all evening, most of which was not an act.

"I'm so sorry to bring you into all this," I said.

"Perhaps I can help," she whispered. "Follow me."

We walked through the halls of the castle, which was on lockdown. Even the guards looked at us differently. I waited in the corridor as she went into her new bedroom and brought something out.

"A book?"

"It's called *The Field Guide to Life and Death*. It catalogs every berry and mushroom you could possibly find in the wild and tells you which ones are poisonous and which are edible."

"That would be useful in the field, but I would think an assassin would be more discreet, likely with a potion."

"Probably. But the authors were the same ones who sold it to me in the marketplace this afternoon. They'll be there tomorrow. We might be able to bring them to the castle to see if they can help."

"When were you in the marketplace? The castle was on lockdown the moment we returned."

"This afternoon. I snuck out."

"How?"

"Dressed as a servant. It helps that nobody recognizes me yet."

I smiled and looked at her, standing outside her bedroom door. I started to lean in to kiss her when my father came pounding down the hall.

"Oslo! Is she with you? There she is. Have you begun to celebrate early? Both of you, don't move."

"Oh no," I said.

"What?" asked Sanna. "We weren't doing anything wrong."

"You're a suspect. We both are," I said.

We stared as he passed one torchlight ring after another, and saw that he was marching down the hall with a guard. "You laughed at me!" he yelled as he pointed. "You said a princess-to-be would never attempt to assassinate her king."

"Please, Father, what's happened?"

Grabbing, then assaulting the guard, Father thrust him forward to provide an explanation. "Tell him."

"I was stationed by the gate this afternoon," said the guard with his eyes focused on my chest. "She said she was a servant, looking to go home to see her mother."

"Fool," muttered Father. "After I ordered a lockdown."

"She was at the marketplace, Father."

"And that proves her innocence? There's no better place to buy poison!"

"Your Majesty, I would never—" started Sanna.

"Arrest her," my father told the guard.

"You will do no such thing," commanded my mother, coming from the other end of the hall. "There's no evidence that she is an assassin, and we should be so lucky to have such a patient daughter-in-law."

"Search her room," grumbled the king to the guard.

The guard glanced at my mother, who didn't protest. "Yes, Your Majesty," he responded, entering the room.

"If he finds nothing, you will apologize to her, Ulffr," declared my mother.

My father scoffed and fidgeted.

The guard was back quickly. "She hasn't even unpacked, sir. There's nothing."

"Thank you," said Sanna to my mother as my father pounded off.

"I'm so sorry," said my mother.

I instructed the guard to go to the marketplace the next morning, find whoever was selling *The Field Guide to Life and Death*, and bring them back to the castle.

———

"Is he eating breakfast now?" asked Lavender as we walked with her sister and Sanna to the dining hall.

"Yes, so we should hurry."

"Wait—" resisted the gifted Canadian. "If we are to aid this cause, I will request full immunity from Svalbardian law throughout the process. As prince, will you grant this?"

"Yes, that's granted. But why do you believe you would break any law helping to save the king's life?"

Lavender shivered and looked downward. Marigold, seeing this, resisted any attempt at humor and spoke on her sister's behalf. "My sister mentioned Polaris. We were exiled from Canada, Lavender nearly executed, for actions almost identical to what we have agreed to do with your father."

"Canadian law, then, is flawed," I said.

"Agreed," said Marigold.

"If it would help, the royal family will provide recompense," I offered, desperately trying to politely end this conversation and find my father.

"That won't be necessary," said Lavender.

"That will be very gracious, Prince Oslo," said Marigold. "We accept."

This delay was making me increasingly anxious, but had the negotiating not occurred, I might not have stumbled on a new theory. "So, you were exiled?"

"Yes," answered Lavender.

"At any time did you desire to . . . to kill Polaris?"

"No. Only in my most angered state could I come close. It was always impossible however, because a modest level of my own restraint would not have allowed me to do so, even given an opportunity. I don't desire to, and would not, kill Polaris. Or anyone. But I also don't think he should be in power."

"Yes, but what if you were without this self-restraint?" I asked. "Then Lavender, would it have been possible?"

"I suppose, but it would take an unstable mind."

"There's one in every family," I said thoughtfully. "Hurry. Let's find my father."

Lavender, Marigold, Sanna, and I reached the entrance to the dining hall. The door was closed, guarded by my mother. Behind the door, we heard my father shouting.

Mother raised a hand to signal for us to enter quietly, then opened the door and quickly led us through. My father was viciously chastising Quinby. He had apparently wandered off, then wandered back, and claimed there was nothing more to it.

We walked slowly toward the tester, who was standing ten steps or so in front of Father and facing him respectfully.

The king was not eating, but his food was in front of him. He had not yet taken a bite. To my surprise, Quinby was not at all nervous in the fashion he had been just prior to his disappearance, and not even in any other way one would expect as he was reprimanded by his sovereign. Quinby was by some means at peace, yet was still to be punished heavily with a tongue-lashing.

"Ulffr," interrupted my mother. "We have guests that pertain to this matter."

"All I see are two additional suspects. Two girls from another land. What are you, Canadian?"

"Have we all become suspects?" asked my mother. "Quinby, Sanna, your own son, and now two visitors whose names you have not yet heard?"

"I need not know their names to have them killed," responded Father. "All of the suspects if necessary."

"Your son says the Canadians can help. Would you like to ask them any questions, or would you simply prefer everyone slaughtered at this time?"

Throughout this argument Lavender and Marigold were quiet and calm, though I did notice Lavender glancing down at her arms occasionally, and at Marigold.

"Immunity," Lavender whispered to me as we all stood five across alongside Quinby, directly facing, but with a bit of formal distance from, the king seated in front of his food. "Complete and total immunity."

"Yes," I agreed, unsure if I would even be able to provide it against my father's will. "Father, this is Lavender, and this is Marigold. They do not wish to kill you any more than Sanna does."

"Oh, my son, my naïve son." He pretended to console himself. "You cannot simply trust people on their word and allow strangers into the castle."

"Father, Sanna found these girls because they can help. They'll know if you are to be poisoned or not. It's something they were able to explore during exile."

"Exile?" asked my father.

"Yes, let's talk about exile. Let's discuss the Svalbardian policy of exile," I said.

Lavender looked at me carefully. I noticed Quinby's look of concern as well when his lips tightened and he blinked out of rhythm. That's when I knew my instincts were leading me on the right path. Lavender was the next to speak, and with sudden frustration. "Svalbard has an exile custom as well? I believed this country to be more sophisticated."

"You, foreigner, are not to speak in this fashion," snarled my father as my strategy developed around his hypersensitivity and stubborn reluctance to discuss the methods in which his own actions may have contributed to this plot. "You are a child, and not of this kingdom. You don't understand the necessity and benefits to the greater good that a proper exile code will provide." Even from some distance, the ten steps forward that separated the king from us five, I could now see the white sections above his irises. I had to keep my father in an irritated, vocal state so that he would reveal more.

"All right then, Father. Why not explain to the girls your policy of exile, so that they, and I, may understand it further."

"Why now, boy? What's the matter with you?"

"Lavender's just convinced me it's a terrible policy. But we can discuss it later." I shrugged. "Or I can just abolish it the day I become king."

He shook his head. "It's a policy that has existed for quite some time. But it was my father who founded the Royal Asylum on Emberland, a large island to the southwest. There he placed any Svalbard prone to laziness, drink, gambling, and any other addictions or addictive tendencies. Our society has been strengthened tremendously because of it. We have become more industrious and productive, and Svalbard has significantly increased its ratio of production to consumption, fully funding the Royal Asylum and even providing improved facilities and caretaking every season."

"Now I will explain the true story," announced my mother, waiting for my father to finish without actually listening. "One of the more compassionless kings of our country's history, your grandfather, examined the Svalbardian economy of his time, and deduced, probably accurately, that much of the nation's resources were used to provide for the weak of mind. So, he sought to separate them from society, stripping them away from our mainland and shipping them off to the asylum to the far south. But you see, an exile goes well beyond the individual victim." There was no doubt that this facet of exile was well understood by our Canadian guests, yet my mother added, "Their families would also be victims, as often fathers were torn from their wives and children, and mothers from their babies, with no real help provided. Oh, and not a true Svalbard lives who refers to it as the 'Royal Asylum on Emberland,'" continued the queen. "It's called the 'King's Closet.'"

I looked at Quinby and noticed he had stopped blinking. Now I could see the whites of *his* eyes. "I've long thought it was a need for comfort that eats at the weak-minded. Would you agree, Quinby?"

"I don't know that this is true, my *prince*," he said, punching the word and staring hard at the stone floor.

My father provided a diplomatic display of defense for his Canadian guests. "The Royal Asylum is hardly as they describe it. Due to the exceptionally tropical climate and still-active volcanoes that have formed the soil,

Emberland is a very warm island, and many choose to live there voluntarily. Often those with addictions and mental health issues prefer extremes. They're hardly suffering. Free or institutionalized, Emberland attracts the unstable—those who seek a paradise land of instant gratification."

"Instant?" inquired Marigold.

My mother explained: "In its heat, it's the most extreme climate within Svalbard's empire, and therefore attracts her most unbalanced people. Even the skies are unstable, with unpredictable storms and intense wind and rain. Still, the pariahs of the mainland migrate to Emberland either by king's force or their own false hopes of a painless, blissful life. In either case, the king is happy to be rid of them."

"What's all this to do with the matter at hand?" asked the king.

"Motives, Father. Our Canadian guests have been through something similar."

Lavender spoke. "Your Majesty, from my own experience, desiring a perfectly homogenized society is an indication of intolerance. Acting upon it is an indication of insanity." Although she explained that she would never desire to kill Polaris, she might have had several choice words she'd wish Polaris to hear . . . and my father was the available substitute.

My mother was exuberant. "Well said! Girl, continue to speak."

"She will not!" yelled my father. "She is a child, so I will forgive her words. However, I will not grant this should she continue."

"Yes, I am a child to you," continued Lavender, disregarding the warning. "I am fifteen seasons of age, my sister only recently seventeen."

"Another birthday alone." Marigold glanced at Quinby on her left side, who stood slack-jawed, staring at his king.

"Do we not argue enough, Erika?" proposed my father. "Or do you simply enjoy it?"

"No, not at all, Ulffr. It's distressingly unpleasant. All arguing is miserable, but a delight compared to allowing a fool to voice an unchallenged opinion."

My father scoffed under his breath and gathered his emotions, which was good news for Lavender. His level of anger was linked to my ability to keep my promise to her. Perhaps he sensed the confrontation elevating into an intervention, and though enraged understood it would be necessary to defend himself calmly and intelligently to defuse Lavender and my mother's unified attacks.

"What's in your arms, girl?" asked the king of Sanna.

"That's why the Canadians are here, Your Majesty," she answered. "This book will tell you what wild food is poisonous. They wrote it."

Marigold pitched: "That's just one of many copies of an illustrated text we have authored on the topic of edible and poisoned aliments, mostly wild. It includes mushrooms, berries, seeds, and almost anything we receive from the soil . . . wild or farmed. If Your Majesty would be interested in funding its further development and publication, we would be open to negotiation."

"Bring it to me," said the king as Sanna approached and handed him her copy of the text. Too proud to accept help from those who had insulted him, and desperately seeking leverage over the group that had formed this spontaneous confrontation, the king drifted into a new lecture on Svalbardian history. Flipping through the pages, he questioned: "This book of yours . . . where do you think this variety of flora originates? Nature? Common ignorance if so. No. Every weed, flower, grain, and mushroom originates here, in this country, discovered below Svalbardian soil in the Seed Bank."

"The Seed Bank is only a legend, Father," I said as my mother sighed in irritation alongside me.

"It is documented!" he yelled, trying to regain control.

"Well, then, I hope our guests enjoy lengthy stories on the subject of seeds," warned Mother.

The king started, "Thousands of seasons past, the known world was dark and savage. The landscape had hardly the vegetation to support her herbivores, and in some regions was nothing more than empty soil, sand, or mountain. Nourishment was scarcely found in a peaceful fashion. The seas held fish and the land had creatures to hunt, but many, many varieties of predatory beings briefly blossomed and quickly disappeared in the constant exchange of blood and meat. The limited foliage was mostly inedible to humans, and what was edible was hardly in any density that could support an omnivorous lifestyle. The creatures of the known world, even its humans, were able to consider only survival. And when survival is the only ambition, there is no room in the world for culture . . . if you do not believe me, spend a holiday in Siberia. Yet out of this dark, prehistorically savage era, an Old Svalbardian tribe discovered a passageway deep beneath the earth. There, they found seeds. Many, many species, and even tiny, airborne spores were sealed in containers, too well-organized for coincidence. It was clearly a gift from the earth to a chosen people. This was the Seed Bank, discovered in what is now Svalbard. The seeds were exhumed and cultivated. Once they began to grow, our chosen land was filled with a variety of beautiful vegetation. The seeds declared diversity itself, with nearly every kind representing a new form of life." To Lavender he continued: "Our people began cultivating crops. The earth's chosen Svalbardian tribe began settling the oldest city in our world, Kildebyen, where you now ungratefully stand."

To soften his insult, I turned to her and said, "Again, this is all legend and myth."

Father finished: "Every seed in this book, every wild plant that repopulated the barren wastes of the known world as our ancestors found it claims its origin here in Svalbard."

"May I?" asked the queen, walking the ten paces to approach Father. As she did, he held out the book as if to discard it, not transfer it to his wife. She took it from him and began to examine the text.

Lavender continued with a relentless determination I wouldn't have understood if she had not informed me prior that she herself had been exiled. "You are pompous about your country's gift of diverse plant life, comparing it to your ancient people, yet you do not tolerate diversity in your own people?"

"Are you still correcting a king?" he asked.

"It's humiliating for us both, is it not?" she answered.

"Then you still do not understand!" screamed Father. "And what if one seed, just one seed in our Seed Bank, were afflicted with mold? It would have spread this mold to the other seeds, ruining the entire vault! Our world would remain in cultural darkness, with barbarians and cannibals still consuming each other rather than grain or fruit! It's no different in the context of Svalbard's policy of exile. Insanity is as contagious as mold moving from seed to seed." He made his point and continued, merely to prevent anyone else from speaking: "We are a country of Svalbards. If we encourage people to identify with their anomalies, what motivation is there for self-improvement? That is why we send our weak to the Asylum."

"Anomalies?" asked Lavender. "Not all anomalies are bad. Some could benefit you greatly if you were more tolerant."

"Yes," I added, "such as a Canadian girl with a unique gift who may save you from assassination, Father."

"So, Lavender," said my mother. "Is his meal poisoned or not?"

"I'll know when someone tries to eat it. I'll be his majesty's taste tester if he'll allow it."

"Go right ahead," said my father.

She took his fork, picked up a bit of fowl and a slice of the fried potato, and brought it to her mouth. She didn't eat it.

"No. It's safe."

Quinby smiled and relaxed.

"You didn't even eat it."

"There," she said picking the food off with her teeth and chewing.

The remaining intervention party stood facing him. I said, "Come, Lavender, Marigold. Thank you for your time. Now you have met the King of Svalbard."

As we exited the room, I overheard Quinby ask Father if he was dismissed, to which Father's response was, "Yes, but be sure to return for dinner. The guards are instructed to monitor you closely outside your quarters and not allow you to leave the castle."

I led Lavender, Marigold, and Sanna not to the exit, but to a quiet section of the castle. "We may still be of use," said Lavender.

"Yes, I agree," I said. "If you're willing, I would like for you to stay with us through dinner."

"That would be my suggestion as well," whispered Lavender. "Marigold, is everything all right?"

"Quinby . . . Lavender, did you see a glow about Quinby?" she asked, concerned, as we four stood alone looking down the long stone halls and over our shoulders.

"No," responded Lavender. "There were no glows in the room, red, white, pale yellow, rainbow-striped, anything."

"Can we examine the food as it's being prepared?" I asked. "Perhaps a poison would be revealed."

"It's not likely," answered Lavender. "I wouldn't know a poison in a food until an attempt to consume it is made. I cannot recognize free toxins in the kitchen any more than anyone else can."

"We should wait, then, and observe Father during dinner?" I asked.

"That would help him survive only one meal," suggested Sanna.

"That would help me survive one meal as well," responded Marigold. "I'm famished. What are royal Svalbardian desserts like?"

Lavender said, "Prince Oslo, I don't believe my gift is required to reveal the assassin."

"I'm not leaving until I see the queen's bedroom," said Marigold.

"Marigold," whined Lavender.

"No, I agree, unfortunately. It's clearly Quinby," she responded, shifting again to seriousness. "We've learned to use my sister's sense, but we've also learned how not to use it. Until dinner is served, we'll likely be bound to act without any benefit from the gift. Though I'd still like to find out what a queen's bedroom looks like."

"First we should figure out whom Quinby would have a greater allegiance to than his king," I said. "If we can figure that out, we'll have our suspect."

"What if he's not trying to kill the king?" suggested Sanna. "We haven't even considered that he may be trying to kill your mother."

"My mother. A mother! Oh, that's it. Sanna, I think you figured it out." I stood stunned for a moment. "Follow me."

We sprinted back to the dining hall to find my father, head down, gobbling his food alone. "The first good meal I've had in days, and I can't eat it without constant interruptions. What is it, boy?"

"Father, where did Mother go? Where's Quinby?"

"They both went back to their bedrooms. Quinby's not allowed to wander right now, and your mother said she needed a bath. What's the commotion?"

As we sprinted out the door to hurry to my mother's bedroom, I could hear my father mumble, "You'd best not disturb her, son."

We saw her down the corridor just as she was entering her room. She didn't see us and disappeared behind her door.

"She's glowing," said Lavender. She and Marigold sprinted ahead faster than I could keep up. It seemed they had run for their lives before. They banged on the locked door and shouted for the queen, which got the attention of a guard nearby. He hurried over and blocked the girls until I caught up and insisted we enter.

"Oslo!" said my mother, taking her shoes off next to her bed.

"We have to get her out of here," said Lavender. "We have to change something."

"What are you doing? Oslo, I'm perfectly safe in my bedroom!" Sanna, Marigold, and I grabbed her by the arms and physically carried her into the hall.

"It's you, Mother. Someone is trying to kill you."

"What? Why?"

As we got her out in the hall, Lavender was the only one left in the bedroom. "It's gone," she said. "The glow is gone."

Marigold stepped forward, asking, "Your Majesty, could you give my sister and me a moment alone in your bedroom?"

"I'm not sure I like that idea, frankly," my mother responded.

"Neither do I," said the guard. "If someone's in there trying to kill the queen, let me lead the way."

Lavender explained, "Thank you, but that's not necessary. We'll be fine alone, if her majesty will allow me and my sister to search her bedroom."

"It would just be a moment." Marigold smiled.

My mother paused, then nodded for the completely bewildered guard to close the door and allow the Canadians to search the room. We heard the slow grinding of the latch from within as they locked themselves inside.

After a three-minute wait that to my mother must have seemed like an hour, the latch turned back open and the sisters came out.

"Was anyone in there?" asked Sanna.

"No. But here's your killer," said Lavender, presenting a brown container of plainly decorated, thickly blown glass.

"That's my new bath oil," said my mother.

"It would have killed you," explained Marigold.

"No. That can't be. I just got it from Borg. He's made bath oils for me for ages. He just sent it over yesterday on the boat with Oslo when he and Sanna came back from Arbor Beach."

"Borg is trying to kill you?" asked Sanna. "That doesn't seem like him."

"It's not," I said. "Because we didn't bring anything back with us on the boat. Borg didn't send you this. Quinby used the timing to his advantage."

"Quinby is trying to kill me?" my mother asked, dejected. She took a deep breath as she motioned for the guard to leave. "I think I know what this is about. But I'll let him tell you. Is it safe for me to return to my bedroom?"

Lavender looked at her and answered, "Yes. The glow hasn't returned."

"Go find Quinby, then," said Mother.

"You have a lovely bedroom, Your Majesty," said Marigold.

"Yes. Thank you."

Lavender and Marigold seemed to enjoy their hurried tour of the castle. The final stop was the servants' quarters. I silently dismissed the guards outside Quinby's bedroom, and with the flask, the four of us surrounded the door. Sanna, Lavender, and Marigold stood aside, in the hallway so as not to be seen, and I put my ear to the door as I knocked. I heard a shuffling of papers and a response from within: "Coming, one moment!"

Quinby opened the door just enough for a foot. I stepped in with the flask, pretending to try to open it. "The cap's stuck, Quinby. Can you help me?"

"No, don't!" he yelled, jumping back onto his bed.

Lavender, Marigold, and Sanna appeared in the doorway. I sighed and asked, "Why, Quinby?"

"Why? I don't understand. You simply startled me."

"Don't move. Go to the rear corner of the bedroom."

"Oslo, don't kill him!" yelled Lavender.

"What? I have no intention of killing him. I'm not even armed."

"You're lying," said Lavender. "He's glowing white."

"Oslo, put down the poison," said Sanna.

I handed it to Lavender while Quinby shook nervously in the corner of his room.

"Is he still glowing?" asked Marigold.

"Actually, yes."

"Quinby? Don't hurt yourself."

"No, Marigold," I realized. "It's the king. We've set in motion an execution."

"Please, no!" begged the taste tester.

"Quinby, I'm sorry. I never wanted it to come to this, but I can't help it if my father will have you executed when he finds out you tried to kill my mother and blame it on a fellow servant."

Sanna asked, "Oslo? Can't you do better than that?"

"We came to your aid to save a life, not help end one," agreed Lavender.

"What am I supposed to do? He tried to kill my mother."

Lavender shook her head. "Just like Polaris. Find a better way."

Quinby sighed. "I should never have listened to my mother."

"Your mother?" asked Marigold. "I thought you were an orphan."

"I am. I was. I've reunited with her. Almost."

Sanna walked over to his writing desk and uncovered the ink and paper that were stuffed hastily inside the drawer.

She read:

Dear Mother,

I have done what you have asked. I will not cooperate with any further attempt should this fail. I am sorry for your pain and I simply ask that you make no further attempts to write. I am also sorry if this is hurtful, but you have

"It ends there," said Sanna.

"You've found your mother," I said.

"Yes."

Lavender took a step forward and sat on the wooden chair next to Quinby. "It's time to talk. As I predict now, you will be executed. This may be your only chance to save your life."

"Just tell us the truth," I said.

"The truth implicates my mother even more than me."

"So, you can either tell us the truth, or die protecting her. It's your choice."

He took a deep breath. "She's on Emberland, in the King's Closet. She's been there since I was an infant, twenty-five seasons past. She was a servant of your grandfather's. Your father was engaged to Erika when he got my mother pregnant. Erika found out about it and coordinated a convenient solution with her future father-in-law. I would be born and remain in the castle, presumed an orphan. I could live in the castle and have all my needs provided for, though I would never be royalty. I wouldn't even be recognized as family. Worse for my mother, she was sent to the asylum. She was branded insane so no one would listen to her. That's the truth, brother."

"Brother? How long have you known?" I asked.

"Not long. My mother only recently attempted to contact me, through correspondence. She was the one who wanted Erika dead, not me. She knew your father first. She should have been queen, in her mind, and I would have been the prince. My mother hasn't forgotten our turn of fate."

"Quinby?" I said. "That's exactly the sort of thing I could see my family doing. It's also exactly the type of story someone in the asylum would make up. How do you know she's even your mother?"

Sanna said softly, "Oslo . . . your mother knew."

I breathed. "She did. Which means my father knew. And if Quinby is glowing . . . my father would kill his own son."

"And what of the other letters between you and your mother?" asked Marigold.

"Destroyed."

Lavender spoke. "Then all that's left is the vial. If we destroy that, there will be no evidence. We may still avoid an execution."

"Brother," I said. "I've known you all my life. At least, I thought I did."

"Thank you, Oslo. But I didn't even know who I was until recently."

"Our father wondered who could pull your allegiance away from your king. Now I see."

"King Ulffr." He laughed.

"There's one in every family."

Quinby stood and hugged me. "Oslo? Don't let me die."

"You won't. I promise. I have a boat. I can transport you to it safely. I'll figure out the castle guards. You may be on the boat if you wish." I still spoke to Quinby but glanced at the Canadian sisters to explain: "There's a municipality called Jan Mayen Island, a small volcanically formed island to the southwest." Facing Quinby again I continued, "It's roughly half the distance between here and Emberland, where your mother is. I can transport you there tonight while my family is distracted with dinner. I'll simply explain to Father that he is to find another royal taste tester. I must insist, however, that you travel without any documentation of citizenship or domicile within Svalbard. When you set foot on the boat for Jan Mayen, you will essentially be exiled from Svalbard. You know I don't have the power to overrule a king, and the other option seems to be execution."

"Thank you," said Quinby through tears. "Thank you. I accept."

"He's not glowing anymore," said Lavender. "He'll live, for now."

Quinby asked me, "What of my mother? Will she be punished?"

"My grandfather declared her insane. To be rid of her, no doubt, but involuntary asylum in the King's Closet is a lifelong sentence. Without you working as her agent inside the castle, my mother is safe. Your mother's current punishment is sufficient." I turned to face Lavender and Marigold. "I must properly thank you. Please, you're invited to be guests of the castle tonight at dinner."

"We would like to be on the boat as well," said Marigold, wiping away tears.

"We would?" asked Lavender, her eyes dry.

"Yes, we would."

"All right." Lavender shrugged.

I answered, "Anything you wish. You may go with Quinby to Jan Mayen Island."

"You'll have to come back to dine with us sometime soon," said Sanna, hugging the two Canadian sisters.

"Certainly, and maybe take a more relaxed tour of the castle when we come back," said Marigold. "Perhaps it's too much to ask, but if we may find transport to Jan Mayen and spend ten or twenty days there, we could expand our text and return to Svalbard to sell the new edition of *The Field Guide to Life and Death.*"

"For your help, it's granted," I responded. "The days on Jan Mayen, the return to Svalbard, and dinner at the castle. I'll instruct the ship to return in . . . twenty days?"

"That would be wonderful," responded Marigold.

"The boat sails in two hours. Be at the dock by then."

"Thank you, Prince Oslo," said Lavender. "Good-bye for now, and our best wishes to you and your wonderful bride."

8 / The Bog Man

I have been a troublesome subject for the physicians of the King's Closet, not because of my behavior in the asylum, but because to study a subject, it must first be classified. Sometimes they call me a bogey, an unidentified blemish on the human landscape, a failed attempt at an average human standard. My name by birth is Tollund, and those inside or outside the asylum call me the "Bog Man." However, the young children I have encountered, who are the reason I am committed, have commonly called me the "Bogeyman." Call me what you will; I am an evil being by my own standard, the one who carries what I describe as the "Darkness."

All bothered adults were at one time innocent children. To tell you how I became this way, it's important I start at that time in my life. Any evil men or women become so because of an evil being before them who, like a carrier of a plague, passes the disease along to them. And like a disease, greater and prolonged exposure to any evil will simply tire one's defenses until they've contracted the affliction. I have no doubt that by now I have done this to others, much the way my father corrupted me. Perhaps those whom I've afflicted now afflict others, to perpetuate a detestable pedigree. I cannot say.

I had no known account of my mother, and from my earliest memories as a child, my father told me she had died when I was very young. He alone raised me on small Jan Mayen Island, southwest of Svalbard, northeast of Emberland, and directly between the two. My father was a taxidermist, preserving any creature in the known world for either trophy or study, as his clientele requested.

There was a brief time in which my father's business was gainful, twenty-five or thirty seasons past, when the previous King of Svalbard sought to reproduce the legendary Seed Bank, with a menagerie of preserved mobile creatures: birds, rodents, livestock, and even humans. The Svalbardian legend states that the discovery of their Seed Bank many hundreds or thousands of seasons ago brought the world out of darkness, cannibalism, and famine. It was a rapid recovery for the flora of the known world, but her mobile creatures recovered much less quickly. The king desired that, should the world ever fall back into darkness, not only would Svalbard have ready a Seed Bank but a Flesh Bank as well.

For five seasons or so when I was a small child, the King of Svalbard generously compensated any taxidermist who presented him with the male and female of a species new to his Flesh Bank. Father, already the victim of gossip as a man with a son and not a wife, became even more scrutinized as he was seen trapping and caging creatures in both wild and settled areas. Jan Mayen Island is small, with a great variety of birds but not a great variety of humans. The people are a closely intertwined community, and Father, with his actions, was placing himself outside the mainstream.

He was a secretive man, keeping the curtains pulled all day, even restricting by lock and key one of the closets within our home. I understood I was not allowed in this closet. At the time I assumed it contained taxidermy tools not intended for child's play.

He often worked by candle during daylight hours, when opening the curtains could have saved the wax. But he desired none to peer inside our windows and discover the nature of his work. As a result, all the community knew of him was by observing this pariah in the forest, on the mountain, or along the shoreline trapping and caging various creatures. As one would expect, I was without friends. No parent would allow it, and few children desired to know me. Had they visited, the mere shock of our small home filled with preserved and half-preserved creatures would have sent them out of my life permanently.

Business was good. Jan Mayen is home to an extensive variety of birds, both migratory and indigenous. Each species justified its spot in the king's Flesh Bank, and therefore the combined commission on a black gull and a closely related white gull was equal to the combined commission on a wild cat and a venomous serpent. All creatures were valued equally according to the king's scale, with several exceptions. Substantially higher wages were given to anyone able to trap an extremely difficult catch, such as a Featherman.

For the sake of pragmatism, my father sought mostly small birds. I was a priority of his, but unfortunately only in the sense that so many unaided parents have little time, energy, and resources. I needed food first, then love, as was his view, so he worked tirelessly with his creatures to earn money, often ignoring his son. It was this way for five seasons or more, that is, until the old King of Svalbard declared the Flesh Bank a failure.

Not a scientist, the king had commissioned the Flesh Bank to have the ability to, like the Seed Bank, repopulate the world. However, with the limitations of the science of taxidermy, an embalmed creature could at best retain its appearance. After several seasons of the project, the king realized this, which my father, and likely other taxidermists, were expecting would eventually occur. Still, the elimination of the project, when I was ten, was devastating.

He quickly changed from excessively fatigued, productive, and angry, to underworked and frustrated. As a child, I was terrified whenever he was upset. He cursed in anger merely at the sight of flowers, calling them useless, as if they were mocking him. I would stomp on flowers when I would see them, hoping to please him. Flowers to us could not be embalmed, and yet stood still and could be caught effortlessly, while the birds of the island provided little cooperation. Although his trapping and caging continued, many of the birds he caught we now consumed; we had to, simply out of necessity, unable to sell them.

My habit of flower stomping developed inside me to the point that I would do it alone, and not simply to make my father happy. I did it to make myself happy; I suppose I felt a certain empowerment, a certain release of anger. However, I now believe I was merely angering myself further by doing so. Meanwhile, my father worked to develop a method that could save the Flesh Bank, and with it his industry, whether the king desired it or not. There was no communication between him and the king, simply that my father set to develop a means of "living embalmment." The purpose was to either keep the creature alive or sustain its fertility after death.

For every attempt there had to be a gull, a finch, or some creature on which to experiment. As the trial and error of my father's experiments gained momentum, the limiting factor became the constant need for a new test creature. He attempted to breed rodents but was unsuccessful even at keeping them alive while caged within his studio. None of the experiments had worked. They had either no effect on the tormented creature or they killed it. Still, he believed he was making progress, eliminating methods that did not work.

As time passed and his savings from Flesh Bank compensations dwindled, he turned to another resource, his son. To expedite his experiments, he eliminated the collection step, which would have usually involved traveling to the shore to collect a gull. There were no more trips to the shore, and I became his gull. As a child I never questioned that we would always have food. I don't believe he shared that peace. For him, the peacefulness of inevitability was drowned by a sense of urgency, and he became vulnerable to sinning out of necessity. This is how I eventually came to view his decision to do experiments on me.

A typical experiment involved an injection. Father would develop a chemical, collect a syrup, from nature, or heat solids into liquids, and then place them into a crude syringe. He insisted these compounds be injected directly into my bloodstream. No other methods, be they more soothing or pleasant, were ever considered. It was never consumed or spread like a balm; it was always by Father's design injected.

An experiment would begin with hope, a hope he understood was distant, yet when it failed the disappointment and frustration he displayed was as if he had expected success. When he was finished with me, done with my body for the time, I would flee the house in search of flowers to stomp and wait to be called for my next injection. Throughout the cycle he insisted on proprietary secrecy, explaining that should another taxidermist learn of any successful methods, or even of any unsuccessful experiments to avoid, his knowledge could be stolen and along with it a king's compensation lost.

My feet couldn't keep my father's secret. The experiments usually left me feeling unchanged and typically well, but at other times resulted in extreme nausea, numbness, or excessive and uncomfortable energy. That was merely the physical. Being eleven, perhaps twelve seasons of age at the time of these experiments, I revealed my father's actions one day as I stomped a distant neighbor's flower bed. I was in tears, and as always, had recently fled after another failure by my father.

The mother of the home approached me. "What are you doing, boy?"

Through fresh tears I responded: "I don't know."

She spoke with compassion. Had this been my father, I certainly would have been beaten. "Come over here. What's on your arms?"

"Nothing!" I reacted, staying by the flower bed.

"Do you have a rash? You have red prick marks along your arms."

She gently grabbed my wrist. Fleeting as it was, I had never felt a sensation like it in my entire life. Warm and peaceful, her touch transferred to me everything my father never had.

Shelter is what I felt.

"Come now, boy; I'll bring you home. I must discuss with your parents the issue of my flowers and these red marks you have."

"No!" I said, yanking my arm away.

"Boy, act your age! You've ruined my flowers and you may be sick!"

"Don't tell my father!" I yelled, terrified.

"Oh, you're . . . " she stammered. "You're the taxidermist's son. Hello, Tollund. Perhaps I'll visit your father another day, with my husband. We'll address the flowers then. You may go now, and be careful."

I ran home, but couldn't construct even in my own mind a safe place to flee to. The woman would come to our house, with her husband, and I didn't know when. My father would be upset with them and with me, and I now understood I needed shelter.

I arrived home. My father was away. At first, I waited, but in my own anticipation of eventual punishment, sought a place to hide. The only secure location in our home was behind a lock and key. It was my father's taxidermy tools, or so I believed, inside the closet I had never seen opened.

I searched for the key, hoping to hide in the darkness, but found nothing. I attempted to mangle the lock, just slightly, to gain entrance without evidence of tampering. But as my patience dwindled, and my attempts continued, I split the wood near the latch and in doing so had just inflicted myself with the anticipation of a second punishment.

Seeing the chipped wood, hoping as children do that their father won't notice, I attempted to convince myself that the damage was invisible. I eventually realized there would be no lie that would exonerate me, and that surely he'd see the damage.

Conceding the second punishment and seeking shelter, I continued to pry at the wood to bypass the lock.

My father returned home with the ingredients for my next injection. I stepped away from the still-locked door, but he immediately noticed the damage.

"What are you doing, Tollund?" he yelled, discarding a sack he had brought home.

"Nothing."

"Son, I have specifically told you never to open, or attempt to open, that door!"

"I wasn't," I lied.

He smelled of the shore. He approached me in a rage, got right in front of me, and shouted, "Is that so?"

"Yes, Father. I haven't," I continued to lie.

"Tollund, let me be very clear," he screamed, grabbing me. "You are not to be disobedient, and you are not to lie to me."

The room was filled with embalmed creatures, organized more for storage than display. This would be a frightening, shocking sight for any visitor to our house. I of course had grown desensitized to it, although as much as I had become accustomed to these creatures, there was one behind the door I was never expecting to see.

My father shook my body and yelled, spitting on my face as he raged. "Boy, if you will lie, and if you will be disobedient, you will know the last person who was untruthful to me!"

He kicked the slivered door, once, then again, then in frustration as hard as he could until the top portion opened in splinters. Inside the forbidden closet were no taxidermist's tools, but the standing, nude, mounted body of a woman, preserved after twenty or thirty seasons of life. Her eyes were coarsely stitched shut but I imagined they looked like mine.

"No! I'm sorry!" I was drawn to look at the woman's body but knew if I took my eyes off my father, I'd be punished harder.

"Get in!" he yelled, hoisting me over the stubborn bottom section of the door, stuffing me inside the closet with the woman. He closed the top portion, but with a broken latch he couldn't secure it. He reached for a hammer and nails and boarded me inside with slices of the original door. This was my shelter.

I could see the woman. Angles of light sliced through, shining on various sections of her body. I stood; I had to. There wasn't room for me to be positioned around her otherwise. I screamed, I cried, and I stared at her, and as candlelight leaked from the studio into the closet through the cracks in the door, it revealed an unclothed woman's leg or flickered on her cheekbones.

I screamed for minutes but cried for hours. I turned my attention to my father, in the workspace outside of the closet, as he ignored my noises, or celebrated them as successful discipline. He continued to work, now with the sack he had brought home that day.

Inside the sack appeared to be sand from the shoreline. It was grayish black, volcanic like all sand from our island. He painstakingly separated the grains, one by one, filtering only the darkest black particles, discarding the rest.

Once he collected his pure, black mound, which took hours as I was trapped in the closet, he lit a fire in the oven. As if he were a metalworker or welder, he reduced his purified dark product into a hot liquid metal, and as he did, I realized what was next for my veins.

He quickly transferred his liquid metal into the crude syringe and rushed to the closet. He reached in and grabbed whatever part of me he could. In the shallow space I had nowhere to hide, and he immediately acquired my arm. He pulled it through an opening in the splintered wood, and with a squeeze near my inner elbow, he expressed several veins of my forearm. With the syringe in his other hand, he shot the liquid metal into my blood.

It burned, searing my forearm, carrying its heat as it spread throughout my body. I watched this. Black and visible in my bloodstream, I saw the Darkness travel out to my hand as it also spread in the other direction toward my shoulder. Had I known what I know now, I would have made every attempt to amputate my own arm before it reached any farther.

The metal cooled slowly inside me but was still uncomfortably warm when I felt it travel upward in my neck toward my brain. That pain, that horrible pain, forced me to a squatting position near the woman's ankles. I found space I could not find before, driven to the closet floor by the pain.

My father left. Possibly to the wild to find his next experiment, I don't know. He set off before he learned the results of his experiment, the liquid metal, and didn't speak after injecting me with this Darkness. I don't know where he went. In fact, it was the last time I saw him.

I remained in the closet for several hours, still with the embalmed woman standing rigidly beside me. Slowly the heat dissipated from the injection, and the dark color in my veins vanished. I looked the same as I had before the experiment, though I was forever altered inside.

I peered through the cracks at the empty room, my home, wondering if my father would return. As for the female figure, I tried to embrace her body, but nothing was transferable from it, long since deceased. The woman whose flowers I had stomped came to the house, bringing her husband. I yelled and I screamed for their attention; quickly they came to my aid.

I explained everything, though we were first forced to discuss the embalmed body. Because of my age, I understood less about her than they deduced.

We fled before my father would return, and they took me to their home, at first I assumed to repair their flowers. However, the flowers were never discussed. I stayed the night with the family.

The family's four children—aged two, five, nine, and eleven—slept in the upper floor of the house. As a stranger and the one who destroyed their flowers, I felt uncomfortable despite the mother's efforts to console me: "There will be peace tomorrow."

I found this hard to believe, hearing heated voices from the lower floor of their home. It was the sound of angry men. In the early part of the evening, this proper family's father could still be heard from upstairs, then another man, then another, and another, while the mother, her children, and I remained obediently in the upper floor.

Finally, the father and his men left. Those of us upstairs remained and went to sleep. The following morning the family took me to an orphanage, telling me that my father was gone.

———◆———

What I hoped would be an opportunity to develop my first friendships turned into a harsh learning experience.

I was placed in the bunks for boys aged eleven to thirteen and occupied the sixth and newest bed space. They didn't speak with me freely at first, and I didn't realize that this was normal.

I was in the play yard that afternoon where some bulbed weeds grew. Short and jaggedly stemmed, and with thickly-layered yellow petals, they were like flowers to a young child.

Another boy from the bunks noticed as I stomped the bulbs, while the other boys and girls played in the yard. He approached me in my corner and asked, "Your name is Tollund? You're the new boy in our bunks." I didn't know how to respond but wanted to make sure not to be rude. I kissed the boy.

It was an innocent kiss, with no feelings other than appreciation and fondness . . . but a terrible, unfortunate mistake in judgment on my part. I suppose I hoped only to make him feel as I felt when the woman touched my arm, the mother of four whose flowers I stomped, the one who alongside her husband saved me from the closet.

I wanted this, and to fully avoid what my father's actions might have been.

He called over the other boys our age. Already cornered in the yard with my stomped weeds, I had no chance to escape.

"The new one kissed me," he said.

"He kissed you?" asked another boy, all five staring at me.

"Maybe he likes boys," said another.

"Maybe he likes me," said the first. "Maybe I don't like that."

"He's sleeping in our bunks?" said a fourth.

"I didn't mean—" I tried.

"Quiet!" said the first. "Quiet tonight when we beat you, and quiet tomorrow if they ask you about your bruises," he said as he shoved me, then walked off as the others followed.

A properly-raised child would have gone directly to one of the adults in the orphanage, and that's what I now know I should have done. However, any past mistakes I had ever made always resulted in beatings. My reaction was therefore to hide and seek shelter, and tell no one.

While dinner was served in the cafeteria, I hid in the bunks of the boys aged eight to ten. The entire orphanage was eating, which provided the perfect opportunity to disappear. I found a large, dark closet in the younger boys' bunks in which I hid until they returned from their meal.

I hid and I waited. They played for an hour or so, and finally one of the adults visited and told them to settle into their beds for the evening. The candles were snuffed and still I waited another hour, remaining through it all unnoticed inside the closet, until I was finally certain all the younger boys were sleeping.

I don't remember much of the night beyond that, only that I emerged from the closet in the dark to leave the room. I paused briefly and admired one of the boys, only four seasons younger than me. I envied his body, this I remember, because when I leaned over him as he slept, I could see his arms were not prick-scarred as mine were. I found it safe to assume he had never been injected with searing liquid metal by his father. I reached out to touch his smooth arm, and then leaned in closer to smell it. Then the Darkness. All I remember after that point was the Darkness, and waking satisfied the following morning in my bed in the room of the boys my own age. I don't remember how I returned there or if my bunkmates ever followed through with their threat.

The following day I felt well, in fact I remember feeling strong and relaxed. In the play yard I was alone again, but fortunately not harassed by the other boys. I wandered into a corner, poking the previously stomped bulbed weeds with a pointed toe.

"Stop," yelled one of the crushed flowers. "No more, please."

"What?" I responded.

"We don't know why you've stomped us," said the other flower. "Please stop. We're damaged now."

"If you can speak, why now and not before?"

"Cause us no harm," a flower responded, ignoring my question.

"Can other flowers speak?" I asked.

"Darkness," said a flower. "The Darkness. Should not be."

"What darkness?" I asked. "How do you know about the Darkness?"

"The pain of the rest of my life," said the other flower. "The pain now."

"I'm sorry! I won't harm another flower!"

Had I a friend to share this with, I would have certainly brought him quickly to see the flowers that spoke to me. Still, the miracle of a speaking flower could not be concealed. From the corner of the small play yard, I turned away from the flowers and toward the other children. They had already noticed me and were glaring with shamelessly judgmental stares.

"The flowers can speak!" I told the others. "Come, see! Someone, every-one!" None moved. They all stared, some drawing away. They appeared terrified of me, and certainly didn't believe my claim that the flowers had spoken.

I realized I would now never have a friend in the orphanage, and would possibly be beaten that night by the other boys my age. So, I fled. I left, again during dinner, escaping the orphanage and seeking shelter elsewhere.

———————

In my first hours alone, I returned to my recently-abandoned home. My father was gone, I'd been told, forever. By the time I returned, the woman in the closet was gone as well. The curtains were closed as we had left them, and inside were the remains of Father's most recent experiments. The walls were lined with preserved creatures, mostly birds, lifeless and quiet but staring at me from their mounts.

I tried to sleep but could not, though dusk had fallen. Alone in my own home, I considered if the woman's flower bed, which I had stomped, could now speak with me. I left in a hurry.

In the twilight I walked to their home and to her flower bed, which lay motionless, still stomped, and not speaking.

"Hello?" I whispered, kneeling.

There was no response. *Dead?* I thought, *Or maybe these flowers could never speak.*

I didn't want to return to the orphanage or my abandoned home. I still needed shelter, and had only found it for one night of my life, with this family.

Peering through the window unnoticed, I watched them for a short time eating dinner. The father, the mother, and the children—two, five, nine, and eleven—all sat as a family, which could have included me at their table as the eldest of five.

As I watched, the youngest threw his food on the floor and screamed. I noticed how the mother and father immediately addressed the situation, able to balance the child's necessities of both nourishment and love. In the commotion, I entered the home, not at first planning to hide. Quite the opposite, I opened the front door fully planning to ask for a meal, or for some help, but after passing inside realized that in the volume of the child's screams, I was inside their home and yet entirely unnoticed by its six occupants.

I quietly but impulsively diverted my path toward the stairway and proceeded unnoticed to the upper level. I was surprised at how easily I was able to walk into their home and pass into their bedrooms unseen. I don't know why I went upstairs and didn't make my presence known. For no reason, I panicked. I made many mistakes as a child, of course, and when my father reacted to them as he did, I only grew more and more fearful of making additional mistakes.

It became such an issue that I could almost never understand my own excited actions. They were fear based, and as I've learned, we attract that which we fear. I feared that I was not competent, causing me to make further inexplicable errors in judgment.

Whatever the cause, I was an even more nervous child now, because I was unannounced on the upper level of the family's home. Had I casually walked downstairs and attempted to leave, I would likely be noticed, and cause them alarm. They would either consider me an intruder or an incompetent fool. This fear led to my next error in judgment. I had spent hours the prior night hiding in a dark closet in the orphanage, and decided I could do so again until the family was sleeping deeply, after which I would quietly escape unnoticed.

Frantically but quietly wandering the upper level while the family continued their meal, I avoided the parents' room as well as what I believed was the youngest's. I found my shelter in the closet of one of the other children's rooms and waited.

Hours passed. I remained silent in the closet, hoping nothing inside would be needed by the family for the remaining night's preparations. I breathed through my nose and waited. The house grew still, and after allowing several more hours to pass, I emerged from the closet to discover I had chosen the room of the child of five seasons.

Leaving his room, hardly exhaling as I passed his sleeping body, I stopped to admire the cleanliness of his skin. I crept closer, wondering if there was an aroma to it, lowering my nose to his body, and again, the Darkness. I honestly don't recall what happened from that moment on. However, I must have escaped their home successfully, because my next memories were waking in my abandoned home, greeted by stuffed birds and loose taxidermist's tools. Again, I woke feeling strong and vibrant, refreshed and relaxed.

I spent the morning thankful not to have been found by the family whose home I'd silently invaded, feeling even more fortunate to have escaped my own lapses in judgment. But as the day passed, I grew bolder and bolder, believing confidently that, as easily as it was accomplished the prior night, I could do it again. This I believe was no longer simply a lapse in judgment, although it was most certainly that, but had become the fulfillment of an urge. I felt strong the morning after escaping their home, as if I had some control over what would and would not be.

I set off that day near dusk once again. Becoming quickly addicted to the thrill of hiding in someone's closet but not yet prepared to attempt hiding in the parents' bedroom, the intent this time was to find the bedroom of the child of nine seasons, quietly enter his closet without being discovered, and likewise escape when the family had long since retired for the evening. Approaching the house, I saw the same flower bed, which hadn't responded to my words before. This night it began to speak.

"Do not," said one of many stomped flowers.

"You speak now!" I responded. "You're alive! That's wonderful!"

"No," said another.

"Yes, I feared you had died! I'm sorry for what I've done," I said, happy for the opportunity to apologize.

"No," said another, "no," said another, and another, and another, forming a chorus of "no."

Then silence.

"No?" I asked. "No what?"

"Do not," said the flower first to speak. "Do not," it repeated, adding, "Should not be."

"Tell me!" I asked, with just enough restraint not to reveal myself to the proper family inside the home. "Tell me, 'no' what?"

Silence.

"No what?" I persisted, upset.

Silence.

I stared down as my muscles tensed. I stomped them, as I had sworn never again to do. I then diverted my attention to the family inside and awaited my moment.

Eventually their dinner conversation became animated enough for them not to notice as I entered the home again. I breezed up their stairway and into a different bedroom from the night before.

And as before I waited successfully inside what I deduced was the closet of the child of nine. Soon the meal was finished, the day was ending, and every member of the family including the parents retired for the evening.

And as I had the night before, I waited several more hours, now not in fear but in a rush of silent excitement. The thought of being caught, of being punished, and everything I risked in hiding in that closet was so important to the sensations I was feeling. The warm blood rushing through my veins merely as I stood inside the closet . . . It could have been searing liquid metal pumping and it would have only made me feel more invincible. Then, the culmination: the escape.

I emerged from the closet and passed by the child of nine on my path to the bedroom door. All was still as I paused briefly to admire the child, only three or four seasons younger than me. I compared the boy's pure, clean arm with mine, the one that suffered my father's injections. Then, again, the Darkness. I truthfully do not recall what happened next, but I did not wake in my home as I had the night before. I wish that I had.

I awoke with a blow to my head. My next memory was that same night, before the sun had risen, wrapped and shackled in chains and being beaten by the proper family's father. I was in their cellar, with the mother and father, but no children.

"I will beat you until you answer me, Tollund! Why are you here?"

"He's obviously very sick," responded the mother on my behalf.

"Sir?" I asked. "What's happened?"

"What's happened? Should I bring my middle children to this cellar to remind you?" he screamed.

"You're going to wake the little one," said the mother as she gestured toward the stairs and then paused. Again she addressed her husband: "Don't kill the boy. This is not a moral issue." She then left the cellar to console her children, leaving me shackled, confused, and alone with the man.

"Sir, my father would beat me, and I never understood why," I spoke. "I assure you; this is no exception."

"Come with me," said the man calmly, as if I could protest while he picked up my battered body and metal restraints. He looked toward the stairs, where his wife had exited. Because she was no longer in sight, he abrasively carried me to the cellar's lower exit and to the outside into his yard. "Don't speak and I won't beat you."

The man carried me and the weight of my shackles, as heavy as I was, and dragged me in the darkness, still several hours before the dawn, into the deepest part of the forest. He brought me to an isolated peat bog surrounded by thicket and tall trees, and tossed me onto my knees.

"You may scream as loud as you wish now." He interlocked his fingers to swing two combined fists, then struck me on both the left and right cheeks in that order.

I screamed, and as he intended, it didn't help. The bog in the forest was too remote. He lashed me with his bare fingers, and when his fists grew tired he kicked, and when his feet grew tired he found rocks to throw. By all expectations I should not have survived. Although the pain was real, it wasn't until I recognized how tired he was that I realized how long he had been beating me. "Why do you torture me?" I asked, "when you have taken me here to die?"

"I have taken you here to die," said the man, breathing heavily, now squatting and resting, "but even your father died much more easily than this."

"You killed my father?" I asked.

"With others, we did. We killed your father for what he did to your mother and you, and now I'm killing you for what you, for what your yearning, has done to my children. I am trying to kill you."

"Yet I will not die," I responded. "There's no blood. On my skin, or on the ground."

The man looked at his hands in the moonlight by the bog and shook his head in confusion. *Father's final experiment,* I thought. *It was a success. A horrible, horrible, success.*

The man continued to beat me, but no more could he beat the Darkness out than could he beat the life from my body. He tried in one final attempt, but grew tired again, and much more quickly than before. He eventually realized what I had: I would not die.

He spent his remaining energy manipulating my body, still shackled, towing me to the deepest part of the bog. Knee-deep at first . . . then waist . . . eventually in the moonlight I saw my final glimpses of the world above the surface as a child.

Now with his victim entirely submerged, he spent the next hour fully committed to dragging me farther and farther to the deepest, most inaccessible part of the bog. He returned to the surface for air while I did not, the weight of my shackles keeping me submerged. He then dove down again and dragged me a little further until he was satisfied. I felt suffocated, yet I would not drown.

The man left.

Unable to move, unable to breathe, and unable to die, I remained at the bottom of the bog. I felt the sensation of suffocation, the pain of it, but as I suffered, my body resisted death. In time I became accustomed to the nagging, gasping, gagging, unsatisfying attempts at free air, and adjusted to other pains as well, such as the frigid temperature of the bog, knowing all of this could cause me real pain but could not kill me. I wondered at first how many days it would be before I was discovered. There was pressure on my ears initially, though I didn't know if I was shallow below the surface or very, very deep. I had been placed in my position by being dragged along the ground, not by sinking. I could only be as deep as a man could dive. My scalp and eyes burned from the caustic marsh, but the burning eventually subsided like the other tortures and I, still unable to move, wondered now how many seasons it would be before I was discovered.

It burned to open my eyes, and because of the thickness of the bog, I was unable to see even my own shoulder. Bound by shackles, I was unable to move hardly a limb. The only escape was my own mind. Sleep became more recreational than functional, and I began to live my life without continuity, only in a state of dreaming. I had nothing to live for in true reality. No people, no friends, no shelter, and no self. For what I believe was nearly twenty seasons, I existed in my sleep.

In my waking hours I experienced nothing but the bog. In time even the farthest, most distant realms of my mind understood that if not in the bog, I must be dreaming. With that power and lucidity, I could then alter the materials and visitors within my sleeping realm. I began a life of my own as the eldest child of the proper family. I grew older, helping to raise my younger siblings, and eventually I married. I had several children of my own, all while shackled below the surface of the bog. But in my mind's realm I lived an ordinary life, visited my custodial parents, and even tended a flower garden. I had lived this new life for nearly as many seasons as my body lay suspended in the bog. However, my wife, my family . . . it all ended when I was drawn back to reality, by voices above the surface of the marsh.

———————————————

I felt a poke, which at first I believed was a creature, or a branch floating by. It was a strong metal object, hooking my chains, now hoisting me slowly to the surface.

". . . two, one, pull!" came a female voice, followed by grunting.

"It would be nice if Quinby were here to help," said a second female, who spoke well in accented Svalbardian in the same fashion as the first.

I opened my eyes and could only see the murky thickness of the marsh but knew I was being pulled closer and closer to the sunlight.

"Three, two, one, pull!" came the voice again as my head was jolted, striking the underside of what I later learned was a small rowboat.

"Are we trying to save him or are we trying to kill him?"

"It doesn't matter," the other replied. "He's dead; look."

"Ah! Oh, his skin . . . his hair . . . how long has he been dead?"

"But the body is still glowing, a gray glow," said one of the girls. I remember this, but never saw the gray glow she described. She continued: "Please, let's drag him to shore."

The other sighed. "All right, if we must. But I may not be able to cast my eyes on him. This corpse is hideous."

I had lost all sense of time by now, so I counted the strokes as they dragged my body, suspended in the water, not yet fully exhumed from the bog. It took over two hundred slow, hard strokes.

As much as I wanted to, I couldn't speak. My lungs were filled with the bog, but I was thankful the girls continued, slowly as it was, to the solid bank of the bog. They had hooked me with the rowboat's small anchor, and eventually grounded the small vessel, pulled it farther up the shore, and pulled in its anchor chain. With it they pulled my body, surrounded in rusted shackles and chains, and dragged me ashore. My skin felt solid ground and free air for the first time in many seasons.

As soon as the air hit my wet skin, I began to sneeze. I sneezed through my nose, then my mouth, then began coughing, spitting up bog, and heaving until my lungs were clear and I was able to take my first deep gasp as the Bog Man.

The girls shrieked, or at least one shrieked sufficiently for both. I coughed more, and spit up more bog.

"He's alive!" said one. "How is this possible?" I could hear them but not see them. I was only partially ashore, still with my legs and feet wet in the bog.

"Please release me," I pleaded.

My vision was blurred as my eyes adjusted to the light and as fluid cleared from their lower lids. *What's this film on me?* I thought. It was a black, leathery substance. I was older now, no longer a child, and unshaven. I tilted my head downward on my stiff, sore neck to see a scorched, red beard. My hair, what I could see, was like the fiery red of fresh, hot, liquid earth from the volcano of our island. My skin was a dull black, like the same liquid earth after it has cooled, forming the rocks of Jan Mayen, and the sand of its beaches.

"Who are you?" asked the girls.

"Please, please, release me. Tollund is my name. I have been badly beaten and tortured."

"Why is your skin and hair as it is?" asked one. "Black and weathered, with a scorching red beard and hair?"

"And how are you alive?" asked the other, a question I neither chose to satisfy nor was I able.

Frustrated in speaking with people I couldn't see, I finally rolled over on the shore in my shackles to face the girls. "I don't know. Why are your eyes purple?"

"Why were you shackled and tossed into the bog?" the other asked, the one with long, blonde hair, still none of us answering the other's inquiries.

"Ritual sacrifice," I lied. "To the Mother Goddess of the Season of Darkness's solstice. They fed me her herbs and shrubs and tossed me into the bog for her."

"Oh no . . . " said the blonde. "I knew this island was remote, but I thought they were more enlightened than this."

"We'll see what we can do to help," said the darker-haired girl with purple eyes.

They approached my chains, still leaning away when they could, and dragged me farther up the shore by pulling my legs and lower half entirely out from the bog.

"Your shackles are rusted, Tollund," said the one with the purple eyes. "How long have you been submerged?"

"Please release me. It hurts to speak with these rusted chains along my skin."

"Yes, of course," she answered.

The girls rolled me to my side, then gave me a second turn so that my front lay downward, as they searched for a single weak point that they could destroy and set me free.

"Here," said one to the other, as I was on my right side, with the girls at my back. "Get the anchor."

After several swings with the small boat's metal anchor, the rusted chains crumbled, and I was free. They helped loosen them from my body so that I could stand, stretch, and view myself. I was hideous, something evil. I took in the sight of my own arms, my legs, and in devastation I learned what I had hoped was a film from the bog was now my skin. I rubbed and I rubbed as the girls stood back, afraid, but as I did my skin remained a dull, volcanic black, with the texture of an old, tanned hide. My nails were overgrown, both hand and foot, and I stroked a beard that I had never felt until that day. Strands weakly pulled out of their pores, and long, scorched-red beard hairs fell into my fingers. This was the Darkness. It had to be. It had been given to me by my father, then fermented in the bog. It had harvested both my body and my mind.

Watching me shake and squirm back to life, the girls cautiously approached. The one with the blonde hair led, and in one of so few times in my life, a stranger was reaching for me . . . the woman whose flowers I had stomped, the orphan boy initially who also observed me stomping flowers, and now these two girls, younger than me by about fifteen seasons but older than I was when imprisoned in the bog.

The blonde spoke slowly, stating, "Hello, Tollund. My name is Marigold, and this is my sister, Lavender."

"More talking flowers!" I declared and fled. I assumed they weren't real; I assumed it was the Darkness controlling my mind. I ran and didn't look back, not even thanking the girls, and continued through the forest in any direction away from them. They did not follow, although my legs cramped quickly.

Now alone, exhumed, and deep within the forest, I found a discarded leather cap for my head. I brushed off some dirt and tied it around my scalp, sat on some leaves, and pulled the hairs from my beard. Pulling it through, strung between my fingers in strands and clumps, the plucking was effortless and unresisted by the roots. The cap could cover the hair on my scalp, and with my beard mostly gone, I could have been seen as normal, if not for my skin. In denial, I looked and looked at my own skin until it became more and more normal to me, the coal color, the prick-scars on my arm still present from childhood . . . but as the denial faded, I realized I couldn't return to society in sunlight. Only at night could I walk by a stranger unnoticed.

I waited in the forest until darkness fell. Later in the season of light as it was, the skies were not dark for long, though the nights had started to get longer. The Canadian girls were the only ones who knew that I lived and was free. Whether or not that mattered I was yet to discover.

I first quickly went to my home, the home of my father. To my surprise the structure was well-maintained in comparison to when I had stayed there. I wondered if I had a home now or if I would have to return to the forest.

I peered through the window to see a much different cabin. No gulls, no embalmed animals of any kind, no taxidermist's tools. I saw a man of just past twenty seasons; he appeared alone, and I continued on. This was no longer my home and the dark memories I had were not worth another moment.

I found a second dwelling, a new one near my childhood home. I didn't remember the house prior to my time in the bog. It was a large home, which was what I sought. Large homes, after all, have more bedrooms and more closets. I entered the home without exhaling, seeking shelter and a sleeping family. I remember entering a bedroom but that's all. Everything beyond is blank. My memory had worsened; I remember only finding the Darkness.

I woke the following morning in the forest, confused and disoriented but physically quite well. The night had passed, and I was alone aside from the forest flowers. They are what woke me.

"No more," said a small pink-petaled flower near my resting spot.

"No more?" I asked as I woke. "I don't understand. You aren't stomped; you aren't harmed. No more what?"

"No more," the flower repeated. "Never again. It should not be."

"Please explain!" I begged, but the flower only repeated itself.

Determined not to stomp the flower, I left without getting a proper response and wandered to a part of the forest made only of weeds, grasses, and trees, which would not speak to me. I found such a spot and waited until dusk.

I had to revisit the home of my youth. I left the forest as the sun set to see again just how it had changed since I was a child. When I arrived, there was a child sleeping inside the home. He may have been six, seven seasons . . . and he lay peacefully in a bed by the one window with open curtains. His skin was soft and pure, forming a discouraging contrast to my charred, leathery hide. He slept in my own home, or what was once my home, and slept without the nightmares of a sick, violently desperate father. He had nourishment and he had love, and he had the one thing I never found: shelter. He had shelter inside this home, in the common area, and did not feel the need to retreat to any forbidden closet to find it. He had shelter in this home that gave me none for so many seasons. Seeking this I disconnected my gaze through the window, and took my grotesque body, with liquid metal in my veins, scorched red hair covered by a leather cap, overgrown finger and toenails, and muted stained hide for skin and I moved this body with the Darkness inside of it toward the door of the home.

Then, the Light.

I opened the door and was bagged and tackled, attacked, shackled, my head covered, and my ankles bound. I growled at the hands and voices, hoping to use my appearance to strike fear in them, whoever they were, and there were several. I could see nothing; they cloaked me quickly. I had entered a trap.

"Take the boy to the other room," said a man.

The boy responded in ignorant delight: "The Bogeyman!" He was escorted to another place, I believe by his mother.

The man then spoke to me. "Tollund?"

I ceased my growling and began to weep underneath my covering. "Yes, it's me."

"I remember you, Tollund. I remember *of* you, I should say. You visited my middle-elder brothers when I was a small child, then only two seasons of age. Do you remember them, Tollund?"

"Yes, sir."

"Do you remember what you did to them?" he asked.

"No, sir. Truthfully, no."

"How is that possible?" asked another man's voice, an older but familiar one. "Do you remember this?" he snarled, accompanied by a swift punch to my stomach. I was so unable to see that I couldn't prepare for his fist, and so his punch momentarily expelled all free air from my lungs and left me briefly unable to breathe. I was able to hear several others, men mostly, react with pleasure to my pain.

"Yes, sir, I remember that," I gasped once my breath returned. "But no matter how hard I try, I truthfully cannot recall what I did to your family."

"You are not ignorant, and you are not innocent!" shouted the older, violent man as he struck me again, now across the head with what I believe were interlocked fists. I was long ago emotionally broken, but still physically indestructible. "Why won't you die?" he shouted. "By all accounts you should have drowned and long ago decomposed in the bog. I want to know why you are still alive."

"Perhaps he's an incorruptible," sounded a familiar female voice, one of the Canadians who had freed me.

"An incorruptible?" laughed the first, younger, calmer man.

"Smell him," added the Canadian. "An incorruptible won't be rotting, and will not smell of decay. What's his aroma like?"

The younger man complied and responded, "He doesn't smell of decomposition, the bog, or even anything unpleasant. He smells like an ordinary flower."

"I'm not incorruptible. I'm embalmed. If anything, I'm cursed. But part of my curse is genuinely lacking memory of my offenses. Strike me for asking if you must, but what have I done to your middle-elder brothers, sir?"

"You affected them, Tollund. They were too disturbed to live here afterward."

"Tollund, we're going to try to help you," came another familiar female voice, also with a Canadian accent.

"Lavender? Or Marigold?" I finally asked, still under the hood.

"We're both here," one responded.

"Tollund, there's a Royal Asylum on Emberland where we would like to take you," one of them said. "They can help you."

"Can they cure me? My skin, my hair?"

"Your fingernails," added one of the girls.

"Marigold, please," snapped the other.

"Can they cure me?" I asked. "Can they cure the Darkness?"

"Maybe," said a third, unknown, man, reminding me in my hood and restraints that many were present but silent. "But they can give you shelter."

"Then I would very much like to go there. Just not the bog . . . please, anything but the bog."

"We will not take you back to the bog, Tollund," said one of the Canadians.

"Thank you."

———

They kept me hooded, adding muffs so I couldn't hear. They walked me out of my old home, down to the docks where they placed me onto a southbound boat. I was transported to the Royal Asylum on Emberland, but nobody calls it that.

It's the King's Closet.

It's there that I've been able to find treatment. In time, I realized the flowers did not speak to me, and never had, although my physicians and I agree that Lavender and Marigold were real. I've lived with the other committed and sick, and I've formed several friendships.

I don't know what the future holds. Will I die of natural causes? Will I live forever? Can the Darkness be destroyed, or only contained? The physicians have studied me. From the beginning, they needed a new classification for what I am, body and mind: a "bogey." They've been unable to cure me, but make attempts with almost daily injections. Their syringes are slender and sophisticated, not crude, and don't leave prick-scars on my leathery skin.

The asylum is decorated with healthy flowers, none of which speak to me, none of which I've ever desired to stomp. My bedroom has no closet of its own, but I have nourishment and I'm cared for with love. I've finally found shelter.

As I had done in the bog, I've confined reality to my dreams. Self-trained and still able to maintain lucid control over them, I know even in my sleep that if I'm not in the asylum, I must be dreaming. And so I live another life in this realm, as I had done for thousands of nights in the marsh. I've returned to my family so that I may grow old with them. There in my dreams I don't have afflicted skin or hair, prick-marks on my arms, or liquid metal in my veins. There I have a flower garden, and I've watched my children grow up and have been able to provide them with nourishment, love, and shelter.

9 / Marigold

After leaving the castle, Lavender and I boarded as passengers on the prince's yacht.

We sailed into the night.

When the sun rose to break the darkness, Quinby approached us seated on a small bench by the bow. To our good luck, he was appreciative, not vengeful. "If not for you, Marigold and Lavender, I would already have been executed."

"Does the king carry out his killings at dawn?" asked Lavender.

"Well, perhaps I would still be alive. But after breakfast, certainly . . ." The exiled Svalbard laughed. "Thank you for your kindness. I'm relieved to be free of King Ulffr."

I turned to look at Lavender, seated next to me on the ship. I stared with one eyebrow raised and a mocking smile that said, *So exile isn't quite so awful as execution?*

Resisting eye contact and looking only at Quinby but fully aware that I was staring at her, Lavender bit back: "Too subtle, Marigold. That's always been your flaw . . . you're undetectably subtle."

I asked Quinby: "So then you aren't upset with me?"

"Oh no! Considering my intentions compared to yours, I should thank you."

"Intentions?" I asked. "Do you have any intentions that involve me?"

"There you go again with that subtlety," said Lavender. "I understand this is a very small island. The crew claims that you could travel the length tip to tip in a single day's walk and meet every soul who lives there in five."

"And complete our tasks in less than ten. What will we do with the rest of our time?" I asked, as coy as I was able.

"I'm just glad we aren't starting our journey with an enemy sharing such a small island," said Lavender.

"Certainly not," Quinby responded. "You have instead a man who owes you a debt or a favor."

"I can think of—" I started, interrupted loudly by my sister.

"Quinby, when we arrive on the island, do you have any toppen for lodging?"

"Why . . . actually, no. I may have enough to pay for a night or two, but I didn't press the prince for any more generosity beyond my life."

Lavender looked at me to give permission and I responded: "As much as you like. We won't need it in the depths of the forest."

I couldn't have refused, even had I wanted to. It was Lavender's gift that kept us alive and would presumably continue to do so. It was her eyes that earned those wages. She reached through our possessions and dug through our clothing, around the small object we received from the Lichen's stash, several copies of our field guide, and some writing equipment. Beneath our camping gear, she finally recovered the money we had made selling our text in the Kildebyen marketplace. She gave Quinby nearly everything. "You'll need this," she said, tossing the pouch. "Or you'll go from being a servant to a slave."

"Thank you!" responded the former taste tester.

"You'll never eat again!" I exclaimed joyously. "Potentially poisoned food while working as a tester, I mean."

"Marigold, please!" said my sister, driving her palm into her own forehead above a grimaced face.

"All right, I was doing another routine. But you don't have to embarrass me."

"How was I embarrassing you?"

"By doing what you just did."

"Doing what?"

"What you just did."

"I don't even know what you're talking about."

"Why is it after one of my jokes you feel the urge to let everyone know that you don't endorse me as your sister if I try to be funny? I'm sorry if you weren't in the mood. I did sense this, but why must you always have the final word that squelches the joke?"

After a pause, Lavender answered, "Eleven."

"What?" I asked, confused, as was Quinby.

"Eleven," she repeated confidently and calmly. "You say I always need the last word. I say 'eleven.' Eleven is a number."

The three of us laughed, and for a brief moment my sister shared my stage in support.

"I thank you again for the toppen, but will you have fare for your lodging if I accept this?" asked Quinby.

"Our work brings us to the forest," explained Lavender.

"I'll be camping, won't I?" I asked.

"Yes." She sighed. "You know this."

"Have I shared my feelings about camping?"

"You have," said Lavender, "a thousand times. I believe it's the reason trees don't have ears."

"I'm sorry to be rude. Quinby, would you like to sit with us?" He had been standing for the duration of the conversation.

"I, uh . . ." he stammered, "there doesn't appear to be room on the bench."

"There is not," stated Lavender.

"Then I'll stand," I said, approaching Quinby, noticing: "You're quite tall."

"I? I'm . . ."

"How tall are you?" I asked, taking a step closer, now within arm's reach.

"I'm about . . ."

"Stand very close to me, so I can see," I continued.

"Marigold . . ." whined Lavender, sitting alone on the small bench.

"Closer."

"She's poison, you know. If you look up marigold in our field guide, you'll see her under 'poison.'"

"You certainly will," I said as Quinby struggled to return my gaze. "Closer," I continued. Quinby hadn't moved, standing bashfully introverted, but I had advanced close enough for us to touch toes. "Come on, closer."

"Uh . . . how could we . . ."

"Oh, if not for your clothing!" scoffed Lavender. "You could get even closer!"

Finally, the wave I was anticipating hit the boat, and I tumbled into Quinby as we fell to the deck, laughing.

"And there, the motion of the ocean," said Lavender, mocking from her seat.

"I'm just having a little fun, Lavender."

"Fun? I've taken a terrible fall," joked Quinby. "Will you nurse me back to health?"

"All right, but you may be bedridden for days," I teased.

Lavender groaned loudly in disgust.

"Oh, soothe yourself, Lavender. Find a thumb to suck. I'm not planning on abandoning you." Quinby and I separately returned to our feet. "We're outcasts too, you know."

"Now I understand why you wished to be on this boat instead of dining with the royal Svalbardian family," mumbled Lavender, in Canadian, for my ears only.

When we arrived at the dock on the central, eastern part of Jan Mayen Island, Quinby headed south to the inhabited area while Lavender and I went north toward the forest, right into the foothills of a dormant volcano. While I may have whined about flies and loud birds, a volcano was an entirely different issue regarding an unpleasant camping experience. According to the crew, the last eruption was generations ago.

We said farewell to the crew and thanked them, Lavender and I expecting to see them again in twenty days. We embraced Quinby as he thanked us one final time before we set off in different directions.

We wandered the forest first searching for a suitable campground, and through the trees we saw what appeared to be a clearing. We drew closer without realizing there would be a boundary of dry thicket. We mowed through it stepping sideways to better crush our path. The brush tapered as we reached the bank of a murky, probably acidic peat pond with a rowboat, its oars, and a small anchor pulled ashore.

The entire bog was confined to the forest. The abandoned little boat was perhaps meant to cross from one side to the other without getting the traveler's stockings wet. Ours were still intact, but the edges of the bog were deceptively damper than they looked. Having had enough cold, wet feet since leaving Canada, Lavender and I stepped into our second boat of the day to cross the bog and continue our survey of the forest.

Almost directly in the center, with the fatigue of little sleep the night prior now joined by the strain of exercise, Lavender found the energy to yell, "Stop!"

"Gladly," I replied.

"Look! I mean, I see a glow from beneath the surface of the bog. It seems to be the silhouette of a man."

"A red glow or a white glow? Or a pale-yellow glow?"

"A gray glow."

"Gray? If red is life, white is death, and pale yellow is something parasitic, what's gray?"

"I'm not farming equipment, Marigold. I don't come with an instruction manual."

"It can't mean indigestion. We'd see bubbles."

"Gray may be drowning. We should hurry."

Lavender lowered the small anchor until she felt it contact the glowing object. Unable to see the glow as my sister could, my task was to row the boat away from it, then toward it while Lavender dragged the anchor with the hopes of hooking something. Fortunately, on only our third hasty attempt we snagged a solid hook on the man or creature, and together began to pull.

"All right, we'll count down from three," said Lavender.

She said the glow was rising closer to the surface, though the pulling to me seemed futile. "If only Quinby were here," I believe I said.

We dragged a man onshore, believing him dead. His skin was the color of dried volcanic rock, and his hair fire red. He was Tollund, the Bog Man. He claimed to be the victim of ritual sacrifice, which gave us pause, but he was suffering so we set him free. As soon as we released him, he ran off into the forest.

"Lavender, have we just freed a terrible evil?"

"Marigold, I have no idea. But we probably should warn the island." I could see bags under her eyes. She was irritable and poorly rested, and now sleep was even further away. She drew the hood of her robe close and we walked south, into town.

No one recognized our description of the Bog Man, and it's unlikely they would have forgotten him had they ever seen him. But once several of the inhabitants, all fifty or older, heard the name 'Tollund,' they directed us to a particular house. They said he grew up there.

"Impossible," responded the young man who lived in the house. "My father—" he paused, "—Tollund is dead, punished for his offenses to my older brothers."

"So, you know him?" I asked.

"Yes. You claim he lives? It's been . . . it must be twenty seasons."

"He was loose in the forest when we saw him last," explained Lavender. "We mistook him for the victim of a ritual sacrifice to the Goddess of . . ."

"Darkness's solstice," I said.

"Yes, that was it," agreed Lavender.

The young man crossed his arms and tilted his head. "Ritual sacrifice? Do you take us for Siberians?"

"No, not at all. But Tollund said—"

"We're not backward people here."

"I didn't say you were," said Lavender.

"Where are you from, Canada? York probably?"

"North of York," answered my sister. "We grew up on a farm."

He hesitated, then said, "Please girls, come in." Lavender looked at her arms and at me. Free of any glow, we entered his home.

"My name is Per. I am the youngest of four. Tollund took inappropriate interest with two of my older brothers when I was two or three. I don't remember this of course, but was told the story when I became a young man. After my father found Tollund in our home as an intruder, he took him to the bog in the remote forest and ensured he would never pass his sickness on to another child, one of his own, one of my father's, or anyone else's. I live here now because I remember nothing of the events, and to me it is a small but practical home. We assumed the lot when everything was settled."

"Tollund lives, and he's free," said Lavender.

"My father said he was gone and could no longer harm us. But you have freed him, is this correct?"

"We believed him to be drowning," answered Lavender. "Yes, we freed him."

She looked again at her arms, which told me she was nervous, as was I. She said nothing alarming, which meant we were safe for the moment.

Breaking the accusatory tension, Per said, "We should visit my father." Lavender stared at a large, soft, fur-skinned hide, used as a rug in the center of Per's floor. I looked over to see just how tired she was. "Come, girls. It's not safe to be here now."

Per was frustrated with Lavender as we walked. "Keep your head up," he barked.

"I'll know if we're in imminent danger," explained Lavender, defending her sluggishness.

"Please, I won't be responsible for your deaths. And I don't believe I would recognize him, so you must keep looking."

"Oh, you'll know Tollund when you see him," I said. "He has black leathery skin, and hair like lava."

"Yes, yes," said Per, "and a Siberian's skeleton has thorns."

"They do," I said. "Our mother's met one."

"Right," he snipped.

"We've seen Tollund," said Lavender. "And we don't embellish."

"Then why did my father's story not describe him this way?"

"Decades in a bog? That's probably why," guessed Lavender.

"We'll ask my father."

"A moment please," requested my sister, stopping her gait. "We, the liberators of this dark creature, are to meet the man who toiled to destroy it, whose children were victimized by it?"

"Yes," said Per, maintaining stride and forcing me to follow. "And we may meet my brothers as well, the victims. They often visit my parents' home."

Now falling several paces behind, Lavender muttered, "I was created evil."

Before I could console her, a shadow passed overhead. "Did you notice that, Per?"

"What?"

It was night and already dark, but something blocked the moonlight and passed quickly. "A shadow. A flicker of darkness."

"It may have been a bird. We have many flying creatures on this island, and the largest ones circle the highest. What they hunt I don't know, but they never descend low enough for us to see them clearly."

"Nineteen more days," I spoke in Canadian to my sister. "But today's almost over."

We finally arrived at Per's childhood home, where his father and mother lived, and noticed a bed of flowers near their window. Perhaps a family tradition, it was nearly identical to a bed of flowers outside of Per's home from which we came.

He knocked as Lavender and I stood slumped behind him. "Son!" spoke an older man as he opened the door.

Not yet invited in, Per instantly incriminated us, as a child does to win the approval of a parent. "Father, these girls have released Tollund."

"They did—" he said, looking at the two haggard, unimposing teenage girls from Canada standing on his doorstep. "How?"

Sensing his anger growing I tried to quickly explain, "We thought he was drowning."

Lavender added, "And criminals do not often display a label."

"Need they, when they're bound and shackled?" asked the father.

We breathed deeply and exhaled with no defense. Lavender again looked at her arms and at me, but without alarm. "We're sorry," I apologized. "We know what he's done to your family."

"Then you'll help us capture him," said the man. "My name is Nels. We'll lay a trap for him inside Per's home. He'll likely return there."

"We'll need some . . ." started Per, knowing what to say but struggling to say it.

"Bait," finished the father. "Yes, it's horrible; I know. Your neighbor boy. He's six, seven?"

"Matthias. Yes," answered Per. "What of Bergen and Hakon? Do they not want this opportunity for retribution?"

The father answered, "I have lied to your brothers to protect them. Tollund would not die as you now know, yet they would be forever disturbed if they knew this. Even as adults, I believe it best that you and I take care of this without them."

"We shall ask Matthias then," agreed Per.

We returned to Per's home, now only several hours from dawn. Outside the home, where their family's traditional flower bed lay, was the disturbing scene of a young boy stomping stems and petals.

"Matthias, why are you awake? Why are you alone?" asked Per.

"Oh no. We're too late," explained Nels, who approached the boy, knelt, and embraced him while restraining him from stomping any more of the flowers.

When we woke late the following morning, the plan for the next dusk was already laid. A brave boy, Matthias would have a bed in Per's home propped in the window to be visible. Per, Nels, Matthias's father, and some neighborhood men would find an angle hidden from the window's view to wait for Tollund, should he return.

As late as Lavender and I slept on the fur rug, we had several hours of sunlight still remaining.

"Day two of twenty," I joked.

"This is all my fault, Marigold."

"No, it's not. The smallest towns have the darkest secrets."

We waited for evening, and for dinner. All involved in the matter—Per, Nels, Matthias and his parents, and several from the neighborhood—met for an unsettling gathering inside the home that was to serve as Tollund's trap. Matthias's mother brought a meal. Her gesture to prepare her son's favorite food, fowl and fried potatoes, was kind but served a disturbing reminder to the adults of just what the boy had been through the night before. We sat among their company as we began to eat our final meal of the day.

"You know, Matthias, this is the King of Svalbard's favorite meal," I said as we ate.

"He doesn't eat fancy fruits or exotic eggs?" asked the boy.

"No, he doesn't," I explained. "Maybe you will be a king one day. Does Jan Mayen have a king? If not, you will be the first."

"If so, try not to become the son of a thousand roaches," said Lavender in Canadian.

"I'm sorry, what did she say?" asked one of the men at the crowded but quiet dinner table.

"We met the King of Svalbard," I explained. "We know him somewhat, that's all."

"Tell us!" they insisted.

It was a relief for all to discuss another topic, and the group persisted with inquiry while we waited for night. I told them of Prince Oslo, Queen Erika, and of course the castle, and the prince's yacht. I spent a secret and told them of Sanna, their princess-to-be, mentioning casually that she hadn't been introduced to the public yet, even in Svalbard. I didn't mention Quinby, or he would quickly have been labeled a pariah. I absorbed the attention of the group, which I could enjoy and my sister could not. It was the best I could do to help carry her burden.

Dusk finally came, and we set up the house to create the illusion that Matthias, sleeping by the window, was alone in his home. Around sunset he was instructed to climb into the positioned bed, and told that even if he could not sleep, to close his eyes regardless and appear so.

Per and Nels hid by the door to the outside, and Lavender and I in a nearby room. Several other men, three I believe, placed themselves throughout the house underneath furniture and in closets.

We waited, not even certain that anything would happen that evening, but it did. We were visited by the intruder.

When Tollund entered, he was bagged and bound before the door was hardly open. From the other room, we didn't feel the same tension or the climax, just the resolve. The men of this mission had waited an entire day or much longer, and they were not prepared to hesitate. Lavender and I rushed in from the nearby room, and Matthias's mother gathered him and took him directly home. On his way out, he exclaimed almost with romance, "The Bogeyman!"

"Tollund?" said Per once the boy was gone.

Unable to see, and after a brief struggle, Tollund gave in to his shackles and accepted them as he had for twenty seasons in the bog. "It's me," he answered.

A frequent cargo ferry runs between Emberland and Jan Mayen. It uses the small island as a crew rest station before continuing on to Svalbard. The ship supplies Jan Mayen with staples and basic necessities a small island cannot sustain, and also has limited space for passengers. Operating on a freighter's schedule, it typically left the island before dawn, which still provided sufficient time to escort our prisoner to the dock and discuss his delicate travel arrangements with the ship's crew. Our squadron left Per's home and as a unit walked with Tollund, still hooded and bound, but with freedom of stride. He was even muffed around the ears now, I believe, although I'm not sure to what effectiveness.

Lavender and I continued with the group, still feeling a sense of obligation to see Tollund off the island.

"Lavender? Marigold?" A familiar voice caused us to break off.

"Quinby?" We turned, finding him trailing our slow-moving party. I ran to embrace him, as Lavender would say, without subtlety. "Where are you off to?"

The group surrounding Tollund paid little attention aside from Per and Nels, who turned their heads and kept an eye on us. "I'm going to use some of the money you gave me to travel to Emberland," Quinby answered.

"To see your mother? Are you sure?"

"Yes! I'm quite anxious. She doesn't know I'm coming, of course. If I had written her, I would likely travel on the same ferry to Emberland as my correspondence, so there'd be no point."

"What of . . ." I attempted gracefully, wanting not to embarrass him in front of an unintroduced group escorting an unexplained captive. "Well, there were some problems."

"Yes, there will be some still. But I need to see her. I've decided to meet her!" Too excited, Quinby didn't even question our escorted captive, bound and covered in a sack. He continued: "Some say Emberland is a paradise. Queen Erika believed the most unstable are drawn there, but there's much more to Emberland than just their asylum. Perhaps I will find a better life."

I smiled, happy for him.

"I may break ahead," said Quinby. "Forgive me, but farewell!"

"We'll walk with you!" I replied. To Per, I added, "I suppose we can break off now. You don't need us to take Tollund to the boat."

"No, please stay with us," insisted Per, staring.

"Marigold, we're glowing," said Lavender calmly in Canadian.

"White?" I responded in Canadian, trying to match her calmness.

"Yes, but keep walking for now."

"No! We need to change something! At least one condition!"

"We're the only ones glowing, so it can't be Tollund and certainly not Quinby, can it?" continued Lavender in Canadian.

"Girls, I've grown tired of your rudeness," turned Per. "It's quite impolite to speak in a language we cannot all understand."

Another flicker of darkness came across the group. I immediately looked up at the moon and saw a tremendous bird circling overhead.

"I believe our group's in danger," I stated. "I suggest we find cover, or we may be attacked from above."

"Keep walking. We'll be at the dock soon." Per directed to Quinby: "Sir, you may go on ahead. Don't feel it necessary to be polite and stay behind with us."

"Sir, I will go when these girls say it's safe," responded Quinby.

Lavender spoke quickly, "Quinby, leave. You are safe and may only stay so if you flee. But this group must find another direction, or Marigold and I will soon be attacked."

"Who told you?" shouted Per, an entirely calm man until now.

"Marigold, Quinby, run!" yelled Lavender as we broke from the group while Per lunged at us. We slipped free and ran. "The boat!" yelled Lavender. "They'll never release Tollund and we may reach the ferry first!"

Quinby did, but we did not. There were enough men to restrain Tollund and still allow Per and Nels, his father, to give us chase. No one chased Quinby, and he escaped to the ferry. We ran toward the boat, but Per matched our speed. He soon blocked our path, forcing us toward the shoreline.

When we reached the coast, still south of the ship and of the docks, we stirred up a commotion with newly awakened gulls, now screeching and swarming, with Per and Nels shortly behind.

"Please don't kill us," I yelled, only able to see the next moment or so of our lives. By Lavender's head turning left and right, I knew we were still glowing white.

"We're not going to kill you," said a nearby voice as I was tackled from behind.

We were captured.

Per had me restrained, and Nels soon cornered and grabbed Lavender. Tollund and his remaining escorts were out of range to the south, and Quinby separated to the north. "Don't kill us," pleaded Lavender.

"We are not going to kill you," said Per. "But we must turn you over to a judge."

"You released Tollund, he violated Matthias, and if we don't turn you over, we become accomplices," explained Nels, apparently the authority of shackles and the Jan Mayen justice system as well.

"Then they will kill us!" begged Lavender. "Please!"

Another flicker of darkness followed her plea, a longer, more pronounced eclipse. I looked up. "Lavender, I don't believe it will be their justice system that kills us!"

A large bird circled overhead, much lower than before, while the stirred-up gulls still swarmed harmlessly and were becoming less vocal.

"We're no longer glowing," said Lavender, which I did not understand, nor did I have time to contemplate, as the end of her words were met with another longer and disorienting shadow, then a swooping impact.

Lavender and I, and our temporary restrainers, Nels and Per, were scattered along the shoreline. "My name is Horace," came a voice. "Who has attacked these gulls?"

He stood five full times my own height or Lavender's, or at least fourfold taller than Nels or Per. He had knocked all of us to the sand in a swift swoop. I looked at him as best I could, at first believing him to be a tremendous man with wings. He was the size of a pine tree, but eventually I saw him as a colossal bird of prey yet with the arm and leg shapes of a human. He was armored and equipped for battle, standing upright and walking toward us on talons which were large enough to clutch several humans, or quickly shred them.

He wore porous armor over his breast much like what I recognized from Lichen's clearing, and drew an also familiar serrated sword, which he handled like a feather.

"Lavender, are we all right?" I asked.

"Who attacked these gulls?" he demanded. His speaking voice was that of a human's, and certainly male. His plumage was brown with some white, his body a weapon and an impressive specimen. He spread his wings for intimidation and display, blocking a notable portion of my panoramic view from a short distance where he stood. In the moonlight and its reflection from the nearby water, he seemed to be feathered throughout yet scaled on his breast, legs, and sides. I had never seen a true flying creature, or any creature, which grew both feathers and scales in his proportions. It's also worth recording that this creature did not resemble, even in the slightest, the species of Anders and Ylwa, whom we had encountered near arriving in Svalbard.

"No one attacked the gulls," explained Per, getting to his feet.

"We disturbed their sleep," explained Lavender. "We're sorry."

Suddenly the four of us were united again, not against Tollund, and not against one another, but in fear of this infuriated guardian who had prostrated us on the sand.

"Is this day three yet?" I asked Lavender.

Addressing the bird creature, she stated, "Horace, these men want to kill us."

"That's not a matter I'm charged to serve," he responded, followed by a shriek no human could possibly produce, again for display, used to reestablish his direction of the discussion. "None of these birds are harmed?"

"Sir, please," I added, "if you don't help us, we will die." Nels and Per were quiet, not defending themselves. "And none of these birds were harmed."

"If I save you, you will be in my debt," said the bird creature, glancing at our attackers.

"We'll find a way to repay you! We'll do anything, please!" I begged.

"Stand by each other, side to side, and bend at the waist," said the giant.

Per and Nels began to run as Horace sprinted along the sand in a different direction, to gain momentum before taking to the air. I can only imagine what Quinby's view of this would have been if he stopped and watched from up the shore, near the dock. For Lavender and me, the view was of the sand and our feet. Horace gained some altitude, circled once overhead, and swooped again as we braced ourselves for uncertainty.

"We're not glowing," said Lavender as we waited. "Whatever is about to happen to us equates to survival."

Horace snatched us from the ground, one in each of his large talons. He did so swiftly and with grace, and with surprisingly little impact we were airborne with only the wind punishing us and not the backward concept of justice held by a remote, self-enforcing people. Beneath the moonlight we watched Jan Mayen from above as we climbed into the sky. The already small island now appeared smaller and smaller until it vanished beneath the horizon.

10 / The Feathermen

Part One—Horace

A Canadian girl who calls herself Marigold requested I record the events, from my perspective, regarding my encounter with her and her sister, Lavender. A bold request, as from the moment we met they were indebted to me.

It was an arduous return flight home from Jan Mayen Island to Thule. Not because of weather or challenging flight conditions. No, I would have preferred poor visibility or even a turbulent thunderstorm in place of the carriage of these two girls. And it wasn't their weight. When serving a transport mission, I'm loaded with several times these girls' load.

No. It was Marigold.

Climbing quickly through an altitude of fifty perch, the wingless novices spoke and interrupted my navigation. "Thank you, sir. Thank you for saving us." Of course they shouted over the drag of the airflow, each clutching her respective talon tightly. This was completely unnecessary.

"Don't shout," I responded. "I can hear you quite well. And don't clutch my talon so hard. You're safe in my grip. My claws' joints are locked and, if you haven't noticed, forming a harness."

Humans are quite small in comparison to us Feathermen. A coarse guess might be one quarter to one fifth our height, yet they're denser and don't produce lift. The girls were small enough that I could carry one in each grasp. They seemed confident they were not in danger, which was more than I would have expected from another human traveling so precariously exposed to the dark sky over open water. Tucked behind my armor toward my tail feathers as I flapped my wings to climb, they felt it necessary to speak as loudly as required to hear their own voices, so they continued to shout. I thought I had been clear that this irritated me.

Lavender, the girl secured in my left talon, said, "We cannot return to the island. Can you bring us to Svalbard?"

The girl in my right talon protested, squirming, and sticking her arm out into the airflow. The drag caught her, causing a snag and moment of force around my center of gravity. Being so far aft, her leverage was strong, therefore I uncontrollably dove to the right.

I returned level, and once satisfied with my attitude, resumed a climb. "Please. Don't squirm." I sighed.

Marigold apologized and said, "I was going to request we travel to Emberland, not Svalbard."

"Oh, whatever for?" asked Lavender, mocking her sister.

This I did not follow, nor did I care. I nearly laughed. "What makes you believe I'm not destination-bound myself? You're in my debt now, which is a fortune I plan to retrieve. If I were to transport you to wherever you wished, you would be bound over again. We would say good-bye and I would never be repaid for my favors."

"How do you plan . . . how do you expect . . .?" started Lavender.

"I don't know yet. We'll see when we get to Windfall."

"Where?" asked Marigold.

"Windfall. The mountain home of the Feathermen. West. Not far. We may seem to travel more upward than forward, but that won't be the case. We will land at an airfield there."

"I haven't heard of Windfall," said Lavender.

"I haven't either," responded her sister.

"Have you heard of us? Of the Feathermen?"

Lavender answered: "One. But indirectly. A . . . a friend found his fallen body. Literally, the Featherman fell from the sky during a storm. We recognize your porous armor and serrated sword."

"Yes, well, if you could fly, your equipment would be weight efficient as well."

"If I could fly, I would fly to Emberland," whined Marigold.

"Marigold, if we follow your hormones and travel to Emberland, what am I to do?" asked Lavender.

"My ears hurt terribly!" fussed Marigold as we passed through an altitude of one hundred perch, ignoring her sister.

"That's because of the air pressure. Your passages are filled with denser, sea-level air compared to the less dense atmospheric pressure surrounding—"

"Well don't make my ears hurt more," said Marigold, interrupting me for the first of many times to come.

"Fascinating!" Lavender perked up. "I would like to hear more."

"Of course. Air flows from high pressure to low. In fact, that's how we are flying."

"Horace, I can't stand this feeling," whined Marigold.

"Try to equalize the pressure in your ears."

"I can't."

"Stretch your jaw. The tubes in your ears are trying to expand."

Lavender asked, "Sir Horace, do the Feathermen know much about science?"

"Yes, we do. We must, to fly. Weather, math, physics, all of it."

"Physiology?"

"Yes."

She tried to whisper, but I heard her. "Marigold, they may be able to tell me more than any human can about my gift, and where it comes from."

"Your gift?" I asked.

"Oh no, it's not—" She humbly retreated.

"She has a gift," confirmed Marigold.

"No, I don't," lied Lavender.

"She has the ability to see life and death," said the talkative one. "On the beach at Jan Mayen when she pleaded that if you would not rescue us, we would die . . . that was a certainty, not an exaggeration."

"Yes, but I had hoped to shelve it for a while," explained Lavender, "so please, if you would not speak of this?"

I didn't reply, nor did I make any promise. They had yet to repay my favor, and this gift could possibly be quite useful, although I did not yet know how. Marigold answered, "What? Why? Not use your gift? Walk about with your eyes shut?"

"Yes, not use my gift, by not acting upon it," answered Lavender, while I focused on reading the stars and catching a tailwind over open water at four hundred perch. "I'm not certain, but I would like to entertain the possibility that it may be a dark gift, and that it should be ignored. When I use my gift, bad things happen. Our exile, freeing Tollund from the bog . . ."

"Working toward our field guide, sorting out the folks from the Living Cave, saving the Queen of Svalbard, saving Quinby!" In a panicked sarcasm Marigold added, "Fantastic! So, if we're camping in the bush and a volcano's about to blow, you'll see the white glow on your sister, shrug your shoulders, and tell me nothing?"

"Marigold, please, I don't know . . . I only wish to try . . ."

"Because you'll be worried something horrible will happen if you do speak? This would disrupt everything," Marigold murmured, then shouted, "Everything!"

"Stop bickering. I'm trying to navigate back to Thule."

"Thule?" both girls reacted, displeased and in unison.

"Yes, Windfall is a city on the island continent of Thule. Is that not acceptable?"

"Splendid," grumbled Marigold. "The moment my sister decides to terminate use of her gift is the very same moment that I'm also carried, essentially as a prisoner, to a land where the plague mars my unchosen destination."

"Why, where did you want to go?" teased Lavender.

"Lavender, please!" snapped Marigold.

"Plague? I know of no plague anywhere on the island of Thule."

Lavender explained: "Canadians are taught to believe there is a plague infecting all of Thule. I wonder if there's more to this, or if it's true."

"I don't believe so. On occasion, a covert Siberian ship will dock and return home with some captured slaves. From one of the two tribes—Trogs or Petras—the Siberians don't care," I said.

Marigold mocked: "On occasion a Featherman will land and return home with some captured slaves. One of the two girls . . . Lavender or Marigold, the Feathermen don't care."

"Marigold, is this how a Canadian behaves toward the one she is indebted to?" I asked, long drained of my patience and now with my exposed nerves being plucked like a stringed instrument.

"Marigold, really!" corrected the more mature younger sister. "This is tremendously privileged information we are hearing, and it's revealing another of Polaris's lies! Don't interrupt!"

I continued: "The ships leave silently so as not to trigger military action from Canada or Svalbard, and sail back with their captured servants. We don't interfere. The only reason I was patrolling Jan Mayen Island was to protect the gulls. A man lived there seasons ago, a gull catcher. When his son emerged from the bog, we returned to protect the gulls. You caught my attention when you stirred up a flock on the shore. Feathermen are committed to the protection of all other birds, in what we call a cohesion. We are the most advanced of all birds and have committed ourselves to their guardianship. But unlike birds, humans are not in our cohesion. Neither are the . . . whatever classification defines the Trogs or the Petras. Humanlike? Humanoid? Regardless, neither of these two tribes, nor even the Siberians, interfere with Featherman society. So we don't interfere with theirs, whether we agree with their actions or not. We wouldn't dare go into the debt of a human."

"Tell me more about the Trogs and the Petras," said Lavender.

"We don't know much. We live in the cliffs above, along a section on the eastern side of Thule we call the Palisades. They use caves and carved-out passageways through the same mountains for their troglodytic life. We live above; they live below. We believe they have an extensive system of caverns and tunnels, but we cannot be sure. Aerial surveillance would not reveal that, and neither tribe hardly wanders into the open. Although we share an island, we live worlds apart and know very little about each other."

"So then there may still be a plague?" asked a slightly calmer Marigold.

"Not logically. Why would the Siberians risk enslaving the afflicted, and returning to their home to spread the disease?"

"It's another political lie by Polaris," concluded Lavender.

"Who is Polaris?" I asked.

She sighed and answered, "The ancient and often awful autonomous leader of Canada. He uses many lies to control his people, and they seem to prefer it. It's only an assumption, but if Canadians believe there is a plague in Thule, they won't wander far. It creates a divide between Canada and

Siberia. A buffer. But as long as Canadians live in fear, Polaris can control them. I'm sure he knows about the Siberian slave boats."

"I'm cold . . . very cold," Marigold grumbled.

"So am I," Lavender responded.

"Yes, but you have your thick black robe. I'm dressed more stylishly, so I'm colder. Not that you'd tell me if I were freezing to death."

"Marigold, please. It's just the wind up here."

"It's not only the wind," I explained. "The air gets colder at higher altitudes. It's called lapse rate."

"More technical spittle," grumbled Marigold. "Horace, if it's so cold up here, and since my ears still hurt, can we go back down to sea level?"

"There's nowhere to land, and I've found a good tailwind."

"But that wind's making me cold."

"You don't feel a tailwind."

"Then why is it so windy?"

"It's the induced airflow. Now please be quiet. Dawn is coming, and I'm trying to read the stars one last time so we don't get lost."

"I want to go back to sea level. Why is it so bumpy? Can't you fly any smoother than this?"

My patience had vanished. I briefly rocked a wing to gain their attention and began a steep but wings-level descent. Then I tucked my wings for a very steep descent and spiraled a few times for fun. The girls began to scream, as I had planned.

"Climb up!" yelled Lavender.

"Your sister said she wanted to go back to sea level."

"We'll hit the water soon!" said Lavender as Marigold shrieked.

I was fully aware of this. She was right, and so I pitched up hard. Very hard. With all of my excess airspeed from the dive I was able to briefly aim at a star at least thirty degrees above the horizon. And suddenly, silence. The aggressive climb caused the girls to black out, as blood fails to flow and the body slips into unconsciousness. It was harmless, and in little time they woke up and Marigold was complaining again. But for a brief moment I enjoyed some peace.

We continued to cruise back to Windfall at four hundred perch above sea level. The sun was rising behind us and shining on the Palisades, which appeared on the western horizon.

As we flew over the city of Windfall, high in the mountains, even Marigold had kind words to share of what she called her 'most recent prison.' The girls both appreciated the jagged cliffs, the agricultural terraces cleaved into mountain slopes, and our windmill farms. They found it more endearing than resourceful when I mentioned that we use our longest pinions from the trailing edges of our own wings to provide the surfaces of the windmills' sails. They enjoyed the clusters of nests and thatched buildings, and laughed pleasingly from a distance above in the early sunlight, watching other Feathermen strolling about town. Rather than regurgitating the comment that all primary flight students first recite, that is, "From here everyone looks like tiny insects," I remember Lavender instead commented, "You are majestic creatures . . . all different, pleasant shades of white and brown. Like trees." But what really struck them were the calm, white cloud beds whose tops were, at the time, at about three hundred fifty perch and therefore beneath the mountain town's four-hundred-perch elevation, and below our soaring altitude of four hundred fifty.

Contrary to what humans may think, the Feathermen do require a proper distance of smooth terrain to achieve flight, more at higher altitudes due to the decrease in air density. The distance isn't notably hindering, but we do have an airfield at Windfall, and any who believe a Featherman can rotate from a standstill is mistaken.

I circled the field at four hundred fifty perch above sea level, fifty above the field, scanning for other Feathermen below. Observing and hearing no traffic, I descended for the airstrip. I didn't land with my first pass, rather I released the girls into the field's cargo-receiving net. They likely grimaced and complained about their tumble into the ropes, but there was no way I would be able to land safely without freeing my talons. I had warned them of what would happen, and if they complained, I could neither hear them nor feign sympathy. I was already beating the air with my wings, climbing up once more for a second approach, this one to a full stop, finally unlocking and stretching the joints of my claws for landing.

We walked from the strip to my nearby aerie, though we didn't stay long. I had planned to at first, in hopes of sleep, even as dawn had already broken.

"Is this where you live?" asked Lavender.

"Yes, this is my home."

"You don't have a roof?" asked Marigold. "This is little more than a nest on a flat cliffside patch. From above, do you ever confuse your home with, possibly, nothing?"

"No. And why would I require a roof?"

"May we at least build a fire?" asked Lavender.

"We're too close to the airfield. It's prohibited. The smoke could obscure another Featherman's vision on landing."

"Yes, but you live here," said Marigold, shivering. "Do you mean to say that you never build a fire?"

"Why would I require a fire?"

"Because it's freezing cold this high in the mountains!"

"Ah, don't worry," I said. "A warm front approaches."

The girls seemed relieved, but both were now shivering.

I added: "Yes, did you see the system on the horizon?" They confirmed that they had not. I continued: "It's good we landed when we did. It would have been quite hazardous to be caught in that front."

Amazed and curious, Lavender asked, "So what might have happened if we could not have landed here?"

"It depends on how extensive the frontal system is, but we would have likely diverted."

"A diversion sounds pleasant. Where to?" asked Marigold.

"Oh, south probably," I teased. "Maybe to Emberland."

Marigold shook her head and growled briefly, but Lavender said, "Marigold, collect yourself. Warm air is on the horizon."

"Would you like something to eat?" I offered, looking for my bag. "Humans eat seeds, don't they?"

Lavender asked, "The Featherman race strikes me as large birds of prey that have developed arms and legs proportionately like ours, scales in vulnerable areas which I suppose provide thicker protection, and modifications to allow you to speak and stand upright, among much less modest advances."

"Thank you."

"But if you are birds of prey, don't you eat other birds? Or at least other creatures' flesh, and not seed?"

"Physically we can still digest other birds, it is believed. But because we were graced with significant evolution, we have chosen not to. This is the cohesion I mentioned, our race's commitment to protect all other bird creatures. It's illegal to consume another bird. This is by our laws, though we attempt to enforce it on all creatures. It's the one cause worthy of interfering with other cultures, as we feel it's a response to their interference with ours."

Marigold mocked: "Yes, all right, so then if I took a loaf of bread to the pond?"

"We could eat either the loaf or you," I responded, getting a laugh from Lavender, who was tired of her sister's devices.

Marigold persisted. "And then you would return to your flock, circling the compost heaps?"

"We eat mostly fish and seed," I explained. "Fish is better, but seed keeps."

"The King of Svalbard brags of his country's seeds, but himself eats nothing but fowl," said Lavender.

"Noted."

"Forget Svalbard. Take us to Emberland," demanded Marigold.

"No."

"Take us to Emberland, or I will tell every human I know to eat more bird."

"No, Marigold," I repeated. "And stop being manipulative."

"I will stop being manipulative . . . if you take us to Emberland."

"Marigold, stop it," reprimanded her sister. "What of eggs?"

"The eggs of a bird? Certainly not. That's considered an even higher offense than consuming an adult bird. It's often impossible to be absolutely certain when separating the fertilized from the unfertilized eggs."

"So then baked goods are forbidden?" asked Lavender. "You cannot cook them with fish eggs, can you?"

"If you could prepare and consume something quite delicious but composed of human babies, would it not be vulgar and cannibalistic?" I asked.

"I see," said Lavender.

Marigold noted: "It's times like these you realize just how harsh the outside world can be."

"Yes. Wait, what? Do you mean a world without baked goods, or a world where fragile eggs are destroyed for unnecessary consumption? Because the world without baked goods is certainly not the harsher world."

Marigold, silent, looked at me in disbelief.

"Marigold, you disagree with your silence?" I asked.

"You've obviously never had soufflé."

"Marigold, are you trying to get us killed or imprisoned? Enough! Let's try not to get exiled just this once!" said Lavender. Turning to me she pleaded: "I assure you; we have ways of preventing fertilized eggs from entering into our diet."

"I'm still a predator," I admitted. "I understand what is fair. And so, Marigold should hope that I am never hungry in her presence while without another available meat source."

"Sir Horace, when will you release us?" asked the irritating one.

"As I have said, when you have repaid your favor to me."

"I do not want to be here," she whined.

"Why?" asked Lavender. "Is this so different than Kildebyen or Jan Mayen? Unlike Jan Mayen, at least in Windfall no one attempts to kill us, despite your efforts."

"It is terribly different," Marigold pleaded. "But we could be home in Canada for all it matters. If you refuse to employ your gift, I have no safety or security. I'm not accustomed to this. How can I focus on social concerns when my priorities are reduced to breathing, sleeping, and eating? Horace, please forgive my behavior. I am truly lost at the moment."

"Forgiven. At no additional debt. Perhaps some seed and water will help you find comfort."

"So that's your struggle," concluded Lavender as I fetched the jug and seed bag.

"Thank you. Horace, what are these dark, round seeds?" asked Marigold, holding one up to her eye.

"Those? They are actually small nuts, not seeds."

Marigold hesitated. "I'm afraid to try them because they look like little warts. Are they any good?"

"They grow on you," I answered.

Marigold looked at me and smiled.

"I can make jokes too." I smiled back.

"A crinkile jug?" Lavender noted of the water container, politely waiting her turn to speak. "Our family has one. Quite rare."

"Yes, I forget where I found it. On surveillance somewhere, most likely. They're wonderful because they don't rust or shatter, and you don't lose water to evaporation if you can seal it somehow."

"I hear they never fall apart," said Lavender, "or decompose."

"Well, drink to your desire," I said, handing them the jug. "The collection sites will be filled after this frontal system passes. It'll begin to rain soon."

"What?" asked an exhausted Marigold.

"Yes, so drink as much water as you like with your seed. I understand the seed can be dry."

"It will rain?" asked Lavender.

"Of course. What did you believe would happen when I told you of the incoming warm front?"

"Rainbows and sunshine?" said Marigold.

"Yes, but you cannot have a rainbow without moisture," I orated. "It's a result of the refraction—"

"Horace?" she interrupted. "Do you have a clean rag? I'm afraid I'm a bit of a slovenly eater."

"Certainly." I turned and stepped several paces away to rummage through my belongings.

Marigold then whispered to Lavender, I believe too quietly for me to have heard from where I then stood had I been human. Still, as a Featherman I could hear her words clearly. "If you won't exploit your gift, I will!"

Immediately before Lavender's reaction, Marigold continued at normal volume. "Sir Horace, my sister has just informed me that we are to die."

"What? No!" protested Lavender.

"Yes, if we stay here, we will become hypothermic and die. Because of the impending rain. And it will never be possible for us to repay you."

"Marigold, please!" protested her sister.

I played into the desperate deception, wanting just as much to be rid of the girls for a while as Marigold wished to be.

"All right, we shall walk to my sisters'. They have a den, not an aerie. You'll have shelter."

We left my apparently inadequate home behind and set out not by air but along the footpaths through the mountains toward the house of Harriet and Bernadette, my older sisters.

Along our walk I warned: "It won't be brief; they do not live near the airfield."

"We have no choice!" insisted Marigold, optimistically believing she had deceived me. "It's either this or death—" she said, interrupting herself. "So if they don't live near the airfield, we may start a fire?"

"They've always got a log burning. Strong nesting tendencies, those two . . . they do nothing but roost. I wonder if they're even still slender enough for flight . . . but I suppose that's their business. I'm confident you'll be comfortable in their den."

"Do they roost a clutch?" asked Lavender. "Because I would be curious . . ."

"No, not currently. Just the floor beneath them."

"This is our future, Lavender. Living with each other, both overfed, alone, and eggless."

"Yes. You want to go to Emberland to find Quinby," recited Lavender artificially. "You've made your protests perfectly clear."

———————

When we arrived, they did indeed have a log on and a warm den.

"Hello, sisters! I have two most unusual guests."

"Trogs?" asked Harriet. "No, you're not Trogs. Or Petras."

Marigold answered: "I'm human, and this thing is my sister, Lavender."

"Humans! Welcome!" responded Harriet, correcting herself.

She and Bernadette were both in what I affectionately call the mother hen position, with all limbs tucked beneath their wings or body, resting on throw rugs in their warm, sheltered den.

"What brings you to our mountain town?" asked Bernadette.

"We were in danger but were rescued by Sir Horace," said Lavender.

"His bachelor accommodations were unsuitable for us," cited Marigold, straightforward and still bitter.

"My name is Lavender, and this is my recently difficult sister, Marigold."

"You're welcome to stay with us for as long as you wish," said Harriet.

Marigold hurried to the fireplace, and I had an idea. "Harriet? Bernadette? I have an awkward request if you would?"

"Go ahead," they answered.

"Our human guests are not accustomed to this altitude or temperature. They've been shivering violently, and I am morbidly concerned their hypothermia will advance to more dangerous stages." Having the attention of all four I continued, "Would you be comfortable incubating them? Particularly Marigold, who mentioned repeatedly that she was quite cold. They're small enough to tuck beneath you comfortably. You could roost atop them. It may save their lives."

"Is um—" Harriet, the older stuttered. "Of course."

"Yes, whatever's necessary," followed Bernadette.

"Wait, the fire should—" started Marigold.

"No, no, I insist!" I said, careful not to reveal Lavender's gift to my sisters. "Marigold, it could save your lives, which was the concern that brought us here, was it not?"

"Yes, but—" she said, while Lavender was silent.

"Well then, Harriet and Bernadette, thank you. And be sure that Marigold receives the warmth she needs. I will be back after some sleep."

"Oh, I had forgotten," said Bernadette. "They've got you on night patrol, haven't they?"

"Yes. I need sleep. And so do the girls," I said quickly to avoid interruption, adding while exiting, "Oh yes, and if Marigold's condition worsens you will need to strip her clothes and incubate directly to her skin. If her shivering ceases, she has either recovered or advanced to a deadlier stage. Feel free to treat her conservatively, to be safe of course."

"Horace?" was the last word I heard, and from Marigold, as I closed the door behind me and finally, finally was alone again and returning to my aerie.

This was not to last. I returned home to a note—an ominous note, in fact—
left by an old friend of mine named Baker. He must have stopped by my
aerie while I was out. It read:

Dear Horace,

*I haven't heard from you in a while. I hope this finds you healthy
and happy.*

*Things aren't going well for me. I've been researching my anti-
icing fluid and feel as though the formula is worthy, but since my
accident no one will agree to its flight testing.*

*I'm starting to lose sensation in the tip of my damaged wing, and
although I believe the bones are otherwise healed, I also fear a loss of
circulation in this wing. Tendon and nerve damage will render me
soon unable to fly. And barring a last-minute miracle, I may lose the
wing to amputation as well.*

*I wanted to see my research to its completion and realize now
that this culmination will be in a matter of hours. Success or failure,
beyond that I have no plan, and no hope.*

*I believe almost all of the aerodynamic theory, but I've never
been convinced that a Featherman cannot fly into icing conditions.
Either my fluid will work, or it will not.*

*So, I'm writing those I care for to say thank you for your
friendship and love. You've been in my thoughts since the beginning,
and I know the best for you is still to come.*

*But I also know that all experiments begin with excitement, are
then filled with toil and labor, and in the end will be remembered as
either a success or a failure.*

Remember me in your thoughts,
Baker

He wants to kill himself? I thought. I reread his words several times quickly and learned that a suicide note does not contain the words *suicide note* at the top, though the message is there. Meanwhile the warm front had arrived. The rain continued to fall as I studied the tip of one wing. Water was falling as a liquid, but as it struck a surface, even my warm wings, ice was forming. It was freezing rain.

This was possibly the most hazardous weather to a Featherman in flight, aside from a tornado or any phenomenon that is catastrophic even to those on the surface. It occurs when warmer temperatures persist above, as when a warm front slides up and over cooler air, and rain falls as liquid. When the rain falls into freezing temperatures, it becomes supercooled and freezes on contact. If it covers our wings, they lose their aerodynamics and a Featherman could fall out of the sky. And Baker had launched into this weather intentionally. Baker wished to test a fluid that could prevent the ice from forming, making flight into freezing rain possible. It had never been done.

Regardless of the danger he faced, I couldn't follow and launch into freezing rain simply to rescue him. This would be just as suicidal. But something had to be done, so I rushed back to my sisters' den to beg the gifted girl to help.

I threw open the door without a knock, startling the Canadian girls and my sisters. Had I not been so hastened and occupied with Baker's uncertainty, I would have greatly appreciated what happened next . . . though you may read this in disbelief.

It seems Lavender and Marigold, both fully clothed, were indeed resting beneath my sisters and allowing themselves to be incubated. Lavender must have been head forward under Bernadette, and Marigold was feet forward beneath Harriet. I believe all were asleep, but when I startled the room, all four jumped. Instantly Lavender was standing. Bernadette was flapping and tossing feathers about, as was Harriet, yet all that was visible of Marigold was her body.

"I'm going to die!" screamed Marigold, muffled. "I'll suffocate in here! Help! I'm going to die!"

After a second or so, Lavender and Bernadette were calm and upright, but when Harriet continued flapping and hopping, we realized that Marigold's head had become stuck in Harriet's rear—her *cloaca*, to use the technical term—all as a result of waking abruptly.

"Harriet, you've got human legs!" Bernadette laughed.

Harriet continued to jump and stir, unable to stand but fluttering enough almost to seem to levitate. She flapped her wings, flinging out feathers and down, perhaps even shedding a few scales as a result of the stress.

Marigold twisted and twirled, rotating her head inside of poor Harriet's cloaca. Because she twirled half-independently beneath Harriet's levitating body, her skirt fanned out in a conical shape, whirling around with Harriet throughout the room for a brief, unbelievable moment until I contained my laughter and was able to secure the human girl.

While I held Marigold as she panicked, Harriet was able to breathe deeply on her side. I found the opportunity to ask if my sister was prepared for an uncomfortable tug. On a simultaneous count, I pulled while Harriet pushed.

Once Marigold had been expelled and the danger had been avoided, it was safe to laugh. She saw her sister's face; Lavender was breathless. Her eyes shed tears of compulsive laughter as Marigold inhaled, collected herself, and wiped her face, scalp, and neck with several of my sisters' rags.

"Lavender, be careful," I said as Bernadette tended to Harriet, who seemed uninjured. "You shouldn't laugh quite so breathlessly."

"Yes, Lavender," added Marigold, wiping her chin. "I could have died. And it's not as though you would have told me."

I objected: "But Marigold, you didn't. In fact, it may be the funniest moment of my lifetime. Lavender, I meant that if you lose your breath, you may never catch it."

By then she was kneeling, still laughing, mocking: "Help me! Help me! I'm going to die! I'm going to suffocate!"

"Lavender, breathe. You're starting to hyperventilate. It's not safe at this altitude," I advised, but she continued to laugh uncontrollably. Unable to calm Lavender, I asked, "Marigold, would you please slap your sister? Hard."

"With enthusiasm," obliged Marigold, still far from clean.

Crippled with laughter and kneeling, Lavender received her sister's harsh open palm across the face, which smacked away the humor. Lavender put her hand to her cheek and shouted, "Marigold, stop!" But soon the girl began heaving for air.

"Lavender, take deep, slow breaths." She looked at me from her kneeling position, still heaving but following my command. "Good, deep and slow. I'll need you lucid and somber."

"Yes. Although that would have made quite the epitaph."

"Marigold, please!" I insisted. "No jokes!"

"Or what?" she asked. "You'll ask me to slap her again?"

"Good, Lavender," I said as she recovered. "We'll need you alive."

"For what?" she said, exhaling.

———

I thanked my sisters, not immediately answering Lavender's question so as not to reveal her secret gift to Harriet or Bernadette. As we walked, I explained: "We must return to the airfield. I have a friend caught in this weather."

"This doesn't seem safe to fly in," said Lavender, noticing the freezing rain.

"It's very dangerous. And I may need you to steer him from death."

"Wait—" she stopped. "No. I'm sorry; if you're asking me to use my gift, I will not."

I continued to walk, insisting, "Fine then. I was not asking. You are in my debt and this is how you will repay me."

She resumed following me. It was important to hurry, but not possible to run in the deteriorating conditions. We walked along the roads, purposefully at best, and could not have sprinted even in fairer skies. The girls' bodies would not allow it, again because of the altitude.

Lavender recited stubbornly: "You cannot make me speak!"

"And I cannot make Marigold quiet. But you—"

"Be fair!" Marigold injected. "I haven't spoken a word since—"

"Since you just interrupted. Now you're getting caught in my gizzard, like a fishbone? In fact, I think I'll call you that."

"You're going to address me as 'Gizzard?'"

"No, 'Fishbone!' A fishbone gets embedded in your throat and is unwanted and irritating."

"No, that won't do," she responded. "I prefer 'Gizzard.'"

"I'm sorry, Fishbone, but that isn't your decision. The one rule of nicknames is that you don't get to pick your own."

"All right, then," she started calmly, but as she continued, her voice rose to an angry crescendo, "I have a pet name for you, and you're also not permitted to appeal. If you're wondering what it is, here's your clue: I had my head caught in one recently!"

"Marigold, please!" reprimanded her sister, nearly matching Marigold's volume.

"Fishbone, please," I corrected.

Lavender ignored me. "Marigold, where has your mind gone? Who are you today? If you could see yourself, even in a pure silver mirror, you wouldn't recognize your own face."

Marigold was as embarrassed as she was indignant.

I said to Lavender, "Yes, but remember . . . however she acts and however it exhausts me, you are both bound to me, and therefore I'm bound to Marigold until either you or she repays my favor. You did not request your gift any more than I requested the gift of flight, but when you requested my services on Jan Mayen, I obliged. This is no different."

"Please, Lavender!" begged Marigold, still upset but now claiming a drop of humility. "Repay our debt to Horace so that we can be free, and I will be forever in your debt!"

"Tell me more about what's happening," she said calmly. "Who's in danger, and how?"

I sighed. "A friend, I believe suicidal, who hasn't flown since a terrible crash fifty or so days ago. His name is Baker."

"How did the crash occur?" asked Marigold in a labored, deliberate calm.

"He was testing an anti-icing fluid. It would be an incredible break-through for us, as currently none exist. We have methods of de-icing, but that only removes the contamination and is used mostly for groundwork. Anti-icing is a theoretical fluid, something you could dip your body into and soak up with your feathers so as to resist the buildup of ice contamination for a certain length of time. It worked in his laboratory, but not during the in-flight test. If you could call it that . . . He never became airborne . . . There was only the one test, which he conducted on himself, I should mention. Until then he was an accomplished Featherman with a history of safe flight. But the fluid has a filmy texture. It must, to coat a wing. This affected the flow of the air, a factor he neglected, and he never rotated out of ground effect . . . I'm sorry, in height, the first wingspan from the surface. He failed to lift off and crashed into some terrain at the end of the airfield. After his crash, he was different."

As we continued our brisk walk to the airfield, Lavender asked: "How was he different?"

"There was the injury to his wing, but the changes were more mental than physical. In fairness, we Feathermen are quite competitive. Some say that if you don't believe you're the greatest in existence, you shouldn't fly. But almost all believe they are the greatest in existence, if not a sky god.

He developed an immediate inferiority complex, knowing now that he was blemished with an accident in his history. In truth, nobody judged him. Or thought any less of him, really."

"So, an ego dilemma?" asked Marigold.

"Not specifically . . . how should I say this? He became a bit self-righteous to compensate, always talking about safety-this and safety-that. Every divot he could find in the airfield, he'd make a small crusade out of it."

Marigold understood. "If you feel inferior but cannot escape yourself, escape your standards. Shift to another set."

"Exactly! Yes, you're inferior. You understand."

She sighed. "Was that necessary?"

"I'd imagine it's a way of substituting acceptance with affirmation, or of purging the error if there was one. And particularly if someone is prone to brood, they can become obsessive."

"I can see where this is going," said Lavender.

"He's not himself anymore. He's my friend, so this has not been a pleasant change. And now he's airborne, desperately and suicidally testing his fluid again . . . on a minimally healed wing, only because the weather is as his experiment demands."

When we reached the airfield, several others waited beside the edge of the landing area, near or beneath the cargo receiving net. The net is large even compared to a Featherman, and on sturdy but portable pylons. The entire structure is both tall and wide enough for at least twenty Feathermen to stand beneath. My arrival made eight Feathermen, all friends of mine and Baker's.

They had likely found the same note, or there would have been no other reason to come to the airfield, considering the weather.

"Horace!" one of them hollered. "Who are they?"

"Humans," I responded as we approached the concerned group.

"So we can see!" another responded.

"Canadians," I added, pointing. "Lavender and Marigold. I'll explain later. You're here because of Baker, correct?"

I had reached them, now all standing beneath the large net, though with little protection from the cold rain, which came through the holes between the ropes. "Yes," one of them answered somberly. "Did you receive the same note?"

"I did. By my read it was a suicide note. Would you agree?"

"We believe so," said another fellow Featherman. "He mentioned the testing of his fluid, but that only seems to tie in to his hopelessness."

"What have you been discussing?" I asked. "What have you concluded?"

Lavender came forward to listen. I fanned my wings out to shield her and Marigold from the rain. A fellow Featherman spoke. "The cloud bases are at the most thirty perch above the field, and the conditions are freezing drizzle, possibly freezing rain. No Featherman should fly in these conditions, and we would physically restrain any who attempt to take off after Baker, even with the intention of rescuing him."

"I agree. I won't take to the air; don't worry. I've committed myself to this."

"Good," the group's spokesman continued, "because there's no need for multiple fatalities today. Beyond that, there's little we believe we can do, other than keep our sights on the approach ends of the field and help Baker if he returns."

"Do you believe he wants to return?" I asked. "Or that he intends to die?"

"He wrote the letters," a Featherman responded. "We believe he wants to return, but doesn't know how."

"I may know if he will live or die, but not until I see him," announced Lavender.

"Oh, thank you, sister . . . thank you so much." Marigold exhaled.

"But I couldn't see this continent until after Horace saw it," said the gifted girl. "In flight that is, and the same was true of this weather. I may see stranger things than others can, but a Featherman's vision is exponentially more acute than my human range."

"Wait a moment, Lavender," started another Featherman. "What strange things?"

"I will know—" She sighed. "I will see if he is to live or die. We may not have time to explain this further, not that I know much more about the gift myself."

"No, you won't have much time," I confirmed. "Once the ice contaminates his wings, and it'll be quick, Baker will come down and smash into the ground like a large melon."

"And what could a half-bird, half-melon do to save itself?" asked Marigold.

"Descend, glide . . . with enough altitude," another friend answered. "An aerodynamic stall is the concern: detachment and loss of airflow and therefore loss of lift."

"Is it absurd to catch a melon in a large cargo net?" asked Lavender.

"We do it all the time. It would be safer than if he crashed into the airstrip," I added.

"Let's move the net," said a member of the group.

The Feathermen shuffled the square net assembly to the center of the airstrip, two Feathermen per pylon.

Marigold asked: "How is he going to see the airfield? The clouds are so low. We may need to call for him." Immediately without further command, we scattered independently into the flat turf of the field, screeching and squawking to our fullest. But in only seconds Marigold chased us and reprimanded, "No, no, no!" She was quickly short of breath, sprinting forgetfully from beneath the net into the field after us. "Have you never been to an orchestra? The instruments don't play according to haphazard directions; they join together, in unison and in time. Do you have a standard distress call?"

She organized us so that our screech would project into the air. Soon came a response from the sky.

"Ready the net," instructed Lavender.

After another response from the sky, the group called out a second signal. He was closer, but we still couldn't see him.

From the center of the field, one in the Featherman group called, "He's approaching! He's low, and he's slow!"

Not requiring Lavender's command, we lifted and shuffled our net structure toward the threshold of his approach.

"I still can't . . ." said a frustrated and breathless Lavender, who had sprinted and followed the group along the field toward Baker as he approached.

"He's covered in ice!" yelled a Featherman.

"I see him!" shouted the gifted girl. "The net's in the wrong position! That's all I know!"

"It's perfect!" yelled a Featherman. "It's right in line with his flight path!"

"To the right, to the right!" she yelled. "It's not perfect! He's doomed if you don't move!"

"We're at the threshold of the airfield!" argued the same Featherman, as Baker descended further with another screech of distress. "To go right is to go into the trees!"

"Left then!" shouted Lavender. "Change something or he'll die!"

"If he crashes into the clearing, he'd likely live," I told the group, all still gripping their pylon. "If Lavender predicts death, it means he's going to crash into the trees."

"Into the trees, then," conceded the original protester.

By some geometric grace, we fit a square peg into a round hole, shuffling through and around the trees until finally Lavender yelled, "Stop! Don't move! That's the location! You've found it!"

We couldn't settle the net structure because of the trees, and strenuously supporting our respective pylons in pairs, we watched as Baker glided in slowly, appearing larger and larger as he came in with a screech.

"Too high!" yelled a Featherman. "He'll overshoot!"

"Don't move!" insisted Lavender.

Wings teetering, Baker spoke not a word and did appear too high for the net. He seemed positively focused on the threshold—to make the airfield on his own aerodynamic effort that is—and not to land short and fall into our net. He was so close now that even a human could see he was covered to the beak in ice.

Low, heavy, and slow, struggling physically with the icing contamination, Baker pulled his pitch angle higher and higher to stretch his glide into the airstrip. He indeed appeared too high, then, suddenly even to him, he fell from the sky with the aerodynamic capabilities of a fully-ripened melon. He was just short of the net when he stalled, and not a full wingspan above. His inertia carried him forward, tumbling into the net, tossed and beaten but alive and no longer airborne. When he fell into the net, most of his accumulated ice broke off like a smashed glass bottle. After helping him descend from the ropes to the ground, we brushed the remaining ice off his wings and back.

All focus was now on Baker. He wasn't quite crippled in pain, but he clutched his previously injured wing. "It worked! My fluid worked!"

Seeing the chunks of ice on the ground that had come off of him, the other Feathermen were skeptical. They dispersed, noting to Baker that he was now indebted to each of them.

Leaving only me, Baker, and the Canadians, I asked, "Baker, you said your fluid was a success? You nearly crashed."

"Yes, but the ice didn't accumulate, even in the most severe icing conditions, until nearly an hour of continuous flight!" he rejoiced, still clutching his reinjured wing.

"That's incredible. And you took off successfully of course, but how? In your first and only other attempt you didn't even break ground."

"I reduced the fluid's viscosity," he explained. "For more laminar airflow."

"Well then, Baker, I congratulate you. But are you . . . all right? Your letter seemed . . . forgive me, but suicidal."

"Yes, it . . . probably was. I'm very sorry . . . I didn't mean to sound like the suicidal scientist, but I also didn't realize how elated I would be if the formula succeeded. And the fluid worked!"

"Good!" I answered, as convinced as I could be so soon after receiving such a letter. I turned to the girls and added, "Lavender, Marigold, thank you for repaying your favor."

"Can you take us to Emberland now?" asked Marigold optimistically.

"No. Certainly not. You would start a new debt to me, and I wish not to be involved."

"But—"

"Perhaps Baker can take you there. But then you would owe him a favor."

"But now he owes us!" insisted Marigold.

"No, he doesn't," I explained. "Your help today repaid your favor to me; it did not start a new debt from Baker to you. Baker is now in my debt, and you girls are in no one's debt or favor. You are free to walk away."

"From the top of a mountain? You're impossible!" yelled Marigold. "You circle overhead to put the endangered in your debtors' prison, you selfish vulture!"

"Excuse me? I saved your lives on Jan Mayen and used that debt to save a friend. How I'm not walking away with two credits is proof of my unselfishness."

"Yes, um, I greatly appreciate your help, Horace." Baker thanked me nervously.

"Don't fear, Baker; you won't be in my debt for long," I added.

"I'm sorry?"

"Marigold, give Baker your compass," I instructed.

"My what?" she responded, still with irritation toward me but now just confused.

"Your compass," I repeated.

"She has the compass?" Baker said, getting excited.

"I don't know. Do I have a compass?" asked Marigold.

"Yes, the small object I noticed you toying with along our walk as we neared the airstrip to help Baker. Your magnetic compass."

"Oh, my man finder," she corrected.

"You must stop daydreaming of Quinby," Lavender told her sister. "I would be as pleased as Horace if you forfeited your 'man finder' to Baker. You use it only to torture me."

"No, it's known as a compass," I said. "Will you please give the object to Baker?"

"Why not give it directly to you, Horace?" asked Lavender.

"Oh no! Then Baker would still be in my debt, but I would go into debt to you girls. And I will absolutely not go into her debt!" I finished, referring of course to Marigold.

"All right," Marigold resisted, "I will consider a trade, but how will we benefit?"

I sighed and explained, "If you give the compass to Baker, he will be in debt to you. If he then gives it to me, he can clear his debt to me."

"So, you earlier noticed this 'compass' and believe it to be of value," deduced a shrewd Marigold. "And yet you said nothing, but concocted a scheme to walk away with our help and also our compass, yet without debt."

"Yes, of course," I answered. Baker, a Featherman of great scientific interest, could hardly contain his excitement. The fluid was a success and the compass in sight after being lost to our race since before his time or my own. We were the only two living Feathermen to have seen it at that moment. "Are you all right with that?"

"Yes," answered Marigold. "Because whatever value the compass has, it's better to have Baker in our debt than no one."

"I wasn't speaking to you, Marigold." I shifted. "Baker. Are you all right with this? Falling into the debt of these girls? In the debt of humans from another culture, as is ill-advised?"

"Yes, yes!" he said quickly. "Whatever brings the compass back to the Feathermen!"

"Are you certain?" I repeated. "I have found Marigold here quite trying. I would get the compass, but I would share its use."

"Oh, the favors you could earn loaning your new device!" mocked Marigold.

"Yes! Absolutely!" Baker repeated. "I will gladly go into their debt. We can use it to navigate day or night, create more accurate maps of the known world, and more importantly, reestablish our search for Spirit Zero!"

"Horace? Who's Spirit Zero?" asked Lavender.

"Lavender, don't," interceded Marigold. "You know if you ask Horace a question, he'll answer it."

"Not this time, Marigold," I replied. "Not if you don't want to know. Make the trade, and I will be washed of you forever."

"Girls, please!" begged Baker urgently. "I would be honored to go into your debt in exchange for your compass. And as I am a scientist, you will have many, many unique ways you might benefit from having me in your debt."

Lavender asked, "Sir Baker, you need not worry about becoming indebted to us. We offer only—"

"Hooooooold on a moment, Lavender," interrupted Marigold. "Ignore her words, Baker. Would you like our compass?"

"Yes!" he said.

Marigold attempted to hand the compass to me. I resisted. "Oh no! You must hand it to Baker, who must hand it to me."

She sighed and rolled her eyes, then handed it to Baker. He knelt down to receive it with two hands, then stood and handed it to me.

Although I was walking away with the compass, duty and debt free, the most serendipitous result of my improvised scheme was leaving Baker and the girls in each other's company. I was uncertain if Baker was in a condition to be left by himself, but I certainly was. Marigold could ruffle another Featherman's feathers, and through circumstance the gifted girl could monitor if Baker ever became a threat to himself. She could do so for some time, while Baker recovered and found a path to repay his debt to the girls.

And I was already walking away.

"Good-bye, Lavender!" I said, parting. "Good-bye, Baker!"

"Now as for your debt to us, Sir Baker . . ." started Marigold.

Laughing as I walked away, I called back, "I wish you well, Baker!"

As I strode home in the rain, I heard Marigold continue: "Immediately, once this weather improves, we will require transport to Emberland."

I waited in tremendous anticipation for my final laugh as Baker informed Marigold: "Oh, I've hurt my wing badly. I may never fly again."

"Horace!" screamed Marigold.

"And I nearly forgot . . . good-bye to you as well, Fishbone!"

Part Two—Baker

The girls were not awful as my fellow Featherman had suggested, and even Marigold was not without her charm. After falling into their debt so that I could clear my own to Horace, and so that we as a civilization could retrieve the compass, Lavender, Marigold, and I began to walk from the airfield through the cold rain to my laboratory home.

Lavender was the first to speak, asking curiously, "What exactly does the device do?"

"It will guide you north," I answered.

Marigold said, "But we tried that. It was inaccurate, and often unsteady."

"It will guide you to magnetic north. Not true north. They are quite different, and one not near the other."

"Continue?" asked Lavender.

"True north is the rotational axis of the known world. To an extent, this is valuable for navigation but only because there is a bright star almost directly above. But even a bright star is only visible on clear nights, in fair conditions. When the sun shines, which is almost the entire season of light, our navigation is reduced to traveling from one landmark to the next. This is particularly inexact when the wind blows heavily, and for flight over open water. True north is not reliable, and will abandon you, although initially it may seem to be the simple, perfect method because it's collinear with the earth's axis."

"And what's magnetic north?" asked Lavender.

"The location toward which the compass will guide you. Following magnetic north, you can home in on a destination or track directly along a magnetic radial. This is possible in all weather conditions. To a Featherman, and to navigation, it's much safer to invest in magnetic north, as it provides much wiser and more accurate guidance, particularly if you become lost."

"So, what is Spirit Zero?" asked Marigold.

"Spirit Zero is a place you can always return to and start over if needed. It's been many generations since we've lost the compass, and we've been limited to following true north, a false zero. The myth of our past—or science possibly—stated that Spirit Zero existed upon or within magnetic north, or that magnetic north was a spirit, and this spirit had chosen us . . . and was calling us, through the compass. Whether or not it's fact, we can now resume our search for Spirit Zero. From even only a scientific standpoint, it's worthwhile to search for the precise location of magnetic north. This may reveal how the device works, so that we could reproduce it. Then every Featherman could have a compass."

"I would request one as well." Lavender laughed, having just had one in her possession, jokingly implying that it was more useful in our hands. "So then, Spirit Zero? If it's an actual spiritual entity, how does Featherman folklore define it?"

"Physically there are many conflicting image descriptions, none of which claim any significance. But all agree a Spirit Zero would be wise, of course, and pure, entirely knowing, unselfish, and it would devote its entire existence to guide all creatures of the earth."

"I should have been a Spirit Zero," injected Marigold. "But I really didn't study well enough in school."

"I'm sorry?" I asked, confused.

"I blame my mother. For failing to push me harder. But I'm not bitter. I'll probably be a fashion designer instead, and that's all right."

"Or a poor man's trophy wife." Lavender laughed.

"There's no such thing," said Marigold.

"I don't think I understand."

Lavender said: "Baker, ignore her. This is her way of amusing herself."

Rather than taking offense, Marigold asked, "You don't live in an aerie, do you?"

"Oh no, I have a laboratory."

"With a roof," stated Marigold.

"With a roof."

"And a fireplace?" she hoped.

"And a fireplace," I confirmed. "How else could I have prepared my fluid?"

"Please tell me about your fluid, Sir Baker," asked Lavender, still interested.

"With it, water will freeze at almost any temperature. Of course, it will not entirely be water, but a solution of water and fluid from the trunks of the sugar maple tree."

"Sap?" Marigold asked, surprised. "Sweet water?"

"Yes. We can boil it and create different—"

"Syrups," said Marigold.

I continued, "In my experiments, I boiled the fluid from the trees down to different viscosities, then introduced warm water in different concentrations. The various levels of this technique will determine the precise temperature at which the water solution will freeze."

Lavender said, "Incredible. How useful it would be to create ice blocks that would last through the season of light, when it's too warm for them to stay frozen."

"Oh, I'm sorry. The tree fluid can only lower the freezing point, not raise it. But it's still useful."

"Doesn't the fluid wash away in the rain?" she asked.

"Yes, eventually. But not for an hour today. I've found a way to prevent ice formation in flight."

"Such amazing science. When we reach your laboratory, we'll be sure not to touch anything," promised Lavender.

Marigold held her left palm up and smiled, "Yes, I don't want to halt progress. That's why I always stand well clear of it."

———

When we reached and entered my laboratory studio, Marigold commented, "Ah, a real home for a real Featherman."

Lavender asked: "Baker? What is your friend, Horace . . . what is his . . . why is he the way he . . ."

"I knew you didn't care for Horace!" quickly interpreted a gleeful Marigold.

"No warning! With no warning he just plummeted from the sky and rendered us intentionally unconscious!" said Lavender defensively.

"Horace is a stoic," I explained. "Thus, the aerie. Some Feathermen have aeries still, but . . ."

"Yes, homeless ones," interrupted Marigold, turning both my head and Lavender's in confusion. She laughed. "I shouldn't have to defend that claim. If they stay in an aerie, with no walls, doors, or fireplace, they have no home. They're homeless."

I nodded. "I suppose that would be true. Horace is a stoic, but not a true stoic. When you tell yourself to ignore pain so easily, it's difficult not to tell others. A true stoic denies themselves even that indulgence, and that's all the negative comments I'll say about Horace."

Lavender agreed. "But Horace analyzed you, which I feel obliged to bring into our conversation, if I may." I feared she would introduce the topic of my note; fortunately she said instead, "He believes that after your accident, you became somewhat intolerably righteous and hyper-critical."

I admitted with relief: "Yes, and this was true. I was not well. I was insecure."

Ignoring my embarrassment, she persisted on the dreaded topic: "So then the note? You seem quite different from Horace. I suppose not many who campaign as stoics contemplate suicide."

I sighed, humiliated in the presence of my small friends. "Yes. I suppose I should be prepared to discuss the note."

"You seem to be a kind, sensitive creature," stated Marigold genuinely as she found some rags to dry her inconveniently long, wet hair. "I would suggest you consider finding a means of transport to Emberland to—"

"Marigold, please!" shouted Lavender. "Now is hardly the time for your—"

"Stop!" Marigold protested. "The King's Closet!" Shifting to a gentler tone and addressing me she continued, "There's treatment there, if you are not well. They have the professionals and the facilities to help heal the mind, or at least address it. Please consider it."

"I feel well now, but thank you. What . . . what could they possibly do to help me?"

Marigold answered, "First they will probably medicate you for believing you are a large talking bird."

"But I am a large talking bird."

"Yes, but don't tell them you think that."

"Then, well, I'm sorry for the accusation," apologized Lavender, mumbling to her sister. "When you suggested Emberland . . . I mean only to say it's no secret you wish to travel there."

"Yes, and why not?" I proposed. "Have you visited the hot springs?"

Marigold grumbled, "They . . . have . . . hot . . . springs?"

"Yes, and that reminds me. I should start the fireplace. Hot springs, yes. A safe distance downslope from where the lava flows. The authorities keep them clean and comfortable, knowing they are such a delightful attraction for visitors."

Marigold spoke through gritted teeth, "Somewhere, probably in his aerie, sits a Featherman whom my sister would see as glowing white."

Lavender's eyes opened wide. "Oh, that reminds me. Your culture has become quite advanced in science and physiology, correct?"

"I suppose."

"And you're a scientist. I have a peculiar gift that allows me to see glows around creatures when they cycle toward or away from various levels of life and death."

"And I have long, blonde hair, which I brush with my left hand," added Marigold, understanding her sister's direction better than I.

"What can you tell me of heredity?" asked Lavender.

"I . . . I'm sorry. I desire to fulfill my obligation to you. If I had an answer to your question, I would share," I responded.

"Devastating," sarcastically stated Marigold. "I suppose you will have to provide our recompense by finding transport for us to Emberland."

"My wing is ailing, but I hope to repay my debt to your liking."

Marigold added, "Yes, we understand. But however we arrive there, be sure the island is in fact Emberland and not Jan Mayen. We cannot return to Jan Mayen."

"No? Horace speaks occasionally of Jan Mayen. I don't know if I'll ever find the opportunity to travel there if I'm unable to fly, but I've become curious. You did not enjoy your stay, it seems?"

"It wasn't all awful," Lavender said.

"They tried to kill us," said Marigold.

Lavender compromised.

"It was definitely a once-is-enough-in-a-lifetime experience."

———————

Now huddled by the fire, us three in fact, Marigold's long hair began to dry. Lavender reached to gently hold a lock of her sister's strands. "Oh, Marigold, how did this happen?"

"What? Not more feces, I hope. I had expected the rain would cleanse me of that."

"Feces?" I asked.

Lavender beamed, "Oh, it was hysterical! She got her head stuck in—"

"Horace's sister's cloaca," interrupted Marigold. "The moment of my life I may never live down."

"No, you will not!" agreed Lavender. "But it's not feces . . . it's a discoloration near the scalp. A lighter yellow, almost a platinum color at your roots."

Marigold plucked one of her own hairs, held it to her eye, and concluded: "Oh, this is awful," and discarded it in the fire.

"That's likely from a chemical in our fecal waste," I informed her.

Marigold said: "Oh well, had I known that dislodging my head so soon would leave my hair with these tawdry streaks, I would have left it in for another twenty minutes."

Lavender smiled. "This comment will now be added to this story whenever I repeat it, which will be often and on every occasion possible."

"I have a purified form of the substance that streaked your hair. It's here in my laboratory. It would be harmless, and could even out your color."

"Or you might consider a darker color," suggested the shorter and darker-haired Lavender.

"Oh no. You mean use the soot from a fireplace as you do?"

"I was going to do this myself, after our fire is out," explained Lavender, as the girls mocked each other playfully. "You present it as foul, but you are prepared to soak your scalp in a purified form of fecal waste?"

"I am blonde," declared Marigold pompously, yet in intentional self-mockery. "I came out of the womb with blonde hair and earrings. I will go to another form of blonde, but never another color entirely."

"Yes, to have blonde hair is to always have sunshine," said Lavender.

"Precisely."

I laughed at them both while I fetched the solution. "Here, Marigold. This will make you very blonde."

"From gold to platinum? You're quite the alchemist."

"I have yet to attempt the transmutation of lesser metals such as lead into more precious ones, such as silver, gold, or greater."

"Then I shall settle for the hair dye," noted Marigold.

"I've known you long enough to understand it's a futile effort to suggest you cut your hair," said Lavender, "so I will only advise that because your hair is very long, you may exhaust Sir Baker's supply of this chemical dye."

"He can always make more. If it comes from where I think it does."

Her long hair did consume most of my extract, which we successfully applied, allowing thirty minutes to soak while we waited and talked. After rinsing the agents from her corrected hair and drying herself near the fire, Marigold described herself as "transformed." To this Lavender responded, "Louder than before, which I did not believe possible."

"I suppose you girls need sleep. It's past midday, but I should rest from my flight and tend to my wing."

"Midday?" Lavender said. "I could sleep until morning."

I fetched them the blankets and spreads they needed to rest in their chosen bed space, on the floor near the fireplace. I also retrieved a bag of seed for them, with two water jugs. I retired to my bedroom after the pleasant conversation.

The girls did not sleep immediately. They whispered, but I could hear them from my bedroom. I assume their efforts would have effectively hidden their discussion from human ears. What I will retell now I was never intended to know.

"He doesn't have any inclination of suicide that I have noticed," began Marigold.

"Yes, but would we recognize a sign if presented to us?" asked Lavender. "What do we know of suicide?"

"Nothing until now. You . . . are you using your gift again? That is, if he walked off into his room alone, glowing, you would have asserted something, I hope."

"Yes. I would have. No, he was not glowing."

"I hope he feels as improved as I do, after cleaning and warming myself a bit," said Marigold humbly.

"Yes, I hope you're in better spirits. What's been wrong lately? Horace was difficult, but he saved us. The moment we took to the sky, it seemed—"

"I'm terribly sorry," said Marigold, sounding weak. "I was not myself. But I believe I have returned and can hopefully be redeemed with an explanation. Your gift. Your gift is part of my structure of needs. I use it to feel secure and safe. With it I know that my need for survival is met, and I can focus on higher needs."

"Marigold . . ."

Marigold began to sob, crumbling quickly, "And what's even worse? What do I do when my needs are met? I make jokes. As if to mock those who must fulfill their own need for safety, when truly, you do that, for me."

"No, Marigold, that's not you . . ."

"It is! Horace was correct. I am useless. I rely on others and I serve no purpose. And look at how I behaved when, for hardly a day and only to consider the greater good, my younger sister wished to stop using her gift . . . You took the gift from me, and how poorly I acted. As if I were thrust into a life of privation, the kind that Horace leads by choice, to whom I could not so much as contribute a kind word."

"Perhaps my gift is something you have become reliant upon," said Lavender, gathering her thoughts to state her case. "But so what of it?

Shelter is a need. And a dark cloud seems to follow me, but somehow you serve as a traveling shelter."

"What, as in camping equipment?" Marigold sniffed.

Listening from within my bedroom, I sympathized with Marigold's feeling of uselessness. Had my formula failed this day, I would have been a despondent Featherman with a disabled wing . . . if I survived.

Lavender explained, "Your gift is your ability to make me laugh as the world is burning, still while fetching a bucket of water. Marigold, I'm not vain when I say this, but I carry a great weight. My gift is a burden, and yet does not always provide a clear solution. My gift does not always carry its own weight, but you do. And yes, often with your immature jokes, your flamboyance, and your ability to attract attention while I find much needed moments of relief. And what of it, if you help shoulder my load with silly devices in tense or morbid moments? That's not poor timing; that's when I need it most. But that's not exclusively all of the ways you're useful. Your insights, your creativity . . . Marigold, for our whole lives you've been sensitive enough to paint yourself brightly so that I wasn't the only bird with odd feathers in our family. You're my insulation, my buffer . . . the diversion that allows me to hide, breaking from the pressure of what I am, all while supplying acceptance . . . which is not a need anyone can self-provide. If I were hungry, I would need something to eat. If I were in danger, I would seek safety. I can generally fulfill those needs for myself, and when I do, I can begin to seek the first need I cannot self-fulfill: acceptance. Most you meet are like this; they are neither hungry nor in danger, and therefore acceptance is the greatest gift we can give each other. To deny acceptance is to deny bread to the starving. And yet York's entire marketplace stared at me the day I was exiled, wanting absolutely no association with me. Though it meant my death or survival, no one would accept me. But you did. Marigold, it's a fair assumption to believe I would have been executed if not for you. Still, we are too young to be exiled, which I also could not fare alone."

Marigold sniffed. "Thank you. Thank you, Lavender . . . thank you so much. Sleep well."

"You too, sister."

Had my formula not been successful, my heart would have turned to lead. I would say the denial of bread to the starving is very much how I had felt until then.

When they woke, we did some planning. We agreed that if I were to travel with them to Emberland, my debt would be repaid. I also planned to seek some counseling there, to receive treatment for my mental health. The obstacle of my ailing wing meant we would walk, which they surprisingly accepted, quite readily in fact.

They didn't seem to mind at all, even subsequent to my warning that the walk would take days . . . difficult travel down mountain footpaths. "Better than *up* mountain footpaths," they said. They viewed the tour as an opportunity to expand their text, *The Field Guide to Life and Death*. They would catalog the wild foliage that grew on the island of Thule, and Marigold even suggested an appendix to the book that defined what was edible to a Featherman's body and what was not. I was of course to be the full test group but never in actual danger of being poisoned. This they would prevent.

After collecting our belongings and packing several bags of seed and some water, we took a map of the footpaths and set out downslope. We passed the time creating a nicknaming system. They took the final syllable of one's name and added an *a* for the feminine or an *o* for the masculine. We were Dera, Golda, and Kero for our journey together, but before long they tired of the unfamiliar, alternative names and reverted to Lavender, Marigold, and Baker.

It was just past the equinox and the sun was setting more and more inconveniently early. Still, we continued as necessary and camped at a normal hour; with a recently disrupted sleep schedule, the girls were talkative late in the night and difficult to wake early in the morning. We traveled normally the following day, camped again without incident, and set out casually on a third day.

On the third night, we camped near the entrance to a cave. Lavender and Marigold weren't tired and were curious to explore. We were on different sleeping schedules, and I figured they could do what they had already done throughout much of the known world: follow Lavender's gift and remain safe. I went to sleep that night, but I woke up alone. They left some items behind but nothing valuable. I wandered and called for them for several hours that morning but found nothing. I couldn't fit through the entrance to the cave, and could only search outside. I felt an uneasy responsibility, having not found an opportunity to repay my debt to the girls. They had disappeared.

I continued alone to the port and embarked on the ferry to Emberland. There I spent some time in education and recovery before returning, again by ferry, then on foot and alone, to my Featherman home of Windfall. I returned to begin bulk production of my anti-icing fluid.

11 / Grandfather

I can still recall when we first discovered Lavender's gift, and how it affected us. She was hardly five, and Simon had been gone for as many seasons. Marigold was six, my wife and I in our fifties, and our daughter Heather the middle generation, not quite thirty. I had no sons, and because my only daughter was widowed with two girls, I also had no grandsons. There were three generations of four women to share the duties of the farm, and me, a grandfather, to complete the entirety of the men's work. In my youth or if I still had Simon's help it might have been possible, but at my age and with a slowly radiating tear in my abdomen, the burden was often overwhelming.

I was still able to perform my work, though carefully and often very slowly. Some chores fell under a masculine category, and they were my responsibility, not my wife's or my daughter's, and certainly not my granddaughters'. I carry a bulge under my skin I believe to be a tear in my abdominal muscle as the result of heavy lifting, or possibly pulling on a breached mullice calf. I didn't feel the initial tear, and don't know the exact moment I created this chink in my armor. It was as old as my granddaughters, I believe. Fortunately, if I were careful in my work, it would not cause me discomfort. But if I wasn't, I could expand the tear, slightly but permanently. My only available solution was to wear a second belt, below the waist, to hold down the small bulge and gingerly carry my burden.

Young Lavender and Marigold were quite fond of the livestock, as was their mother when she was a child. There are three main breeds on a typical Canadian farm. There's the tollimore, which stand at about waist level to a human. They're independent by nature. They have dark, smooth fur and a large udder to share their milk. There's the ovidon, a flock animal, about the same size as the tollimore. They're usually light gray and provide thick fleece for shearing. The biggest and the strongest by far are the mullice. The mullice are quite different and much more difficult to describe. All three creatures are the result of generations of selective breeding, from some ancient wild creatures, we're left to assume, but it's the mullice that are nature and agriculture's miraculous joint achievement. They can be dark red, rich brown, deep black, even occasionally mottled white. They have teeth like children's fists, horns that curve down, and tusks that curve up. Grazing creatures like the others, they pull more than grain or grass from the soil, sucking up rocks, weeds, decay, and dirt, swallowing it all and turning what they eat into pulsating muscle. They also return something to the earth, and even their large, warm, unsightly manure patties will later be a healthy mound where the tallest grasses grow. These creatures stand as tall as a human and are ten or so times our weight. Their heads are long and broad, swinging slowly on their thick necks. From withers to rump there is a downward slope and a more slender span across the hindquarters than the muscle and power of the fore section. They're a creature of sheer power, a beast of burden but docile and cooperative, except for the bull when the season favors breeding. The mullice are also good for their meat. Each of the creatures has its utility, and each is needed for the farm to survive. But as my granddaughters would learn, nature is never quite fair with the gifts she gives us at birth.

Of all our animals, Lavender's favorite was the old tollimore who had traveled north alongside her mother. We had told her the story, and the gentle creature was to Lavender a faithful friend, the only one of the livestock to return from Heather's visit to Simon. This tollimore also helped a young girl grasp the events around her father, whom she had met so briefly on the day of her birth. She had named her friend Ellie, or rather we encouraged that name, for what she did on the way to Fort Alert, on Ellesmere. As a father and a grandfather, I know better than to allow a child to name a farm animal that could one day be sold or slaughtered, but we allowed one companion creature for Marigold as we did for Lavender. We hoped it would help them cope, if only just a little, with growing up fatherless.

By the time Lavender was five, Ellie was old for her breed, blind, and dry. Without milk or young or any other benefit, an animal's last contribution to their farm is their flesh. With too much delay I feared she would be lost to old age or sickness, and with it her meat. So, as I had done with my own daughter, I knew the time had come to explain to Lavender and Marigold the inequalities of nature and the practical purpose of their friends.

I had decided Ellie was to be slaughtered, though I had not yet carried it through. In preparation for the tears and protests of two children, Lavender to feel particularly betrayed, I first announced the decision to my wife and my daughter Heather.

"Where are the girls?" I asked as we sat in the kitchen.

"Marigold's in the field and Lavender is playing with Ellie in the stables," answered Heather.

"Oh dear."

"What is it?" asked my wife.

"I'm afraid Ellie's time has come."

"Oh dear," replied my wife.

"And what? Are we to eat her?" responded Heather.

"Yes, of course. We can't be emotional, please. I pay for the feed she consumes; she no longer has any—"

"I hope you're hungry, because I refuse."

"Heather, I'll need your help explaining this."

"No. What fault of hers is it that she was born a tollimore? When can a creature not become a member of the family? She kept me alive for days when Lavender was born and . . . and she saved my life from that thorned barbarian! What if an animal saved your life? Would you not spare its?"

"Please, Heather. Did we not have this conversation twenty seasons ago? And before this begins, what do you mean a member of the family? So the women can outvote me five to one?"

"But the girls," responded my wife.

And with that, Lavender burst into the room shouting. "You can't kill her!" She ran to Heather, who picked up and comforted her already-weeping child.

Had I not been the only man of the house, I believe this, and many, many other discussions would have been entirely different . . . how much wood to throw on the fire, how much tardiness to cathedral services should be tolerated for the sake of one's hair, and of course many arguments just as this: What would we serve for dinner? Thankfully, my wife corrected, "Lavender! You aren't to listen in on private adult conversations."

"I wasn't listening! You can't kill her; there are babies!"

"What babies?" asked Heather, I believe only to validate her vote against my decision.

"Ellie's babies. Ellie has three babies."

I felt sorry for Lavender, but I assumed it was her imagination protecting her.

"Lavender, darling," added Heather, still holding, comforting, and encouraging her, as well as exploiting her against me, "are these three babies inside or outside of Ellie?"

"Inside."

I decided then to inquire. "How do you know this, dear?"

"There were three glowing red spots inside of her. They aren't new, but they're all glowing white now, even Ellie!"

My wife suggested, "Lavender, dear. Why don't you show us in the stables what you mean?"

She hopped from her mother's lap and ran off. The adults in the room looked each other in the eye briefly, as if to silently question, *Who will be the first fool to believe her?* After our pause, we followed the girl to Ellie's stable.

Lavender declared, "Do you see? Ellie's glowing white!" She was not, at least not to our eyes. My wife, Heather, and I searched for a light source to explain some glow we couldn't see. It was daylight, but the stables are sheltered, and Ellie was in the shade. Our necks and eyes wandered, and we even squatted to the level of Lavender's eye in search of a glare. We scanned the other creatures of the stables, but none carried a "glow" of any color. Lavender repeated, "Ellie is glowing white. You're not looking at Ellie. Don't you see?"

"Lavender dear, please show us where Ellie is glowing white," said her mother.

"Everywhere! But before she was white, the three babies were glowing red. Now they're white too, but they're in her . . . " she said as she stepped toward Ellie and pointed accurately to the old tollimore's womb.

"Lavender, are any of the other animals glowing red?" inquired my wife.

"Yes."

"Which?" Heather asked.

Lavender then pointed to two pregnant ovidons, a pregnant mullice, and an egg-laying fowl which was incubating a clutch of eggs.

"She just pointed to every maternal creature here," I said, informing the others.

"And Ellie!" she reminded us, adding, "But Ellie is glowing white now, not red like the others and you can't kill her!" She remembered her etiquette and added, "Please." A smart child, she was learning that we couldn't see the colors, so she continued to explain, "On days when I see an animal glow white, they're killed and you cannot do that to Ellie!"

"Lavender, were you listening to our conversation in the kitchen?" I asked.

"No! I already said I wasn't!"

"I believe her now," I told my wife and daughter. "Lavender, are any of the other creatures glowing white?"

"By the feed, the fowl with the green feathers. But that's not Ellie. I'm worried for Ellie."

"That was the bird I had decided to take for lunch," said my wife. "I felt it of no consequence to tell you, so I didn't. I certainly did not inform the girls."

As we all began to understand, Heather asked, "Lavender dear, is my abdomen glowing red?"

"No, I have never seen you glow." The girl giggled.

"Good," answered Heather, not surprised but still pleasantly relieved, followed by a glare in her direction from myself and her mother.

I said, "I believe I understand. If Ellie truly does give us three tollimore by season's end, then perhaps Lavender can predict an animal's life and death."

"Thank you!" said Lavender.

"For what, dear? Because I was the first to believe you?"

"No. Because Ellie's no longer white."

"Incredible," I gasped, now speaking to the adults. "The moment I changed my mind and decided to spare Ellie, Lavender claimed the creature was no longer white."

"And the babies glow red again," pointed Lavender a second time to the womb. She quickly was her normal self again, embracing Ellie, then running back into the field to find her sister. The three adults remained in the stable, again to pause a moment and ask each other silent questions.

My wife broke the silence. "We can check Ellie's temperature. To see if she could in fact be pregnant."

It was elevated, but many possibilities remained in which we could still consider the child's gift unproven. For example, Ellie was not yet showing visual evidence.

We had the green-feathered fowl for lunch, but I don't recall what was consumed for dinner that night. Carrots and vegetable leaves, most likely. However, I do remember the events following the meal.

I say this delicately of my own granddaughters, but until that day we had believed Marigold to be the gifted child. Nothing ethereal—Marigold's ability was her artistry and creativity, particularly with music. As beautifully as she played for a child of only six, her level would have been even more elevated had there not been the delay of realizing her left-hand dominance. I carved a small, custom flute and syrinx for her, both of which she played as if the instruments were fashioned in a professional's workshop and not by a farmer using tools intended to mount hen coops. She also sang well, and young Marigold's ease with song would delight but often intimidate my wife, her instructor, who had limited musical training herself.

The lessons immediately followed dinner, when Heather would occupy herself with the cleanup after the meal. The girls would be with their grandmother, and I would find my only rest of the day.

Much to my own confusion, I had started to weep one night. Thankfully, I was alone.

This was before we discovered Lavender's gift. We weren't desperate; I worked to ensure that. None in my family went hungry even in the seasons of darkness, and with the exception of my abdomen's tear, we were all in fine health. Still, when I lay in bed that night with the door closed, and could hear Marigold's voice performing scales, I broke. It was painfully confusing, why I cried . . . I was not a man of tears and had to look inward to understand why.

It was as if I had been building pressure behind a dam until all that was needed was this fracture and the tears would flow. The emotional crack, a chink in the armor, was sparked nightly by my own granddaughter's harmony, as if her young voice's exact resonance shook some structural flaw in my dam. The first time I wept was the most distressing. Why was I weeping? When would it stop? I tried to hold it within but could not, not with the music from the lesson still reaching my ears and remaining trapped between them.

But it helped. Once my episode was over and not witnessed by the others, I went to sleep and awoke the next morning prepared for labor and pleased to sweat in the field. I couldn't remember feeling more impenetrable or more at peace.

It became almost a nightly exercise, something routinely hygienic. Throughout the day, fear, tension, and pressure would pour into me until, in my bedroom's privacy during Marigold's music lesson, it would seep out and relieve my burden. I made certain to never again stock days and days of pressure without allowing myself relief. It benefited my work, my family, and my health to permit these episodes. They went on for at least a full season, and served me until they were no longer needed, the night we discovered Lavender's gift.

"Marigold, please come with me to the stables," I said after dinner that evening.

"But what of their lesson?" asked my wife.

"Carry on with Lavender. I have a few questions about the livestock I would like to ask Marigold, without Lavender present."

"No!" yelled Lavender, feeling excluded. "That's not fair!"

"Heee," Marigold giggled, feeling favored. "I'll be sure to say hi to Ellie for you!"

"It's just for tonight, and only for a moment, Lavender," said my wife, understanding my intention. The entire course was inverted, and the girl with the purple eyes and no musical ability stayed behind for lessons while her older, euphonious sister went to the stables to discuss life and death. Still, it had to be done; she had to be tested.

"Why are we going to the stables?" she asked as we walked slowly, the sun having set for the evening.

"Marigold, dear, do you remember when we asked you to attempt to write with your left hand?"

"Yes."

"This is similar." Once we reached the stables I continued, "Marigold, do you see a glow about any of the livestock?"

"No," she said after panning, observing most of the animals sleeping.

After pausing to give her a moment I added, "Is Ellie?"

"No."

"Is any creature in the stable glowing then?"

Sensing disappointment and to prove her worth she answered, "Yes!"

"Wonderful! Which?"

Posing with her head to the side, chin up, eyelids relaxed and mouth puckering as a young girl imitates an adult woman, she declared, "Mmmmmmme!"

Some have milk, some have fleece, and some have meat. Marigold did not have her sister's gift. The girls would have the remainder of their lives to determine the fairness of their inequalities; I had to focus on providing. Young Marigold could already bring me to tears with her talent, but I believed Lavender's gift would pull me off my bed, dry my eyes, and stand me upright as a man.

Earlier that day I had nearly slaughtered Ellie, and if she didn't have a name, I would have without discussion. If truly pregnant, her three young head of tollimore would all have been lost. Those aren't always the outcomes for which you can fault a farmer, but they can still be the ones that starve his family. My mind started a blend of planning and daydreaming. Lavender and I could travel the rural area north of York near our farm, even farther if necessary, and help other men in my trade prevent the devastation of missed opportunities, all for a fee of course. To think what I could have done with a child like this in past times. When uncertain if an animal's condition was fatal or not, whether to slaughter before it died and went to waste, whether to spend wages and effort to treat a condition or if the effort was futile, when an animal was fertile . . . oh, and the time I must have wasted pairing livestock that were already pregnant. The girl could have greater benefit to this farm than ten sons, and with only one small mouth to feed.

Yes, we could travel to other farms, give predictions of individual creatures, or entire flocks and herds. As a farmer, I can say with confidence that we're all always ready to invest a modest fee toward improving our profitability. With farms more profitable they would be less at risk to fail, and with farms more productive, our town if not our country could be more secure from hunger. How exactly we would conduct our services I wasn't certain, and Lavender's gift was not yet proven, but I had all of Ellie's gestation to determine both.

During the days following our discovery of Lavender's potential, I viewed the bulge in my abdomen quite differently. I could finally look to the future without fear of how an aging man could continue to support his family as it became more and more unlikely I would physically be able to do so. The longer I considered Lavender's gift and the hope and changes surrounding it, the more I looked back at my then-recent tearful episodes with private shame. They were no longer necessary, and I wanted to believe they had never happened, now that the future looked promising.

Still attempting to verify Lavender's gift, I disorganized and retethered the livestock throughout the stable, then brought in the girl to separate the pregnant from the rest. She was never wrong. Young Lavender grew weary and often confused with my persistent testing and retesting of her gift, and at times I would hide the tests with games or lessons. For example, if a hen incubated a clutch of eggs, I would ask Lavender to perform a counting exercise, tallying the eggs first by their red glows when they were blocked from sight by the hen, then again in plain view after removing their mother. I told her she was learning her numbers.

I conjured every test I could imagine, but because the validity of this potentially celestial gift was so difficult to accept, I vowed not to act upon it until certain. I vowed not to act upon her gift until the birth of Ellie's three predicted offspring. As difficult as my physical work had always been, to bring myself to perform it knowing I may soon be free from strenuous labor made leaving my bedroom each morning all the more purposeless. Still, to declare to my fellow farmers that my granddaughter had the prophetic ability to see life and death . . . I just didn't believe that claim could be made, even if true. And in desperation or greed, could a believer of her gift not become a potential thief, a kidnapper of my granddaughter? If I had a hen that laid golden eggs, I would tell no one, and if knowledge leaked in spite of my silence, I would broil the bird just to have meat before it was stolen.

I developed a plan over the days while waiting for Ellie to birth her young. There would be no claim of the spiritual, only the scientific. My science involved fraudulent devices, such as dried gourds filled with grain which I would shake about, a warped lens, some shears, and other misleading rubbish to create an intriguing bag of "tools." Let the desperate or greedy man steal these tools. He can attempt to decipher them while my granddaughter and I return safely to our farm. Of course, the girl would have to accompany me.

Awaiting my second career, my daily work dragged on, my mind now wandering, sending me to measure Ellie's abdomen twice, often four times each day. She was indeed becoming appropriately larger. Restless one workday, and shamefully impatient, I abandoned the field and returned to measure Ellie once again. *If only I could slaughter this one creature now, as I do with others every day*, I thought. By this time, I would surely be able to sort through the mother's carcass to discover whether or not the creature was truly carrying the three predicted young. Ellie need not be alive, nor her progeny. *Need I more proof*, I wondered, *when I have tested the child forward and backward?*

I knelt before Ellie, who was tethered and feeding on grain. I knew why I waited for her three young, and it was because I, like any other farmer, doubted her fertility. I had proven the girl's gift to myself, but if I could cut open the tollimore and find three little spines inside her body, I could consider the gift proven to the institution of agriculture and use the child to begin my trade. Why wait so many more days? Why wait and waste Lavender's gift? Ellie was one creature; in the days until she gave birth, how many creatures on how many farms could be helped?

And what if there were no young? I would be weeping again every night in my bedroom to the sound of my other granddaughter's song. If that were a possible outcome, the lost labor in my lack of productivity, due to this mental distraction, would be difficult to overcome. It was an agonizing wait, and I wished my mind and spirit would return to some form of productive labor. Of course, the outcome I wished for would be to travel to other farms with the girl, smile as I passed their laborers, possibly share a baked treat or stewed fruits with another farmer and his wife, and inform a man like myself if his livestock were dying or not, or pregnant and with how many. All in exchange for a few tiles, eight or nine . . .

My mind was prematurely determining wages when I heard Marigold shriek, "Lavender, come play with Ellie and me!"

I heard delicate footsteps as Lavender followed Marigold to the gate of the stable. "No! Ellie's glowing white again!"

Glowing white? I hadn't moved, still kneeling by the creature. I saw no white glow, but neither had my wife the day we consumed the fowl with the green feathers. I had made no conscious decision to kill Ellie, at least none that I was aware of, but Lavender maybe knew better than I that I would have done this had the girls not arrived. I didn't understand the gift entirely, but I didn't doubt it. And if I didn't doubt it, why were we not yet visiting other farms?

"Oh, Marigold, she's normal now," I heard from Lavender.

I never turned to look at the girls; I was too humiliated with myself and my weakness. I simply stood, left the stable rigidly, and returned to the house. As I walked toward the bath, I passed my wife and Heather. I announced, "Tomorrow Lavender and I shall be traveling."

One of the farms to the west was our first visit; the wife was a rabid gossip and I hoped she would provide complimentary publicity. Lavender and I often provided our services for no fare, at least initially, while we convinced the skeptics. It was always awkward with a young girl at my side, pretending to use the tools and poking large female mullice in sensitive areas. I would rattle my gourd in the air and hold the warped lens to a creature's nostril, all while its owner looked at me as if I were the one with the horns or the tail. Then I would ask for some distance and pretend to show my granddaughter this unique familial skill while she in fact whispered to me what she saw. The girl's performance was never a concern; she was properly reserved. She knew if she were able to keep our secret, the farmer's wife would almost certainly feed us a fresh, farm-baked dessert.

Before terribly long, just several accurate birth-count predictions, Lavender and I were earning enough tiles to provide for the entire family. We quite easily covered the family and farm's expenses for the day and saved the surplus for the girls' futures. The day we discovered Lavender's gift and the day we visited our first farm had changed our lives forever.

Not all moments created by Lavender's gift were pleasant, nor were they appreciated. A difficult visit, and the nearest Lavender ever came to revealing herself, was a visit to the Tustin Farm, near our own. We had made our predictions and the farmer was pleased, sharing some conversation with us afterward in his kitchen while his wife and daughter of about eighteen seasons served fresh pastries. The man had three sons, all fortunate enough to be working in the field at the time, spared from the awkward moment. There was a secret in the room, one which my granddaughter was unknowingly about to reveal.

"What does it feel like to be pregnant?" asked Lavender of the farmer's daughter.

"Lavender, sweetheart," I stammered.

A brief pause, then the daughter's pale face and defenseless lips confirmed it.

"She learns of this before we do?" yelled the mother. "You're pregnant and you confess to a tiny stranger before you inform your own parents?"

"The Rotner boy!" yelled the father.

"Oh, you're too young," said the mother.

"I didn't tell anyone!" said the pregnant teenager defensively.

Already pacing the kitchen, not knowing for what he was searching, the father screamed irrationally, "Rotner and his boy must give me land for this . . . or I will kill him if I don't kill you first!"

"Darvis!" yelled the wife at her husband.

"Don't worry," Lavender said to the pregnant teen. "He's not really going to kill you; you're glowing red, not white."

"We should go, dear," I tried again, this time attempting to pick her up.

"I'm glowing what?" asked the teen of Lavender. "Why are you here, anyhow?"

"Now, Lavender!" I insisted.

"Wait," she demanded, "I may be pregnant one day too and I want to know how it feels!"

The farmer's daughter answered in somber sarcasm, "How do you think it feels?"

I gathered the child and we left at once. I don't remember, but I don't believe I ever settled my compensation with the future grandfather. It was payment enough to leave not a moment later.

That experience was more than enough to deter me from wanting to try Lavender's gift on humans. Our wages were steady and abundant already, and it wouldn't have been realistic to expect to keep our secret while working on anything but livestock. And of course, five was not a healthy age to be asked to forecast the fate of any pregnant or dying human. She was too young, and evidently, I wasn't able to articulate these issues to her with any wisdom of my own.

"I don't understand. When you told that man his mullice was to bear twins, he was very happy," Lavender stated as we walked home, "But when his daughter was pregnant, everybody became angry."

"You see Lavender, mullice have various utilities, or many ways to bring tiles. A farmer can sell them, breed them, eat them if he needs to, or use them to protect his land. When they graze, they consume small rocks and weeds, which helps the soil. So, more mullice are better."

"Are more people bad?"

"Oh no," I said, entering a whirlpool, "but when a mullice has a baby, a farmer can earn tiles. If his daughter has a child and is not married, he loses tiles."

"Like Mother?" she asked.

"N-n-no," I answered, trying now to think more abundantly and speak more sparingly.

"Why not? She's not married and you have to pay for her and for us."

"Yes, but you see, Lavender, your mother will be married again one day." Shamefully, these were my actual chosen words.

Lavender's eyes, her beautiful, valuable eyes, began to tear at the thought of change, as any child's would. Too distracted by the thought of her mother's remarriage, she fortunately failed to digest my misguided explanation of marriage, its purpose, and gender inequalities.

"Girls are wonderful," I blurted.

Crying, she asked, "I help you earn tiles, right?"

"Oh certainly!" I exclaimed, jubilant and thinking I had resolved her concern. "You help greatly, and how wonderful it is that you do."

"So, what about Marigold? Is that why you never take her along with us?"

Was there no way out for me? I wondered.

"Darling, do you remember twenty or thirty days past, when your sister found me playing with Ellie? And she called for you, and you briefly saw Ellie glowing white?"

"Yes."

"Lavender, tiles can make a good person bad. They can make you fear things that will not harm you, and they make families clash like you witnessed today. Sometimes someone in a family can earn more than another, and the family argues. Sometimes someone in a town can earn more than another and the town argues. Even countries . . . "

"So why did Ellie stop glowing white that day?"

At last, I was guiding her thoughts. "Because even though sometimes people forget about the things more important than tiles, sometimes they also remember before doing harm."

———————

As days and seasons passed, business continued. I transformed from a lesser-known farmer into a prosperous, well-respected man able to provide singular, benevolent services. For this I never struggled with our lie, and Lavender kept it well. Rarely would someone question her presence as we traveled, and if they did, I gave the defensive, rehearsed response, "Cannot a man with no sons and no grandsons teach his granddaughter the apprenticeship of his trade?" On her own she would add, "When we're done, will there be dessert?"

Eventually Ellie did give birth, to three healthy tollimore as predicted. She milked for a while, then became dry again and bore no more young. We allowed her to die naturally when she was ready and buried her in the soil of the family plot. She was laid near the most recently deceased, Simon, whose grave was a tombstone without a body, having died in battle. Ellie lived peacefully for two seasons past her practical utility, which was never in return for her milk or her meat, or even her companionship to Lavender, but for the role she played in our discovery of the girl's gift. The gift would have revealed itself in time, but I believe a sense of purpose is not limited to humans. Every creature must justify its existence to itself, or it will not be satisfied. Feel free to challenge my claim, but remember I tend a farm. Whether it's the insect who must lay its eggs before it expires or the farmer who must support his family, the simplest to most complex minds will not be at peace without purpose. What remained to be seen was not Lavender's ability, but its direction. At the time, none outside our family knew of her gift, but with so many services within its potential, my only concern for the girl was whether or not she would ever be able to satisfy the sense of purpose she would develop as she grew older. If not, she would never find peace. If so, she would be blessed with the same peace she provided to me, as only because of her, my burden had been relieved, and my purpose had been fulfilled.

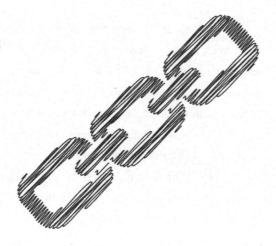

12 / Agrippin

I first discovered my gift at four seasons, when my younger brother was an infant and hardly thirty or forty days had passed since his birth. When his eyes closed and he was lying in his bassinet, my mother, laughing quietly, called me over to share in her amusement.

"Look, Agrippin. Do you see his lips moving? He's suckling. He's dreaming of milk."

Though she stood beside me, fully clothed and not nursing her sleeping youngest, I saw an image of her bare breast above my infant brother's head. In these images, he was present and nursed from the breast, his image's lips moving.

"Look, Mother! Over his head, it's you! You should nurse him and make the dream real."

Confused at first and unable to see the image herself, over time we would realize I had the ability to observe the dreams of others as the images took form in their minds. As a child, this ability was difficult to validate to an adult, but when my father would wake from a nap and I would tell him what he had dreamt of, it became impossible to deny . . . and quickly he would learn to sleep behind a locked door.

"I always knew there was something special about those luminous orange eyes," my mother eventually declared.

None in my family, nor any other known Siberian, has a comparable gift. My gift's origin remains undiscovered to this day, but the knowledge of it quickly reached the Siberian military. By six seasons I was drafted into their intelligence division, hardly seeing and hardly knowing my family from the day I was conscripted. My parents found relief in this, as I was quite a fortunate one. I was thorned, as the rest in my family and as most Siberians are. However, even every thorned mother and father fear they carry the dormant hereditary gene that would yield an unthorned offspring, who would be forcibly taken for a lifetime of slavery . . . mining, pulling crops from the soil, or otherwise. The thorned can expect a military youth, longer if they or their superiors prefer. I was blessed with added fortune because of my gift. My purpose was strategy; I was not given a weapon or expected to lay my life down for my nation.

I spent my days and seasons in service of the Siberian military, though this often meant I would work more against my country's own people than against enemies from other states. When a peasant was noted or accused of dissent, be it acting or speaking against his country, he would be immediately taken into custody, restrained, and handed to me, even when I was a young child. Before my service, the man would likely be tortured if not killed, all based on a rumor. This tactic of the Siberian military dictatorship was practiced even without sufficient evidence, done to make a point, and to control their country through fear. When the distrusted were delivered to me, I would speak with them and record their words . . . a confusing strategy when your interrogator is eight, perhaps ten. However, the true information would be recorded when I would return at night, while the suspect, still in custody, slept. Dreams typically represent fears or desires. If a suspect dreamt of torture and execution, they were likely freed, as the military's effectiveness was considered to have reached the prisoner, controlling his mind effectively. If they dreamt of revolt, or anything heroic in which they either freed our slaves or assassinated our constituents, they would be executed . . . and I would be commended for identifying and silencing a threat before it became active.

This was painfully taxing. But I rationalized that, before my time, the man would have likely been beaten in exchange for his information. Or he might have been killed with even less information, a case for which I was merely used to justify what was to happen regardless.

Also difficult for such a young mind was the sexuality of so many dreams I was forced to observe, which will therefore be a presence in the story you read. Bizarre, often outlandish, lewd insights into the adult human mind. Things that would be difficult to separate by fear or desire, as no one would admit either way if questioned in their waking hours. As an intelligence officer I was high ranking, and even as a child able to find camaraderie with the other officers and dignitaries. Over a rowdy meal or bawdy gambling lasting late into the night . . . which was a schedule I was accustomed to . . . they would beg I retell the lewdest dreams I could recall observing, and in full detail. Of course, none of these men who listened would allow me to observe their dreams.

Meeting Her

I was nineteen seasons old with the depleted, tired eyes of a slave of sixty-five when I met Lavender and her sister, Marigold.

I had woken one day in the early evening, as was typical, though it was the season of darkness and so the sun was hidden regardless of the time of day. I had a file and a mission that awaited my attention, the result of a recent disturbance in one of the women's slave quarters.

Excerpts of the file read as follows:

Slave number: *00398871*
Slave name: *Lavender*
Captured: *Originally by a Petra tribe in a Palisades cave along southeast Thule, traded to Siberian ownership during Thulian slave-harvesting*
Nationality: *Siberia via Canada*
Serving: *Ore mine A45, Mainland Siberia*
Quartering: *Siberian women's camps*
Abilities: *Fluent in Canadian, Svalbardian, not yet Siberian*
Skills and uses: *Experienced wet nurse*
Family in service: *One sister, Marigold, slave number 00398870*

There was an essentially identical file with excerpts nearly the same aside from a different slave number, 00398870, and a different name: 'Marigold.' But it was Lavender's file that had recent writing at the bottom, suggesting that her abilities, skills, and uses be reevaluated. *Am I to determine if she's become dry?* I thought, not having yet met the woman. *There must be someone more appropriate for that sort of thing.*

I continued, reading the file's second page to find a description of the disturbance from several nights earlier.

Event Report

Event: *Death of slave 00228574*
Location: *Siberian women's camp near A45, Mainland Siberia*

Cause of death: *Contaminated food*
Labor-safety event: *None*
Insubordinate event: *Not believed at this time*

Description of event: *Slaves 00228574, 00398870, 00398871 and five others sharing quartering. Slave 00228574 and five others are Siberian-speaking-only natives. Slaves 00398870 and 00398871 are Canadian-born Siberians, and speak only Canadian and Svalbardian. Dinner had been served, but not yet consumed. Slave 00398871 became excited, seemingly to urge the others not to consume their meal. By description of the other five women, none consumed their dinner but slave 00228574. Slave 00398871 urgently attempted to prevent slave 00228574 from doing so, upon which slave 00228574 by the account of the other five became protective of her meal. Likely believing slave 00398871 was attempting to take her meal, slave 00228574 quickly ate as much as she was able before the other slaves physically restrained her. Within minutes, slave 00228574 was vomiting and within hours she was dead. Immediately reacting to the commotion, the guard responded prior to the death of slave 00228574 and alerted the cook, who disposed of his stock and attempted to alert other cooks in nearby quarters. This was somewhat successful, and likely prevented many slave deaths due to the contamination, but not all. In total, thirty-seven of the eighty potentially exposed slaves consumed the tainted stock, and all exposed to the contamination died, the other forty-three surviving.*

Action taken: *Tampering is not suspected. Unintentional mishandling of bulk stock is believed to be the cause of contamination. Suggest the stock officers and cooks involved be briefed. Of all forty-one surviving Siberian-speaking slave women, none claimed they were aware any contamination existed in their dinner. However, when questioned,*

slave 00398870 and her sister, slave 00398871, were elusive through
their language barrier to discuss how they were able to alert others of
the contamination and therefore save much of the slave population
potentially exposed. Suggest they be brought in for interrogation.

As I finished assembling my uniform, a knock came on my door. I heard the voice of another intelligence officer. "Are you awake yet, Agrippin? We're ready and waiting."

"Yes, Velorik," I answered. "I've just read the file."

I left my quarters and stepped out onto the base to meet the older, more diversely experienced officer. We walked through the dry, brittle mud under a half moon and along torchlit paths to the interrogation offices.

"They're here," he said as we approached the dull, low-ceilinged, almost portable structure built possibly in half a day. "How's your Canadian?"

"Still fluent," I answered. It was the end of Velorik's day and the beginning of mine. He was rushing as I still dragged myself into the waking world to begin. "I may have forgotten a few words, but nothing that would prevent communication. Yours?"

He paused, prepared to open the door to the building for me, and answered, "'Working proficiency,' according to my most recent evaluation. It's more difficult for us older folks, you know. We have more clutter." He smiled, tapping on his temple.

"I'll lead, then."

We walked down a narrow hallway, saluting a guard who allowed us into the room where slaves 00398870 and 00398871 waited to be interrogated. Ten or so candles were lit to combat the seasonal darkness. I also saw a faint, dim, but shimmering purple glow coming from two eyes on the other side of a cold rectangular table.

I quickly turned away, shielding my own eyes and their orange glow, whispering to Velorik in the dark room and in Siberian: "This won't do. I'll fetch a stronger light."

I returned with a lantern, holding it near my face and reentering the room. Velorik sat in the right seat across from the girls as Marigold and Lavender sat to their left and right respectively. I sat down and faced Lavender. I gathered not a word was spoken in the awkward moment while I had fetched the light, not even an introduction.

"Hello, Lavender and Marigold. My name is Agrippin and this man is Velorik. We're intelligence officers, and we have some questions for you."

Marigold slouched back in her chair, which teetered on its rear legs, and stared at the low, plain ceiling. Lavender stared at the table with her arms folded, tapping the fingers of her left hand high on her slender right arm.

"So. What are the epaulettes for?" teased Marigold, commenting on our uniforms. "Do officers wear them just so everybody knows?"

Lavender added: "Never mind her. She has a fashion sense."

"Epaulettes are passé, just so you're aware," suggested Marigold.

"Fortunately, it seems the plain woolen dress will never go out of fashion," remarked Velorik about the young women's slave garments. "Although I see the bonnet has fallen out of favor."

The girls ignored him. They were wearing their standard-issue thick-fabric, grainy gray working dresses. They were not wearing their bonnets; I don't understand how Marigold could have labored without one considering her hair. It was long and whitish blonde, falling over the back of her chair nearly to the floor. Lavender's hair was dark brown, shoulder length and cut to avoid her eyes.

I opened their file, read, and questioned in Canadian, "You both are— uh, experienced wet nurses?"

The girls burst into laughter, looked at each other, and continued laughing.

"What is a wet nurse?" Velorik asked quietly in Siberian.

I provided him with the Siberian term, and he immediately shifted from indifference to anger, staring quietly now at the girls as they ignored him.

"How old are you?" I asked, rather than bothering with the file.

"Seventeen," answered Marigold.

"And I recently turned sixteen in your slave mines," responded Lavender, sending a challenging stare directly into my eyes.

"Happy birthday," Velorik added coldly, in Canadian with his thick Siberian accent.

"So please, tell us how you were captured," I asked.

They looked at each other. Marigold began, "On Thule. We were traveling with a Featherman but had difficulty sleeping. So, we left our camp, intending to return, and wandered into a cave. We stumbled around a bit curiously, and saw what we believed were some flickering lights further inside. We went deeper to search for the lights, finding that they were little human-like creatures, scurrying around the caverns. Their bodies glowed in the darkness."

"Their bodies did not glow," corrected Velorik. "It was a bioluminescent scum they bathe in, one that coats their skin. The lakes and puddles in their caverns breed a film that gives off light in darkness. The Trogs and the Petras bathe in this film, to cover themselves so they can see and be seen."

"So, you were harvested by the Petras, who sold you to Siberia? And not by the Trogs?" I asked, referencing their files.

The girls looked at each other, uncertain, and shrugged their reply.

"It does not matter," Velorik concluded. "Trogs and Petras are the same, like Siberians and Canadians."

"In what way are we the same?" Marigold laughed.

Lavender added, also laughing, "You invade our country as predictably as the leaves fall. You have thorns and gray skin, and think you're the same as us?"

"Silver," corrected Velorik.

"Yes, fine. But as for your colors, I've never seen a Canadian with orange eyes before," she added, staring at me.

"Or red, or purple," I muttered to Velorik in Siberian.

"So, you believe—" he responded, suppressing his excitement.

"I'm certain. They glow like my own. She mentioned the color of mine and may have already noticed their shimmering as well, possibly not. But I believe her eyes must be a part of how she knew the meal was tainted."

"Wait. We'll discuss that, and Polaris, but later," replied Velorik. In Canadian, he added, "The Trogs and the Petras share a lineage—"

"So does the fish and the bigger fish that eats it, if you go back far enough," interrupted Lavender.

Velorik ignored her and continued, "The Trogs and the Petras are noticeably similar in appearance if you have ever seen them in the light. They may be able to tell each other apart, but to a Canadian or Siberian they simply look like small, human-like cave-dwelling creatures with bristly hairs, large eyes, and a light greenish skin. They speak separate languages that share no root with any language you would hear outside their caves, only to each other. This is because they were once part of a single existence."

The girls stared dully at Velorik. As if he awaited a prompt, I asked, "What happened?"

"They were a unified tribe until a collapse in their mine separated them, isolating their tunnels and cultures from each other for ages. Eventually they re-expanded their channels and were reunited, but by then they spoke different languages and were unable to find peace, yet they were the same."

"You're going somewhere with this," droned Marigold.

Velorik finished, "Yes. This is no different than the Siberians and the Canadians."

"You said the Trogs and the Petras bore a resemblance." Lavender snickered, shaking her head. She pointed to me and my fellow officer noting, "You two have sharp thorns sprouting out from your gray skin. I have never seen a Canadian with thorns."

"But there are unthorned Siberians, without the silver skin," I said. "A Canadian is nothing more than an unthorned Siberian, by their heredity."

"Therefore, all Canadians are truant Siberian slaves," concluded Velorik.

"Except us," laughed Marigold. "We're right here."

My stomach grew queasy as I prepared to defend the indefensible. Without any nausea of his own, Velorik explained, "From a hereditary view, two unthorned Siberian slaves will certainly give birth to an unthorned slave child, each and every time. Two thorned Siberians will most likely give birth to a thorned child, but not necessarily. They might have an unthorned boy or girl, which will therefore be harvested into the slave ranks."

"What of a mixed couple?" asked Marigold. My heart beat hard with a little embarrassment as she asked, "For example, Agrippin and Lavender. What if they were to have a child?"

"Well then Agrippin would find himself in a great deal of trouble." Velorik laughed.

Looking directly at Lavender, clumsily forgetting it was Marigold who had asked, I added, "Our child might be thorned or not. It would be less likely to be thorned than if both its parents were."

She smiled awkwardly yet did not blush, and politely but insincerely responded: "Okay, then. That's very interesting."

"I've watched many dreams in which thorned Siberian men fantasize about a romance with the tender, sanguine skin of an unthorned slave woman," I noted to Velorik in Siberian.

"Yes, well there are two right here. And we both know it wasn't true when I said you'd find yourself in a great deal of trouble."

Ignoring the disrespect in a language they didn't understand, Marigold said to her sister, laughing: "Still, even if there were a chance the baby could have thorns, I don't know if I'd take that risk. Giving birth seems torture enough without the—"

"The thorns come later, as the bones grow," I interrupted.

Marigold smirked, "So then you've decided that all of us without thorns are to be your slaves? Why, because you can't milk a tollimore without getting kicked?"

Holding my palms out to show the girls, I mumbled, "Actually no thorns grow from—"

Velorik interrupted loudly with his thick accent. "The Siberian military is the strongest in the world! Her children were chosen as the sole recipient of the gift of thorns! Even our land is rich with metal ore, for weapons. And in the northern sea sits Severnaya Siberia, an optimal location for our naval base and the ideal geographic protection for the mainland. These signs are too strong to be considered coincidence. They indicate our destiny, to rule the world."

The girls looked at each other and laughed. "Ha. 'Destiny.'"

Velorik, not typically an angry man, grew frustrated. "Our society is unlike yours. It does not exalt the individual, and we are stronger as a nation because all individuals accept their birth-given service. The ore needs to be mined and the crops need to be picked. And meanwhile, those born more equipped for battle are free but serve the destined Siberian army."

"We've heard this, what has it been, four times now?" asked Lavender, smiling at her sister.

"And for all we know, the Petras were the fifth, but we couldn't understand their language."

Lavender explained: "Four times from four different cultures, all believing themselves to be the chosen race. The King of Svalbard believes the discovery of their seed bank has made their people and their country the most significant. Many Feathermen believe a force they call Spirit Zero is contacting them through a device, an instrument. You say your thorns indicate you are chosen to rule the known world, and Polaris preaches essentially the same message as the others."

Marigold teased: "So yes, Velorik. Like the Trogs are to the Petras, we're not all that different."

Velorik smiled. "Yes. Polaris." Addressing Lavender, he said: "We have given you much information, and now I am curious to learn from you. What does Polaris preach to his people regarding their origin?"

"Don't ask me. Marigold knows her quatrains better than I do."

Marigold recited:

Above this word there is no text
I come from heaven's Northern Star
Its rays on earth's terrain reflects
Abandoning its home afar

She explained: "Polaris claims to come from the heavens, from a star in the sky. He claims to have brought this light with him, blessing the nomads and uncivilized men and women with it. He claims to have freed them from darkness as they became the early Canadians. They settled York under his religious and social leadership, ages past."

Velorik asked the girls, "And which is the North Star?"

"The one beneath which the world rotates on its axis," answered Lavender.

"Correct. But as for your leader's true origin, your Canadian education has failed you, I'm afraid," smiled Velorik. "And if you are not a product of your education, you will be a victim of your environment."

Marigold glanced at her fingernails. The girls were not bothered, nor did they show offense. Rather they sensed Velorik expected a certain defensive reaction which he would use to explain their error, and they refused to provide it.

He explained, "Girls, all Canadians are merely truant Siberian slaves. All of them, including Polaris."

"Of course!" reacted Lavender, appreciating the epiphany Velorik had handed her. "It's all so clear!"

"Incredible!" agreed Marigold as the girls looked at each other with excited smiles. "So, what then? Canada's redeemer and defender was merely an escaped slave?"

"Yes, and as I have said, Canadians and Siberians are as close as the Trogs and the Petras," added Velorik, although somewhat confused. I believe he expected them to resist a while and cling to their beliefs, but when they didn't, he seemed to instead mistake their celebration and excitement for the shift in allegiance he had been slowly attempting to foster in them.

Lavender asked: "So what was the separating event? For the Siberians and the Canadians, how did the caverns collapse to form the two cultures?"

"The most successful slave break in Siberian history," I answered.

Velorik continued, "Yes, and Polaris led this escape. He was a Siberian, and a genetic curiosity. Red eyes yet without albinism . . . he lacked thorns and was therefore a young slave. He led a large group of his fellow slaves through the darkness to the sea, where they took to the water by raft. We believe they used the North Star to navigate these waters."

I added, "So when he says he came directly from a star in the sky, there's some truth to it."

Velorik mumbled to me in Siberian, "We should know. It's how our ships invade Canada."

"I don't think a single Canadian knows this, except Polaris," said Lavender.

"Yes, but he's not Canadian. He's Siberian," insisted Velorik.

"How did they escape?" she asked.

"Fire. They simply set everything they possibly could on fire, in incredible synchronization and we believe with a type of oil slaves had access to at the time."

"Much of Siberia burned," I added.

Velorik finished: "And now you see how all of these slaves' descendants . . . all of them," he punctuated staring at Marigold then at Lavender, "are Siberian slaves living in delinquency."

Velorik was entirely serious, but the girls couldn't receive him that way. "Please. It's been ages. Polaris is ancient. Older than any of us by countless seasons." Marigold laughed.

"You can have him back," joked Lavender. "The rest are Canadian now."

"We will take Polaris back . . . eventually," insisted Velorik. "But it's not so simple. If a brush fire is ignored, it may spread beyond one's ability to contain it."

"Our father died in one of your neurotic attempts to combat this 'brush fire,'" mocked Lavender, somehow with condescending, satirical tone and not with a taint of personal grief.

Her sister added: "Yes, and you portray Polaris as a false witness and a blasphemer. Perhaps this is true. Yet through our father and through others we have heard of Siberian practices such as ritual sacrifice and even necromancy. So, every Canadian owes Polaris a debt of gratitude for pulling Canada's pilgrims and therefore her descendants away from these abominations."

"And slavery," added Lavender.

"Yes! If not for Polaris, today we would be Siberian slaves!" laughed Marigold.

"You are Siberian slaves!" Velorik insisted in frustration.

"Right. Thanks for explaining my joke to me."

"He thinks he's smarter than you," said Lavender. "But that's no surprise. Siberians are much more prejudiced than Canadians."

Laughing smugly, Velorik responded: "But don't you see? That very statement is prejudice itself."

The girls grimaced and shook their heads. Facing him, Marigold said, "Velorik . . . oh, simple Velorik . . . twice in a row?"

Lavender said, "I don't know if Polaris was the first slave to slip through your obsessive fingers, but he wasn't the last. Again, this we know from our father, a Canadian soldier killed by the Siberian thorn."

"Girls, I will not tolerate disrespect," said Velorik.

"What will you do, then, to punish us?" asked Marigold. "Enslave us and force us to work the mines?"

"How, in your position, can you be so flippant?" Velorik wondered.

She answered, "You may not know this, but we were exiled from Canada."

Lavender explained, "The King of Svalbard didn't care much for me before he even knew my name. A small mob on Jan Mayen Island attempted to kill us."

"But we were saved, thankfully, by possibly the least hospitable Featherman alive," laughed Marigold.

"Yes, so it's nice to finally feel wanted. If we burn a bridge to even one other country, we'll have to learn to tread water in our sleep."

"And so, you are disrespectful to your masters? You believe you are unconditionally welcome within Siberia because you are our captives? You are slaves!" insisted Velorik, unable to control their minds.

"We have free will," commented Lavender. "What else would we be but happy?"

Marigold added, "And you don't seem happy, Velorik. If you wish to obtain free will like us, you must find an agent to release you from the tyranny of petty concerns. Our current situation certainly forces the dismissal of these; yours invites them."

Velorik grew quite upset. Still, without screaming, he said heatedly: "Free will? You do not have free will! If I say you must do something, then you must do it!"

Marigold stated calmly, "No, that's freedom. Freedom may exist beyond our limitations, but free will exists within them."

"You have neither. You have only limitations, and I am but one of your many, many masters!"

"Yes, but to be the master is to be the slave," mocked Lavender.

"Oh, excellent!" celebrated an excitedly joyous Marigold as she turned to speak to her sister. "Well done. If we ever see Brother Lichen again, we'll have to remember—"

"Who? Never mind. Lavender, Marigold, I am free. You are not. Is this not plainly obvious to you, or has your Canadian education failed you once again?"

Lavender teased, "You're a slave to your epaulettes. You're no freer than an ovidon tied to a cart."

Too neurotic and myopic to realize the girls' device, Velorik did not see the value that their mockery possessed. Belittling your aggressor's point of view through sheer unaffected laughter can snatch their weapon, dismantle it in front of their eyes, and return it to them in pieces. It is, however, not the most respectful form of peacekeeping, so this approach may instead serve as the spark to an explosion. But, if you are willing to declare yourself independent and invincible, you will be prepared for that. And the girls most certainly were. They made it clear to Velorik that any woven web would entangle none but its weaver. They remained invincible, which Velorik found quite unnerving. I, however, was silently seduced.

"I will tie you to a cart, and you will tell me who is the slave!" he insisted.

"No," defied Lavender with alluring confidence. "We know you want us alive or we wouldn't be here."

"Yes, you're demanding obedience. But what is your threat exactly?" mocked Marigold. "Because if you can't find one that's effective, you may want to consider a rewards-based system. Food, clothing, jewelry . . . "

Lavender admitted: "We're slaves in the sense that you understand. You can make us work, you can feed us poison, and you can kill us. We possess nothing external, yet you are not satisfied with even that level of control. So, we present you with the tyrant's dilemma: you want to control our minds, but you cannot. But to admit that would be to admit helplessness in the matter, and to you nothing could be worse. You'd rather attack and attempt to control reality itself than admit helplessness. And you can never embrace helplessness because you're a tyrant. It's so unsettling and disturbing to you . . . and what's worse . . . think of the other things you cannot control. They're the most important things, and therefore the most unsettling to admit a helpless relationship. Life. Death. These are two things I know better than you may realize. You're one who must have control to be settled, but you'll never find it and as a result you leave yourself so bothered, so emotional because of this helpless self-inflicted dilemma that you unravel, becoming unable to control your own mind. And because all we have as slaves is our minds, we have become free, and you have become a slave."

"Tied to a cart," punctuated Marigold, smacking the table and smiling. "And I would suggest not wagering your own sanity to control our minds. We've already delivered two to an asylum."

I didn't know who these two were and did not ask. But their statement was as valid as it was hyperbole. My own definition of *insane* is one without adequate self-control or one who has a need for too much.

As the girls continued to mock the man, I said very little. They were fighting fire with water—a flood really—and Velorik failed to adapt. And so, he did the only thing he or any other Siberian officer was trained to do, which was dispatch more fire.

"All a slave has is their mind? What about family? I can easily arrange for one of you and not the other to be transported to a very, very distant slave camp. Yet in my kindness thus far, I have not."

Marigold said, words saturated in mockery, "Oh, thank you so much! Such kindness. Now I'll begin to form an obedient, loyal, emotional bond with you. In return I believe you will show favor to us."

"Can we call you 'Father'?" Lavender chimed in, topping her sister with heavily-soaked sarcasm. She sighed. "I know why you wished to speak with us. And yes, you can punish us. And yes, we would be devastated if you separated us. But you might have done that if we were perfectly behaved, simply to fulfill your own needs. And if you do, you cannot rely on my help in any way."

"Why did you not tell us of your gift?" I asked.

"I certainly begged her," Marigold noted. "I knew it could keep us from the mines, but she was afraid it would be exploited. And here we are."

"Every time I use my gift it seems something devastating is possible," explained Lavender.

"Please. Tell us the specific nature of your gift," I requested.

She exhaled, relieved and now smiling while speaking directly to me, "I've waited a long time to find another like myself. Would you please tell me the nature of your gift before I discuss mine?"

I looked at Velorik, a little stunned. In Siberian, I asked him, "How should I respond? She's noticed my eyes."

He answered while the girls stared impatiently, "She claims she has never met another with a gift? Distract her . . . tell her of their leader. That will give me a moment to think."

"You've never known another with a gift?" I asked. "But, what about Polaris?"

"Uh—" stammered a confused Lavender.

"Yes, his eyes are a unique red color, but he doesn't have any exclusive visions the rest of Canada cannot see," said Marigold. "Does he?"

"Perhaps nothing powerful, but yes, he does have a gift," I said.

Lavender squinted and grimaced, almost grunting with her palm pressing against her forehead: "That man is one deception after the next! Well, I suppose some sort of jealous cleansing is now the most recent theory emerging as to his hidden motives for my persecution. If this is true, I may never know. His agenda seems to be to conceal his agenda."

"Tell us your gift, and we will tell you about Polaris's gift and Agrippin's as well," blurted Velorik.

"Tell me Agrippin's gift, then I will tell you mine, then you will tell me Polaris's," bargained Lavender.

In Siberian, I noted to Velorik, "This is a futile exchange. Once she knows I can read her dreams she'll know she won't be able to hold a secret."

"Agreed," he responded to the girl, ignoring me. "Agrippin can observe your dreams. He can see them in images as you are sleeping."

"Incredible! Thank you. I was unsure that it would even be different from my own, and how interesting that it is. All right. I can view life and death. I knew the women in our quarters—all of them, in fact—were going to die under the circumstances of the moment. So, unable to speak Siberian, Marigold and I did what we could to adjust their circumstances, but one was determined to consume her poison. And she did. So, what does a dream look like to you? Can you hear them?"

"No," I replied. "They look to me just like my own dreams seem as I'm having them. I cannot hear the dreams, so I have studied the art of reading lips. And Lavender, when you see life and death, what do you see?"

"Various colored glows depending on the level of life or death. If someone is near death, a white glow. If a woman or an animal is pregnant, a red glow."

"Polaris?" asked Marigold.

"He can see through smoke and fog, clouds, vapors," answered Velorik.

Lavender and I looked at each other and snickered, laughing through our noses. "Completely useless," I joked.

"I certainly wouldn't trade," she added.

"Well, not entirely useless," reminded Velorik. "It undoubtedly helped his escape, able to set so much of Siberia ablaze yet lead his followers to the sea. In fact, it helped again from there. That was one of the reasons we were unable to follow him by ship, because of the sea fog."

"All right, but how often will that gift be useful?" asked Lavender.

"Yes, but it is still a gift," he responded pleasantly. With a certain maturity, he continued his mission, forgetting the girls' recent insults. "I am relieved to hear that you believed you had never met another gifted one. And I am sorry, but I am also relieved to hear that Polaris has exiled you. It tells us he is not breeding the gifted as we feared. The Siberian thorn has been an advantage for centuries, but we believe future battles will be won with these gifts, not with our thorns."

"Oh!" said Marigold, jumping in her seat. Her jaw dropped ecstatically, and she covered her blonde hair with her palms, incredibly excited. She turned her head frantically back and forth from me to her sister, and I believe this time my heart stopped beating entirely while I awaited her next words. "That's why we're here?"

"Oh no . . ." said Lavender as she hunched her shoulders, looked down at her knees and pressed her palms into her lap.

"Oh yes!" Marigold smiled, pointing to me. "He's going to make me an aunt!"

Velorik fanned the misunderstanding by standing to leave, joking, "Well, my workday is over, but you can go alone from here, Agrippin. Your workday is just beginning!"

"It sure is!" Marigold laughed. As Velorik left the room, Marigold hollered, "Wait, wait! Velorik! What am I to do? Stay with them and watch? Wait!"

He left without a reply. The moment he was gone, I explained, "We . . . they . . . " I swallowed and cleared my throat, finishing, "It's not the Siberian army's intent to breed us, Lavender."

Admittedly I was a little hurt by how relieved she was, but understandably it would have been forced.

"So?" she asked.

"So, we believe you have already given us the information we desire, and we thank you for doing so, but I will still be observing your dreams tonight. Both of you."

"Oh, well that's not any better," protested Marigold.

"That's much better," insisted Lavender.

"No, I mean, you were right, Lavender. As slaves, all we have is our minds, but now not even those."

"You must rest eventually," I noted, not mentioning the variety of chemicals I had access to that could be used to forcibly induce sleep. "You won't be returning to your slave quarters. Because you are aware your dreams are to be observed, we'll set up a separate room with a clean, plush, comfortable bed. You may request a specific meal if you like, a dessert, or a warm bath, and have every comfort you wish. In the way Velorik understands slavery, you would be my master. After all, we're more likely to have honest dreams when we're most relaxed."

"Tie me to the cart," said Marigold with a smile. "You had me at 'comfortable bed.'"

"Before we begin, I must ask a few questions, so I can better understand your dreams. Lavender first. What are some of your pleasures, your interests . . . if you would, please tell me some of your favorites . . . favorite meal, favorite flower, anything . . . "

"Some questions! And you claim you aren't trying to breed us?" joked Lavender.

With that hint of flirtation from the girl with the beautiful eyes, I pushed away my awkwardness and decided to flirt back a bit. "Let's start with a simple question. Lavender, would you please describe your most romantic fantasy?"

First Night of Dreams

We left the briefing office and walked back through the seasonal darkness and the brittle mud. I escorted Lavender and Marigold to the sleep observation quarters just beside my own assigned residence. A separate building, the sleep quarters were effectively my office right next to my military home. A guard stood outside. Inside was a suite designed for luxury and comfort, all engineered to dismantle a suspect's mind for the sake of intrusion. The guard saluted and signaled to me that the room was prepared, and indeed it was.

"Ah, finally a warm bath," said Marigold.

"You first," offered Lavender. "I'll begin with some treats."

"So will I," said Marigold, grabbing a handful of small Siberian finger pastries and bringing a tray to the tub. She drew the bath curtain, herself behind it, tossed her slave dress overtop the curtain rail and plunged into the warm water eating her pastries.

The room was filled with twenty or thirty candles, plenty to eat, soft decoration, one plush bed in the center against the wall, and a wooden chair in the far corner. It wasn't the only room in the building, but was sealed off to appear so.

It was fit for a general's wife, but most commonly used to observe criminals.

Trying to recall what filth had slept here last, I approached the bed to smell-test the sheets. "They've been cleaned," I informed Lavender, who was eating from the generous arrangement left out for the girls on a polished fine metal platter atop a dark wood chest.

"The bed's certainly big enough for two people," she said. Still somewhat guarded, she added, "Marigold . . . that is, Marigold and I will fit comfortably beside each other in the bed."

"It's been so long." Marigold sighed behind the bath curtain. She pulled it aside just enough for another view of the room, adding, "Yes, a real bed."

"Anything we can do for the sake of your comfort. Remember I will see the images of your dreams, but there is nothing, no matter how lewd, offensive, or embarrassing, that I haven't seen in another form many, many times already." Lavender turned to listen. "And that's because many of the repeating symbols, characters, and themes are classically true from one mind to the next. Dreams permit the subconscious to wander, seemingly aimlessly, and uninhibitedly."

"Marigold wanders aimlessly and uninhibitedly," said Lavender, nodding toward the bath.

"Then she is in the impulse-driven region of the mind," I added.

In a flash, Marigold pulled her bath curtain entirely, sitting nude in the tub but covering her private areas with her knees bent and together. With her right arm across her chest, she whipped her head around, spraying Lavender and me generously with her long, soaked hair. In another flash the curtain was pulled closed, the metal rings dragging along the curtain rod, and Marigold resumed her bath.

"Thank you, Marigold." I nodded. "I'll return in an hour or so to spend the night in my chair there in the corner. Would you like me to bring anything when I return? Anything?"

They made no further request. When I returned, I found they had already lain down in the bed. They had snuffed most of the candles and were sleeping but had not yet begun to dream. With so little light and tucked so well under their covers, I couldn't identify which body was Lavender's and which was Marigold's. And I would need to if I were to record their dreams with any purpose.

I approached the right side of the bed to see a cover sheet tucked to the chin, with little more exposed than a gentle face, short, dark, wet hair, and the damp bathwater stain on the pillow. I smiled a moment as her eyes rested, sharing the relief she must feel whenever she closed them. I stayed near her and held still a moment, and another. I stopped staring only when I realized that in the room's darkness I could see the reflection of the orange glow from my eyes off her cheek. *She wouldn't appreciate this*, I thought, backing away from within a breath of her lips, settling into my chair in the corner of the room.

I waited a while for the dreams to begin, end, and begin again, watching tediously while neither dreamed, then scribbling frantically when they both dreamed at the same time. I had hoped to find myself in one of Lavender's dreams, in almost any capacity, only to learn if she had formed any thoughts of me. Rather her dreams were more symbolic and distressful, eerie and nightmarish. It was difficult to watch her suffer knowing how easily I could have woken her from one of these horrors. But it was my task to record, not to interrupt. And my image made no appearance in her dreams, casual or sexual. If there was any sexual content observed, though not of me, it was on Marigold's part.

When the girls woke in the morning, it meant my workday neared its end. They left their suite and we walked across the dry mud again to the same briefing room we had met in the day prior.

Velorik had not yet arrived. I was quite prepared to return to my quarters and sleep while the waking world did whatever it does without me. We sat as we had before, across the table, and I began to rub my eyes with fatigue. When I finished and lifted my chin, I saw the girls both staring at me, cringing.

"What?"

"The thorns coming from your knuckles . . ." explained Marigold. "They came awfully close to your eyes."

I was silently hurt when I looked at Lavender and saw that she was still cringing somewhat. "Think of them as fingernails. You wouldn't scratch your eyes with your own fingernails."

They cringed again at the comparison, hurting me further, but not for long. The girls began to ask about their dreams.

"Do you recall any of them?" I wondered.

"No," they answered.

"I'll begin with Marigold," I said, pulling out my notes as she smiled. "Dream Two—"

"What about Dream One?" she asked.

"Dream One," I complied. "Peeling carrots with difficulty using a dull knife."

"Ah, the subconscious. The dark, inaccessible side of my mind," joked Marigold.

"Dream Two," I continued. "Marigold, have you ever been to the Svalbardian Royal Castle?"

"Kilde-av-Kimen? Yes, we have. Somewhat recently. You could say we took the grand tour."

"So, your memory of the layout is still accurate? Because in your dream you revealed much of what you remember from there. These are the images the Siberian military really, really appreciates."

"Oh dear . . ." she said, Lavender now nervous as well. Marigold asked, "What was I doing in the castle?"

"Running, nude, chasing a man."

"Quinby!" Lavender laughed. "Marigold, not even your dreams are subtle!"

"I don't know his name, but he was dressed as a Canadian soldier. He appeared injured, but would disappear whenever you approached him."

She sunk down, leaned forward, placed her head gently on the table, and covered her face with her hands and long hair. "That was my father."

"Ah, the one who yesterday you said died in battle? That would make sense. He seemed to characterize the 'elusive father' symbol. This is common in female dreams, and usually indicates the absence of the authoritative father."

Marigold picked her head up and asked, "I was chasing my father? But why in Kilde-av-Kimen?"

Lavender added to the embarrassment. "And why nude?"

Marigold sunk again into the table. "Oh, and you saw me nude."

"For the second time," Lavender said, reminding Marigold of the mischievous splash from her bath.

"In your dream, yes. Your fifth dream may answer your question." Reading my notes, I continued: "Tall male present, Svalbardian, age twenty-two to twenty-nine. Marigold is quite drawn to the male but only until very close, when she is quickly and strongly repelled, fearful."

"That's Quinby," commented Lavender.

I continued: "Nature of Marigold's behavior toward the male seems to indicate he is the classic 'impregnator.' Possible relationship to Dream Two." I breathed deeply, looked up from my file to Marigold and said, "Well, I have two more that don't involve peeling carrots."

Already squirming uncomfortably, Marigold responded: "Continue if you must."

"Dream Three. An older man argues with Marigold over mundane chores. The issues seem to be that of obedience, independence, and mutual respect. Setting is a farm, and the older man may represent the authoritative father."

"Our grandfather. He didn't spend a lot of time with me growing up. Plenty with Lavender, though."

"Wait," said Lavender. "So now you have a sketch of Kilde-av-Kimen and our family's home in Canada?" Turning to her sister she noted, "This is awful."

"Oh, just wait until it's your turn," said Marigold.

"One more first," I continued. "A complicated one, so please don't react before I can explain . . . Dream Four, an inviting form approaches warmly with a smile. Arms are open and the form is somewhat androgynous, with both male and female anatomy."

"A hermaph—" began Marigold.

Expecting her to protest, I raised my hand. "Please. I must explain. It's the merging of the opposites. This was possibly your one dream without sexual content."

"What about the carro . . . oh, never mind." Lavender caught herself and returned to silence.

"So what then, Siberia and Canada?" asked Marigold.

"Most likely. The Trogs and the Petras, less likely. Or possibly a fear, such as Velorik's threat made yesterday regarding separating you and Lavender. Do you see yourself and your sister as opposites?"

"Yes, actually," she agreed. "*Complements* may be the more appropriate term."

"All right. Lavender?"

"Please."

"Dream Three, nighttime in the forest. Alone at a campsite, Lavender carries the trunk of a large pine tree toward a campfire. The tree would be much too large to carry if not a dream. She places the tree in the fire, and it begins to burn. She stands back and laments the loss of the tree."

Marigold pleaded: "Just to even things out a bit, please tell me the pine tree is some sort of phallic symbol."

"No. The tree symbol usually represents growth and personal development."

"Of course," whined Marigold.

Lavender smiled. "But really it could be anything."

"Well, yes."

"So, the symbols? The characters?" asked Marigold. "The father, the tree? Those are symbols?"

"Yes. All part of our shared human inheritance, which is why they're so common in folklore and mythology. The guardian spook, the milking mother, the creature of living earth, the warrior, the leviathan, the tragic couple, the royal house, the disturbed and undead, the sky warrior, the alchemist . . ."

Listing the symbols, I wondered again if I could find myself in Lavender's subconscious.

Could I play a role?

I wished desperately that, through our gifts if necessary, we might have a place as the divine couple . . . and we would occupy an already-existing root in her mind, a place in her dreams, and a role in her waking world.

Lavender wondered about another symbol. "So then what is the fire? In my dream, as I burned the tree?"

"The fire symbol? It recurred again in Dream Four. The setting is similar, in the wilderness, although the fire burns higher, stronger, and less controlled. This was odd . . . you are facing the fire from a safe distance, focused intently on the fire itself. It's night or at least dark in your dream, and although the fire is the sole source of light, a large, looming shadow stretches from your feet and is cast toward the fire," I said, turning my notes around to show her a sketch of what I saw. "By all rules of optics, the shadow should have been cast behind you. In the dream you attempted to walk the circumference around the fire, always facing it, but no matter where you moved, the darkness adjusted to be radially between you and the fire, so that you could not reach the flame without walking through your shadow."

"Yes, but it's a dream," said Marigold dismissively.

"The rules of light may not apply to the shadow, but it does have its own rules to abide by."

Lavender said: "I'm fearful to ask what it may mean, Agrippin. Your tone sounds concerned."

"Lavender . . . yes . . . I . . . I wonder why your shadow was so large in your dream. Have you . . . have you killed another, or done anything you deeply regret?"

Discouraged, she sighed and answered: "Yes, but not as a murderer. I'm haunted by the dead slave woman in my quarters, the inadvertent trouble we stirred up on Jan Mayen Island, an older Canadian I unsuccessfully rushed to the hospital . . . "

Marigold wrapped her arm firmly around her troubled sister's shoulders.

Across the table I glanced down at my own arm and counted no less than five thorns between the elbow and the wrist.

Lavender didn't allow an extended moment of sympathy. She collected herself and asked, "So then, what is the fire?"

I answered: "I think it would be irresponsible for me even to discuss it. After being overwhelmed with so much information yesterday regarding Polaris and his abilities, and his method of using oil to set Siberia ablaze in the slave outbreak . . . even all these candles and lanterns we use in this time of seasonal darkness . . . It could be anything, and is probably several things. It's too convoluted even to attempt—"

"But in my first dream, the fire was something that destroyed my tree . . . my hope of growth, and of development."

"Such as the loss of a father," reflected Marigold.

"Or exile," commented Lavender.

"Yes, or the exploitation of a gift," I added.

"Well, I still enjoyed my warm bath," joked Marigold, breaking the disturbing tension.

I finally heard Velorik's voice from the hall, chatting with the guard.

"Excuse me a moment," I said to the girls, leaving them in the interrogation room and finding my fellow officer.

"Velorik! Good morning," I called out in Siberian.

"Good morning, Agrippin. So, what do Canadian girls dream about?"

"Oh, the same as any other . . . although I saw the blonde nude," I joked.

He laughed, asking: "So what have we learned from the reevaluation of their skills and abilities?"

"We can say confidently that they aren't wet nurses."

"You might know, having seen one of them nude."

"Lavender has already discussed her gift . . . beyond that, based on my questioning and analyses I would say she has a technical, organized mind."

"And the blonde?" he asked. "Is she gifted in any way that may be useful to us?"

"No, I don't believe she has any gift like her sister's. Even her mind is different. She is more of a performer or an artist, more an aesthete."

He joked: "Ah, so she is doubly useless."

"No, I wouldn't say that."

"Oh, please understand me," he placated, poorly. "An aesthete such as the blonde will never provide anything essential to survival. Remove the useful one's gift and her technical, practical mind may still be that of a physician, engineer, or mathematician."

"Or front liner, or ditch digger," I added.

Never intending to begin a dispute, he said: "Should the front liner or ditch digger not be respected for their work?"

"They should. Should the musician not be respected as much as the physician?"

"You've fallen for her, haven't you?" Not understanding exactly whom he meant, my heart had yet another arrhythmic lapse as he teased: "Yes, you've fallen for the useless blonde."

I answered truthfully: "Oh no. I haven't fallen for Marigold."

"Well, if you want her, take her. She's a slave, and if she keeps you happy, she's not entirely useless. Besides, our interest is with the gifted girl."

"Oh." I sighed. "What interest?"

"This will be my second briefing of the morning. Come, I'll explain as I inform the girls."

I followed Velorik nervously back into the briefing room, where the girls waited. A decision had been made by a committee of officers, and I was marginalized yet again from participating in the discussion. But I was their aesthete, their servant artist, and because of my craft I often slept while they formed their decisions.

Velorik began: "Lavender, Marigold . . . you will be returning to Canada."

Marigold perked up at his words, while Lavender remained cynical, stating: "Then we'll be returning as your slaves. If we return free, Polaris will execute us on sight."

"Your father died in battle, as you have said," commented Velorik.

"Yes."

"And you have said that you have found a way to be a slave yet have free will."

"Yes."

"And you have also said, 'You can have Polaris back,' correct?" he asked.

"Yes, this is all true," agreed Lavender.

"'You invade our country as predictably as the leaves fall'?"

"Yes, I said this. So?"

"So, we would like you to guide an initiative. The ships are being prepared and the troops assembled as we speak. Hundreds of ships, thousands of men. Thorned Siberian soldiers awaiting your guidance."

Speaking in Siberian, I demanded, "An invasion? Velorik, when was this decided? How many are to be dispatched, all but the laundry guard?"

Marigold's excitement turned to shock, while Lavender calculated quickly.

"Agrippin, please, they will know your sentiment by your tone," Velorik responded calmly in our native tongue.

"My tone? So what of my tone!" I was tired, needing sleep, and loud in my impatience. I wasn't pleased to learn of the plan to invade Canada, but I shouldn't have been surprised. It seems each of my country's recent generations has had a perceived need to go into battle, with or without cause, so that they may produce their own military heroes, establish their identity, and have someone to honor and emulate for their next battle.

"You'll be traveling with them," he turned to inform me. "The girls don't speak a drop of Siberian, and you are our highest-testing Canadian translator. But more important, we need you to stay inside the mind of the gifted slave girl, in the event she considers anything insubordinate."

"Is everything all right?" mocked Marigold.

"A moment, please," I responded, turning to Velorik and continuing in Siberian: "And why do you think she would . . . oh, you still believe you can control her mind, don't you?"

"No, but you can read her thoughts as she sleeps. And you have been very effective in the past at identifying and silencing threats while they are still dormant. Now please, allow me to speak with the girls."

"Yes, please," I insisted. "Feed them your propaganda."

"Propaganda?" said Marigold, hearing a familiar word.

"Yes, we have this word as well in the Canadian language," noted Lavender.

"See what you've done?" he turned, upset as I smiled. In Canadian he addressed, "No, it sounds the same, but is a different word, with a different meaning."

"Such as 'counterintelligence.'" I smiled.

Velorik glared angrily at me. As the girls had done the day prior, I returned his gaze with an invincible smile.

He continued: "Lavender, the violence could end. You're no longer a Canadian, having been exiled. If allegiance is an issue, it should not be, considering your sentiment towards Polaris. Your father died defending Canada, so why inflict this upon another family? If you watch over our army, you could guide it from danger, just as you saved so many slaves. You would save not only Siberian lives but if the initiative is swift, overwhelming, and decisive, the Canadian military will lay down their weapons and many Canadian lives will be saved as well."

"You're right," agreed Lavender. "These battles occur so frequently. Your country persists and persists, and seems to advance and retreat from Canadian shores as stubbornly as the tide. I don't expect this to change. It would end the constant fighting if you simply absorbed Canada within your empire. And if Canada fell to your rule, I don't see how this would be any worse than if Polaris continues his reign. And no, I have no allegiance to him. So let it be Siberian rule, and let the violence end."

"WHAT?" shouted Marigold as I stared at the gifted girl. "But they will bring slavery, and other atrocities! No allegiance? No family? No . . . no, no . . . oh no, Lavender . . . "

Lavender didn't turn to face her sister, choosing rather to stare downward, gazing at the cold table of the interrogation room.

Like me, however, she knew that what was going to happen would do so without concern over how we personally felt about it. Shocked with what seemed to be a hasty, potentially world-altering decision made by both the Siberian commanders and the young, gifted woman, I believed Lavender to be stepping forward into her own tremendous, looming shadow, approaching the fire.

"Wonderful," commented Velorik. "An excellent decision. We sail tomorrow morning, and Agrippin will be your escort for the entire campaign." He turned to Marigold and explained, "You will be spending a great deal of time with him. You girls may spend the day and sleep the night again in the suite." He then turned to me and said in Siberian: "Stay inside the gifted girl's mind. If she deceives us, you will be accountable."

Second Night of Dreams

I woke that evening and immediately visited the suite in the quarters beside my own to find the girls behaving quite normally. For Marigold, this meant she had returned to bordering on the absurd. And it also meant she was no longer affected by her sister's consent to lead a tremendous Siberian invasion of their homeland. This shift was possibly based on a more recent private discussion between the sisters; I did not know. Now their flippancy was bothering me, as it had troubled Velorik earlier. I was tied to two carts, now moving in opposite directions. If Lavender were to obediently follow Velorik and the other commanders' orders, I would be unable to explain Marigold's ease. But that was not the matter; rather the scale of the invasion and the exploitation of her gift was the trouble. The second cart, which better explained both Marigold and Lavender's coy smiles, said that Lavender had only agreed in word to Velorik, and was not going to follow through with any level of obedience to the man. If this were the case, as Velorik warned, I would be expected to detect the disobedience or be held accountable.

Within minutes of lying down in their plush bed to sleep beside each other, Marigold was snoring loudly. When Lavender elbowed her, she mumbled something about peeling carrots.

I laughed as Lavender groaned in frustration, turned away and pressed her pillow over her ear. I've heard plenty of snoring, and this wasn't genuine. Marigold hadn't snored at all the previous night. I approached her and shook her shoulder. "You're snoring, dear. Rather loudly."

"What? What?" She pretended. "But the carrots . . . I was almost done this time."

I laughed and lied, "Yes, I saw."

You don't dream while you snore.

"It seems I've got a bit of a snoring issue," she continued. "I can sleep in another room if it will help."

I paused, considered her offer, and glanced at Lavender, whose pillow was still pressed over her ear. "Yes. Yes, Marigold, thank you. I believe it would help."

"No need. I'll go to another room," said Lavender, getting up from the comfortable bed.

"Well, Lavender, the problem is the only other room is mine. In my quarters just next door."

"So, I'll sleep on your bed. You can watch Marigold finish peeling her carrots."

"Actually, I can't." I wasn't lying, nor was I playing the situation to my favor. If she were to leave, my work would take me to wherever she slept. "I would have to follow you."

"Come on, then," she said unenthusiastically.

Lavender and I stood outside on the doorstep. I told the guard not to bother Marigold and glanced over at my nearby quarters and back at Lavender. "Is there anywhere you'd like to go? The market is closed but the base has a small shop."

"Something warm to drink might be nice."

"I . . . I have something in my quarters," I offered, already forgetting my patience.

"All right, show me the way. It might be nice to share what we know about the origin of our gifts."

"Then I'll be unable to do much of the talking," I answered as we walked. "I'm not withholding anything. Siberia genuinely knows very little of how one is born with a pair of shimmering eyes. If they knew more, I assure you they would have bred a new army."

"I don't know anything, either. I wonder what Polaris knows."

"Our military lives in constant fear that he knows much more about the gifts than we do, and that he'll harness them first."

"He seems more interested in eradicating those with a gift than breeding us. So, I suppose we should start a fire?"

"We should?" I asked.

"Yes, to boil some water." She laughed.

We spent some time talking, hours in fact. She told me of her recent travels with her sister; I entertained her with stories of the most unusual dreamers and most outlandish visions I had watched.

She went to sleep in my bed, and I began again hoping to find myself in her subconscious. I wasn't present in her first dream, and I don't envy the man who was. It was Polaris, and he was tied with a noose around his neck in the gallows, under Lavender's control.

The rope was slack, and his weight was on his feet, not yet the victim of execution. He was glowing white, revealing to me her vision, which no one else had seen but her. It was an aura, an almost heavenly light shining off him like energy. It didn't flicker or pulse like a fire; it glowed. She was troubled in her dream, as the crowd observing the impending execution was boisterous but torn. Some seemed to want him dead, others wanted him alive, and his fate was in Lavender's hands. The dream may have revealed her desire to kill the man who exiled her, or possibly it revealed a fear that she would one day kill him.

Or that she was afraid she desired to kill him and couldn't hide it. Certainly this is a dream the Siberian military would not want interrupted, but I took not a single written note as the girl's sleeping body seemed unstill and disturbed. I've seen dreams that should've been more disturbing than this, but I couldn't bear it.

"Lavender," I whispered, touching her shoulder, waking her before Polaris was hung. "Lavender, dear, you're having a terrible dream."

"What?" She jerked. "Oh, thank you." She breathed deeply several times and repositioned herself under the sheets.

Several hours and three indifferent episodes later, another male form entered what was Lavender's fifth dream. I knew immediately there would be potential. I recognized an indiscriminate male, which likely was the classic symbol of the lover. She was embracing the man gently, her head and cheek on his chest. She leaned away to look at him and smile, unblocking his face. I almost shouted with excitement as I recognized myself; I was finally in her subconscious. *Oh, it's me! It's me, without thorns!* I thought. Then I almost cried in dejection, realizing: *Oh, it's me . . . without thorns.*

I stood up quietly. I watched the dream imagery above her body and patiently approached it, all while minding my steps. The figures were smiling, their arms intertwined. I knew I could bring this from her subconscious into her conscious, waking mind if the images stayed amorous. If I were to ignore the dream and never mention it to her, she would likely forget it. But if she awoke during the dream, she might remember it forever.

The unthorned image of me closed its eyes as Lavender's image closed hers. I was poised at the side of the bed. I watched the images intently . . . they were going to kiss. I saw the reflection of my orange eyes again on her sleeping cheek, and found her chin resting on the mattress.

The images were hardly an instant away from kissing . . . I reached out to gently lift Lavender's chin with my hand, intending to bring my lips to hers while she slept, breaking her dream and willing it to life.

But I didn't. I backed away to watch the imagined reality, trying only my skill at lipreading. The image of Lavender seemed to mouth the words, "Kiss me," yet I could do nothing but watch.

She kissed in her dream, then startled and awoke. I looked down at my feet, certain I had done nothing wrong. The guilt of our thoughts kept my eyes on the floor.

"Did you see that?" she asked.

"Yes."

"You did? I can hardly hear you."

"Yes," I said, a little louder.

"Can you come here?"

I stepped to the side of her bed and knelt, finding her by following her eyes glowing in the dark. I told her: "It's all right. I might have had the same dream myself."

"What if I were to tell you it was a good dream?"

"Then I would do this." I leaned in and pressed my lips to hers. She wrapped her hand carefully behind my neck and opened her lips for mine while I moved my hand from her chin to the side of her face.

"Stop," she said quietly.

I felt a surge of denial, wanting to believe she wasn't rejecting me so quickly. "I'm sorry. Did I prick your cheek? I'm so sorry."

"No, that's not it. We just can't continue."

"I'm so sorry. I shouldn't have. I've been thinking about you. But I shouldn't have been so bold."

"No, that's not what I meant. I saw a brief, red glow. If we had continued, we wouldn't have stopped."

"The red glow is gone now?"

"Yes. It was only a warning."

"Oh. And red means . . ."

She smiled. "I think you know what it means, intelligence officer."

"So, we would have . . ." I paused. "Lavender, may I ask you something?"

"Yes."

"Have you thought about what our child would be like? If we were to have one."

"Unhappy."

"Why?"

"You're serious? I enjoyed your kiss, but a child?"

"It wouldn't be so absurd, you and me."

"On our own, maybe. But like this? If you're serious, I'm going to start thinking the Siberian army really is trying to breed a gifted child."

"No. We could keep the child for our own," I suggested.

"Agrippin . . ."

"We may be the only gifted people in the known world aside from Polaris. We could have a gifted child. Our own gifted child. Or greater . . . a holy child in a holy family. One the world desperately needs, born to strike peace between the Canadians and Siberians."

"What a wonderful life, when our child is taken from us and its gift is exploited by your country. Besides, I would like to know this child's father a little better first."

"I'm so sorry. I ruined the feeling in the room."

"Wait," she said, gripping my hand as I tried to go back to my chair.

"Yes?"

"I can't get pregnant from a kiss."

I could see the glow of my eyes on her cheeks, and she could see the glow of hers on mine. We closed them together, and when we did, the room was entirely dark.

Fetters

Lavender, Marigold, and I as their constant escort clung to one another as a small unit. We were transported by ferry from the mainland to a naval base on Severnaya. With Velorik's intermittent presence and the entire absence of sunlight, we were hooded and rushed onto a tremendous, armored ship docked among smaller ones. We were not to be seen. I don't believe we were . . . and the girls were not to become an object of curiosity to the other soldiers.

I had never deployed, nor had I ever witnessed our naval fleet. There weren't hundreds of ships as Velorik's boasting had suggested, but the fleet wasn't far shy, and even in the darkness I was able to count enough to conquer a younger nation. The docked armada rocked gently with the tide, almost colliding rail to rail and plank to plank, with empty masts waving farewell to the island. The slave girls were fettered and chained to the very structure of their room, a private prisoner cell toward the stern of the ship. The quarters had been carefully converted to be suitable for a prisoner of the highest profile, be they the King of Svalbard or Polaris himself, should he ever return to his native home as our captive. Their chains were slack enough to reach their beds but not the door to their quarters. Even once we launched, they were not free to roam the deck, as I was. There was a third bed and a wooden chair, also mine, in a far corner of the room.

I felt like a child, frustrated with complex authority figures who refused to be direct and honest. My inability to understand the waking world made me feel all the more immature, yet had it been an abstract symbolic dream, I could have construed a more lucid explanation. Nothing made sense. The Siberian army had only begun to research Lavender's gift and, I assumed, proclaim false faith in her guidance. I had yet to determine the sisters' true intentions, but I could not doubt the staggeringly large fleet of warships prepared for launch from an island of Severnaya.

"We're sailing now, aren't we?" asked Lavender shortly after the push. "I feel a different motion." She lay on her bed, as did Marigold, shackles dangling from their mattresses and connecting to attachment panels bolted to the wall.

"Yes. I wonder where Velorik is."

"Is he on this boat, or another?" asked Marigold.

"This is the generals' boat, and every officer's other than the various ship captains."

"When . . . when do I begin?" asked Lavender, Marigold turning quietly away from her pillow to face her.

I rose from my chair to leave, noting: "I'll find Velorik."

I stumbled onto the deck for a sight I don't often see. The boat was not entirely officers; some better-blistered hands were needed to move the vessel through the water. Simply watching the work of the other side of the army, the greater-numbered but lesser-ranking, was a vision into a world as different as that of the dream realm. I had no understanding why a boat would require so much rope, so many metal devices inside which I would dare not rest a hand, or so much tension in the knots and in the voices of the crew.

We sailed not as the lead ship but tucked within the fleet. We moved dangerously close to the other warships, which were carrying thousands of soldiers, livestock, supplies, fresh water, weaponry, and whatever the Siberian army required to stage their pre-battle ritual and launch their attack, both of which I had also never witnessed. The ships, numbering nearly a hundred, were guided by the North Star.

I walked with Velorik back from his quarters. "She asked what is expected of her. It might be best to brief her and Marigold."

"Marigold." He laughed. "It's fortunate for the slave girls that you have taken a fondness for the useless one. Otherwise, she'd be left behind and the sisters separated. But don't let all of that bright, blonde hair distract you from staying in the conscious mind of the gifted one."

I denied nothing, allowing him to continue to believe I had been carrying an intrigue with Marigold. Evidently, it was to her benefit that Velorik believed this.

When we entered their room, he looked directly at Marigold and asked mockingly: "So Marigold, how has Agrippin been treating you?"

"Wonderfully," she replied calmly. "Agrippin has treated me very kindly."

Believing he understood more than he did, he turned to me and smiled mischievously.

He then moved toward Lavender and told her, "I will be speaking to you on behalf of the commanding generals."

She asked: "They don't speak Canadian?"

Velorik lied, "Yes, in fact they all speak quite well. And they certainly believe in your ability to steer their army from death. With you, they are pleased that they will not march into defeat. However, they also believe in your ability to command life and death and will therefore, for their own protection and security of their nation, be unable to visit you."

"It doesn't work like that," I mumbled, drawing a soft laugh from the girls.

"Yes, I tried to tell them," said Velorik defensively. "But they do believe in your gift and your guidance. They are here, on this ship. And this is the flagship. You are the flag officer of the entire fleet of over a hundred ships."

In Siberian, I asked, "Really, Velorik? Those who don't allow pockets on maids' uniforms trust a girl they will not meet?"

He answered in Siberian, "Agrippin, you are too young to be this old. What is the problem now?"

"How were so many ships and soldiers readied so quickly? Or were we invading Canada regardless? Are the commanders following her gift, or are they using her as a rallying cry to inspire the front lines to fight, believing they have a divine layer of protection from death?"

"They genuinely trust her gift," he answered, seeming honest by my detection. "Of course, they will not allow her to guide them into the mouth of a volcano, and neither will you, so stay inside her head. But when have you become so untrusting, and so cynical of your own commanders?"

I continued in our native language, while the girls stared impatiently. "I . . . I have seen the minds of many who did not trust us. I'm sorry; it's just difficult to believe they would follow this gift."

"Of course, and you have never witnessed a necromancer's work. You will on the eve of the attack. Then you will understand the faith they place in her."

"All right, enough," protested Marigold. "What under the stars are you discussing?"

"I believe I heard a word that sounded like *necromancy*," stated Lavender with a bewildered look.

"We were just discussing when you would begin to guide the fleet," I lied, testing Velorik's reaction.

Still speaking in Siberian, he responded, "Agrippin, that's not to happen until we reach land. The stars are safe enough guidance for now."

"Nonsense. She's the flag officer, is she not?" I said. "Or was that a title meant for flattery, only to foster allegiance?"

Velorik grimaced, squeezed his eyebrow, and spoke to Marigold. "Please, stay here in the quarters with Agrippin." He switched back again to Siberian and said to me: "If you would like some time with her, you need only ask."

"Yes, you take Lavender out on deck. I will stay here with Marigold," I said, in Canadian, walking to her mattress and standing beside it.

Velorik responded in Siberian, "Very well. Enjoy her without inhibition. I'll explain what I mean later." He then pulled a key to release the gifted girl's fetters.

Lavender glanced back at her sister and me, confused. Once she was free, Velorik glanced back as well and smiled. I sat at the foot of Marigold's bed as she lay on it, also confused but not flinching. Velorik escorted Lavender out of the quarters, and as they left, I hollered, "Be sure to keep us safe, Lavender."

The door shut. Alone with me now in the quarters and confused, Marigold instantly demanded: "What's happening and what are your intentions?"

"Has Lavender . . . mentioned me?"

"Yes. So don't you dare hurt her," warned the older sister, smiling in relief.

"Thank you . . . the other night, for helping me be alone with her."

"I was helping her, not you."

"Still, thank you."

"All right, up and off the foot of my bed. What was that about just now, when Velorik was here?"

"Oh, of course." I stood, stepped away and answered, "He thinks . . ." I sighed, expecting all variety of laughter from Marigold. "He believes I've taken a strong liking to you, and that I've taken advantage of your position as a slave. He doesn't know I care for Lavender."

"Oh, how dramatically complicated." She smiled, entertained. "This makes your attraction to my sister all the more interesting."

"No. It's more distressing than this. I don't know if he was serious, but he mentioned that you wouldn't be here if I had not had an interest in you."

"Oh dear. So they might have left me behind, and separated me from my sister? Well, how would they expect her cooperation if they had done that?"

"I don't know. I don't understand quite a bit of what they are attempting."

"So, when Velorik offered that you stay here with me just then?"

"I had to accept. Or you lose the one value he finds useful in you."

Marigold was disgusted, and this seemed not easily accomplished. Upset but calm, she asked, "So, right now? He thinks we're together?"

"Dramatically complicated, yes."

"Oh, I hope he's not out on the deck mocking Lavender with this."

"And I hope he doesn't take too long to return. If he doesn't come back before I start complaining, I'll be very upset."

She smiled. "You really have been spending time with my sister. That's something I would say."

It was approximately another half hour, but not as awkward as it could have been. Marigold and I did eventually discuss greater things, such as the impending invasion, the trip at sea, and even her time aboard the yacht of the Prince of Svalbard. Then there was a knock at the door, and Velorik's voice warning: "We're entering, if that's all right."

Lavender shoved open the door and looked me directly in the eye, purple to orange, but with the standard mixed anger and favor that forms jealous heat. I smiled in return, not to mock her, but pleased to know I could correct the anger. She didn't mind the fact that Marigold still lay in her bed fully clothed and I was across the room uninvolved, with no evidence of misbehavior.

Velorik glanced at me and noticed a smile on my face, but misplaced its source. He wasn't pleased with me and therefore simply stated his business. "Lavender said there were no glows, but that she was able to see a storm on the horizon the crew did not, even with their tools. She has guided us in an easterly diversion to avoid this." Lavender continued to shine a focused beam of angry purple light in my direction, Marigold was silent, and I smiled at Lavender. Velorik bent to reshackle Lavender as she stood rigidly. He stated in Siberian: "Nearly time for them to sleep, Agrippin. You've had your fun with the useless one; now remember to keep to the dreams of the gifted one." He wished the girls good night and left.

The door to our quarters shut behind Velorik and instantly it was Lavender's turn to demand an explanation. "Has something happened? What! Why, Agrippin, when you sent me with Velorik to the deck did you drift over to my sister's bed?"

"He believes I have been exploiting Marigold," I answered.

"Have you?"

"No, of course not," answered Marigold. "Look at you!" She smiled, teasing her sister. "He's helping us, Lavender. You can trust him."

Wander

On our first night on the ship, Lavender and Marigold's dreams were of constant wander. It wasn't long before Velorik came knocking on our door.

"Look!" he pointed, speaking to me in Siberian while holding the door open to the darkness. "Can you see? The bed of fog?"

"So?" I asked.

"She steered us into thick fog; she will steer us out. Safely."

"Don't wake her up."

"Why? Is she revealing something through a dream?"

"Yes," I lied. "You can stay if you whisper while I observe."

"No, I'll leave you to your work. But as soon as she's awake, we need her."

"The commanders truly are trusting her gift, aren't they? That's not like them."

"Yes, Agrippin, they are. You just will not be at peace until you find a disparaging explanation for your superiors' motives?"

"I'm sorry. I do not dissent; I'm simply under a great deal of pressure. I must stay within the gifted one's mind or be held responsible if she becomes deceitful. It's difficult to do so when I'm not able to understand the minds of her masters."

"It's not hard to understand. They believe our future wars will be fought using these gifts and don't want to wait another season to strike. They believe we're in a race to harness these powers. Yes, if the invasion is a failure, many Siberian men will perish. But not a single commander would be lost. They would return to Siberia and rebuild our numbers. Or, if the weapon cooperates and we are victorious, they will be remembered as the heroes that finally recaptured Polaris. They will carve up the Canadian landscape for their own governorships, possibly leaving a district for me or even for you."

"They would give me no land. I am one of their weapons."

"Don't you wish to know what I meant when I said to enjoy the useless one without inhibition?" Velorik abruptly shifted.

"Oh yes, of course," I said.

"I'm sorry I did not explain, but I wanted your time with her to be enjoyed." He looked somberly at me, sighed, and paused before continuing, "She's to die. The night before the battle. I'm sorry; I know she's been your plaything."

I stared silently ahead at Lavender and Marigold's sleeping bodies, watching Marigold stir but not wake.

Velorik continued in a whisper: "Agrippin, you are not to know. I've only recently been informed by the commanders."

"And how do these commanders, who have refused to visit these quarters, even know about a girl who has not had the freedom to leave her bedside?"

"They have known for several days ... Agrippin, I'm sorry. It's certainly not my decision. I've tried to assist your intrigue, but they questioned why my supplies request called for two leg irons."

"And I would question why it would call for a single one."

"The poor girl. She has no comprehension that she will be killed."

"Lavender's gift will warn her in time, you realize. Why, if I may? Why will she be killed?"

"Agrippin, there will be other slave girls. You mustn't, you really mustn't develop deeper feelings for them."

Calmly I repeated: "Why is she to be killed? And how would they know about her unless you told them?"

"Agrippin, stop!" he said through his teeth. "What's become of you? You're distrusting and neurotic. She's their slave, not yours. She's useless. Her only purpose will be as a sacrifice during the rituals on the eve of battle. Rarely do the soldiers witness such inspiration, to all view the first kill of their enemy. She may stay as she has been, with her sister. That is until the night before we attack, so as not to test the allegiance of the gifted one."

"She will glow by then. And when did she become a Canadian? Her slave file reads of her nationality: 'Siberia via Canada.' And what need do the soldiers have for such a savage ritual?"

"Agrippin, you've never been asked to take a sword into battle. You've never faced death, and I hope for your future that if you're ever asked to do so, you're able to do it bravely. But you've been an officer from early childhood, so please understand that there is no shame behind the courage a soldier must find, however they find it, to march into battle and possibly the face of death. I ... I am sorry I have told you of the girl. It's true that there may be no place for genuine friendships in a professional environment and that your friends may place you in the most compromising position."

"Velorik, thank you. And I'm sorry. In your greater maturity you have been very tolerant of me, and even of the girls' insults. For this, I swear to you that you'll find no trouble for revealing her misfortune to me. I'll tell no one."

My promise was broken almost before the door closed behind him.

"Lavender, is Marigold glowing?" I asked, shaking her to wake her up.

She opened her eyes and looked over at her sister. "No, of course not."

Marigold wondered nervously, "Oh dear. What was your discussion with Velorik about?"

"You were awake?"

"Yes, I heard everything. But you spoke in Siberian."

I became horribly ashamed to reveal the exact danger. As I explained Marigold's situation, the waking world became so absurd that it could not help but come into focus.

"We could tell them I'm pregnant with your child," suggested Marigold, nearly panicked. "They may spare it, an officer's. And the child's father and aunt would be gifted . . ."

"If they intended to breed the gifted, Agrippin and I would have already been forced together," noted Lavender.

"Well in hindsight, that wasn't necessary!" snapped Marigold.

"We . . . we never . . ." I began.

"I'm sorry," Marigold said quickly, pulling hard on her chain. "But even my sister's gift does little good when I'm shackled to a wall."

Lavender acquired a deliberate calm, reacting to her sister's escalation. "Regarding children, Agrippin, I would never bear the child of a man who served the ones who wished to kill my sister."

Marigold sputtered, "Are they breeding you or not? Because if you have a girl, be sure to name her Marigold, after her dead aunt."

I answered, "No, they're not. Your sister meant only of any future we may have, beyond the Siberian army."

"Sometimes I forget you're Siberian." Marigold laughed nervously, tears flowing down her cheeks.

Lavender asked: "Agrippin, we appreciate this information, even if it's difficult to receive. But search yourself . . . why did you tell us this?"

"Because . . . because I'm ready. Rather, I'm almost ready, and needed your push. The ritual will be the night prior to the battle. It always is. It won't be at sea. Once we make land in Canada and certainly before the ritual . . . I'll be ready then. We can all walk away."

As Marigold dried her cheeks, Lavender marched toward me, nearly reaching the limit of her chain yet ignoring it. She found the soft patches of my neck between the thorns near my collarbone, pulling my lips toward hers and kissing with something deeper, something more appreciative than passion. My heart jumped.

We drifted in the darkness for days, on the sea of no one's country. As much as we wished to escape, we understood our situation and even our lives as no greater in value than Canadian peasants, or the Siberian soldiers preparing to invade their land.

Lavender guided the ships east when Canada was west, north when it was south, and nowhere when it was somewhere. During the wanderings the armada emptied several supply ships, which had to return light to Severnaya. When Velorik confided that the generals were growing impatient and distrustful, Lavender said privately, "Then I have stalled neither too much nor too little. Tell them, or tell Velorik to tell them, I have said to sail directly to the nearest Canadian shores from here."

Landfall and Betrayal

Land travel was little different than being at sea. Lavender, Marigold, and I remained together. We traveled by carriage, to which the girls were again fettered. We slept in the carriage and were occasionally visited by Velorik, who unwittingly fed information to Lavender through his trust in me. In this we found a way to gauge the commanders' patience, and determine if their faith in Lavender continued. We tested this faith to the highest extent possible, while the army's supplies dwindled, and still hoped desperately for a silent retreat.

We had approached shore northwest of Ellesmere Island, well west of Fort Alert, and wandered south generally toward York ... thousands of men through dense forest. Still, our carriage of three passengers—occasionally four—remained an island in the darkness among the standing army.

On occasion we saw a flicker of moonlight and the image of a great bird high overhead. It was almost certainly following us, and I only wondered what divination the necromancer made from its flight path.

The ritual would mark our escape. If it occurred, we knew battle would be the following day. Lavender would have marched the army as aimlessly as she could, and we would have done our part. Marigold would be set for sacrifice. Able to do no further and greater good, we would defect.

The Siberians had found a broad field, and hundreds of canvas tents were pitched for the night. Lavender, Marigold, and I waited in our carriage for Velorik. Lavender asked: "Agrippin, did you once tell us that a thorned Siberian won't have thorns as an infant?"

I paused, hoping she had given some thought to our future and the possibility of a child. "Yes. Their birth is the same as for any other newborn. There are no thorned infants."

"And when do the thorns come?"

"Typically not before the child's first birthday. Even if a mother is thorned and a child is not, Siberian women will have at least a full season with their child before it is taken from them."

"Sometimes less." Lavender sighed.

"What?" asked Marigold, tense.

"Our mother. She tells the story of when I was born, and how she rescued a Canadian boy from a Siberian woman. It seems she may have stolen a child from its mother."

"Oh, and the thorns were not yet . . . Where was this?"

"Here in Canada. In the forests, like here, but to the northeast, by Fort Alert."

"I wonder what happened to the boy after he disappeared," Marigold said nervously.

Lavender answered: "Maybe he's a soldier here in this camp, preparing to invade Canada. I don't think we'll ever know."

Velorik came solemnly to our carriage to brief me, but spoke in Canadian for all to hear. He sat to my right. Across from him sat Marigold; across from me sat Lavender.

"Lavender, thank you for your gift and its services," he began.

Sensing much, much more to his message, I interrupted. "Where have the soldiers gone?"

"To the clearing. The gathering has begun," he answered.

"The ritual?" I asked.

"Yes. If you are quiet, you might hear the livestock vocalizing their responses to the necromancer's music. As I had begun, Lavender, the Siberian army has appreciated your assistance. Undoubtedly, they will appreciate your future service as well, and have decided to begin to compensate you, possibly allowing even certain freedoms. You have kept us from harm, but we have wandered extensively."

"It was necessary," Lavender said defensively.

Marigold's hands shook; her eyes focused on Velorik. I removed my sleeved coat, exposing my arms.

"Yes," responded Velorik. "And we are within a day's march of York, by our estimation. We no longer expect you to steer us from death. It is impossible now to do that for our army. Casualties are an expectation of war, and of peacetime as well." He looked at Marigold, breathed deeply, and pulled the key to the fetters out of his pocket. I made certain to see the key before I did anything. "Marigold, I need you to come with me," he said.

"Velorik!" shouted Lavender. "You're glowing! Be careful!"

"Me?" he asked skeptically. "Are you sure it's me?"

"Lavender, would you please hold my coat?" I asked slowly.

"What? No—" she began, posturing anxiously to quickly reject it. I stood, hunching inside the carriage, ignoring her and holding the coat open to block her view of Velorik. I tossed the coat over her head and stumbled intentionally rearward. I wrapped my right forearm across Velorik's neck and shredded violently. With no more than a soft grunt I sawed the thorns of my forearm across his jugular, sinking deep into his neck and tearing the skin and throat to ribbons.

Marigold witnessed everything. Lavender was quick to toss the coat aside, exposing herself to Velorik's spurting blood.

"Oh no . . ." Lavender groaned. "Agrippin, no! No!"

Velorik tugged his chest with his fingernails and died with a cough. His eyes bulged, as did Marigold's, who was equally surprised at how their fates had just been swapped.

"We . . . we only needed his key, Agrippin," said Marigold thanklessly.

I pried it out of Velorik's hand and scrambled to unfetter the girls from the carriage. "And you think he would have given it to us voluntarily?"

"He might have. He trusted you," she answered.

"Siberian officers trust no one."

"Agrippin, I would have rather died than this," declared Lavender.

"Yes," drawled a stunned Marigold.

"If we don't go now, you *will* die. Velorik was your escort to the ritual, Marigold. They'll wonder where he is soon."

"You were to obtain the key, and we would all simply walk off into the darkness," said Marigold. "No captors and no slaves. We'd travel to York, open the cathedral doors, and warn Polaris himself."

"And that's exactly what we're going to do, but we need to go quickly."

"Agrippin, please don't follow us," requested Lavender.

"What?" I nearly screamed. "I free you; I save your sister . . . do you not care for me?"

Calmly and painfully, she said, "I'm going to have nightmares from this for ages."

"So, you really want me to go another way? Where? Lavender, where am I going to go?"

"You can't go anywhere if you're tied to a cart, Agrippin."

"Oh, not this again. I can't believe this. I watched every one of your dreams. How did I not see this betrayal coming?"

"Betrayal? Agrippin, your friend is dead, your arm is covered in his blood, and you think I'm the one betraying you?"

"Murdering Velorik was never supposed to be an option," said Marigold.

"What is this nonsense? Now you're mourning the loss of your captor? You manipulated me. We shared not a single honest kiss, did we, Lavender?"

Marigold stood up and bumped her head on the inside of the carriage. "No! I can see right through to the other side of my sister, and I promise, it all changed only a moment ago."

"Wait," said Lavender. "Never mind any of us. Agrippin, never mind you and me. Never mind what kind of child we would have. No soldier in the Siberian camps cares about you and me. No mother or father sleeping in their home in York right now cares about us. What's the best action each of us can take, right now, to save as many lives as possible?"

They both looked at me. "The best thing . . . I can do . . . is to stall the army for as long as possible while you sneak off to warn Polaris."

"Thank you, Agrippin," said Lavender. "For this, I love you."

"You'd better hurry." I sighed. "Go now, and I will not follow."

"Good-bye, Agrippin." Marigold stepped out of the carriage. "Thank you."

Before Lavender followed her, I asked, "Wait. How did you hide your plans from me? In the beginning."

"We didn't hide our plans from you. It was simply camouflaged, to your eyes at least."

"Your dreams were of aimless wandering," I said.

"As you described the subconscious itself. The one symbol to confuse you the most, and yet it was without symbolism. It was direct and honest. Our plan all along was to wander aimlessly."

"And I took it as the subconscious. You did it to protect me, didn't you?"

"So you would have nothing to report but what we all already knew. We knew no one would be harmed that way, and your commanders could not dispute my directions if their army wandered safely as Marigold and I did in our dreams. Remember, at the time we were uncertain if we should trust you."

"And now you'll have nightmares about me."

"No. I'll still dream of you fondly. And every kiss was honest, Agrippin," she whispered, pausing, then kissing me before she left. "Thank you," she said.

I held my hands across my eyes, unable to face her or her departure. "Yes. Good-bye, Lavender."

Rogue

I sat in the carriage alone with Velorik's warm corpse. There was no place for a thorned man of any age, living or dead, outside of Siberia. Lavender and Marigold were set to warn York, and I truly hoped their country would defend itself. I was already on Canadian soil. If the invasion failed and I left a defeated Siberian army now or later, I could not wander the marketplace of Kildebyen, let alone York. No man or woman, not a single one who shares this genetic burden, this archaic body-weapon, exists beyond Siberian borders except while carrying flag and sword. I would be known immediately and distrusted for an eternity simply on sight, wherever I traveled. And the panic I might cause, a rogue Siberian soldier wandering small towns beyond his homeland.

I looked out of the carriage for a lingering trace of Lavender or Marigold but found nothing. Slaves 00398870 and 00398871 had run off in their slave dresses into the darkness. I heard the low notes of the necromancer's music and the screams of the livestock in the distance, calling and vocalizing their distress. I abandoned Velorik and walked toward the ceremony. Thousands of Siberian soldiers, all fellow thorned men, sat around the ritual like a tremendous fire pit watching a bare-chested necromancer drain blood from livestock into buckets, then bang low-pitched drums and play high-pitched flutes to attract ghosts of fallen soldiers, feeding them the blood as an offering to gain their service in battle. I found the generals, separated and guarded, and approached them quietly so as not to disturb anyone's appreciation of the display.

"Velorik is dead," I told them.

"What?" one asked. "Yes, I see you have blood on you."

"Attempts to save him. Lavender and Marigold are his murderers."

"I see," he responded. "So, she can command life and death."

"Yes. And they disappeared like vapor, according to Velorik's dying words. I wasn't there when they killed him."

"Then there is nothing we can do," he concluded. "Agrippin, we will question you another day. Come, sit with us now, and enjoy the ceremony."

You may have known from the time I shared Lavender and Marigold's files that I was set to defect. It was as difficult to leave the Siberian army as it was to say good-bye to Lavender, and yet in every way unalike. After the ritual, the army began its feast and prepared to invade York. Meanwhile, I searched Velorik's tent for several surprising treasures: the slave files of Lavender and Marigold and a few personal effects taken from them at the time of their capture. I took the papers, leaving no written record of slaves 00398870 and 00398871 in the Siberian file. In the trove I also found a dark robe and a book called *The Field Guide to Life and Death*. From there

I escaped, quite uneventfully and even comfortably, as it was common for me to be awake while the world slept. The glow from my eyes helped me mind my steps as I stumbled urgently but quietly through the forest. Eventually I would use their book to survive in the bush. The dark hooded robe was a tight fit but a useful method of hiding my identity as I defected, and for every one of the days following.

I cannot say where I was bound, or I would be hunted by my former master and punished, likely killed. If you consider this my paranoia, then you are not Polaris, the other gifted Siberian to escape long before me and still with a bounty on his head today.

I understand that my former master may one day capture me, and that day may be tomorrow. I cannot be terribly difficult to find. If a man with glowing orange eyes causes a panic in your town—that is, until he's recognized as a lonely rogue soldier and defector—then you have found me. If you see a young man, or maybe one day an old man, with thorns protruding from his gray skin, and he is the only creature like this you've ever seen in your small town so far from Siberia, then you have seen me. Or if you saw no thorns because that man was walking underneath the shadow of a dark robe fit for a smaller frame, worn even as the sun beat down in the height of the season of light, then you've seen me and you have found my escort, Lavender's abandoned shadow.

And so I wander, like a dream with little promise of a conclusion. I only hope tomorrow will not be the day I'm found by my former master, but rather the day I am reunited with my former love.

13 / Marigold

Lavender and I fled directly for the trees, confident that Agrippin would brood for a moment, then do his part to prevent anyone from following us. We were alone aside from the flickering light of the full moon, cold in our slave dresses and in the peak of the season of darkness. We ran through the darkest part of the forest under a clear sky, the air dry, and the stark canopy of the Canadian woods, guided only by the moon, the stars, and the faint shimmer of light from Lavender's eyes. If we could see a half step ahead we were fortunate, getting a warning of twisted roots, rocks, bushes, or tree trunks only as our shins nearly collided with them. For this my left hand was in Lavender's right, combining our balance and dexterity, each frequently catching the other from falling as we stumbled slowly and quietly through the forest. When we sensed we had distanced ourselves sufficiently from the Siberian camp, we paused a moment to wonder if we were being pursued.

"You don't have gifted ears, do you?" Lavender asked, whispering.

"I hear nothing. You?"

"Nothing. I believe it's safe to speak quietly."

"So which direction is York?"

We read the stars and soon revised our track slightly to the southeast. Looking up, we believed we were alone. Not a breeze, a flap of a wing, or a single creature disturbed us in the forest, as even the flies were dead for the season.

After several moments of slow travel through densely spaced but clean, leafless oaks and maples, I teased: "Agrippin's a good man, thorns and all."

"I'm not sure it matters. I doubt I'll ever see him again."

"So, too good for a murderer?"

"One of us ought to be," she replied, squeezing my hand a bit, perhaps involuntarily.

"Attempted murder if you are referring to Quinby, as I'm sure you are."

"Yes. Of a king. What do you really see in . . . never mind."

"No, what? He should've been the prince. Aside from his regal error, do you not approve?"

"None of that matters. Marigold, do you believe we can both survive this?"

"I relinquish that burden on you."

"Well, we aren't glowing of course, but we've just defected from the Siberian forces. I cannot think of any act they might consider to be higher treason than ours. They're set to invade the town of York, which we hope to warn. Yet this is also the town from which we are exiled, to be executed on sight if we return. Polaris wishes me dead whether the law supports him or not."

"We're fortunate for your gift, then." I gave a false sense of optimism.

"You're avoiding the subject. We may find ourselves pressed between two situations which we will be unable to change, only for me to warn of the white glow yet have no recourse. We may become trapped in an inescapable situation."

"So be it," I chanted. "And we already are. No other Canadians know they are threatened, and we simply don't have a choice but to warn them, whatever our . . ." I sighed. "Whatever our *fate*."

"So be it?" she replied, sending a shiver up my already chilled spine as our resolve fought to exorcise our fear.

"So be it," we agreed.

We stumbled only a few more dark steps before she asked, "So you still consider us Canadians?"

"From the roots to the tips," I answered as calmly and confidently as I could. I could feel a tremble in my younger sister's hand.

We passed the next few moments and several hundred half steps of forest in silence, pretending we didn't detect anything but strength and determination from each other.

Eventually a shadow flickered in the moonlight, and the silence was broken.

"That's certainly a Featherman," whispered Lavender.

"Or a winged Siberian."

"Oh, thank all of nature itself that they don't have wings. Thorns are enough."

"Ow!" I winced.

"What was that?" asked Lavender. She and I both reacted to an object that struck me on the head. "Are you all right?"

"Actually, yes. I'm not sure how, but something just fell from a tree."

"No, it was the Featherman," she explained, having seen something I did not. "He swooped low over the trees, blocking the moon an instant before you reacted."

"Can you see the forest floor? If you can find the object that struck me, we might know whether we're being attacked, aided, or just prodded for amusement."

We knelt and spread our palms along the dirt, probing the ground for the projectile. Lavender stood up with a small cloth sack. "Seed," she said, clenching the palm-sized bag.

"I'll have some." I shrugged. "Any theories?"

I grabbed a small handful of seeds from the open pouch as Lavender remembered: "He's unable to land here because of the trees."

"He's trying to signal us."

We looked upward to find the Featherman indeed circling above silently. Lavender added, "And he must know our situation, because he flies low to the forest and has the sense not to vocalize or produce noise in any way."

"Yes, but do we follow?"

"Wait. There's a folded note buried in the seed." As the Featherman circled patiently above, she strained to read, with her shimmer of light:

Fellow Feathermen, rejoice! Spirit Zero does exist!

> *To find Spirit Zero, use the magnetic compass. When you grow near, expect certain errors in your instrument. You must expect a 'dip,' as I have discovered the radials collect within Spirit Zero itself, a flightless entity that will force the final moments of your search to be on the ground, not airborne. The magnetic compass has been retrieved, and currently scientist Baker is working to reverse-engineer the device so that its design is available to all Feathermen.*

"Marigold, this is incredible! They've found their Spirit Zero!"

"Ugh, it's Horace overhead, isn't it?"

"Yes, but he's trying to guide us—"

We both ducked abruptly as the Featherman swooped overhead again, rattling the treetops. With it, something hit my side. "Ow!" I nearly screamed. "Oh, right in my ribs."

Lavender asked, laughing, "Another small sack of seed? And he struck you with both of them? We can be certain it's Horace who flies above." She tilted her head skyward to wave, and he rocked his wings in the moonlight.

He had passed so low over the treetops that his wake rattled free many of the still unfallen but crisp leaves, which then floated slowly to our feet. I was uninjured. "He's guiding us to Spirit Zero. I'm intrigued to be led there, but I'm uncertain how this being can or will assist us to warn York. And he seems to lead us east, not to York, in the southeast."

"Yes, but—" began Lavender.

"We'll follow and once a clearing allows this Featherman to land, we can at the very least speak with him."

She added: "Yes, and Horace, or whoever it is, might carry us in their talons to York whether we encounter Spirit Zero or not. Such speed would drastically increase the town's readiness and defense." Our voices reached him. Lavender looked up at the large creature. "Oh, and he's rocking his wings again! He hears us and we need not shout! Wonderful!"

"Still hardly worth going into a Featherman's debt." I paused, cringing when I realized what I had said. I then questioned the sky: "Oh, are you out of seed sacks?"

We seemed to walk endlessly as the Featherman guided us, so long in fact that a shimmer began in the sky.

The dawn of the Celestial Lights had just begun around us and in the direction of our course.

"Lavender, this is taking quite some time," I noted, growing anxious to find a clearing.

She replied: "When we homed in on the Living Cave, before we met our father . . . the glows guided us. They propelled us with their warning. These Celestial Lights are no different, except that we walk toward them."

We continued to walk as the shimmering intensified, outshining even the brightest stars, even the moon. Translucent jades and familiar purples, textured like a liquid or a polished metal, danced in the sky. In the calm air, the Featherman flew rigidly overhead, circling and recircling. Lavender's hand remained in mine until we realized the lights had overwhelmed even the season of darkness, and we could walk comfortably. In the illumination of the colored lights I saw an elated smile on my sister's face. We had released each other's hand, now able to run. Even the Featherman adjusted his speed, seeing our path in colored light. It was thousands and thousands of strides, but hardly a fraction of what our worn feet had sustained since our exile.

We continued, wondering whom or what we might find at the end of our steps, and if indeed we would satisfy our curiosity about Spirit Zero. We might have forgotten about York in the moment; I know I did, reassured simply that the lights continued to intensify as we, with joy, traveled to visit their realm while departing our own.

Finally, the clearing.

"Brother Lichen!" shouted Lavender, abandoning control of her voice.

"Sister Lavender! And Sister Marigold!" He pivoted from a distance, placing stone fists in the ground to turn toward us. The jades and purples were reflected in his dark surface. His appearance was that of smooth cobblestones resting at the floor of a shallow stream as clear water trickled over them. He was as we remembered him, yet now in an entirely new atmosphere. "You appear surprised! Of course, it's me; this is the Lichen's clearing! The lake, its surface now frozen, the signposts you staked, the berries, the mushrooms," he added, holding an arm to the sky. "Oh, but you were not here to see the lights! Aren't they beautiful?"

Lavender stuttered, "Y-You're Spirit Zero? You're the genuine Celestial?"

He laughed humbly, "Had I known this when we last met, I would have certainly mentioned it. Although Brother and Sister Featherman are convinced, I must say I'm still somewhat in disbelief. Oh, and here's one

now! It seems to be Horace, a kind Featherman, and my most frequent
visitor. He holds the device you retrieved from my pile, but has discovered
a new use for it." The Featherman, now confirmed as Horace, approached
the clearing for a landing.

"Kind?" I asked.

"Yes, and he has spoken of you," explained Brother Lichen. "He's
appreciative of the device, which he calls a compass."

Horace landed along the opposite side of the clearing. He slowed from
the speed of flight but maintained his haste along the ground. He rushed to
Lichen, moving now by talon to soil only, wings folded behind him.

We found each other, us four, Horace and Lichen nearly equal in
stature and looming over Lavender and me. We all began to speak at once,
and it took a moment to untangle the lines of inquiry. Lavender wished to
understand Lichen's status as Spirit Zero, but little remained unexplained
aside from the trust the Featherman race placed in his wisdom, from
thousands of seasons of existence and thousands of words from dying
human minds, caught between life and death. In hindsight it was not
surprising that Brother Lichen was Spirit Zero, as he had already served us
in this very respect shortly after our exile.

There was a competitive moment between Horace and me. I wished
to explain that we required his assistance—debt and favor system be
forsaken—in being transported to York. After wasting time bickering,
Horace finally snapped his beak shut, glanced at Spirit Zero, hung his head
slightly, and muttered, "To be last is to be first. You first, Marigold, please."

I was too stunned to speak. "No, please, you, Horace."

"No, Marigold, you begin," he replied.

Lavender sighed and said: "We have escaped from a massive Siberian
movement which is set to invade York, the Canadian capital south to southwest of here. The town is unaware and needs to be warned."

Horace spoke his part. "A human with green eyes, like yours are purple,
recently traveled to Windfall. He called himself a merchant but appeared

more like a herdsman, with his entourage of mullice, ovidons, and tollimore. They traveled by foot and hoof, mind you, up the mountains, specifically to find me. He would not give his name but knew mine and knew yours both. His request was that the Feathermen's surveillance shift and follow a Siberian armada which at the time had yet to launch or even assemble."

"I'm . . . I'm sorry, what?" Lavender pleaded.

"A human who knew of you requested I follow the Siberian invasion. I'm aware of their movement, but only through him, warned prior to their launch. He predicted it. We have been monitoring them from the dark sky, and have specifically been asked by this man with green eyes to follow you as you fled."

Lavender asked, "And so you're here? But how did he know we would flee?"

Horace replied, "How did he know my name? Or where to find me, and that I knew of you? For that matter, how can you sort life from death?"

"So, is he in your debt now?" I asked, thinking that I was questioning the old Horace, who no longer existed.

"To give is to receive," he replied, staring downward into my eyes.

"Oh, this is quite the improvement, Horace." I commended him with more than a bit of patronization. He took it well.

"So then, this man . . ." my sister mumbled.

"Lavender, you don't remember this. You were drugged the day you were arrested. But there was a man, a poor merchant with noticeable green eyes. They were indeed like yours, as Agrippin's are orange, and Polaris's red, in fact brighter than Polaris's."

"The man who . . . the peddler who suggested a split sentence?"

"Effectively exiling us, but saving your life," I finished, excited by the realization. "Amazing! So that was no accident. There was nothing casual or circumstantial about his presence. He planted himself in advance to—"

"To guard me," she finished. "So, what is his gift, exactly? What can he see?"

Brother Lichen added, "If he's always present when necessary, he must have an understanding of what will and will not happen. I may enjoy an exalted title as the Feathermen apply it to me, but I certainly would not claim omniscience."

"I *am* always present when necessary," came a friendly but unfamiliar shout from somewhere in the forest.

Our heads turned as we searched for the owner of the voice. Horace seemed to turn only once, accurately locating it.

"Might I meet my fellow gifted friend?" shouted Lavender.

"Yes!" replied the man, nearer than before. We heard a clumsy rustling from within the trees, then a disheveled man in stained, shabby garments emerged. He was heavy and far from polished or even groomed; by my look he was fifty or so seasons aged. He seemed to struggle to reach us as we all stared, but he came, panting, to meet us in the clearing. "You two . . . you two are younger than I am, and you certainly cover a lot of land." He tried to catch his breath quickly for conversation's sake. "I must warn you, this will be a difficult exchange, particularly for you, Lavender."

"Sir, you have beautiful eyes," she noted, guarded, ignoring his warning. "What do they see?"

"Oh, a large bird, a stone creature, two young Canadian women, a clearing around a lake, and a forest full of trees."

"Of course. But what is your gift?" she persisted.

"Timing," he said. "Certainly not running."

"Sir, I know of a Siberian named Agrippin with the gift to read dreams. Polaris, leader of Canada, sees smoke, fog, and other vapor obstructions as if they were clear air. I see indications of life and death, of pregnancy, and occasionally of something new I did not previously know about my gift, but always some presence or absence of life. This is my sister, Marigold. She is without a gift but has been vital to my survival, as I understand you have been as well. Sir, please respond; what do you see with your gifted eyes?"

He stared, green to purple, locked in eye contact holding Lavender suspended. He did not speak.

She continued, "Sir, am I simply to accept that you will not reveal your gift? I will persist infinitely, so if you would, please tell me."

Horace recalled: "It was this way when I wished to learn his name. Don't waste any more of your time."

"Forgive me," the green-eyed man said. "I don't wish to be rude. You may deduce my gift simply by my defense of its secrecy as I forecast that the events of your travels, which include this moment now, will find their place in print. There cannot exist a record of my identity in this document, as it would make it possible for Polaris to persecute me."

"Yes!" I blurted. "He persecutes the gifted, and keeps his own gift secret from his people."

"This is true. Of the persecution, and of the secrecy. Polaris is a man of multiple metaphors, but to a gifted Canadian he's an old, old pine tree. While the non-gifted are in awe of his strength and power, they are blind to his methods of maintaining it. He sheds countless needles to the soil below, each so acidic that it scorches the earth beneath his canopy. No competing sapling may grow in the acid of his shade; he does not allow it. Worse, the soil of the Canadian people is burned, and they are numb to it. I have lived a life keeping my roots above this dirt, above the acid and persecution."

"Stop!" insisted Lavender. "You wish not to be recorded so you may avoid persecution, but what of me? This print you predict: who will author it?"

He was silent.

"Please, who will author it?" she persisted. "Because if you could be killed for your inclusion in such a text of our journey, what of the gifted girl whose name is on every page?"

"I'm so sorry. In my silence I am only, like you, following my gift," said the ungroomed man.

"So then why are you here?" protested Lavender. "If you predict and pursue a gift-guided sense of time and place, why this clearing, why this night? You certainly hurried to arrive, as if this ethereal timing was not a foregone certainty."

He smiled and began with his purpose. "Because I have informatio—"

"Oh, well that's a nice change," interrupted Lavender, frustrated.

He smiled serenely and continued: "that is important to share before you take to the sky. As you warn the people of York, guide the refugees to this clearing. The lake has a thin sheet of ice, with water for drinking underneath, and the soil here provides some nourishment as well. With your signposts and with Sir Lichen's assistance, we will begin tonight picking and sorting the berries and the mushrooms, the edible from the poison. I have a herd of livestock east of here, grazing and sleeping. They are mullice, ovidons, and tollimore. I'll drive them to this clearing before the camp forms, and it will surely form. Send your family to me, Lavender, Marigold. Do this and your mother can retrieve her livestock if she chooses. I should say, their lineage."

"I cannot even begin to collect the ricochets of confusion in my mind at this moment." Lavender stared at him.

"I met your mother near the time of your birth. She left some livestock in my care, but I only ever intended to borrow them, breed them for sixteen seasons to increase their numbers, and return them tomorrow to the refugees of this battle. It will not be enough for all, but the fleece, milk, and meat may help the needy while the able-bodied rebuild. Your family can retrieve what the desperate do not need."

Lavender asked: "Are you my father?"

He laughed. "No, oh no. I met your mother within a day or so of your birth, and helped her to your father. But you and I do share a common, third parent."

Horace and I had a laugh at this. Lichen looked inquisitive, and Lavender of course asked: "A third parent? Are you prepared to explain, or was that, like your gift and your name, a secret?"

"The gift. I simply meant the gift."

Lavender demanded, "Tell me the origin of our gift."

"I do not know," he answered.

She groaned. "You lie. You know, and you won't tell."

He replied: "Question your mother about the events of your birth, and she might know more than I can say." After a silence he continued: "I cannot promise any answers; again, I'm only following my gift. But you may ask any questions you have while I'm here. The worst response will be silence."

Lavender declared: "I might have a thousand questions. But what does it matter? Horace, Marigold, are we prepared to take to the sky?"

Brother Lichen pleaded: "Horace, please, when you have helped the girls, involve the Feathermen. Retrieve as many as can be quickly readied, and come to the aid of the humans as they wage war. Both Siberian and Canadian."

"Yes, Spirit Zero," he replied obligingly.

"Involve Baker," added the green-eyed man. "Once you carry the girls to York, you'll need to immediately fly a fair distance to Windfall, then speak with Baker while assembling a party and a plan. Time will be short, but sufficient."

"Baker cannot fly," Horace explained.

The man with green eyes knew. "Yes, I understand. But speak with him for insights as to how he may help his able-winged Feathermen neutralize this battle."

Lichen and the green-eyed man stayed in the clearing to prepare the predicted refugee camp. As on Jan Mayen, Lavender and I stood hip to hip and bent at the waist, bracing for the careful but firm snatch of Horace's talons. He returned to the opposite side of the Lichen's superficially frozen lake and found the stretch of clearing needed to take to the air. He returned in flight, passed low over the clearing, and plucked us into the sky.

Within seconds of ascending above the clearing and relying on Horace's compass-based navigation, Lavender said regretfully: "I should have asked if Polaris has exterminated other gifted men and women in the past. It sounds like he has."

"You may find the opportunity to ask him yourself," I replied.

Shivering now in her slave dress with the induced air stripping our bodies of heat, Lavender said: "We'll have Brother Horace to protect us. We can face Polaris with a tremendous armed predator-warrior by our side and therefore certainly not fear execution."

A silent pause led me to question our vessel: "Horace, you can hear us, correct? You'll be by our side when we confront Polaris?"

"I . . . I cannot say. Where will you find him?"

"Inside the cathedral, likely," replied Lavender. She then realized, "But both the green-eyed man and Brother Lichen instructed you to return immediately."

"I'm sorry," said Horace, genuinely torn. "We should have asked the Spirit and the gifted man while we were on the ground. I pray that this will not prove a costly error for your confrontation of Polaris."

"We can rely on my gift, then. It will be our escort, and you can return to Windfall to mobilize the Feathermen," she said to Horace.

"So be it?" I asked.

"So be it." She nodded.

From above, the city of York appeared quiet and asleep. By our estimate it was midway between midnight and morning, and yet still days until the next sunrise. The Siberians would advance from the north and northwest, but for the moment they likely slept in their camps, a day's march from the Canadian capital. Horace found a sandy bank and warned us to expect a tumble, then counted from three so that we could brace for the drop on his release. He was careful, and we tumbled unbruised. He never landed. As we had agreed, he dropped us into the soft mound at his slowest possible speed, and pulled his beak high into the air again, away from land. He had produced time for us, and the flight seemed a miracle. "We would hardly be a third of the way," said Lavender to me on the ground while we watched the Featherman depart. "Thank you, Horace." He rocked his wings again in the moonlight as he departed for his long return flight to Windfall.

We walked from the south gate into the city of York. The Celestial Lights were still visible to the northeast, but now with their source some distance away, they were more present on the horizon than overhead. The prominent light came from mounted torches lining the empty streets.

Our intent was to warn Polaris.

We would warn him and escape to the north, warn our family, and flee with them to the Lichen's clearing. Of course, we had no reason not to notify the first passerby, a lone woman, forty or so in age, head down and walking southward toward us.

"Madam?" I called.

She flinched, afraid because of the hour of what we might want. "Please, I have nothing."

Lavender spoke with a soft, unthreatening voice, "Madam, we have just learned that this town will be invaded by Siberia. Please tell anyone you know—your family, your neighbors—and have them escape to the northeast, toward the Celestial Lights. There they will be safe and find nourishment and supplies."

Accelerating her gait, she deflected, "If Siberia is set to invade, I'll be safer here. Polaris will protect our town. He always has."

We sighed, discouraged as the woman continued on. Lavender noted: "Nobody is up at this hour, and two fools wandering the night street warning of the end of time will accomplish very little."

"Straight to the cathedral," I declared.

We passed not another resident of York on our way.

From a distance we noticed two standing night guards, and remained clear of their view to discuss our approach.

"We simply tell them we must warn Polaris of a Siberian invasion. What more is necessary?" said Lavender.

"I predict one guard will detain us while the other tells Polaris that some girl with purple eyes wants to speak to him. He'll lock his inner door and command the guard to return to the cathedral entrance and execute us both."

"All right, all right. So, what do we do?"

"Your name is Sanna and mine is Erika." I smiled as she squinted. "You speak only Svalbardian, and with a thick accent. We are new to Canada, very poor and fresh from Kildebyen. We need a warm place to stay."

"Oh, you're going to flirt your way in." She groaned.

"Yes, and you're going to keep your eyes shut so they don't recognize you."

"But then I won't see the glows that predict if we'll be killed."

I answered, "But if the guards see your eyes, I predict we will be killed."

We approached the cathedral guards, cold and underclothed in our identical gray slave dresses, Lavender's eyes shut and therefore her hand in mine for guidance. The guards were pointing and laughing quietly the moment they saw us.

I cleared my throat and spoke first to take the lead. I greeted them in Svalbardian. "Hello, sirs. My name is Erika, and this is my friend Sanna. Forgive us for intruding, but we have just arrived from Svalbard. Do you speak Svalbardian?"

"Erika? And Sanna? As the queen and princess!" said one of the guards.

"What did she say? What language are you speaking?" asked the other.

"Ah, wonderful!" I continued. "You speak Svalbardian! Yes, Erika and Sanna." I laughed. "The same as the royals, but we're certainly not royalty.

We are very poor, coming to Canada for labor. But we don't speak a word of Canadian. Our bags were stolen, and we have no tops—"

"Tiles, not tops," corrected Lavender in Svalbardian and in character.

"Oh yes, tiles," I said. "Thank you."

Had neither guard spoken Svalbardian, I would have attempted a broken Canadian with a thick accent, but splitting the guards worked much better. The non-bilingual one asked: "What are they saying?"

The Svalbardian-speaking one answered, smiling mischievously in a quiet Canadian, "They need our help. No bags, no currency of any kind, and"—he turned to us and asked in Svalbardian—"and girls, do you not have a place to stay?"

"Nowhere," I replied, yanking Lavender's hand and walking up a step to the cathedral entrance, closer to the guards. "Had our belongings not been stolen, we might have found an inn, and work in the morning, with some good fortune. Please, we have been taken advantage of and have been left with nothing. We don't even have proper clothing," I added, fanning my dress. "So, we come to the cathedral."

"Is your friend all right?" asked the Svalbardian-speaking guard.

"A temporary blindness. Well, we hope," answered Lavender.

"She's blind," he explained to the other guard.

"She's blind?" He laughed. "Oh, this is too easy. Nobody will be awake for several hours . . . let's bring the poor girls inside . . . and warm them up."

"I don't know," said the other. "Their story is odd."

"Is there a problem?" asked Lavender. "We simply need warmth and shelter."

"In Svalbard, no weapons can be carried into the houses of worship." I turned my back on the Svalbardian-speaking but skeptical guard, backing into him. I pulled my hair away in a clump, exposing my neck while arching my back. I lied: "Often worshippers are patted and searched before they are allowed to enter."

He choked a bit on his own tongue and so I took another half step closer as he noted: "Svalbardian hair certainly can be long, and a very light blonde."

Hearing his Canadian perfectly, Lavender nearly laughed, understanding my hair as neither Svalbardian nor my own natural color since using Baker's dye.

The less skeptical guard was eagerly opening the heavy entranceway, signaling with his palm and wide smile for us to enter. I grabbed Lavender's hand, and with her eyes still shut I guided her inside the warm house of worship.

During cathedral services in the season of darkness, the nave is lined with hundreds, sometimes thousands, of high-mounted candles. The hall was empty aside from us four, two guards and two pretend Svalbards, and lined economically with no more than a hundred candles, spaced to minimally light the sanctuary while not in use.

"Polaris is your king, yes?" I asked.

"Oh no, not exactly," answered the guard.

"They do not have a king," added Lavender.

"So then there is no castle?" I asked. "But where does the king—I am so sorry—where does Polaris stay?"

"What did they ask?" wondered the eager guard.

"Oh, they just wanted to know where Polaris sleeps," he answered.

"Oh, down below?" he revealed, flicking a thumb to the rear stairwell.

"Don't!" corrected the guard. "Oh, I'm sorry. They don't speak Canadian, so why would it matter?"

"Thank you so much for helping, and I am so sorry to persist," I went on, fanning my dress again, "but as you can see our dresses have been dirtied from our travels," which was a true statement, considering they were dusted in soil from Horace's release of us into the soft mound. "And we are quite cold. For our health and to wash our clothing when we are done, might we find a hot bath? Warm water would be best for our skin, and for Sanna's eyes. If there is a fee of any kind, to the cathedral or to you personally, we would be pleased to labor away any debt we accrue for your help."

"Oh . . . uh, a warm bath?" stammered the guard who understood, switching to Canadian. Put out, he sighed and listed: "Firewood, pots, towels, a tub . . ."

"Two nude girls!" said the eager one.

"Wait here, please," responded the nervous guard. Remembering his Svalbardian he repeated, "I am sorry. Wait here, please. We will start a fire and a warm bath. Be comfortable; it will take us some time."

———————

They disappeared into a narrow hallway in the middle of the left side of the nave.

"You can open your eyes now, Lavender," I whispered, returning to Canadian.

"You sure have a fondness for men in uniforms, don't you?" she teased. She looked at herself and at me and confirmed, "Not glowing." I had almost forgotten that possibility. She searched the floor and near the tallest candles found a long, metal object. It was almost as long as we were tall, a polished metal rod with a curved bell shape at the end.

"A candle snuffer?" I asked.

"We must find Polaris while the guards are drawing the bath. If he scrambles for a weapon before we're able to warn him, I would like something to defend myself."

I shrugged and grabbed a candle snuffer of my own. There were several lining the cathedral, which, at times, might have a thousand candles to snuff.

With my other hand I grabbed a small candle. We found the stairwell at the rear of the cathedral. "Lavender, wait. If we find him in his sleep, and the guards return, we'll be trapped between them and the catacombs."

"Still not glowing," she said over her shoulder, prowling down the stairs.

The air took on a dank, musty odor as we reached the bottom stair. We struggled to maintain our silence without coughing. Quietly and quickly, and with two purple glowing eyes and a single candle, we searched the lower floor until we found a thick reinforced metal-and-wood door.

"Locked," I whispered, pushing gently at the barrier. "And probably latched, bolted, boarded, and guarded by a three-headed jackal on the other side. What should we do?"

Lavender knocked on the door. "Polaris?"

"All right. We could try that."

"Polaris!"

After a cough and a snort behind the thick door, then some shuffling, we heard an ancient voice speak, "What?"

"Polaris, we must speak with you," I replied, tense.

"Who are you? What is it?"

"The Siberians, sir. They're invading."

After a squeak from the ropes of his bedding and some further shuffling from within, he unlatched his door and opened it.

"You!" he nearly shouted, looking up to find two glowing purple eyes in the dark underground hall. His red eyes had a faint trace of light remaining, but little compared to Lavender's. He retreated hardly a step into his room, but Lavender became another creature, enraged and triggered by the red eyes.

She lunged for him, candle snuffer held diagonally to pass through the door into his chambers, springing from the floor and tossing him on the ground. She was on top of the old man, snarling, knees holding the snuffer across his chest and her hands around his neck prepared to squeeze.

"Lavender! We came to warn the man, not kill him!"

He gagged and kicked, legs frail but free. "I saw the glow. He was going to reach for a weapon. Then no one could have been warned. Please! Secure his legs so he's forced to listen."

I set aside the candle and with my own snuffer held down his thighs, squatting across his shins. He couldn't move. He was simply too old and frail to resist. He was flat on his chamber floor, wearing a red-and-white robe.

"You!" he said once more in disbelief, finding breath to speak. "You were swallowed into the sea, were you not? Are you Death herself? How dare you come for my celestial spirit!"

Lavender raised her arm high in the darkness and slapped Polaris across the face with the force of hundreds of days of exile. She slapped him a second time, not as forcefully, a third, a fourth, and seemed unable to find the satisfaction she expected to attain.

"Lavender!" I begged, still restraining Polaris's legs.

"Celestial?" she snarled over him. "You aren't from the heavens. We know you're nothing more than an escaped Siberian slave."

"And so are we, now," I said. "Polaris, the Siberians will soon invade York. They're a day or less within range."

"How do you know this? Is that why you came? Did you lead them here?"

Again, Lavender struck Polaris hard across the face and shouted, "We are here to do your work, you fool! Protect your people! Mobilize your military! Flee the town before it's invaded! And tell them the truth about what you are!"

"What did you claim of me? That I'm an escaped Siberian slave, not from the sky above? Girls, you may only be executed once. Sink to blasphemy, and I will attach additional punishments to your family, beginning with your mother."

Quickly, to prevent another outburst from Lavender, I said, "Polaris, if you continue to deny and deceive, then you fail in protecting your people."

"Protect my people? If I'm to believe what you just said, you led the Siberians to our doorstep, did you not?"

"Does any of this matter?" I questioned. "Warn your army; warn your people. Preserve your town and with it your command role."

He paused in silence, seeming to accept our advice until Lavender protested: "No. Then he only perpetuates himself. Have you killed any other gifted children like me?"

"Of course I have. So go ahead. Kill me. Make our society better. Kill me, and I won't be able to do it again. If this must end, why not kill me? But first, look at how Siberian babies are separated into thorned and unthorned. One stays with his family and his society, and the other is stripped away and thrown into slavery. I escaped this to start a new country where there are no privileged and subjugated classes. Where there wouldn't be two groups, separated by birth, one inevitably controlling the other. Without me, you do realize you and your sister would be in different classes, don't you?"

"Don't listen to him, Lavender," I said. "Polaris, just stop talking and warn your army."

He ignored me and continued: "That's how a tyrannical class structure begins. Your very existence, Lavender, everyone born with a gift, threatens the balance we escaped Siberia to achieve. Could I allow that to happen here? You were persecuted, but never should you believe I held a personal hatred for you, as you seem to have for me. You were persecuted simply for your gift. Considering you were not aware of how your existence threatens our society, I commend your actions. Attacking me might seem noble. But when I was a Siberian slave, I didn't just escape for freedom. I knew they would use me and other gifted men and women to create an army of gods. I don't lie to my people for my own sake. I keep my gift and other secrets to protect the people of Canada. Kill me for lying if you wish. Kill me like I've killed gifted people of the past as they were born. But expect your home to fall into cold chaos if you do, as Siberia turns the known world into its slave camp. Without me there would be no one to persecute the gifted, so you and any other gifted children would be safe. Until we become Siberia. But go ahead if that's what you think the people want. Kill me. Do it."

Nervous, I warned: "Lavender, we aren't here to become him."

She said: "You are but a poor representative of a greater institution, Polaris. There are fine Canadians, you simply are not one. But we've come to save everyone."

Wanting to get away before the guards searched for Erika and Sanna, I said: "You've been warned, Polaris. Save your people and lead them to a clearing to the northeast. Tell them to follow the Celestial Lights. Warn your military and have them defend an empty town. Devise a trap, an ambush, or whatever you decide. You are their commander. Remember that Siberia will be here within the day from the north and northwest. But know that you cannot rely on our silence if we ever learn we are pursued. We will leave this cathedral and return to exile, but should you or your men follow in any way, the entire known world will learn your authority does not extend beyond that of an ordinary man."

Lavender added, "Don't pursue us, our family, or any other gifted man or woman if you wish to preserve our silence."

"I accept," said Polaris from the floor. "But someday, I promise, you will learn the true burden of self-perpetuation."

With a count to three, Lavender and I released Polaris so that we could escape quickly up the stairway.

During our count, he attempted to disrupt our concentration. "Why, oh why did I not kill the infant Lavender when I had the opportunity?" Still our counting continued in synchronization. We sprung to our feet with 'three,' and Lavender swung her candle snuffer, striking his ankle with the bell-shaped end before he could stand. He winced and grabbed his ankle, unable to follow.

We rushed through the house of worship and through the large doors to the outside. We sprinted as best we could with tired legs, heading north to find our family.

Once well beyond the city limits and into the rural districts, convinced we were not being followed, I finally found the opportunity to ask: "Lavender, were the attacks necessary? The slaps, and the farewell swing of the snuffer?"

"He won't need both ankles to warn his men," she said defensively.

"Yes, but you seemed set to kill him, the sort of misdeed for which you dismissed Agrippin. You once declared to the Prince of Svalbard that never, even in your most angered state, would you be beyond self-control enough to desire to kill Polaris. You were beyond self-control. If we face him again, remember the effect he has on you."

"Quite the opposite," she denied. "I was in complete control, and I stand by my words to the prince because I did not kill Polaris. Marigold, you didn't see, but he glowed the entire time we held him to the floor. Yes, I was enraged, but not beyond control. I was the cause of the white glow. And I found so many ways to justify it. I could have easily driven the bar of the snuffer into his neck, or its small end into his eye socket and through to the floor. Even his throat was exposed to me. I was a short lapse of self-control from killing him. But the white glow that explained all of this to me . . . I don't know . . . maybe I expected a tainted white, another color entirely, or even no glow around the old man. I have since Svalbard, and before then, distilled Polaris in my mind to pure evil, believing evil is never murdered but rather eradicated. When he glowed white, I realized that I had not Polaris as my enemy, and no enemy but myself."

"Words of Brother Lichen. Polaris then owes him the debt of his life. Yes, okay, but the slaps seemed unnecessary."

Still settling from what she would not admit as a temporary loss of sanity she disagreed.

"They were my alternative. And it does not matter, because I hope to never face the man again."

We reached the farm. In the darkness it looked so similar to what we remembered, a reminder that we hadn't even been away a full season.

This very day the season past, we lived there, yet to move to York's marketplace, yet to reveal Lavender's gift to society, and therefore yet to be exiled.

"Dare we rejoice?" I asked.

"We've warned Polaris, we seem to have escaped the Siberians, and all we must do is reunite with our family and escape to Lichen's clearing," recited Lavender.

"Good. Nothing could possibly go wrong."

"Marigold, please."

We banged open the door, finding the dark kitchen, expecting to wake our family in our search for something to ease our hunger. "What's this?" I whined loudly, sorting through the pantry. "Disgusting dried mushrooms . . . nothing but preserved vegetables?"

"Is it too much to ask for the occasional pastry?" asked Lavender, also loudly, searching for something to drink.

"You know it is. We beg for it whenever someone heads to market. But when they return, it's stale bread every time."

"Oh, that garlic loaf that Grandfather likes?" said Lavender, moaning dramatically. Finding a pitcher, she groaned. "Oh, and where was this water drawn from? A small puddle in the field between two mounds of mullice manure?"

Finally, some shuffling started in the bedrooms. Lavender and I glanced at each other and smiled.

"Wait!" shouted Grandfather from across the house.

"No, it's the girls!" shouted Grandmother near him.

"Impossible!" responded Grandfather as his wife stampeded for the kitchen. "You've had a dream!"

"Girls!" she shouted in the darkness, reaching us. "Lavender, Marigold, is that you?"

Grandfather arrived quickly behind her, fearing he need protect his wife. "Lavender? Marigold? You're not dead? You're alive! You're alive!"

"No! We're the spirits of Lavender and Marigold!" I said with a nasal vibrato, waving my arms.

"The hungry spirits," joked Lavender.

"Yes, and when one dies, she is given a hideous gray dress," I added in a casual voice, posing to display the garment.

There was a stunned pause of disbelief as our grandparents stared.

Finally, Lavender explained: "We're joking. We just thought we'd surprise you this way."

They lunged toward us for an embrace and quite quickly all were crying and speaking loudly. Mother soon arrived with a lantern and we shared embraces. I had been waiting for another look at the scar on her cheek. After escaping Siberia, I understood it quite differently than before. We then sat again as a family, briefly.

They noticed my altered hair color, and Lavender explained, "Oh, it was hysterical! She got her head caught in—"

"The cloaca of a giant bird," I interrupted. "I found nothing interesting inside. Besides, our journey was filled with much more unbelievable moments than that. Like Lavender getting her first kiss. *Finally.*"

They offered anything edible they could find, our grandmother noting that we appeared gaunt.

"Well, we spent many days wandering the bush, and more recently in a Siberian slave camp, where the meals were occasionally poisonous," explained Lavender.

While we quickly ate some bread and dried vegetables, Grandfather asked, "Girls, what are you doing here? You could be killed if anyone sees you."

"We're here to warn the town of an impending Siberian invasion," answered Lavender.

"Oh no . . ." gasped Grandmother.

I answered, "We have to flee east toward the lights. You'll see them on the horizon, where there will be a refugee camp. Mother, do you remember the green-eyed man who helped you find Father shortly before Lavender was born?"

"Yes, of course."

"He's bred the livestock you left with him. He would like to return the lineage to us."

Grandfather resisted. "No, we must stay and fight if Siberia is invading."

"The military will handle that, and is expecting them. It was delicate, but we've warned Polaris. The Siberians will invade from a direction which will place this home as one of the first attacked," I explained. "There's nothing more I would desire right now than to find my old bed and sleep until the sun rises, days from now. But any nonessential distractions must be avoided."

"Why did you not write?" blurted Mother, overwhelmed.

"Why did you do nothing to pursue and protect your children?" snapped Lavender, tired and hungry. "Or was our exile simply too much of an embarrassment and an inconvenience for you?"

"Yes, we should avoid nonessential distractions. Such as these," I mumbled ineffectively, as the bickering began.

"We were told you were dead!" said Mother. "We received a notice from the Canadian military that you were seen eaten by a huge creature!"

"We were hunted," I noted. "By Polaris's men. Our exile was not sufficient for him, so he sent a party to kill us. When his men watched us walk into the mouth of the sea creature, he must have ceased his search. Had we written home, he might have known we were still alive and would have resumed his pursuit."

Lavender announced: "Mother, you're glowing red. You're pregnant."

"What?" she asked, flustered.

"No, not genuinely." Lavender smirked. "But now we know you have a lover."

The joy of the reunion quickly dissolving, Mother snapped, "Lavender!"

Disappointed with their own child for a different reason, Grandmother and Grandfather said: "Heather!"

"Marigold!" I contributed for my own sake, as all eyes turned toward me. "Please listen, because speaking of the sea creature, brace yourself, if you're ready?"

"Continue, quickly," prompted Grandfather.

"Simon is alive," blurted Lavender again.

"Yes, well, in a way," I added.

"A complicated triangle for our mother," mocked my sister.

"Lavender, behave!" corrected Grandmother.

"I was exiled! Nearly executed if not for Marigold! And what do you do? Do you do anything? Let your two young daughters run off into the bush while you stay in your warm home? Why not follow us? Why not stay a family? You picked a farm, shelter, sustenance, and comfort over your own daughters and granddaughters! You did nothing! All of you!"

She nearly collapsed in fatigue, frustration, and tears. Mother fled the room, and Lavender was comforted by her modestly apologetic grandparents.

Mother returned quickly, with a box. She was now in tears as well, torn to shreds by the judgment of failure as a mother. It had been issued by the worst possible accuser, a struggling child. She slammed the box on the table in the kitchen, and through streaming tears she exclaimed, "Here's your *nothing!*" She ran off to gather her belongings for our departure.

"What are these?" I asked, plucking a bead from the box, holding it near the lantern. The box was filled with them, small beads painted in the exact design of that over the entranceway of our brief business in the York marketplace, the Mystic Garden. Black specs in the middle, and concentric circles of purple and white around them.

"Lavender, within days of your exile we thought you both to be dead," explained Grandmother. "Your mother grieved in a terrible way. She found beads identical to these when we went through your belongings in the rental you left by the marketplace. She began replicating these beads, painting more so as not to forget you. Rather it was so that Canada would not forget you. She sells the beads in the market, a self-respecting but pathetic effort because she never makes much money and is often harassed by Polaris and his men. They understand it as an act of defiance, which it is, as well as an accusation of injustice. But when they extend this injustice, turning over her cart or threatening her, she absorbs it, careful not to move or speak. As you remember, if she commits even the smallest crime, the punishment would not be as it would for most Canadians. Because she journeyed to Simon for your birth, and the associated punishment for treason, she would be killed by a very jealous man in Polaris should she stumble in her path to follow any other of his laws."

I agreed. "Jealous is entirely correct. Of Polaris, that is. That shriveled, desiccated man we now know has a gift similar to Lavender's only not quite as powerful or useful. He also has been, we assume for as long as he's been alive, eliminating others with a gift of their own."

"Precisely how your mother markets her beads," Grandfather explained, still comforting Lavender, who sobbed quietly as tears streamed from her face. "As a protection from the dry bitterness of jealousy. She remembers Polaris's jealousy of Lavender as a newborn."

I added, "Polaris is not what he claims to be. He's not from the sky above. He's an escaped Siberian slave."

"What?" Grandfather reacted.

"We don't have time to explain everything. We should gather our belongings and head for the Celestial Lights, to the east."

Lavender stood and admitted: "First I must apologize to my mother."

Mother emerged from behind the kitchen wall, having heard her. She asked: "Is Simon truly alive?"

"Yes," answered Lavender. "Trapped inside the sea creature. His situation is not your fault or mine, and had he died, this would not have been our fault either. The fort had ample medics. He wishes you would know that you have his blessing should you choose to remarry. He'd prefer that you were happy."

———————

Our mother and grandparents returned to their bedrooms to collect any valuables and traveling necessities as we prepared to abandon our home for Brother Lichen's clearing. Having been gone long enough to have our own non-sentimental belongings mostly discarded or given away, Lavender and I collected very little and anxiously awaited our family's departure. I changed into warm fleece garments, but Lavender didn't bother to change out of her slave dress. I placed a thick coat around her.

"Polaris warned I would learn the burden of self-perpetuation."

"He wished only that you feel apologetic for existing, to aid his cause of your elimination," I explained.

"Marigold, a battle will begin later this day. There will be many deaths, and my life is of no more value than theirs."

"So what then, are we not escaping to Lichen's clearing now?" I asked.

"You should go ahead. I will rejoin you and our family. But if I go to the Celestial Lights now, the burden, the self-perpetuation Polaris warns of, waits to ensnare me. In this battle—in any battle—there will be injured, there will be dying . . . those who will live and those who will not. Soldiers who do not forsake their own responsibilities. I can assist them, sorting the living from the dying, containing the casualties from greater numbers. I'm not sure what I will do exactly, maybe find the medics' tent . . . but I'm no good to any of them if I run off to the clearing with our family, forsaking the responsibility of my gift."

"And I'm no good to you in the Lichen's clearing."

"No, don't!" she melted. "No, Marigold, don't!"

"Lavender, when will you stop crying?"

"Marigold, I need you to listen! Don't follow me! Do you understand? Don't follow me, Marigold!"

I grabbed her cheeks with my palms and waited a moment for her to open her eyes. More tears fell down my fingers as I stared closely, still waiting for her eyelids to open. Soon they did, and I searched deep inside the lavender irises to find my image. Illuminated by her eyes' shimmer of light, I saw my distorted reflection.

"So, I'm glowing. I've glowed white before."

Our family gathered by the door, each of us with a small personal bag and a warm coat. Lavender pretended as though she had not been weeping and faced away from them. I faced toward them.

"Let's go," commanded Grandfather, reaching for the door.

"Wait," I said calmly. "Lavender and I will first return to York, then rejoin you in the refugee camp. Go east-northeast toward the lights. You will find it."

"York?" questioned Grandfather. "That's where they'll attack."

I explained: "Yes, so there will be many casualties. She and I must sort them out, living from dying." Behind me Lavender breathed deeply, still trying to hide her state.

Our mother questioned: "Lavender, are you and Marigold to be among the dying? I will not grieve my daughters' deaths twice."

"No, she's not glowing, and neither am I," I lied, now struggling to resist tears of my own. Fortunately, it was dark, and I could hide reddening eyes with a steady voice.

"This all makes me nervous," declared Grandfather. "But I trust your gift. We'll find you again in the camp, or, hopefully, if Canada finds victory, maybe your help will be enough for Polaris to expunge your record and we will find you back here on the farm."

"Be careful, girls," insisted Grandmother as we embraced and said our good-byes. Lavender turned to embrace each of the three quickly, holding her head down to hide her eyes.

My sister headed south as I trailed after her. If I caught up, she hurried to maintain a slight lead. I knew she was displeased with me, now seeing her sister as a fool and an emotional burden. We had improperly bid farewell to our family, misleading them when we declared we believed we would see them again.

Finally, some distance from our farm, still in the rural districts but not yet to York's northern limits, Lavender stopped and confronted me. "Our family was not glowing, Marigold. Nor were you. Just to be clear—because I will not leave this to interpretation or miscommunication—do you understand that you are currently glowing white, in this moment, and that I am forecasting you will die? And that this change occurred when you insisted that you would follow me?"

"Yes, of course."

"You're a fool. Worse, you're a fool of knowledge. You understand your mistake and insist upon it. Was it difficult to lie to them like that?"

"They would have it no other way. Grandfather at least would have certainly followed uselessly, only to have gotten himself killed. How irritating that would have been . . . a stubborn family member wanting only to help and not abandon their sister." I paused, adding, "How painfully irritating!"

Breathing irregularly, she shook her head and groaned. She collapsed to her knees in the soil and cried into her hands: "Marigold, you imbecile! Every time I attempt to do what I believe is right, the outcome is always so wrong! Marigold, you're going to die!"

"Yes, I know. I glow white, and I'm afraid. So, we should not ask, 'What will become of us?' The question must be, 'What will we do?'"

She looked up, offended, then back at the ground. In the absurdity of the situation I announced: "Today we lay to rest our dear sister Lavender."

"Marigold? Stop this!" she demanded, still on her knees.

"But more important, we bury her awful wooden shoes. In life, her more stylish sister attempted to introduce fashionable choices for Lavender's feet."

"Marigold?"

I persisted: "I remember a time, this was back on the farm, by the way . . . Lavender was only eleven. I was twelve, possibly thirteen . . . no, twelve . . . so then Lavender would have been ten . . ."

"Marigold!"

"Excuse me, it's not possible to interrupt one's own funeral," I quietly explained, then continued loudly: "Yes, Lavender was ten and . . . wait, that wasn't Lavender! I'm so sorry, everyone. I was thinking of somebody else entirely. I knew I should have written my words down, but I truly wished to speak from the heart today."

She looked at me in pain, her expression begging me to stop.

I said softly: "Lavender, it may not be fitting or well attended, but you deserve at least an outcast's eulogy."

She looked at me, weeping more than before.

"All right, I'll stop eulogizing. But will *you* ever stop crying?" Without a reply I continued: "Oh well, I suppose you should be permitted to cry at a funeral."

She screamed: "Your funeral! Your funeral! *I* have no other choice! Marigold, this is *your* funeral!"

I knelt by her side, placed an arm around her and said, "So be it."

She stood and embraced me with her full strength, our two thick, warm coats pressed together as she sobbed and said: "Marigold, thank you so much. Thank you so much for your sacrifices. I love you."

"I love you too, sister."

"You'll be laughing with me right until the end, won't you?" She sniffed.

"Or *at* you."

"Marigold, please." She smiled.

"Let's head south to York to see how we can help."

When we arrived in the denser part of town, it was morning but eerily it could have been the beginning of any other day in the season of darkness. People were plodding about their normal business of routine survival. Torches burned on street-side posts to guide them. We were discouraged to realize that the way we might best help was the way we thought we already had.

"Marigold, this is going to be a bloodbath. Everybody here is glowing white."

"They don't know of the invasion?"

"Polaris," she grunted. "Polaris, Polaris, always Polaris."

"He told no one." I came to the realization, sinking into a shocked, calm numbness like a heavy stone dropped into the center of a cold pond. "Why? Why tell no one?"

"I know I didn't kill him. I left a man who was certainly not in a white glow."

"Unless . . . he's using them as bait. To trap the Siberian army once and for all."

"We have a town to warn."

"Then I'm glad I followed. We should separate. Two mouths can warn twice as many townspeople. And I can be quite loud."

"Marigold, if you leave my side, I won't be able to warn you if you're set to die."

"Do I still glow?"

"Yes. Yes, we do. We have both glowed white steadily since leaving the farm. We glow white, and everybody here glows white. Not a single person is free of the glow."

"Because we have yet to warn them," I suggested optimistically.

She held her hands together across her nose and mouth. Looking to me she inhaled and said: "We may never see each other alive again. I just hope we can save a few lives before we—"

"We already have. Three in fact, all family. So far, a gain of one."

We embraced again, understanding it to be our final farewell.

———————

We divided the town in half. I didn't want my sister to have to face Polaris ever again, so I took the half with the cathedral. I was alone now, without Lavender's aid.

I survived Windfall when she stopped using her gift. I can survive this as well or at least warn as many people as I can, I told myself.

Denial was the fashionable reaction initially, as I started with a father and daughter walking together.

"Excuse me, sir?"

"Yes?"

"I don't think you should take your child to the academy today. Siberia will invade our town. It won't be long before their army is at the north gate."

He turned his head left and right, holding his young daughter's hand. "I don't see anybody—"

"You're the first I've informed."

He laughed confidently. "That's absurd. I would have heard some warning."

"That's a strange thing to say to someone who's warning you," I rebutted, figuring if he wished to laugh at me, I could oblige.

"If what you say is true, Polaris will mobilize his soldiers and we'll be safe." He walked off, his daughter quietly petitioning, "But she says not to go . . ."

As it was early in the day, few townspeople had left their homes.

Next was an elderly couple standing by their doorstep. They moved slowly, as if afraid to fall; I couldn't tell if they were arriving or departing. "Madam?" I hollered. "Sir?"

"Yes, young lady?" replied the older man.

"I must warn you that York will be invaded by Siberians within the day. You must escape town. Head northeast toward the Celestial Lights and you will survive."

The woman sternly replied: "My hearing is not what it once was, but I'm certain I would have heard a bell or a horn."

"Or some sort of warning," said the older man, reprimanding me. "Girl, do you believe it humorous to play tricks on an old man and woman?"

The woman chastised me as well. "One day when you are as old as I am now, I hope a young girl mocks you, wanting to send you wandering into the forest for a laugh."

"Thank you." I left.

Learning quickly I was limited by a lack of authority, I found a mother and infant I thought I would certainly be able to convince. She was walking slowly while holding her child and an empty sack, south in the direction of the market. "Madam?"

"Yes?"

"Madam, I see you have a beaded necklace. Do you know my mother, Heather?"

"I think so. Is she the one with the scar on her cheek? If so, she sold me this."

"Yes, that's her. Do you like the necklace?"

"I do, but my child is always tugging on it, so I don't often wear it. When I bought the beads, your mother told me the scar was from a confrontation with a Siberian."

"It was. And the beads are modeled in the likeness of my sister's eyes. Lavender."

"Lavender, who was killed?"

"No, no! We survived! I'm her sister, Marigold, and we've returned to warn York that the Siberians will invade, and the town must evacuate."

"I remember you girls, from your business."

"Yes!" I exclaimed, feeling so close to convincing her. "The Mystic Garden. Were you a patron?"

"Yes, of course! When I was early in the pregnancy with my child, Lavender verified I was indeed carrying. She even told me it was to be a single birth, not twins, and was clear to say that she could not verify the gender. It was a boy," she said, pulling away part of the wrap that covered the child's face in the cool air.

"He's beautiful. So, if you trust my sister's gift, you must flee York. I was only a moment ago standing with her as she predicted the entire town was to die if they do not flee. Please, madam."

"I do trust your sister's gift. That's why I wear these beads. Will they not protect me?" she bargained.

"No. No, those beads will not protect you from death. It doesn't work like that."

Still she haggled. "So what must I do for my family to survive without fleeing our home?"

"Regretfully, there's no comfortable fix, madam. But there is a solution! Leave York. Head northeast toward the Celestial Lights. You'll be safe."

I left her as she pondered. I had not the time to wait while she weighed the idea of death in her home against a difficult life in a refugee camp. And because acceptance of the inconvenient truth would require the most difficult change of all, a change of one's lifestyle, her emotional progression stalled illogically in a phase of bargaining, as if there were any way she could continue to survive in the same fashion she had been living.

And the fact that she believed she could bargain against this ominous warning suggested she may have actually been in an earlier stage, one of denial.

I had no idea when Siberia was going to strike, and so far I had tallied zero successes in three tries. I was tempted to increase my ratio to one in four simply by fleeing myself and allowing the skeptical to be slaughtered. But instead, I focused on my lack of authority.

I stood in front of the cathedral. I had warned any passerby of the coming invasion, but it had still been a waste of breath. I might have been zero in ten by the end of my walk, wondering if Lavender found any success of her own.

I stared at the centerpiece of the town that awaited invasion, its roof like a turned-over hull from the Siberian warship that had carried me home. I looked left and right, having traveled a bit of the town, wondering if Lavender was in my periphery. She wasn't. I wondered also why the doors were now unguarded, or if Polaris had warned all armed men of the invasion, including the cathedral guards.

The door was heavy, and the nave was dark and empty. There were no worshippers, and only several flickering candles lit. I found a snuffer again and proceeded inward.

A silhouette passed slowly left to right across the far end of the nave, searched urgently for something, and swept back right to left. "Hello!" I called.

The shadow froze when it heard me, and faced me only briefly . . . but its eyes gave it away. Two red flickers like dim candles at eye level drifted to the left as the shadow said nothing, escaping into the earth down the stairwell.

The shadow was hobbled, but I was not. I sprinted impulsively through the nave, needing to grab this shade and make it step into the light. I needed his authority, York needed his leadership, and yet for all I knew, he looked for a dagger for my throat.

"Polaris!" I shouted from the top of the stairwell. "Polaris! Why did you not warn York!"

He called up from below, "Where's your sister?"

"Why did you not warn your people? Why not protect them?" I insisted, pounding each stair as I descended.

I reached the bottom of the stairwell cloaked in darkness and breathing the fumes of rot. Not a single candle was lit, nor was there a trace of his red, glowing eyes. I looked left and right so quickly that when I attempted to step forward down the hallway, I walked into the side wall, losing the little orientation I had.

"Where's your sister?" he asked, but in my disorientation, I couldn't locate him. His voice echoed, coming from within any of the many rooms attached to the underground hall.

"She's not with me. We separated when we realized you had warned no one."

"Good. She would have killed me, had you not controlled her anger."

"At the time I thought you were going to warn your people. Otherwise, I might not have bothered stopping her."

"I owe you my life. And you came back to help. It's too bad you're not gifted, as your sister," he remarked. He did not sound near. "But you aren't useless, Marigold. You would make a good leader if you had a gift. Come closer. Let me help you."

"Help me? You don't intend to kill me?" I asked, holding the snuffer in my right hand with my left palm to the hallway wall, stepping deeper in, feeling for open doors. He didn't respond. "If you won't warn your people, I will. I've already mobilized hundreds," I lied. "They're fleeing the city. They'll ask where you were when it mattered, and I'll be forced to tell them the truth about you. Soon they will know you as a traitor."

"Yes, you know my secret. You and Lavender are the only ones who do outside of Siberia. But leave the cathedral as you are, and you die by the Siberian thorn, like your father. Or you can live. I can give you a gift to help you survive. But I can only give it to you in total darkness. Follow me to the catacombs."

"I'd have to be fairly stupid to do that, Polaris."

"I'm not trying to lock you in. I just need darkness to give you the gift."

"Come up. Come up and warn your people. Why do you leave them to perish?"

"To trap the Siberian army. It was the same during the slave break. Not all survived, but they won't change history. I'll tell you the source of the gift, and you'll understand everything, Marigold. Come deeper in. We can find peace between us."

"Come up, Polaris. Your country needs you."

"Do you know the source of the gift?"

"That's the least of my concerns right now." I carefully searched the man's bedroom, which I recognized even in the dark, remembering the layout and where his garments were stored. He was not in the room; he was farther down the hall.

"It's the Celestial Lights. But as I've discovered, it must soak the eyes of a newborn when they first open for any gift to be instilled. The lights are given but one opportunity to trigger a biological response that permanently alters one's genetic makeup. You likely have this dormant potential, Marigold, but unlike your sister, you've missed your opportunity to activate your gift. What could your gift have been? To see gold and precious stones underneath the soil? To see spirits walking the earth?"

"To see people for what they truly are?" I replied, finding one of the old man's folded robes.

He persisted, a bit more desperate. "There's a way to activate a gift after infancy. I know how. You can have a gift like your sister, but you have to come with me to the catacombs."

"Why would you want me to have a gift?"

"I'll need someone to save me when this is all over. I can give you a gift that will help you survive this battle. Your sister broke my ankle, Marigold. But I've positioned my soldiers where I need them, and I plan to remain below the cathedral until the fighting has ended. Our numbers will never match theirs; I need to trap them first, then send my army in. I'll need someone with gifted vision to find me when the fighting's over. Please, a gift for a life."

"You sound like you may finally speak the truth."

"I do."

"And yet only in the dark, to someone who already knows your secrets."

"Please, Marigold. I need someone to keep me alive. Just come closer."

"If you won't save your people, I will," I said, ignoring his offer. Grabbing the robe, I planned to escape back up the stairwell. But in a moment of weakness and curiosity I wondered if there were any truth to what he was saying. I looked back down into the dark hallway and saw two flickers of red deep in the darkness. He had come out from his hiding place, not chasing me but emerging as he heard me leaving. He stood in the hallway and stared for a moment. His eyes blinked once, briefly creating total darkness, then reopened as my gaze stayed fixed. I felt a strain in my pupils, then a shiver in my spine. My heart thumped twice, then I finally regained myself again and ascended into the nave. I shouted back as I left, "It won't work, Polaris. I'm not going to let you trap me in the catacombs. Soon your people will know the truth about you."

This was the last time I was in his presence. I went up the stairwell with one of his robes in hand, prepared to exploit his authority.

———

I emerged from the cathedral wearing Polaris's robe. In the darkness the townspeople saw first the robe and not the one within. There were no more than ten within view of me, walking by the cathedral incidentally. All quickly turned to face me, most knelt, and in a blink of a red or purple eye their numbers doubled. I had yet to speak, and they had yet to fear the unusual.

I waited another moment, checking the heavy cathedral door behind me for any possibility that Polaris pursued. He did not; the door remained closed. I pressed my silence just far enough before someone would, from a distance, notice that the person in Polaris's robe was an imposter.

I spoke. "People of York, hear me! Polaris is gone! He has taken repose in the catacombs. His robe passes to me."

A bold man drew near, "And who are you?"

Hiding my nervousness, I called out, "His final message was to warn you."

The bold man called back: "If Polaris has died, why do you wear the red robe of war, and not the black robe of mourning?" He was much closer than any other in the crowd, and I could see him as a man of forty or fifty, strong and with gray hair, now climbing the steps to approach me at the cathedral entrance. The rest stood far from the structure, silently awaiting resolution.

I announced: "There is no time to mourn. Siberia invades today, and we must evacuate our town before their numbers overwhelm us!"

He was four or five steps away. I couldn't hide my fear any longer from the stranger, nor could I pretend to only address the crowd. I adjusted my line of sight to prepare myself to be attacked. My pupils dilated, my eyelids opened to their fullest, and I stared the man in the eye out of fear that my lingering white glow was finally to be fulfilled.

He dropped to his knees before me, begging forgiveness. With his nose to the step he cried: "Please, please! I was not doubting you! I never doubted the truth of your words!"

"Rise and stand beside me," I commanded, confused but improvising. He obliged yet covered his eyes. He would not raise his head, even as he approached. I told him: "Please, sir. Convince them we must flee our homes."

"We must flee our homes!"

"Tell them we must leave town and head toward the Celestial Lights."

"We must follow the lights! She is the Celestial One herself! Polaris lives within her! Her eyes burn with a renewed flame, red as his!"

"I'm sorry, what?"

He turned to face me, gazed into my eyes again, but covered his own once more and fell again to his knees. He shouted to the crowd, wanting to earn his forgiveness: "Polaris has passed his authority to this girl! Polaris lives forever! *She* lives forever!"

I cupped my hands and held them to my face, blocking any light from the stars above, the torches that lined the street, and the veil of Celestial Lights far off on the horizon. I breathed as if awaiting a physician's diagnosis and opened my eyes within my palms to find a fire's reflection flickering on my fingers.

The light emanated from my eyes, the only possible source.

I uncupped my palms and whispered, "Sir, please, rise again and tell me the color of my eyes."

He chose not to lift his nose from the step, answering, "You are celestial. You come from the heavens, from a star in the sky. I need not dare gaze into your eyes again to know that they are still red, red as a moment ago, red as Polaris."

All blood rushed from my head hearing this, so strongly that I was left with a ringing in my ears, drowning out the noise of the crowd as they began to react. I was afflicted. Polaris had found a way to perpetuate himself, and I had become his vessel. I was so afraid now, so disturbed and violated that I even took a moment to question my own thoughts, while the bells in my ears continued to toll. He had altered my nature. Was my mind still my own? Had I become evil? What would this crowd now do? Could they accept me, or was I bound to be forced into the role of their victim of persecution, their savior, or both? Overwhelmed with more self-doubt than I had ever experienced, I remembered my sister and finally understood what a moment in her life is like. I just hoped she was more successful than me, warning people on the other side of town.

Curious, the crowd drew near. Regarding me as Polaris's chosen successor, with his robe and eyes, they stood around the lowest step. Only the brave man, kneeling, terrified, remained beside me. I bent my knees in nausea, nearly fainting as the ringing in my ears ceased and some blood began to return to my head.

"We must flee to the northeast. Siberia will invade, and we'll be slaughtered if we don't evacuate," I warned in a shaking voice.

They stood frozen, now seeming much greater in number, almost a hundred. "Who says this?" someone hollered from deep within the crowd. "Does the man beside you do your speaking? Declare your authority!"

"Is authority necessary to have knowledge of an invasion, to warn others and to save them? Would you not listen? Cannot a commoner do this?" I pleaded.

"A commoner cannot wear that robe, girl!" he hollered again.

I was dumb of speech, and a silent crowd stared. I understood what Lavender faced when she stood trial before this same group, charged with blasphemy. I now also understood Polaris. "I am the Celestial One!" I declared, receiving applause. I awaited its waning, continuing: "The light within me comes from Polaris himself, who comes from the heavens." Polaris had won at least this victory. I declared him to the crowd, trembling silently beneath my robe in both desperation and self-doubt. "We are to flee the Siberian attack, finding safety beneath the Celestial Lights, which shine on the northeastern horizon. Canada, find your children! Find your husband, your wife, your neighbor, your father, your mother, your sister, your brother! Return home quickly, warn all others along the way! Blow every horn! Ring every bell! Do not stay and fight in the darkness! Follow the lights, follow into the light!"

They mobilized, successfully warned, successfully convinced. But they were only the first hundred, hopefully set to warn many others, but still only representing a fraction of York. It was doubtful that the warning would include anyone from the remote rural districts. With so many left to warn, I could not leave the cathedral to save myself. I no longer felt it necessary to survive, nor did I feel worthy.

I turned to face the heavy cathedral doors behind me, opened them and returned inside. I scanned the nave for Polaris but found no one. He seemed determined not to leave his underground bunker until the battle was over, and yet neither he nor I nor anyone already warned knew the exact moment Siberia would reach York. Before our escape, Velorik had mentioned that dwindling supplies would force them to invade today, and I believed them to now be an hour, at least, from York.

Inside the dark, empty cathedral, I searched for a device to gather a new crowd, to refill the street and send them forth to the Lichen as I had with my first one hundred converts. To them, these were my candles now, my walls, my floor, my vaulted ceiling, and my altar, the altar which I had believed since childhood would be where I would stand when I wed. I ascended from the worship level into my choir loft, searching for a musical instrument of penetrating volume. I found a long horn with a useless loop of tubing in its center, a decorative touch to a functional and explosive siren. In the choir loft I also noticed a pull-string to an access door in the ceiling I had never seen before. I pulled up a ladder from the common area and rested its bottom in the loft to climb up and see where the opening led. After a bit of one-handed crawling, twisting, and climbing, I was on the cathedral roof, under the stars and high above the town.

From my roof I could see much more. I looked to Lavender's half of York, straining in an attempt to find her, but again found nothing. I looked to the northern horizon for the Siberians but also found nothing, and worse, I realized in the darkness I would not see them when they reached the borders of the town. In the northeast were the beautiful Celestial Lights, hovering over the Lichen's clearing. Beneath me some men and women moved quickly in that direction, but others, in ignorance or denial, seemed to act as they would any other day. The horn was my last hope.

I licked the mouthpiece and blew a short note followed by a steady note of increasing urgency. I blew the two notes again, and a third time. I blew the horn as loudly as my lungs would allow in the cool air, reaching the farthest Canadian I could have hoped, and even one more I wished I hadn't warned.

The town burst into flames. As instantly as a horn could blow, in a synchronization that only one specific escaped Siberian slave would understand, a perfect fire ring bloomed around the circumference of the

Canadian capital. I paused for a breath and realized the horn had also resonated underground, beneath me and beneath the nave, beneath the earth, in the darkness.

It was an unnaturally round fire, and no accident. I don't know the technology, but there is no doubt it preexisted, developed likely in secrecy by one who understood this day might come. Lavender and I had been many times frustrated in our attempts to kindle campfires with crude tools, and often it takes many minutes. This vast fire formed a circular moat around a large town, and again I say I don't know how it exploded so quickly, but it could not have been possible without an oil.

I cannot explain *how* the fire burned, but I do believe I can answer *why*. What insights to the human mind would explain why an oil, in this intentional combustion, would be tolerated even though it threatened the fragile boundary between life and death? If we, the narrators, could break through the binding of the page and speak directly to the reader, I might ask, "Brother Lichen, *why* does the tragic fire burn?"

Brother Lichen might say, "It only burns with our permission, and to stop it we must simply overcome ourselves. We have no enemy but us."

All of York was trapped, and I stood on the roof with what had become a useless horn. The fire encroached quickly, set to scorch all earth within its area, but brought with it a beneficial light, which allowed me to see reaches beyond what was earlier in my scope.

I strained my eyes again to the north, now realizing the Siberians had begun their invasion and crossed York's limits. They had arrived, finally, and yet much sooner than I anticipated. I could see that they were caught as the wall of fire was triggered, the eager trapped inside, the unfortunate in the middle burning to their deaths, and the trailing soldiers safe but wondering now what was expected of them.

My task was complete. I could not warn a single man or woman of York better than a raging fire, nor could my horn. From my rooftop I scanned the tremendous ring, still with some time before it spread inward. I saw no break in the wall of fire. If any part of the barrier was thin, it would quickly fill and correct itself. Swiveling my head, I wondered what sort of oil Polaris used for this devastating weapon, wondering what fuel would burn without smoke. I then realized there was of course smoke; I simply could not see it because of my new eyes.

The Siberian forces to the far north of town seemed disoriented. But in a berserker's mentality many pushed through the wall of fire, unable to see and unwilling to disobey their command. From the northeast, appearing beyond the fire and from within the veil of the Celestial Lights, was another race set to involve itself in the humans, their war, and their fire.

The sky was filled with more Feathermen than I knew existed. Between the shimmering of greens and purples on the horizon as well as the light of a fire that prevented human escape on the ground, hundreds of silhouettes approached our town in flight, in piercing V formations.

One Featherman, possibly Horace, flew in front of all the others, possibly with compass in hand. He formed the keystone of the group, with several of his cohesion trailing on either side. Behind them, another V, and another, at least ten. These ten or more groups were one in front of the other, forming a linear procession.

They seemed to approach slowly, which as they grew near only reminded me of the illusion of a large object moving incredibly quickly far from the eye. While the Siberians foolishly continued to penetrate the wall of fire—some successfully—a large portion of the Canadian townspeople still remained within, waiting to either burn or be slaughtered by the Siberian thorn. When the Feathermen reached the sky above the fire, the lead group broke away, then the next, and the next. Within each group, five or seven Feathermen also dispersed, swooping over and swarming the Canadian capital.

I suppose standing on the rooftop of the cathedral made me the easiest pluck of the city. Without warning, there was a gentle impact as I was snatched by a talon. Airborne above the city, I had escaped the white glow.

"Lavender!" I shouted to the unfamiliar Featherman. "You have a second talon! Return for my sister!"

"I will take you to Spirit Zero," he replied, committed to a previous command, and deflecting mine. "We will take all Canadians to Spirit Zero. You may search for her in the clearing, under the lights."

———————

I was one of the first refugees to reach Brother Lichen's clearing, at least one of the first humans. The Feathermen had already established a presence there. As tremendous armed guardians, they lined the perimeter of the field. They were too imposing and capable, and too great in number for the Siberians to pose any threat, should their thorned attack be redirected toward the Celestial Lights.

The Feathermen had assembled several great cushioned structures, nets similar to the pylon-mounted one at the airfield in Windfall. For this mission they expected human cargo, and were prepared.

I was released from flight into a soft cushion, stuffed appropriately with down and resting on the net. I descended safely to the ground as my escort disappeared into the sky, returning to York to pluck another Canadian. I discarded Polaris's robe. If I could have discarded my eyes as well, I might have.

My gaze swept across the clearing, briefly taking in the beauty of the Celestial Lights. I returned my line of sight to ground level in search of Lavender. More Feathermen swooped down, releasing their Canadians safely onto cushions. The first to be rescued hoped to find a family member among the next to be saved.

"Marigold!" shouted a very familiar voice.

"Lavender!" I responded, turning my head. "Oh, hello," I corrected, realizing I had responded to my mother's call. I ran to them where they were waiting anxiously.

"You have found Sir Lichen's clearing!" said Grandfather. "We were the first family to arrive, and have spoken with an incredible stone creature whom you know well. Oh, and these Feathermen! Thank the stars they are on our side of the battle."

"Yes, thank the stars for that," I mumbled. "Also thank Lichen, and Marigold, and Lavender."

"Where's Lavender, dear?" asked my grandmother. "You didn't separate, did you?"

"What . . . what is . . ." My mother squinted, coming closer.

"My eyes?" I asked.

She laughed. "Are they red? Marigold, you leave and return with a new hair color, then you leave and return with a new eye color. Will you be green-skinned the next time we see you?"

"Like the Trogs or the Petras." I smiled.

"Who?" asked Grandfather.

"How did you do this?" my mother wondered. "I hope you didn't poison your vision simply for effect."

I sighed without an answer.

"Where's Lavender?" persisted Grandmother.

I explained all that I could, trying like any young adult not to worry them with more information than they needed.

"Well, I suppose we stay here at the camp, enjoy the beautiful lights, and wait patiently for Lavender to be delivered by the Feathermen." Grandfather shrugged.

"Yes, patiently," I attempted, suppressing panic. They might have been accustomed to her absence, but I was much more comfortable by her side. Hoping to distract myself, I asked, "Grandfather, have you retrieved our livestock from the man with the green eyes?"

"Perhaps later. We'll see how this camp forms, and where the group's needs are. There are still only sparse, small clumps of people wandering the clearing," he noted, although more arrived steadily as the Feathermen swooped low overhead, then returned to York for more. "I don't see him. He was here in the clearing earlier, much earlier that is, and seemed busy. But while we wait for Lavender, come, follow me."

Grandfather led our family across the clearing to the opposite end of its pond.

"Sister Marigold!"

"Brother Lichen!"

Two Feathermen drained enormous buckets into the pond as the Lichen observed. As a Featherman stands so many times taller than a human, their buckets are proportionately larger, containing perhaps the volume of one of our smaller homes. There were hundreds of these giant buckets stacked along the trees at the perimeter of the clearing. "These are colleagues of Brother Baker," Lichen said.

"Yes, I know Baker well," I noted. They looked at me oddly from their height above, surprised. "I've spent time in his laboratory. I have been to Windfall."

"Tell her what you'll be doing," said my excited grandfather to the Feathermen.

One explained: "Brother Baker is unable to fly and could not come here to Spirit Zero, but his innovations are present. We've exhausted our full stock of concentrated anti-icing fluid, made from the juice of the maple tree. To be converted from its extracted and condensed form into a usable solution, it lacked only dilution with water in Spirit Zero's lake."

"To melt the lake so that refugees can drink?" I asked. "It's hardly frozen, and only in its upper layer."

"No, that's not our goal," answered a Featherman.

"You're speaking to a musician," my mother teased, taking advantage of having already heard this explanation before my arrival.

"Thank you, Mother," I murmured.

"I'm sorry." She laughed. "I'm just so thrilled to see you again! And soon Lavender as well!"

The panic surged in me, but I continued to suffocate it to save them from concern.

The Feathermen explained: "We work to suppress the freezing level of the resulting solution, which will be the lake, so that the fluid's new freezing point will be just above the current temperature of York."

"And we've just been told what that is," explained the other, draining a bucket of the syrupy concentrate into the water. "The temperature was taken in the first wave of Feathermen as they rescued Canadian humans from overhead."

"I should have paid better attention when Baker explained scientific things," I confessed.

"A steep temperature inversion is today's prevailing condition," explained the first Featherman. "We are extremely fortunate. Not only does it allow smoother air for the Featherman to control his flight with precision as he rescues a Canadian, but it allows him to carry this fluid in its liquid state, based on the temperature here and on our equations, in the warmer air two hundred to two hundred and fifty perch above York. Then, if our formulas are accurate, he can dump an overwhelming volume of fluid from above, which will fall in an agitated, super-cooled state."

"It will remain a liquid as it falls into colder temperatures, temperatures below its own rendered freezing point, until it strikes an object," added the other. "Then it will freeze aggressively on impact."

"Freezing rain." I remembered. "Baker's vocation."

"Exactly," they confirmed.

"Incredible. The fluid designed to combat freezing rain can be used to produce it?"

"Because the fluid's properties will react from sky to ground and in an inversion, we can operate the science backward or forward." They nodded.

"And in its volume and abundance, the ice flood will neutralize Brother Siberian as he invades," explained the Lichen. "I am told a human would survive a strong ice storm . . . Brother Siberian will be waist-deep and immobilized in the frozen fluid. The Feathermen can manage him from there without violence."

"I'm lost," said Mother.

I explained: "York burns. They're fighting fire with water, so the whole world doesn't burn."

A Featherman added: "And if the people of York are willing to tolerate such an unfortunate combustion, then science may be our last hope."

"And what of the Canadian military? Are they absent from all this?" asked my grandfather.

"Cowards," mumbled my mother, who would be a war widow if not for the Host.

I disagreed. "No, it was Polaris. He may have lied to them, sending them west or south. They'll attack once they see the fire, now that the Siberian forces are crippled." I turned to face the only two Feathermen on the ground and asked, "If I gave a description, do you believe you would be able to find and rescue my sister?"

"With the time it would take to circle overhead, we could probably save two human lives," one answered.

The other added: "And if we fail to focus on this mission, we fail to save thousands of human lives."

I accepted their refusal. "Letting many die to save herself . . . that's not why Lavender went back to York one final time."

Brother Lichen stated: "She was prepared for this, Marigold. I have seen many humans die, but none so bravely."

"Is something wrong with Lavender?" asked my grandmother.

I began weeping so much I couldn't speak. My knees shaking, I had to sit. My mother, my grandfather, and my grandmother had lost us both once before, then we returned, and now they were left with one.

They were devastated but had already grieved, and had a healthy, calloused strength to support me—even my mother who was in tears as well.

With her arm around me, my grandmother said, "Dear, she may be alive, and she may not die. There's nothing we can do but wait and allow the Feathermen to do their work, and pray that they will find your sister."

"No!" I shouted. "She's a grain of sand on the seashore! And that's what she wants to be!" My cheeks were so wet that my face was becoming cold. I wiped my eyes with my forearm and protested. "No. I won't accept that." I was insistent, walking toward the drop sites where Feathermen were continuously releasing fresh refugees.

My grandfather chased after me, while my mother, my grandmother, Brother Lichen, and the two scientist-Feathermen stared. When he attempted to gently grab my arm from behind, I flicked his grasp away, sobbing, and shouted: "If Lavender's going to be killed, I'm going to live the rest of my life knowing it wasn't because her sister sat on her arse and did nothing!"

I kept walking but my grandfather more sternly now held both of my arms. Again, I flicked him away while the rest stared. "Marigold, tell us where you're going! If *you're* going to die, *I'm* not going to live the rest of my life knowing I let you kill yourself in a state of madness."

"I will not walk this earth with half a soul. I'm returning to York to find my sister." He halted when I explained: "Not alone, of course. With a Featherman. I know one who can help."

———

I asked Brother Lichen to follow me further around the lake where more large buckets were stacked, waiting along the clearing's tree line. I ran ahead when I saw Horace, while Brother Lichen trailed slowly.

"Fishbone!" he replied. "I'm trying to line up the buckets. Go away."

"Oh, so you're only nice to me in front of Spirit Zero. I see. Well, he'll be here soon, and I need you to save Lavender. Now."

"Marigold, is she not here in the crowd? York now burns badly. Many Siberians are trapped inside, along with only a few remaining Canadians. We're just discussing the next stage in our plan."

"You're the only Featherman who knows what she looks like."

"And if she wants to survive, we need to neutralize the fire."

"But Horace, can you spare yourself for just this one mission? Find another Featherman to line the buckets. I will be forever in your debt . . . or never in your debt. Whichever you prefer."

He explained, "No, I do not believe I can. As I have stated, *York burns badly.* There is far too much smoke billowing from the fires, and the town is nearly invisible beneath it. I cannot see through smoke, so . . ."

"I can!" I shouted, pointing with both hands to my red eyes. "Snatch me into the sky and we will find her together. You have two talons, and we weigh much less together than one of these buckets. I'll guide us through the smoke."

"What have you done to yourself now?" he asked, looking down. "I cannot help. We move as a cohesion to the next stage of our rescue of your town, which requires certain flight formations, proper filling and loading of the buckets, pickup timing . . . Marigold, perhaps this is her destiny."

"Oh no! Oh no!" I was livid, battling an inflamed temper not common to me. "Don't you dare feed me this *destiny* nonsense! She could have easily claimed herself a 'chosen one,' but she didn't. She needs your help, now."

"No," he replied.

I looked over my shoulder. Brother Lichen was a few seconds from arriving. "It looks like it's going to rain," I stated calmly to Horace.

"What?"

"It looks like it's going to rain," I repeated deliberately.

"You fell from a tree, didn't you?"

"It looks like it's going to rain," I said once more.

He looked up at the clear sky, confused and irritated. "Marigold, are you—"

"I know," I said preemptively. "Not a cloud. But now for the rest of your life, every time you hear any one of your fellow Feathermen say, 'It looks like it's going to rain,' you'll be programmed to recall the night you either helped saved Lavender, or the night you walked away and let her die. It's a trick I learned from my father."

"Still manipulating, I see." He groaned.

"Oh, that's nothing." I smiled as Lichen arrived. "Spirit Zero, what should Brother Horace do? Save Sister Lavender with my assistance or be one of many, many Feathermen—a drop in the bucket if you will—to perform a task which could realistically spare his help?"

The cohesion of Feathermen knew the second stage of their rescue was soon to begin, and all had made many, many trips between the clearing under the Celestial Lights and the fire burning around the Canadian capital. Their most recent cycles were more difficult as the smoke and fire progressed, inward I'm sure. They had begun to return to the clearing, landing and walking, resting their wings only briefly before preparing to return with a much heavier, high-drag load.

Spirit Zero spoke to Horace. "You are the most advanced creatures in the known world, and you have proven that today. You have greater physical gifts than the humans, and you have a much more advanced social and scientific structure. To you the humans are as the crowned elk once were to them. In your heroism today you have accepted the responsibility of stewardship, as stewards of all lesser creatures." As he spoke, a few fellow Feathermen gathered around to listen. "The humans are by a significant gap the most advanced of all the creatures beneath you, and will be the most complicated and challenging of your stewardships. Today you have advanced your own race even further by accepting into your cohesion more than the obvious brothers and sisters of your race, more than simply other feathered creatures. So, while you are to be commended for your efforts, which were only possible through the advanced state of your race, I will humbly request that you, Horace, help Marigold rescue her sister."

"Oh, thank you! Thank you!"

Feathermen continued to come over to listen as Brother Lichen spoke. "The individual suffers as does the group. They understand that they are of no more importance than another, but Sisters Marigold and Lavender brought you to me, so please bring Sister Lavender now to me, so that she may not die but instead begin again. Brother Horace, take Sister Marigold to York to accomplish this."

"I'll take over what Horace was doing," said a Featherman from the group.

Defeated, Horace said, "You will be in my debt forever, Fishbone. And I will collect."

"Stop!" insisted Spirit Zero. "Who here saves the Canadians, and soon the Siberians, simply to benefit? Who here believes that collectively you act only to indebt entire cultures to your own?" More Feathermen steadily arrived as he spoke, returning from York and finding an opportunity to congregate near the Lichen. Many, many were present now, and all were silent. He looked around slowly, and none responded, but even the body language of another species can speak loudly. They had helped us tremendously but were guilty of Spirit Zero's accusation. "Then listen to a few more words, and quickly return to the matter at hand. You have feathers to wear, scales to protect vulnerable parts, wings to fly, and whatever you need. You are noble and your home is in the purity of the air, above where the humans sow and reap. But are you stewards? Stewardship accepts responsibility; dominion seeks earthly reward. The most advanced form of life must have stewardship over all other creatures, not dominion, or how could it call itself advanced? You live in a structure of debts and favors. Abandon it. You focus on fairness, so that all may receive the same, but you neglect justice, which provides based on need. It's through justice, not fairness, that we find peace. Assist those in need for the sake of justice, and therefore to serve peace, which you have done so well today in your assistance of lesser creatures."

He did not preach for long, but the Feathermen gathered near, eager to hear his words. These words came through the Lichen, a pure creature, but as most of his wisdom, they were likely a modified echo of those who had died, poisoned in his clearing. He preached to the birds, and the birds listened. Horace had listened. It was nothing short of a miracle.

"All right, *lesser creature*," conceded Horace. "Are you ready?"

"Yes!"

He groaned under his breath and turned away as the flock of Feathermen, hundreds at least, parted to make way for his exit. Lichen held his large, stone hand low to the soil, palm up, and I stood on it. Horace moved quickly to a suitable stretch of flat land, began his sprint, and took off into the air. Spirit Zero held me high above the clearing, his arm stretched into the sky. Horace was now circling into position. I looked down from Lichen's palm, seeing the tremendous and numerous buckets, the syrup-altered lake, thousands of Canadians, who all, including my family, took notice and looked back curiously, and almost as many Feathermen immediately beneath me.

I looked up and saw Horace approaching under the veil of green and purple Celestial Lights. I bent carefully into position as Horace gently snatched me from Lichen's outstretched palm, carrying me in his locked right talon into the sky for a hopeful return to York.

"I trust your gift, but I'm going to fly blind once we're in the smoke. I'll be listening for your commands," Horace said.

"I'll keep it simple. Up, down, left, and right."

We quickly found York on the horizon. Before I was able to see the wavering of the tips of the flames, I saw what appeared to be a town glowing in lava. When we got closer, the impression of lava changed to naked, sweeping fires. *Give me a candle snuffer large enough . . .*

I was unable to see any smoke. Even with the expanse of the fire, I was still surprised how high and far we were from York when Horace began to worry about the loss of visibility. But I knew, as we both began coughing.

"Continue to fly straight," I instructed. "We're safe and well clear of terrain."

"No! Our path carries us through the unbreathable smoke. We cannot survive this for very long."

"Then fly as necessary to avoid the smoke! I'll search for Lavender."

He wandered and meandered above, but would not descend close to the terrain, claiming a loss of altitude would put us again inside the opaque fumes. I explained that as any clear day, I could distinguish little detail from our high altitude. I saw buildings ablaze and only a few people, all rushing aimlessly and hopelessly through the scarce untorched sections of town.

He continued to wander north. I was able to see the Canadian military, now present and battling the Siberian forces. Some Siberians had forced their way through the northern perimeter of the fire, most dead as a result, but the greater numbers were all north where the Canadians opposed them, north of the fire, and forced to drift continuously northward, as the fire spread slowly to ruin more and more land, which became uninhabitable even as battlegrounds.

"What do you see, Marigold? I can't see the surface, and I see little more than black and gray clouds contaminating the sky."

"I see a town nearly destroyed. The second stage must begin soon, if York is to survive in a rebuildable state."

"It will begin soon. They didn't wait. The moment we departed the clearing, the first Featherman was to take a loaded bucket into the sky and will therefore arrive shortly to neutralize everything that burns. They'll release the fluid from above our current altitude, placing us in their way. Hurry please, because we'll soon be evading more than deadly smoke."

"I see a Canadian every several streets, all running desperately. Can you fly lower? I can't see if any of them may be Lavender."

"No, I cannot. Look for the way they move from above. Do you recognize your sister's gait?"

"No. No, I don't."

Frustrated, Horace sighed as if our entire mission had been hatched in poor judgment.

"Down," I instructed.

"No." He resisted.

"You claimed to trust my gift, and we established commands for a reason. Down."

"No. We'll be unable to breathe in the smoke."

"Then grab a deep inhale for the descent, and when you become weary, climb again to a higher altitude. Horace, we must dive deeper!"

He complied and dove excessively fast, nearly pooling all my blood in my nose, eyes, and forehead as we entered a rapid low pass over the city. He saw nothing but smoke I assume, but his speed was designed to span as much of York as possible in one breath.

He continued to rush above the city, and I saw very little but realized I was reaching the limit of my air. Foolishly I attempted to breathe, seeing no smoke but forgetting why, and therefore quickly gagging and purging the contaminants from my lungs. I was nearly asphyxiated, but as a Featherman and a stoic, Horace still had not reached his limit.

"Horace!" I gasped. "Up! Up!"

He climbed aggressively; with my throbbing head I was unsure when it was safe again to breathe. His excess speed allowed a rapid climb, and when I felt the pitch return to level, I breathed in what volume I could, gasping and regaining my breath.

"Did you see her?" he asked.

"Yes," I wheezed. "I believe so. If I did, she's alive. In a small group, huddled by the clearing before the cathedral."

We took less than another moment to regain my air. Horace urged, "Ready?"

"Yes. Down."

"Wait!" he remembered. "You said a small group? How many? I may not have a wide enough grasp in my talon if there are too many."

"Five?" I guessed. "They're huddled close. Please try."

We breathed our fill of warm, dry air again and descended into the smoke I couldn't see. Horace flew much slower on this second approach, knowing accuracy and timing would be the concern.

I guided him down, left, down, down, and further down as I had hardly the air left in my lungs to push out another word.

"Look directly at your target," he gasped as we descended too slowly for my lungs. "If they appear to rise in your field of vision, our angle is too low and steep. If they appear to move downward by your reference, tell me to go downward because we will be otherwise too high."

"Down . . ." I forced out from my lungs, now with the air so sucked from them that the walls of the organs seemed to collapse and touch each other.

I stared at the group with my eyes focused as we approached. I'm certain I did not allow my eyelids to close or even to sag, but still my vision seemed shaded and grainy.

Then all was black.

I was unconscious. I don't know for how long.

"Marigold? Marigold, are you okay?"

"Hmmm . . ."

"Marigold, do you hear me?"

I breathed slowly. I inhaled through my mouth a deep, deep, pleasing breath, but reacted by coughing more than once.

"Oh, thank you, thank you! I thought you might have died!"

"What?" I asked, disoriented. I opened my eyes to first realize we were soaring again beneath the stars and above the black terrain, well away from the fire but not yet rejoined with the Celestial Lights. I turned to face the talon to my left. "Lavender! Lavender, you're alive!"

"Yes! So are you!" she confirmed, as relieved as I was.

There were three others sharing space with Lavender in Horace's left talon, pressed together but uninjured. She told me what had happened, after I explained why my eyes had been altered since we last were together. She detailed how the green-eyed man had returned to York and found her. Together their gifts guided them to survive the fire as it persisted. They were able to eventually huddle in front of the cathedral, safe only by the nature of the wide clearing in front of it. No clutter was nearby, therefore nothing burned. They could avoid the flames and even the smoke while waiting for rescue. They gathered several townspeople—the three others who were locked inside of Horace's cramped left talon as we journeyed back to the Lichen's clearing. The man with the green eyes huddled with them until we arrived, shielding them as much as possible from the heat, acting as a protective barrier around the four. Horace descended based on my final command and did not realize I was left unconscious. He continued in his profile and track, descending as I had last guided him. Eventually he was beneath the smoke and low over the commons, able to maneuver successfully by his own eye to find the huddled five. According to both Lavender and Horace, in the final instant before Horace nimbly plucked the group from the ground, the green-eyed man broke from the huddle, seemingly bound for the cathedral, even as it began to burn. The green-eyed man, Lavender's protective barrier, had helped as long as possible, as long as was necessary, then was gone. They did not know if he survived, but could not understand how it would be possible if he had. Horace claimed that the man's sacrifice was necessary, explaining that his talon was unable to fit another refugee.

Lavender described the last several moments as miraculous, but also excruciating and awful. She glowed white—they all did as they waited on the ground—but the man with the green eyes insisted that no harm would come to them. Then, unable to celebrate for the time between their rescue and my return to consciousness, Lavender believed she was staring at her sister's cold corpse and also knew the green-eyed man had likely left himself to the fire.

The three others in Lavender's talon described a sight I am sorry I was not able to see. As we departed York, bound for the Lichen's clearing, formations of Feathermen arrived and medicated the human's disaster with their buckets, focusing on the northern section of town and north of the fire, where the Siberian and Canadian battle continued. The liquid solution was successful, they explained, claiming they could see floods of ice sweeping over the earth like ink spilling on rags, soaking every pore and coating each feature of the terrain, instantly snuffing any fire it touched. It crystallized and glowed eerily. It was bluish yellow but not green; it formed around soldiers, trees, buildings, carts, and carriages as stalagmites of ice. Siberian and Canadian warriors were equalized, coated but not often killed by it. They were immobilized by the ice, unable to continue fighting on the frozen battlefield.

Horace's release of his five newest refugees marked the first rescues in quite some time. The Feathermen had abandoned their aid of the individuals, now focusing on the town as an entity, and even the countries involved as a cohesion. And so, we held the entire large and crowded refugee camp's attention as we were released together into a drop site.

The three townspeople from Lavender's huddle were the first to dismount. Isolated shouts came from family members who had all but given up hope. Following the isolated cheers, the crowd celebrated collectively. Our family was waiting directly beneath the drop site.

Thousands and thousands of Canadians were focused on our return. I dismounted first, met by thunderous applause. Covered in soot, I embraced my family as the cheering continued. Quickly the crowd silenced itself, however, and watched as a humble girl, not tall or strong, with short dark hair and unusual purple eyes carefully stepped from the drop site to the ground. If my applause was thunder, hers was an earthquake. They understood what had happened, and they recognized what she had done for them. We all smiled—our grandmother, grandfather, mother, Lavender, and I—but covered our ears for a moment in the overwhelming celebration. The voice of our nation was boisterous and exuberant, no longer the crowd of our past that once stared in indifferent silence, cold and detached as Lavender was nearly executed in front of them. In this moment now, all would have given their lives for her without hesitation. Hands rose into the air, and some even held a small, painted bead between their thumb and first finger.

Brother Lichen held his arm in the air as well, delighting in the curious human behavior. He waved from a distance across the clearing, separated from the human crowd, allowing them their moment. His stone face smiled, pleased to see his Sister Lavender.

She embraced our mother, both of them breaking into tears and apologizing for any foolish bickering of the past. She embraced our grandfather, joking that from henceforth she would only use her gift on livestock. She embraced our grandmother, thanking her for the education and the upbringing, without which we would have never understood the world we were tossed into. And she embraced me, thanking me for bringing her to the clearing beneath the Celestial Lights, for reuniting her with her sister, her family, and her country, and for being by her side throughout our journey. Then, when she faced the overwhelming crowd wondering whom she would embrace next, an unknown man approached her to speak.

He was nobody we had seen in our travels, and nobody we remembered from our days at home. The man seemed simply to be a nearby, inspired, motivated member representing the crowd. "Lavender, my name is Theodorus. Lavender, you're a good person. From all of us, thank you."

She was already weeping joyously, but nearly collapsed into me as I stood by her side while the man spoke these words. She could have filled one of the Feathermen's buckets simply with the deluge she left on my shoulder. She emptied herself of pressure, expectation, fear, and self-doubt. She had succeeded. Through the support of others and not by her own self-perpetuating design, she had survived.

Like bread to the starving, she finally found acceptance from more than just her sister.

———————————

"What now?" asked my grandfather. Our family sat privately, in our own corner of the refugees' clearing, snacking on our ration of the clearing's wild harvest. Most families had found some of their own separation as the camp's celebration faded, and the lineage of our family's livestock intermingled with the crowd like distant relatives visiting for a holiday. I think we all knew this day would be celebrated as one. Brother ovidon, Brother mullice, and Sister tollimore were not asked for their flesh this day. With the condition of York's rural districts uncertain, these creatures might be needed for breeding and rebuilding. Their fleece and milk were already in use, but like generations past when meat was a luxury, these Canadians would be eating mushrooms for a while. The battle continued, we were told, and the Feathermen still drained the lake to extinguish the fires. Much of the Siberian army fled, and between the fire and the ice, I'm surprised they didn't attempt to flee sooner. But the Feathermen would not allow it, neutralizing and capturing each soldier from both armies, like they had for the townspeople they'd dropped in the Lichen's clearing. The generals of the two opposing forces would not be escorted to the clearing or even returned home; instead, they would be taken to Windfall, where the Feathermen would force the leaders of both armies into dialogue for the final stage of their plan.

Lavender explained: "The crowd's support was wonderful. But if ninety-nine of one hundred love me and the one hundredth wishes me dead, I'm vulnerable."

"Who?" asked my mother in disbelief.

I answered, "Polaris seemed convinced he could live by retreating to the dead. We don't know if he succeeded. But what I know of him, I would say he found a way to continue to exist."

"He won't survive much longer once this crowd learns of his reprehensible actions. But even if he's killed, the respectable dead may not want his company either," my grandmother declared bitterly. In an effort of contrived sympathy and to withdraw her judgment somewhat, she added, "If he had died ages ago, he would have been better remembered. But whether he lives or dies, I can say with great confidence that you girls need no longer worry about any sentence of exile."

"Yes, but when they learn of Polaris's true nature, his lack of authority or wisdom, the lies and the exploitation, there may be riots in an already crippled town, as well as violent, unstable bids by his feverishly hopeful successors. I would only be a focus of controversy until peace is restored. And that's just the Canadians. We defected from the Siberians, who have pursued Polaris for generations since his escape," said Lavender.

I added, "There was even a small mob on Jan Mayen Island which we left unsatisfied. Sadly, it was always Lavender they really wished to kill."

Lavender said, "We still may have to wander a bit. When it's safe, hopefully, we can return to York. Me particularly. As she says, I don't believe Marigold would be hunted."

"So where will you go? Will you write?" asked Mother.

"Yes, since you have mentioned writing . . . I stole a correspondence between the Queen of Svalbard and the new princess there," I revealed, a smile creeping unevenly across my lips.

"What?" asked Lavender. "When? Oh, when we were in Queen Erika's chamber?"

"Wait—" began my mother, a bit jealous. "When were you—the queen? Really?"

"And where is this letter now?" asked Lavender.

I answered, "Probably in some file stashed with other papers somewhere on mainland Siberia. It was taken from me when we were enslaved."

"You stole a private letter written by Queen Erika?" asked an amused Lavender in disbelief.

"Yes, of course. I also stole a private necklace, but the Siberians took that from me as well, those thieves. A beautiful piece—it really matched my eye color at the time." I paused, explaining, "I'm joking. I didn't steal anything but the letter."

Grandfather asked, "So what did it say? Do you remember?"

"Oh, absolutely," I answered. "I memorized the entire text well before it was confiscated. I'm glad I did. It was on the subject of Emberland, where I promise you I'm bound next, and I will write. York will be a bit of a frontier while it's rebuilt, and I have suffered enough cold fingertips and frozen toes. Enough of this season of darkness. Enough camping, enough of the bush, and enough of the slave camps. As for the letter, I recited it to myself many times, in both Svalbardian and translated into our own language. It's what helped me through our Siberian captivity without losing hope. In Canadian it would read:

Dearest Sanna,

> *In my welcoming you to the family, I feel obliged to warn you cautiously of both a member of your new family and a member of our empire.*
>
> *King Ulffr and the island of Emberland are the most likely sources of grief for the Svalbardian Royal House and the Svalbardian Royal Empire. Both act on pleasure principle, seeking immediate gratification.*

My family began to laugh at my recitation and the calculating, lashing words of the queen. Interrupting my recollection, I smiled. "Emberland sounds wonderful, doesn't it?"

"I may join you," said my mother.

"It gets worse." I laughed and continued:

I defied this sort of upbringing with our Oslo, and I hope that your marriage may benefit as a result. However, when the time comes for my grandchildren, you must consider how you raise them. If they are to be raised without consideration for how their actions affect others, they may only be suitable for life on Emberland.

But for now, we have Ulffr within our family, and Svalbard has Emberland within its empire, and I do love them both. I warn you extensively only so that you may be able to do the same.

With Love,
Queen Erika

"'With love.'" My grandparents laughed. "Marigold, if you stole this letter, now how will Princess Sanna ever know to hate Emberland and her king?"

"This would be even more humorous if you knew Sanna," said Lavender, smiling. "She could accept Polaris for who he is."

"Marigold, you are going to Emberland, then?" asked my mother.

"You heard the letter. Of course I am."

Lavender added, "For much of our journey she wished to make it our next destination, but it never was. Now I'd wager she would swim there if necessary."

"Then I will join you, if you don't mind," said Mother. "When my daughters last left my side, I failed to follow."

"Yes, of course!" I said. "It would be wonderful! If I'm going to meet Quinby's insane mother, he'll have to meet mine."

Mother asked, "What? Who? Who are all of these people?"

"Oh, I'll explain as we're swimming across the sea," I joked. "Now that our journey's ended, I have quite a bit to tell you."

"All right. We'll discuss it . . . *on the ferry,*" Mother agreed. "Mother, Father?" she asked.

"Oh no," my grandmother answered. "We'll return to the farm and rest, and do what we can to help our neighbors as York rebuilds. Hopefully, the fire and the Siberians didn't bother with the rural districts, and with a few empty rooms we may be able to lodge those who have lost their homes."

"Lavender?" asked my mother, now excited for the journey.

"If you're going to Emberland, be sure to visit the King's Closet. Mother, you will meet another interesting creature when you do. His name is Tollund. He's a troubled child at heart and I'm certain he would greatly appreciate visitors."

"So . . . then . . . you won't join us?" Mother asked, dejected.

"I should be uncharted for a while," Lavender reminded her. "I'll return, so don't fear for me. I have my gift. I've considered a physician's academy . . . I would prefer not to say where, but I've long considered medicine. Not herbs and poisons; we have already worked with those, but surgery rather. Marigold, do you remember when we ran into the sea?"

"The Host?"

"Yes. I have to find the next use for my gift. With it, and some knowledge of surgery, I might learn how to heal."

"You could repair my abdomen," said Grandfather hopefully.

"I've thought of that," she nodded, possibly also considering our father and his worse torn flesh. "Yes, absolutely, if I learn that it's possible."

"Marigold, how do you plan to use your new gift?" asked Grandmother.

"By bathing in the hot springs on Emberland, pretending I cannot see through the steam that would normally provide the other bathers with privacy."

Lavender said good-bye to each of us. My mother provided her younger daughter with the clothing and supplies she had packed for herself when we fled the farm.

Lavender would leave directly from the clearing, a bit safer for her this way we believed, and the rest of my family and I would return to the farm before my mother and I embarked for an extended recreational journey to Emberland.

Leaving our family aside briefly in the crowded refugee camp, Lavender and I set across the clearing to bid farewell to Brother Lichen. He spoke first as we approached him near his lake. "Sisters Lavender and Marigold! Peace and all good! How afraid I might have been before knowing you if this many humans had found their way to my clearing. I never believed the monster whose soil poisoned so many could now host a banquet celebration of the needy. Have you noticed your signs? Your posts? They still stand and still guide the visitors to that which is right and good and away from that which is wrong and bad."

"So do you, Spirit Zero," said Lavender.

"Yes, and the man with the green eyes has certainly helped these people as well," I said. "He and Baker are the heroes the Canadians will never know to celebrate."

"Yes, they will," said Brother Lichen. "You've reminded me . . . the man with the green eyes gave me a note a moment before he left my clearing to return to York. He asked that I give it to you when you were prepared to leave here, and no sooner. I didn't know what this meant until now." Lichen's large stone fist extended and spread its fingers to reveal a small note addressed to Lavender and me. As we reached for it, he asked Lavender: "So, a nomad when we met and a nomad again as we say our farewells?"

"Yes," she answered cautiously. "Does this mean I am to follow the tracks of the crowned elk?"

Lichen smiled, remembering his friends. I anxiously retrieved the note written by the green-eyed man, and together Lavender and I read it.

"So, he survived?" asked Lavender. "No, not necessarily," she remembered. "His gift may have shown him the events beyond his own death and allowed that he plan accordingly."

Looking to the bottom, I read, "He leaves his name, which earlier he would not reveal for fear of persecution. Now it seems it doesn't matter."

We looked at each other somberly in a moment of respect, which Lavender broke, stating, "So *you* are the author of the book he mentioned? The book he predicted would detail the events of our journey?"

Overwhelmed at first, I answered, "Yes, apparently I've been trusted with this duty. And the note also states that the purpose should be to publish a text available to any of the Svalbardian empire, Siberia, Canada, and the Feathermen. We will therefore 'encourage an understanding of the recent events, and of Polaris's role in the destruction. This task as much as any brick or beam will rebuild York,' he writes, and specifically states that this is necessary, 'for public perception to not again fall against Lavender's favor, while also eliminating the persecution of the gifted.'"

Lavender said, "It also appears you are *one* of the authors. He left behind correspondences for some of the others we passed along our way."

"But who is Commander Markham?" I continued to read. "Oh, the man who chased us into the sea. I don't know that I'd care to speak with *him*."

The words the green-eyed man left behind were more notes and scribbles than a formal letter. Lavender found a patch of words on the page and read, "He claims Markham will be peaceful and that he was merely following orders."

"Oh, and it also says that I should take editorial command of this publication. That I will need to, for it to carry a semblance and coherence."

"Yes, that would be true," agreed Lavender. "Just to mention one simple detail, the Svalbards have their calendar system and we have our own. And so do the Feathermen . . . and the Siberians . . . yes, it will be necessary to make adjustments."

"And fill the gaps of people's memories, of course," I added, also deciding, "If I am to take command of this text, I will make myself an artist."

"Marigold, you are an artist," said my sister.

"Then it will be easy."

"Marigold, please." She smiled with a roll of her eyes.

I added, "There's such responsibility to this undertaking, but so much potential! I can attach symbols to focal characters and metaphors to concepts or events, such as the fire that burned our forever-altered city. The fire-bringer may classically have been regarded as progress and wisdom, but knowing what we know now, and with the pen in my hand, it will show quite the opposite. But don't worry, Lavender. I will join you with a metaphor, life and death of course, but I won't allow this to reduce you beneath your character, as so many on our journey have wished to do. In fact, this thought has given me a clever hook for the book's opening." Unrelated to the symbols, I continued, "The story of Lavender and Marigold shall be told by all of us. So, Brother Lichen, both the note I read and my own judgment agree that you must be one of our authors."

He smiled. "I will begin writing my chapter immediately."

I continued: "And Lavender, if I am to edit this text, I can choose your fate, your destiny. I can pick where and how it will end. Looking into the past from our perspective, even a plain set of eyes sees that it should not have been necessary for you to perish in the combustion. I will influence the events that have occurred and with my words insist that you survive the fire."

She did not answer.

Acknowledgments

I would like to thank everyone who played a role in bringing this story to life. Thank you to Deb Staples, Jerome Eyquem, Jonathan Denton, Barbara Bohan, Eric Langstedt, Brett Sills, Alan Noah, the CamCat team, and of course, my entire family.

About the Author

Clinton Festa's works span a wide range of formats from sketch comedy to epic drama. He began his writing career as a cartoonist and writer for his campus humor magazine, the *Cornell Lunatic*. As a playwright, his works have been performed around the United States and Canada, and several of his comedy sketches have placed in national competitions. He wrote and directed *The Malone Family in the Enchanted Forest*, a seven-episode podcast series produced by the Cary Playwrights' Forum. Clinton continues to write a variety of new works and looks forward to sharing them with fans, friends, and family.

Clinton is a former airline pilot and current aviation professional who has won several awards for his work in aviation safety. He runs a small charity called Sentences Book Donations which is an online book drive for people in prisons and juvenile detention centers.

He currently resides in Greensboro, North Carolina with his wife and children.

For Further Discussion

1. If you had a gift to see things others couldn't, what would it be?

2. If you were Marigold or Lavender, what would you have done differently, if anything?

3. If you were dying, would you wait inside the Host and hope for a cure or go naturally?

4. Would you want Agrippin to watch your dreams?

5. Which narrator was your favorite? Which was your least favorite?

6. Do you think the narrators were reliable? Were there any you didn't trust?

7. What time period do you think this story takes place in? What evidence from the novel supports this?

8. Just for fun: You're invited to Sanna and Oslo's royal wedding. What character from the story do you bring as your plus one?

Inspiration for *Ancient Canada*

Ancient Canada was inspired by many people and places I encountered throughout my travels in aviation. It was also significantly inspired by conversations with my wife as well as the life of St. Francis of Assisi. The Saint served as direct inspiration for the Lichen character.

The original idea for the story came years ago while visiting a friend in New York City. Looking for a place to eat lunch, the neighborhood was full of wonderful restaurants with food from around the world. Thinking about different cultural traditions–food, language, clothing, mythology–led to the idea of an alternate Arctic Circle.

Not wanting to infringe on true cultural traditions, the story of *Ancient Canada* borrows only the geography of the North and tells its own story of mythology. Other sources of inspiration include *The Odyssey* and *The Canterbury Tales.*

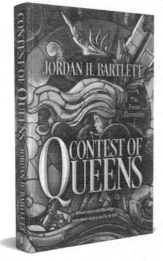
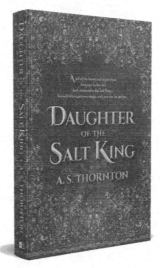
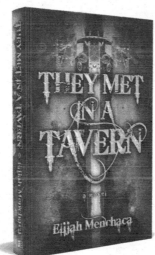

CamCat Books

VISIT US ONLINE FOR
MORE BOOKS TO LIVE IN:
CAMCATBOOKS.COM

FOLLOW US

CamCatBooks   @CamCatBooks   @CamCat_Books